THE SWENSEN CONNECTION

BOOK 1: BEGINNINGS

STEVEN E. WILDE

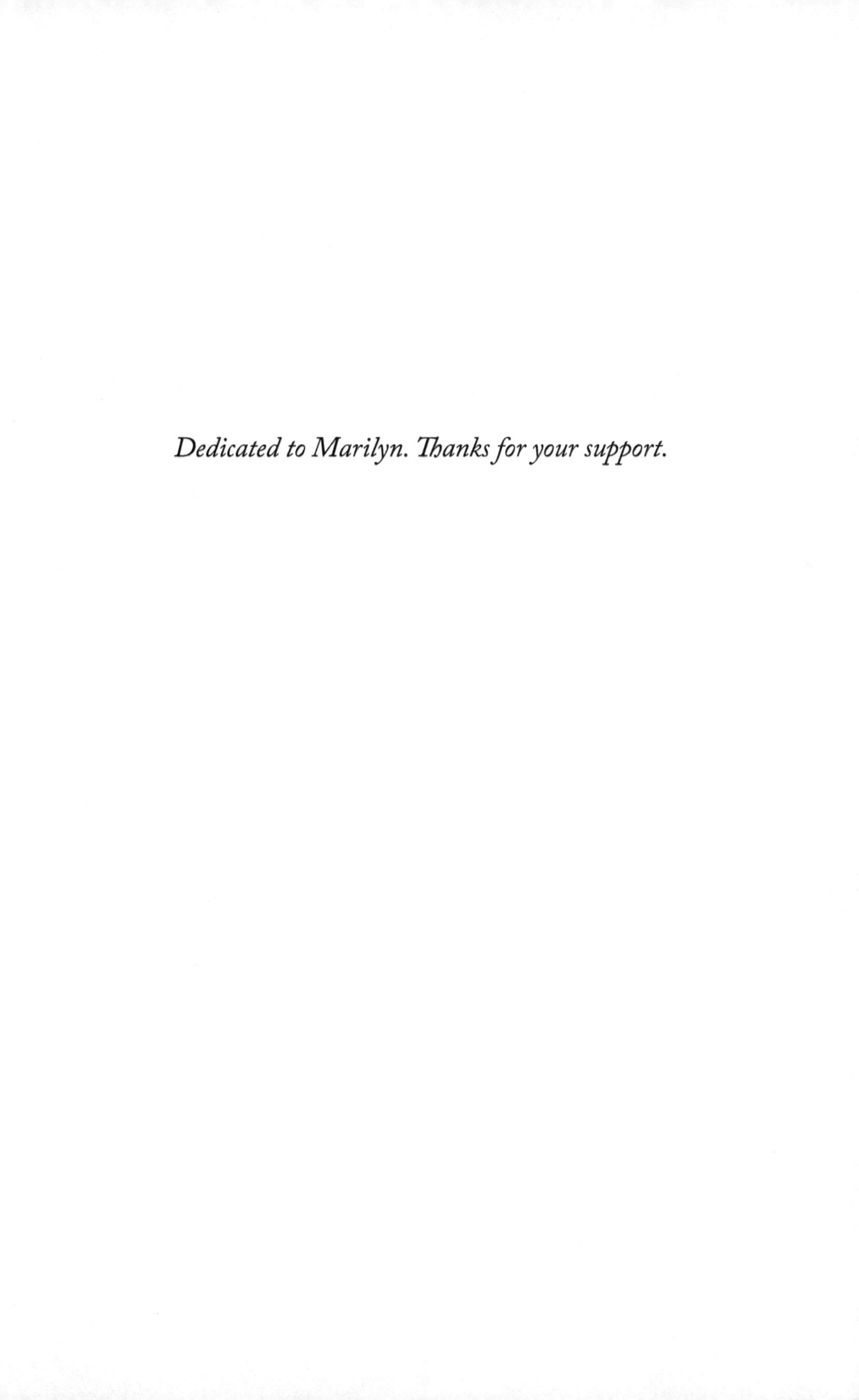

Dedicated to Marilyn. Thanks for your support.

Prologue

Salt Lake City, Utah
Rice-Eccles Football Stadium, University of Utah Campus
Present Day—Agent Rainbow

"Hey, Rainbow," Ollie said as his CIA associate moved into the bleachers and sat by him. Oliver Tanner was a CIA analyst who helped agents plan their assignments and obtain the resources they needed to complete them. Rainbow was a veteran agent who ran other agents and sometimes had his own missions. He also functioned as a recruiter whenever he or Ollie saw someone they liked.

"Hello Ollie," Rainbow said. "I'm here. What did you want me to see?"

"Don't you just love a college football game?" Ollie asked, lifting his head and sniffing the air, as though there was something special about it. "This is a key game for the PAC-12 conference. The University of Utah won the PAC-12 South division and Oregon State won the PAC-12 North division. This is the conference championship game and whoever wins goes to the Rose Bowl in Pasadena."

"I'm more of an SEC fan," Rainbow said. "Give me Alabama or Georgia, and I'm all eyes and ears. So, why am I here?"

"See the two cheerleaders talking below us on the sideline?" Ollie asked, pointing to two cute young women standing at the bottom of the bleachers, talking animatedly.

"Yeah. What about them? They're cute, like all college cheerleaders."

"Keep an eye on the brunette. I think there's something special about her."

Ollie settled in to watch the game, eating popcorn from a tall paper bag. Rainbow had trouble concentrating on the game or the cheerleaders. He had an agent in a difficult situation in Nicaragua, who he needed to extract before he got hurt.

Rainbow glanced periodically at the cheerleaders, particularly the cute brunette. She was tall, probably five foot ten, athletic, and more attractive each time he focused on her. What did Ollie want him to see?

"Who is she?" Rainbow asked during half-time, while they waited for the second half of the game to begin.

"Her name is Mary Slade. Single. Studying political science and criminal justice."

"So? What? You think we should recruit her because of her interest in criminal behavior?"

"That's what attracted me to her," Ollie said. "But it's the over-all package that kept my interest."

"You have the hots for her?"

"No. No. She's intelligent, self-confident, physically fit, knows martial arts . . ."

"She looks full of herself. Okay. What do you want me to do? Interview her?"

As they watched, the players entered the field to get ready for the second half of the game. Two of the Oregon State players stopped to talk to her and her fellow cheerleader. They must have weighed in the two-hundred-fifty-pound range each. She stepped away from them as though trying to ignore them, but they moved around her to force her to look at them.

One of them poked her in the chest with his fat finger. She reached up and grabbed his finger, twisting it so hard, Rainbow thought he heard bones crack. Then she grabbed his arm with both hands and threw him behind her. His feet left the ground in the process and he landed hard on his back. His teammate knelt by him and inspected his finger, then turned his head to give Mary a dirty look. He spoke to her, but Rainbow couldn't tell what was said.

She took a step toward the second player, now on his knees on the grass, and calmly kicked him between the legs. She backed away as he fell flat on his face and curled into a ball. After a couple of minutes, he got to his knees, said something to her and cast a nasty look in her direction. She went back to him and kicked him in the face, breaking his nose and knocking him unconscious. Then she walked away, pulling her shocked friend with her, acting as though nothing had happened, and leaving the two men lying on the ground.

When another player noticed the two prone men, he called the coach over. The coach looked them over, tried to talk to them, then, shaking his head, told some of the other players to carry them to the locker room. They didn't return to the game.

"Okay," Rainbow said, "I'll have her come in for an interview."

1

Langley, Virginia; Hilton Inn Meeting Room
Mary Slade

"Hi folks," Rainbow said when Mary and her parents entered the meeting room in the local Hilton Inn. "Thank you for meeting with me. My name is Ren Bloosey."

"You work for the CIA, right?" Mr. Slade asked nervously. Mr. Bloosey didn't acknowledge the question. "Why is the CIA interested in us? In particular, our daughter?"

"Fine. I'll get right to the point," Bloosey said. "I'm a recruiter. We're always looking for new young talent. Your daughter has come to our attention as a possible recruit."

Mr. Slade looked at his daughter questioningly. "Did you tell someone you were interested in working for the CIA?" he asked her.

"No, Dad. But I did complete a questionnaire for one of my classes that asked if I would be interested in working in the criminal justice system. Naturally, I said yes, since that's what I'm studying."

"I thought you just wanted to be a court clerk, or something," Mrs. Slade said, staring at Mary, her hands twisting nervously in her lap.

"No Mom. But I was considering applying to the police academy after I graduate."

"You want to be a street cop?" her dad asked.

"I want to make a difference," Mary said, looking at her mother. "You've taught me to be honest and to help other people. There's too much greed and corruption in the world. I want to change that. I know I'm just one person, but if I can make a difference in one person's life, I will feel like I have accomplished something. And I think I have it in me to help lots of people. I hadn't considered working for the CIA, but if that's a possibility, maybe I can make a bigger difference than I could if I were a street cop."

"That's a nice speech, Mary," Bloosey said. "Do you mind if I call you Mary?"

"No. That's fine," Mary said, looking at her mom rather than at Bloosey.

"Mary, we'd like to give you a test, to see if you have the aptitude to work for us. I'm already convinced you do, just from watching and talking to you. But we have to go through this procedure before we can hire anyone."

"What is this procedure?" Mary asked, now making eye contact with him.

"Honey, I thought you wanted to become a nurse." Her mother said.

"Mom, that was years ago. I've grown up since then and have thought it through some more."

"The first step is a written exam," Bloosey said. "If you pass that, we do a psychological evaluation. If you pass that, we contract with you for a six-week training program. Assuming you don't drop out of the training program, we hire you and give you an assignment that fits your particular skills and interests."

"What kind of assignment?"

"I can't give you specifics, you understand. Some of what we do is clandestine and involves overseas travel. Most of our women work as analysts, translators, code-breakers, or couriers."

"How long would this process take?"

"The longest process is the training, so, if we begin now, you could get your first assignment in about two months."

"What about school?" Mrs. Slade asked, frantically. "She'd have to drop out of school to do what you're suggesting."

"Mrs. Slade, if Mary has the aptitude to work for us, she'll get better training and a better education from us than she could possibly get in school, no matter how good their programs are. What do you say?"

"I don't know," Mr. Slade said.

"I'm against it," Mrs. Slade said.

"What's your reservation?" Bloosey asked Mr. Slade.

"We lost Mary's sister to some violent men in high school. We'll worry about losing our only remaining child to violence, especially if she takes on a dangerous job."

"I see," Bloosey said. "What do you think, Mary?"

"I've taken martial arts and gymnastics for years, to keep myself in good shape, physically, because of Shelley's death. I don't want to back away from a challenge that I think I can handle, even if there's an element of danger associated with it, and I like the idea of seeing the world."

Bloosey looked at Mary, thinking about her comments. She wore a concerned expression, so he waited for her to explain. "Can I drop out if it doesn't look like something I want to do?" She asked.

"You can, but once you begin training, it will be harder. We'll need a commitment to finish the program. Then, once you pass all the tests and accept an offer of work, you have to sign a non-disclosure agreement and commitment, that are binding for life."

"So I won't give away any secrets?" Mary asked.

Bloosey nodded. "We own you after that," he said.

"Can I take the test?" Mary pleaded with her mom.

"I don't know," Mrs. Slade said, looking into her daughter's bright, intelligent eyes. "Oh, alright. As long as we discuss it again after you get the test scores. I don't want you doing anything dangerous."

"Mom, walking down the street is dangerous. Riding in a car is dangerous. Life is inherently dangerous."

"Okay. Okay. You've made your point."

"When can I take the test?" Mary asked Bloosey.

"Today, if you want to. We'll have to go to the office, but I can get you back to your hotel in time for dinner."

"Then let's do it, Mr. Bloosey."

"Okay, but please call me Rainbow, or agent Rainbow," Bloosey said. All three of the Slades gave Rainbow a funny look.

They left Mary's parents at the hotel and drove to the George Bush Center for Intelligence. They got Mary a visitor pass at the front desk—Rainbow signed for it—took her to a room where a middle-aged woman signed her in, had her fill out an information sheet about herself, then handed her a booklet that reminded her of a college exam. She was directed to a desk and told to complete the exam and return it to the woman. Ollie and Rainbow would check on her in a couple of hours.

When Rainbow returned, she told him she was on the last problem. He returned a few minutes later and spoke to the woman, who was in the process of scoring Mary's exam.

"Excellent," the woman said a few moments later, writing something on the front of the exam booklet and handing it to Rainbow.

"That's great," he said, looking at the score and thumbing through the pages. He went to Mary, took her by the forearm, and led her from the room.

"How did I do?" Mary asked.

"You did excellent," Rainbow said, smiling. "You noticed that some of the questions are multiple choice and others are story problems—case studies, if you will. They're scored based on your approach to solving the case. There's no one right answer, so nobody ever gets one hundred percent. You passed with an excellent score. Your instincts are good. Now, we just need to convince your parents to let you continue, unless you want to continue without their permission."

"I should talk to them," she said.

"Probably a wise choice." He smiled at her.

Rainbow drove her back to the hotel and left her with her parents, with a promise to call her in two days to see what she decided. He gave her a business card with his phone number on it just in case she had questions or made her decision before he called her. She called him the next day, from the hotel, before she got on a plane to go home, and said she was ready to begin. He told her to stay, instead of going home, and show up the next day, to begin. Her parents could send her anything she needed from home.

2

Salt Lake City, Utah; Lee Kay Public Shooting Range
Taylor Swensen

"What are we doing, Ollie?" Rainbow asked as he walked to the check-in counter where Ollie was getting directions.

"I thought we'd shoot some shotguns, then rifles," Ollie said, chuckling. "We could also do some archery if you want."

"Let's skip the archery. But why here? We have better facilities in Virginia."

"You liked my last suggestion, so I thought I'd show you another candidate."

"You know it's not cheap to fly out here every time you want to show me someone. You've got a female skeet shooter for me?" Rainbow laughed at his own joke. Ollie didn't.

"No, but Taylor Swensen is a dead-eye with a rifle."

"Taylor? Male or female?"

"All male, and quite a hunk, if I do say so myself."

"Since when are you into guys, Ollie?"

"I'm not, but this guy is a head turner, both his looks and his shooting. Follow me and you'll see."

They walked out to the shooting range and Rainbow followed Ollie to one of the shooting stations. He handed Rainbow a pair of binoculars, then pointed to the young man holding a twelve-gauge shotgun a few feet away in the shooting position, just loading his rifle. He wore a light jacket to keep the chill off and stood in an inch of snow from a recent storm.

"Pull," Taylor Swensen said, and two targets flew through the air from left to right, about a hundred yards away. He fired twice and both targets exploded, one after the other, in rapid succession. He quickly reloaded.

"Pull," he said again and repeated the process.

"Change the trajectory," he said.

"Ready," someone replied.

"Pull," he said, and repeated the process yet again.

This continued until he had fired on twenty targets from the left, the right and both directions at the same time, hitting all twenty.

He checked his rifle, setting the safety, then turned around to get his gun case.

"Taylor Swensen?" Ollie asked.

"Yes?" Taylor said, looking at the two strangers. "What can I do for you?" he asked.

"You can show my friend, here, how well you shoot with a sniper rifle," Ollie said

Taylor grinned. "Sorry, I left my sniper rifle in my other pants. What are you talking about? I don't have a sniper rifle."

"But I do," Ollie said and held a small briefcase out in front of him, toward Taylor.

"You're joking, right?"

"No joke. We'd like to see you assemble this rifle and shoot at a target we've set up, with the permission of the range, at one thousand feet. Think you can do it?"

"I've never tried it, but I don't know why I wouldn't be able to, if the rifle is sighted in properly."

"It is. Go ahead."

Taylor took the briefcase, opened it on a bench, and admired the disassembled rifle in packing material. "It's pretty," he said, giving Ollie a suspicious look. He removed the components, one at a time and assembled them, as if he'd done it a hundred times.

"I can tell you know your way around guns," Rainbow said, drawing a look from Taylor.

"I've handled a few," Taylor said.

"You won't need that," Ollie said, when Taylor picked up a silencer, the last component in the case.

"Okay," Taylor said, loading a high velocity bullet from the case into the chamber. "Now where is the target?"

"About four degrees to the left of that transmission tower out there."

Taylor looked through the scope on the rifle and found the target.

"It's a silhouette of a man," Taylor said, turning to look at Ollie. "Is that what you want me to shoot?"

"It is," Ollie said, "and be forewarned, the head is an exploding target, so don't be surprised."

"Okay, who are you guys?" Taylor asked, pointing the muzzle of the rifle toward the ground. "FBI, CIA? Terrorists? What?"

"You caught us out" Ollie said. "We're not terrorists. Now let's see you shoot"

Okay, FBI or CIA. Taylor lined up his shot again. This was a new weapon and a long-range shot—almost two miles—so he took his time, checked the wind, then his breathing, and gently pulled the trigger. The response was almost instantaneous, even at that distance. He could see the head explode, even before he took his eye away from the sights.

"Great!" Ollie exclaimed from behind him. He turned around to see the two men looking out at the target. Rainbow had the binoculars to his eyes and they were both smiling.

"Right between the eyes," Rainbow said, lowering the binoculars. "Was that where you were aiming?"

"Yes," Taylor said. "Does that surprise you?"

"Not at all. It tells me we need to talk some more, but not here. Are you free for dinner?"

"Sure. We can leave from here and you can drop me off at my apartment when we're done. I don't have my ride with me."

"You came with someone else?"

"A friend. I'll just tell him where I'm going and then I'll be ready. Do you want me to clean the rifle?" He asked Ollie as he disassembled it.

"I'll take care of that, thank you," Ollie said as he helped Taylor put the disassembled gun back in its case, each component in its correct position in the packing material.

They rode in Rainbow's rental car, arriving at the University of Utah campus a few minutes later, parked in the Student Union parking lot and walked to the Panorama Room on the upper level, overlooking the Salt Lake valley. It was Taylor's suggestion, since it was Friday night and they had all-you-can-eat shrimp on ice, which was Taylor's favorite.

They went through the buffet line and found a table by a window that overlooked the campus and downtown Salt Lake City. It was out of earshot of the other diners, a difficult feat since the Friday night buffet was so popular.

"I'm Oliver Tanner," Ollie said, holding out his hand. "Please call me Ollie."

"And I'm Ren Bloosey," Rainbow said, "but I prefer to be called Rainbow. Agent Rainbow also works."

"Okay. Ollie and Rainbow. What do you want to talk about?"

"Tell us about your background and your ambitions," Ollie said.

"Okay. You already know I'm Taylor Swensen. I'm studying

Nuclear Engineering. I'll graduate in a year and a half, if I stay in school. My hobby is computer graphics animation. I want to design virtual reality games and get filthy rich, so I can be a playboy and live on an island in the Pacific."

"Where did you learn to shoot like that?"

"Here and there. I took a gun safety course as a boy scout, liked shooting, so I got a membership at a gun club and started shooting every week. I've won several local and regional competitions with hand guns and rifles."

"How's your social life?" Rainbow asked.

"Why is that important?"

"It may not be, but we take everything into consideration when making decisions."

"Okay, I'm currently dating the daughter of a wealthy businessman. Her father started a technology company in college with a friend and it grew beyond their wildest dreams. He bought out his partner, spun off two other businesses and sold the original business for over fifty million dollars.

"My parents died in an auto accident when I was ten and I went to live with an aunt and uncle. No siblings, my uncle died two years ago and I put my aunt in a rest home at age eighty. Now, I spend all my time either in school or shooting."

"What about the girlfriend?"

"Brooke is flamboyant. Growing up with money made her a little careless. She likes to wear expensive clothes and jewelry. We were on a date and she was kidnapped. I was taken along with her to keep me from reporting it. She was wearing at least a quarter of a million dollars in jewelry at the time." He stopped talking.

"How did that turn out? You're here to tell us about it."

"I was tied up tightly and dropped in a corner of the building where we were being held. One of the kidnappers was assigned to watch me while the other three teased her. They took her jewelry, then stripped her. Looking for more jewelry, they said. One of the men apparently decided he couldn't resist her charms and had started to get physical with her. That's when I finally got myself untied. I hit the guy watching me while he was distracted by the action with Brooke. I took his handgun, took aim and shot the guy about to rape her."

"This was from across the room, under stress." Rainbow clarified.

"Yeah. I figure I was about fifty feet away and hit him between the eyes. The other men acted like they had no clue where the shot came from. That gave me time to get to her and get her out of the way."

"Was she hurt?"

"Not by my shot. I missed her by at least three inches. But she became hysterical from the blood, gore and physical attention. I ran to her as she ran to me. We hunkered down and waited to see if my shot would attract attention. In about ten minutes, I heard sirens. Five more minutes and police entered the building to settle the conflict with the remaining kidnappers."

"But you held them off?"

"I think they were afraid of me."

"That makes sense. Alone and tied up. No way you could do what you did."

"What happened to the girl? Are you still dating her?"

"Yeah. For now. Her dad offered me a reward, which I turned down."

"Why? I thought you wanted to get filthy rich."

"I don't need his handout. I did what I did because it was the right thing to do. I'm a hard worker. I'll earn my riches through my own efforts."

"Noble," Ollie said.

"Now, why were you looking for me?" Taylor asked, already suspecting why two men from the U.S. clandestine services would be seeking him out.

"You're intelligent," Ollie said. "I'm sure you've already figured out that we want to bring you in for testing, to see if you'd be a good addition to our service."

"FBI or CIA?"

"CIA."

"What kind of testing?"

"Physical, intellectual, psychological."

"And if I pass your tests?"

"We'll offer you a job."

"What kind of job?"

"The test results will help us place you. But based on what I've seen so far, I think you'll end up as a field agent. So, are you interested in taking an aptitude test to see if you'd make a good member of our team?" Rainbow asked.

"Sure. Why not?' What do I need to do?"

"We'll arrange for you to come to Virginia to take the test. We'll go from there."

The next day, a courier arrived at his dorm room with a package that contained an open-ended, round-trip ticket in his name, to Virginia, along with an instruction sheet on what to bring with him and how to contact Ollie.

Taylor went to Langley two days later, passed their test, then entered their training program three days after that. Physical conditioning, obstacle course work, tracking, memory development, target shooting and psychological evaluation, so intense that he went to bed exhausted every night. At the end of his six-week training, he was hired as an assassin and assigned to go to London with another agent. Their mission: find and stop a man recruiting young people to join a terrorist cell targeting government employees and facilities.

Rainbow

"What's the matter?" Ollie asked. seeing the look in Rainbow's eyes after they'd given Taylor his first assignment.

"He looks too good. I worry that something will go wrong; something we're not seeing. What about the girl he was dating? Is he going to drop out and go home to her and her dad's money?"

"I spoke to Taylor about her at lunch yesterday," Ollie said. "He told me he was never really interested in having a long-term relationship with her. He was dating her to get her dad's attention. He thought he could convince her dad to set him up in business. After we spoke to him, he postponed that ambition for future consideration. The father tried to give him a reward, but he turned it down."

"He said that."

"Yeah. Then he turned down the offer of a job working for one of her dad's companies in lieu of working for us."

"Really? That sounds like what I was wanting to hear."

3

On paper, the agent with Taylor, Greg Talbot, was his mentor. In reality, the outcome of this assignment would determine if Taylor would need a partner on his next assignment or was good enough to be on his own. Rainbow suspected the latter would be the case.

As soon as they arrived at the Gatwick airport, Greg got on the phone.

"Who are you calling?" Taylor asked. "I thought we would go to see the station chief."

"We don't need the station," Greg said. "I have contacts in London who will have the information we need."

"Is Sean Connor there?" Greg asked, when someone answered the phone. "Yeah, that's him. Can you put him on? Thanks. Sean? Greg Talbot here. No. No. Don't worry about it. I need to talk to you. I can be there in fifteen minutes. Will you wait for me? Thanks, Sean. There's a beer in it for you."

"Who's Sean?" Taylor asked.

"Ex-con trying to keep his nose clean. We help each other whenever I'm in town. He gives me information in exchange for beer. Sometimes cash. Depends on his situation and current needs."

Sean

They entered the Lucky Pig pub and went to the bar. The bartender must have recognized Talbot, since he nodded toward the left, where a short man, with a scar forming a dimple on his right cheek, sat alone at a table. His clothes were ragged and his hair, held in place by a Gatsby cap, was long, stringy, and dirty. Talbot moved to Sean's table and sat. Taylor sat next to him on the bench.

"Who's this?" Sean asked. He sounded suspicious, even angry.

"Sean, this is Taylor. He's helping me on this trip. We're looking for information."

"You're always looking for information."

"And you always have what we need. That's why I like you so much."

Sean choked out a laugh. "Right, enough with the flattery. What do you need?"

"Someone is recruiting young men for a terrorist cell. We need to find the recruiter and stop him. What can you tell us?"

"What's in it for me?"

"What do you need?"

"A million pounds Sterling . . . Short of that, I need to get my teeth checked. I got a bad tooth."

"That could be expensive," Talbot said. "Your information better be really good."

"You know my information is always good. Don't hold back on me, bloke."

"We're good Sean. Tell me what you've got. Is he here now?" Talbot asked.

"No."

"How do we find him?"

"He comes in pretty regular 'bout sixteen thirty hours to have a pint. He asks around, that's why I know what he's doing. He's not very careful for a terrorist."

"Okay, we'll come back. Here's the dentist's contact information." Talbot handed Sean the name and phone number of the

CIA station. "Just tell them Greg said to give you the name and number for the company dentist. We'll follow up with you before we leave town to see how it went." Talbot turned toward the bartender and raised his hand in the air. "The usual for Sean," he said. The bartender nodded.

Talbot and Taylor stood and headed for the door without waiting.

"What's the story on the 'company dentist'?" Taylor asked when they were back on the street.

"One of my contacts is a dentist in London, who trades favors for referrals. I don't know how good his work is, but he doesn't charge much when it's for me. If Sean calls the number I gave him, and uses my name, the person who answers the phone will put him in contact with the dentist, who will then bill me."

"So there really is a dentist?"

"There really is. Of course, I should probably make a call to grease the skids." Talbot got on his phone and placed a call. He spoke for a few minutes, then disconnected.

"He gets fair-to-good dental work and we get excellent information." Talbot said when Taylor stared at him.

Talbot took Taylor to a nearby men's clothing store to kill a few hours while they passed the time, waiting to return to The Lucky Pig. Talbot told Taylor he'd get better results if he looked more like a local, so Taylor bought a tweed pullover, a pair of Argyle socks, a sports coat with patched elbows, and a Gatsby hat to add to his wardrobe.

They returned at four twenty, Taylor wearing his new clothes, and found a booth on the side of the bar opposite the door, where they could hopefully hear, regardless of where the terrorist sat. Talbot picked up two pints of brew and brought them to the table, setting one in front of Taylor. Taylor pushed it back to Greg, frowning.

"Drink it." Greg said, pushing it back toward Taylor. "You'll fit in better."

"I don't drink alcohol," Taylor said, pushing it toward the center of the table, not toward Greg, but away from himself.

"What do you want?"

"I'll have fruit juice if they have it."

Talbot laughed out loud. "Boy, you'll get more information if you drink with the boys. You think about that."

Taylor thought about it and didn't like the implication. Would he really be a better agent if he drank alcohol? He remembered as a teen being challenged by friends to drink a beer. He had taken two swallows of the ghastly drink and promptly vomited on one of his friends. They never tried again to get him to drink. "I may have to rethink this business," he mumbled.

"Water," Taylor called to the barkeeper, halfway across the room. The waiter frowned at him, then filled a glass with water and left it on the bar for Taylor to pick up. A few minutes later, Talbot motioned toward the door, where a man had just entered. He was stoop-shouldered, bearded, and wearing a long black robe that reached almost to the floor. The man didn't sit; He wandered around the room, speaking a few words to a few of the customers, and palming coins handed to him, as though he were a beggar. Good cover. When he passed Talbot and Taylor, he held out his hand and gave them an undecipherable look. When neither of them gave him a coin, he walked on. After making the rounds, he was back at the entrance. When he left, Greg gulped down the last of his drink, dropped some money on the table, stood and followed. Taylor hurried to keep up.

Outside the pub, Talbot looked around until he spotted the terrorist a block away, turning a corner. They followed, quickly. He had entered a dead-end alley, with only closed doors on either side. The terrorist stood about halfway down the alley, facing them. They stopped.

"Americans," the terrorist said in passible British English. "I saw you in the bar. What do you want?"

"We just want to know who you are," Talbot said with a strong British accent. Taylor had to look at his associate to see if he had suddenly morphed into an English Bobby. Seeing that he hadn't, he looked back at the terrorist and waited for Talbot to make a move.

Talbot started walking again, slowly, toward the terrorist. Suddenly, the terrorist held a gun in his hand, pointed at them. "You're not English, you're American. CIA?"

"We need to know why you're recruiting young men. Are you planning an attack? Where?"

Just as suddenly, the terrorist started shooting at them. Taylor dropped to his stomach on the dirty asphalt. Talbot stood his ground. The terrorist's aim was terrible. The bullets passed all around them, but not close. Taylor wondered if that was intentional. Talbot pulled his gun and took one shot, from the hip, hitting the terrorist in the head. He went down immediately and didn't get up.

Talbot turned and left the alley. Taylor followed, dusting the dirt off his clothes.

"Do we just leave him there?" Taylor asked.

"Word will spread fast that whatever he was doing will draw the wrong kind of attention. We don't normally leave a mess for someone else to clean up, but in this case, the message it will send is worth the trouble."

"Will there be trouble? For us, I mean?"

"The ambassador may be asked questions. Maybe even the CIA station chief, but they'll cover for us. We just need to get as far away from here as we can before the authorities show up."

"How will the authorities know we shot him?"

"They'll canvas the area, including the bar, and someone will mention that we followed him out. They'll guess that we're American and contact the embassy to find out who we are. They won't find out."

Taylor had to think about that. "How long did it take you to pick up the British accent?" he asked.

"Not long. With your knowledge of languages, you should be able to pick it up in no time. You'll be spending a lot of time in British colonies, so you should have lots of opportunities to hear others. Just listen and practice. Maybe record some conversations and play them a few times until you get the various accents right."

"We're done here," Taylor said into the phone a short time later. "I'll get a flight back tomorrow."

"Agent Talbot already sent in a report on the shooting in London," Ollie said. "Good work. Don't come here. Catch a flight to Singapore. The Southeast Asia station chief has the file on your next assignment. It's another terrorist, but this one you'll do on your own."

"Really? I don't have contacts in Singapore, like Talbot has in London."

"That's fine. You'll make your own contacts. The station chief will have suggestions."

"Yes, sir," Taylor said. He had reservations about this approach. He would much rather have a partner for one more mission. But he understood that he needed to find his own contacts as soon as possible. He was resourceful. He had training. And Ollie trusted him. He could do this.

4

"Here's the file," the station chief said in his British accent. Taylor repeated what the chief had said, trying to mimic the accent.

"That's good," the chief said. "You'll pick it up in no time. The note they sent with the file said that this is your first solo assignment, and only your second assignment since you finished your training, so I'm supposed to give you whatever help I can. What do you need?"

"Can you tell me who to go to for information? On my first assignment, my partner knew someone who was familiar with the people in the area."

"I can't provide much help there. Tell me what kind of people you need and maybe I can tell you where to find them."

"Greg said to find ex-cons, recovering alcoholics, gamblers, prostitutes, anyone who will trade favors for information and who I think I can trust."

"Now, you've got me there," the station chief said. "I don't know how many of that kind of people would be trustworthy. Let me ask one of the other agents here."

"Send him to the courthouse," Taylor overheard from the adjacent room. Taylor picked up his case file and was ready to leave, but decided to wait until the chief returned.

"I heard what he said." Taylor said. "Give me the address for the courthouse and I'll spend some time down there; see what I can do on my own." He spoke with more confidence than he actually felt.

"Feel free to return if you don't find someone who can help."

"Thank you."

"Anything else you need? Weapons, ammunition?"

Because Taylor had flown into Singapore, he didn't have a gun. So, he took him up on his offer, selected a nine-millimeter Beretta with three clips of ammo and stuffed them in his bag.

"Don't try to take those into the courthouse," he was told. "They'll confiscate the gun and arrest you for carrying."

"Good to know. Thanks."

The next morning, he was at the courthouse when the doors opened for business. He didn't know what to do or what to expect, so he played it by ear.

"Which way to the courtroom?" He asked one of the security guards manning the metal detector at the entrance.

"Rooms two and three will be in use today," the guard said. "Down that hall to the right," he added, pointing

Taylor found the room marked 'Courtroom 2' and opened the door slowly, not knowing what to expect. There were a few people spread around the room; some looked like attorneys, some like vagrants or regular citizens. He sat on the back row, near the door and spent the morning listening to cases. He had no inspiration about what to do. He heard cases involving drugs, theft, breaking and entering and arson. He even heard a preliminary hearing on murder. Some were plea bargained. Some were held over for trial. Some were dismissed. But he didn't know what to do about any of them and he didn't feel good approaching any of the people appearing before the judge.

When the judge recessed for lunch, Taylor was the first one out the door. He went looking for food. When all he found was vending machines, with cakes, candy bars and drinks—he didn't want to leave the building in search of food and miss a potential contact—he bought a Snickers bar and a Coke and carried them to Courtroom 3 to consume.

He was immediately approached by an officer of the court and told that he couldn't eat in the courtroom, so he found a chair in the hallway, to finish his meager lunch, then returned to the courtroom for the afternoon session. Receiving no inspiration before the end of the day, he went looking for food and a room. The room part was easy—he had a referral from the station chief—and he found food without much trouble. He went to bed early and rose early the next morning. He returned to the courthouse to repeat the process.

Late in the day, one case caught his attention. A woman had been charged with prostitution and had been acquitted, since no one would testify against her. The prosecution was incensed; they said they had witnesses, but the witnesses refused to testify against her. As the judge dismissed the case, Taylor left the room and waited for her in the hallway. As she passed, her head held high, self-confidence evident in her demeanor, Taylor made his decision and approached her.

Ponloc

"Excuse me," he said. "Can I speak with you for a moment?"

She ignored him and kept walking, with only a slight hesitation. He hurried to keep up with her.

"Excuse me," he said again. "Can I buy you a drink?"

She finally stopped and turned toward him.

"Why are you bothering me?" she asked.

"Because I saw you in court and have a proposition for you that I think you'll be interested in."

She laughed out loud and studied his face.

"Aren't you the funny one? Do you work for the prosecutor?" Her speech had a slight British accent, which he tried to mimic sub vocally.

"What?"

"I said . . ."

"I heard what you said. Why did you say it?" He asked, practicing his newly-acquired accent.

"If you were in the courtroom, you know that I was charged with prostitution and you just offered me a proposition. Why?"

"I'm sorry. That's not the kind of proposition I meant. I need information and I think you might be able to help me."

"Why do you think that?"

"Just a gut feeling. I've been here for two days, trying to find someone who might have information that I need. When I heard your case, I got this feeling that you were the person I was looking for. You're attractive. You have self-confidence. No one would testify against you. You obviously know people who respect you . . . or fear you. Will you hear me out?"

She sighed, like he was trying her patience, "I can tell you're trying to acquire a British accent. You've got a way to go, but I'm impressed. What do you want?" she finally asked.

"First of all, my name is Taylor. Taylor Swensen."

"American?"

"Yes," he said, nodding, "I work for our government. Can I ask your name?"

"Ponloc." She spelled it for him.

"Is that a given name or surname?"

"Just Ponloc."

"Can I buy you a drink?"

"No."

"Can we find a place to sit and talk?"

"Is this going to take long?"

"It doesn't have to." He looked around for a place to sit. He couldn't see one close by.

She studied him for a few more moments. "You intrigue me," she finally said. "Okay, I'll let you buy me a drink and I'll listen to your proposition. Then I'll decide whether to help you, ignore you, or call the police. You realize that the police are very intolerant in Singapore, don't you?"

"I've heard that. I promise. This is a legitimate business offer. Where would you like to go?"

"Oh, I get to choose?"

"Anywhere you want."

She hesitated again when they got to his car and he got in, expecting her to follow. She was attractive, but he wasn't interested in a relationship with her. He might have been, under different circumstances—he liked her exotic looks—but not now.

"Come on," he said. "I'm not a kidnapper, nor do I have designs on you."

She thought about that for another few moments. "Why not?"

"Why not what?"

"Why don't you want me? You said I was attractive? I've heard you Americans worship beauty."

"I'm attracted to beautiful women, just like anyone else. And, I agree, you are a beautiful woman; but I don't mix business and pleasure. What I need now is information."

She studied him for another minute, then got in the passenger side and directed him to a nearby bar. They found an empty table and she ordered a drink. He told the waiter he'd have water.

"You're not drinking with me?" she asked, giving him a curious look.

"I don't drink alcohol," he said.

"Why not?"

"Dulls my senses," he said, realizing that he needed to find a better reason than that. Most people that he would interact with would expect him to drink with them. "I can't afford to not be at my best. Besides. I hate the taste of alcohol. It upsets my system."

"Ahh, can't hold your liquor. There's a story there."

"There is, an embarrassing one."

She smiled, like his answer impressed her. He wasn't trying to be macho. Or, it just wasn't worth pursuing. "Okay, what's your proposition?"

"I need information. I'm willing to pay for it."

"What information?"

"You're a native of Singapore? How old are you?"

"I am, and my age is none of your business."

"I'm guessing twenty-two. Close?"

"Close."

"Okay. That might work against us. If you were older, you'd know more people."

"Why do I need to know more people?"

"Because I want to know about a specific person. Do you know a terrorist who's recruiting young men for an attack?"

"Wow. That's pretty specific information."

"Yes, it is. Do you?"

"How will you pay for this information?"

"So, you have the information," he said, concluding that she did from the way she answered. "That's good. The payment is negotiable. What do you think the information is worth?"

"A night with me in my apartment, and I choose the entertainment."

"Can we negotiate, or come up with an alternative payment that's just as acceptable to you?"

"Do you object to spending the night in my apartment, or me choosing the entertainment?"

"I'm more concerned about your choice of entertainment."

"Why?"

"Because you've been charged with prostitution. I don't know if the charge is valid, but I don't want to find out."

"Alright. I think I'm pretty firm on the place, but I may let you help with the entertainment."

"Then you have a deal. Should we shake on it?" he asked, holding out his hand.

She took his hand, pulled him across the table, and kissed him on the lips. She was stronger than she looked. "It's a deal," she said.

5

Russia—eight years earlier
Dmitri Pavlovich

"Should I worry about the changes taking place in the government?" Dmitri asked his mentor and current supervisor in the USB, Aleksey Vladoroski.

"The changes are being led by the USB's sixth service, of which we are a part," said Vladoroski. "Most of the changes appear to be infighting between the security services, but some are definitely cases of corruption at high levels of the government. The SEB, FSB, FSO, and even the USB have been affected, but it seems the situation is settling down. We should not be affected. Are you worried about your customers in Northern Africa and the Middle East?"

"I am. We bring in a huge profit that supports Russian industry. I hope we are immune from the purges."

"You realize that the sixth service is the most powerful and secretive organization within the government, don't you?"

"I do. And we've worked hard to establish trade relations with the Arab nations and their radical anti-West extremists. I hope that's not lost on those in power. We are important to the long-range goals of the Russian Federation."

"I'm sure they realize that your customers in Africa and the Middle East are important to our county's long-term goals. I bring it up whenever I have an opportunity, to help them remember. So, what help do you need from me?"

"My biggest problem is the American CIA. Normally they focus on my customers, but lately they've been watching my activities as well."

"But you've been able to handle them so far, haven't you?"

"So far I've identified and eliminated two of their agents, but they keep sending more."

"And you have plenty of muscle to help control the situation, don't you?"

"We've hired plenty of mercenaries to help with protection; but it's eating into our profits. I worry that the Americans will come up with someone, eventually, who will be lucky enough to get past them and get too close to me."

"I don't see that happening, unless you become careless. And you're not careless, so we're safe. Just don't become complacent or let your guard down."

6

As soon as they entered her apartment, Ponloc locked the door behind them. She went to the kitchen, opened a cupboard and brought out a bottle of amber liquid, along with two glasses. He saw that the label said vodka, before she turned it away from him.

"Excuse me for a few minutes, while I freshen up," she said. "Make yourself at home, but don't leave." She left him and went down a hallway. He wandered around her apartment, looking at her modern furniture and color-coordinated interior design. The furniture looked expensive and comfortable. The apartment was in a modern building in a good part of town.

He could hear when the shower stopped running. A few minutes later, she returned to find him sitting on her couch. She wore only a short, black, lace negligee with spaghetti-straps, that left little to his imagination. She poured some vodka into the two glasses, then brought them into the living room, set them on the low table by the couch, then sat close to him.

"All set," she said. "Now let's get started." She leaned into him and kissed him on the lips. She smelled of soap and flowers, and tasted of alcohol.

"I think we need to set some ground rules here," he said. "We agreed to negotiate."

"What do you want?" she asked, acting perturbed, but keeping her head close to his, her lips close to his face. "What are your conditions?"

"No alcohol and no sex. I'll agree to anything else."

"What?" she sounded insulted. "Those are the first things men insist on having whenever I bring them here."

"Well, you'll find that I'm not like other men."

"Are you gay?"

"Definitely not. Just particular about those two things, and anything that leads inevitably to them, like too much physical contact. Now, what do *you* want to do?"

"There's nothing left that can keep my attention," she said.

"Okay, give me the information I asked for and I'll leave, so you can get on with finding someone who'll do those things with you."

"No. No. I'm more intrigued than ever. You're American. You're looking for a terrorist. Are you CIA?"

"I can't tell you," he said, "or . . ."

"I'll have to kill you," they said at the same time. Then they both laughed.

"I've seen American movies, so I know about your CIA."

"The movies make working for the CIA look glamorous and use only beautiful people. It's not like that."

"You're a handsome man," she said. "You fit the image."

"Thank you, but I'm just an ordinary guy. Now, you're very pretty," he said. "I bet you know a lot of men. Do you socialize much?"

"I like to socialize and I like men. Is this leading to a question about the terrorist?"

"You implied you know who I'm looking for. Is it someone you like? Are you going to have trouble telling me who it is?"

"I'm pretty sure I know who you're looking for. No, it shouldn't be a problem telling you who he is. In fact, I'll take you to him if you want."

"You'd do that? Even if it's dangerous?"

While they talked, she took his hand and led him to the bedroom. He went along, thinking she was getting information for him. She removed her nightie—she was, indeed, a gorgeous woman—then started undressing him. As soon as he realized what she was doing, he stopped her by placing his hand on hers.

"You're violating our agreement," he said and backed away from her, while she tried to stop him by holding onto his arm. He looked her in the eyes. "You're doing it on purpose, aren't you?"

"I need to make love to you, Taylor. Please?"

"That's not what we agreed. That's not what I want."

"But, I need it. I crave it. I'm what you Americans call a nympho."

"Maybe what you need is help controlling your compulsive disorder."

"What do you mean? Do you think I can turn off my passions like a light switch?"

"I think that with some help, some guidance, you can control your sexual disorder and funnel your energy into more useful pursuits. You could use your energy as a weapon instead of a crutch."

"You call it a disorder. Does that mean you believe there is help for it, that I can control it?"

"I do believe that. Would you like that? I think I know who can help, if you're interested and willing to commit to following some professional advice."

"What's it going to cost me?"

"This is where we can help each other. We can make it part of our deal."

"Meaning what? I give you the information you want and you help me with my self-control?"

He nodded and smiled.

"That's an intriguing idea," she said. "Do you think the CIA would hire me if I could control my passion and use it as a weapon?"

"I know if I could trust you, I'd visit you whenever I come to Singapore and need information."

She thought some more. "Maybe I'll agree to make this part of our deal. How do we do that?"

"Let me make a call, then you can take me to our terrorist friend."

"Deal!" she said, then pulled him to her and kissed him again. He was distracted by her body being in close contact with his and distanced himself from her only with effort. He called the office and spoke to the chief's executive assistant for a few minutes, dressing as well as he could with one hand. She helped him. The station chief had told him about the local resources that they used periodically when negotiating with informants. A behavioral therapist was one of them.

"It's all set up," he said when he disconnected. "The company has a female therapist and you have an appointment tomorrow at ten. Here's the name and address. Give them my name when you check in and everything will be billed to me."

"I can't let you pay for it."

"I get a special deal, so don't question it or try to pay for the appointment. If they want to schedule a follow up, or multiple visits, do it. I'll check back with you next time I'm in town to see how you're doing."

"Is this going to be dangerous?" Taylor asked as they got in his car. She said she didn't have a car because it was so hard to get around Singapore in a private car.

"I don't know if he's dangerous. I've only met him once and

I've heard the rumors about him. I think he's a front man for Al Qaeda, an organizer. He only deals with the recruits; he doesn't plan the missions."

"So, he may be dangerous and he may surround himself with protection. Is that a fair assessment?"

"I'm sorry. I don't know. I only know how to find him because he asked me to refer young people to him."

"What kind of young people?"

"Anyone who seemed unhappy, disillusioned, or looking for something in their life."

"That sounds like a good come-on for a terrorist cell."

She directed him to a neighborhood that was more rundown than he expected to find in a modern city like Singapore. There were barefoot children playing in dirty cobblestone streets. The buildings were older, more rundown, some crumbling. Graffiti covered many walls. Robed men sat on stoops smoking, drinking or just talking.

She had him pull over to the curb near an intersection where an open-air market occupied one corner.

"I think this is the right place," she said.

He studied her, trying to decide if he could trust her, even now. She could be leading him into a dangerous situation; but he believed she would not let herself get caught in the middle of a gun fight, where she could be injured or killed. He'd brought his Beretta and ammo.

She led him into the corner market through a wide, arched, open doorway. There was a long counter in front and to the left of them, with glass display cases, filled with food, mostly salads and meat dishes. Flies buzzed around some of the dishes in the open-air display case. There were three metal tables set up in the open area in front of the counter, with two metal folding chairs set up at each. No one was seated at any of the tables or milling around the market.

Three older women stood behind the counter, wearing burkas. Two appeared to be preparing food on a flat counter in front of them, while the third, an older, short, plump woman, stood looking at Ponloc and Taylor, expectantly.

Ponloc asked for Josef in a foreign language—Persian or Farsi, he guessed. The woman at the counter registered a look of recognition, as though Ponloc's voice triggered a memory, or her request for Josef offended her, then yelled something in a language Taylor didn't understand, pointing to the exit. Ponloc yelled something back.

"Stupid woman," Ponloc said to Taylor.

"What was that?" Taylor asked.

"She said, 'He's mine. You can't have him.', so I said, 'I don't want your mule. Just get him out here.'"

The older woman stopped, looked pensive, then called something into the back room. When nothing happened, the woman went to the back room.

A small, thin man entered from the back, followed by the woman who had gone to get him. He looked proud, but Taylor could sense that the woman was the boss and he was doing what she told him to do—her mule.

The man spoke a few words to Ponloc, then looked at Taylor expectantly.

"English," Ponloc said.

"I am Josef," the man said. "You want to see me?"

"I'm Taylor," Taylor said, trying for a British accent and failing. "I need information. You are recruiting young men for a suicide mission. What is it?"

"You are mistaken. I am seeking young people, boys and girls, to attend school in Saudi Arabia."

"Yet you recruit youth of any nationality, not just Middle Easterners. Why is that?"

"I want our youth—all youth—to be educated in our beliefs and religion. We have schools where they will learn the words of the Prophet, instead of what this government thinks they need to know."

"So you say. You do not have an attack planned against the Singapore government?"

"No, we do not," Josef said, but Taylor could see the perspiration standing out on Josef's forehead. His hands fidgeted, and he shifted his weight from one foot to the other, nervously.

Josef's eyes wandered to the three women behind the counter. Taylor's eyes followed. Josef nodded to the women, then turned toward the back and started to leave.

Taylor drew his gun and pointed it at Josef. "Stop, Josef," he said. Suddenly, the three women behind the counter pulled guns from under the counter and pointed them at Taylor and Ponloc. Taylor pulled Ponloc to the floor, just as automatic weapon fire poured out across the room, shattering the quiet of the neighborhood and punching holes in the stuccoed walls behind where they had been standing. The women weren't aiming the guns. The way the guns jerked, it looked like they barely had them under control. Taylor turned one of the tables over and pulled Ponloc behind it for protection.

As bullets continued to fly around the room, with no apparent target, Taylor pulled his Beretta from his belt and took a shot, dropping Josef before he could leave the room. The women who had wielded the automatic weapons let them drop from their hands as they turned to assist Josef, and started to wail. The guns clattered to the floor. Taylor and Ponloc scrambled out to the sidewalk on hands and knees, stood, and ran to his car. Taylor fully expected a barrage of gunfire to follow them, but, for whatever reason, it did not.

Taylor started the car, did a U-turn in the street and headed back the way they had come. He was drawing a lot of attention from the old men on the street.

"That was easier than I thought it would be," he said, then looked at Ponloc, briefly. The blood had drained from her face. He worried that she might faint. "Put your head down," he said. She just stared straight ahead, so he reached over, put his hand on the back of her neck and pushed her head down toward her lap. When he let go, she started to straighten up, so he pushed her head down further, leaving his hand there until he was satisfied that she would leave it down.

"Are you okay?" he asked after a minute.

"Did you have to shoot him?" she asked.

"They shot at us first, in case you didn't notice. And those weapons would be illegal in the United States."

"They probably are here, too." She said. "I've just never seen anyone shot before. I think it put me in shock."

"Well, it looks like they're not going to follow us," he said, just as two black SUVs entered from a side street at high speed and chased after them, gaining quickly. Catching the movement in his rear-view mirror, he turned to look behind them.

"Forget what I just said. Look back and tell me what you see," he said, shifting his eyes back to the rear-view mirror. She sat up and turned in her seat.

"Two cars, at least four people, maybe six, guns out the windows, pointed at us."

"That's what I thought," he said as he hit the gas pedal and they accelerated up the street. Luckily, there was no traffic on the street at the time.

At the next intersection, he made a quick left turn, almost hitting a police car. The driver turned on his lights and siren and flipped a U-turn, ending up behind the first SUV. "Stop and pull over," Taylor heard over a police blowhorn. Then there was a screech of metal on metal and one of the SUVs careened up onto the sidewalk and hit a telephone pole, the police car, unable to stop, ran into the back of the SUV.

Taylor continued, making quick turns, trying to lose the other SUV. Then a second police car pulled up behind the second SUV and did the same thing. This time, however, the SUV flew up onto the sidewalk and crashed through the front wall and window of a shoe store before it stopped. The policeman was able to stop before he hit the SUV.

When a third police car continued to follow them, Taylor handed his gun and ammo to Ponloc.

"Put these under your seat," he said. As soon as she did, he slowed and pulled over, waiting for the police to do their thing. Taylor showed the policeman his international license that had 'US Diplomat' stamped across the face.

"Wait here," the policeman said, then went back to his car and got on the radio. A few minutes later, he returned and handed Taylor his license.

"Here you go, Mr. Swensen. It appears that you were being chased and were trying to outrun your pursuers. In the future, we ask that you stay out of this particular neighborhood, to avoid the undesirable element here, and obey all traffic laws. Speed endangers innocent pedestrians."

"Yes, sir, it does. I have no reason to return to this neighborhood."

The policeman walked away and Taylor drove off, careful to

stay within the speed limit. He followed Ponloc into her apartment. She offered him a drink, again, and he declined, again. She poured herself a full glass and drank the whole thing without stopping for breath. Finally, she looked him in the eyes again.

"Thank you, Taylor, for an exciting afternoon. Please keep your promise to visit me."

"I will. Please follow through with tomorrow's appointment."

"Definitely."

Taylor drove to the agency office and called Langley to report in.

"I usually get a written report, Taylor," Ollie said. "Just dictate your report to a secretary and send it to me. Unless there is anything of a confidential nature, then type it up yourself."

"Everything is confidential, isn't it?"

"Technically, yes. But you can write it so that what the secretary sees doesn't put her in danger of having too much classified information."

"Okay. I'll work with that. What's next?"

"Get to Sydney and talk to the station chief. He has your next assignment."

"Yes, sir. I'll take the next available flight out."

"After you file your report."

"Yes, sir."

7

Sydney, Australia—Mary

"Are you ready for lunch?" Mary asked Katie, the receptionist.

"As soon as Ricky gets here," Katie, the receptionist said. "Where should we go this time?"

This had become a regular routine; every time Mary was in Sydney to deliver documents to the station chief. Mary, Ricky and Katie would go to lunch together at least once each trip, sometimes twice, depending on the workload.

"How about the little place on the corner? We haven't been there for a while."

"Works for me." As soon as Ricky showed up, Katie stuck her head in the chief's office door and told him they were going out for lunch.

"Be careful," the chief said.

"Mary's going with us so we'll be fine." Mary had established a reputation at the office a few weeks earlier when she'd been accosted on the sidewalk by a man demanding her purse.

"In your dreams," she had said and walked way.

The man had made the mistake of grabbing her shoulder to turn her around and she had swung around, hitting him in the side of the head hard enough to not only knock him down, but knock him out. A passerby had called the police and Mary had waited to explain herself. The police had determined that the guy had robbed four other single women in the previous three weeks. They hauled him away. She showed them her diplomatic credentials, gave them a verbal testimony, and was allowed to walk away.

The three women walked down the sidewalk to the small restaurant on the corner. Mary noticed two men watching them, they were all three young and pretty, talking animatedly. They entered the restaurant and found a booth near the back. Mary sat on the bench facing the door, while the other two sat together facing her.

Mary noticed when the two men entered, looked around, and walked toward them. They had just ordered their food when the men reached the table. Ricky excused herself and walked toward the ladies' room at the back.

Mary thought of the two men as number one and number two, number one being the larger and tougher looking of the two. Number one rested his forearm on the back of the booth behind Katie and leaned over to talk to them.

"Hello ladies," he said. "Want to go somewhere to get to know each other better?"

"We want to eat our lunch in peace, without you disturbing us," Mary said.

"That's not very friendly," he said, as number two stepped over and rested his arm behind Mary.

"Please leave us alone," Katie said.

"We're not doing anything illegal. We're just trying to be friendly. We can tell you ladies are from out of town. American?"

"None of your business," Mary said. "Now go away."

"Or what?"

"You don't want to find out."

"Oh, aren't you a feisty one?" number two said and reached over to take Mary's chin in his fingers.

Mary took his hand off her chin and pushed it away from her. He grabbed her right wrist with his left hand and tried to pull her up out of her seat. She took his middle finger in her left hand, the one on her wrist, and bent it back until she could tell from his expression that it had hurt. He let go of her wrist, then reached toward her neck with his left hand.

She stood out of the booth to face him. He was a couple of inches taller. He reached out again to put his arm around her neck. He never made it. She swung her fist around and hit him in the side of the head, hard enough to knock him down.

"Bruno!" Mary heard someone say, likely one of the waitresses. A large man stepped out from behind the counter and approached as number two staggered to his feet. Number one took a step toward Mary, swinging his fist at her head. She blocked his arm with her own arm, then kicked him between the legs. He fell to the floor next to number two.

Bruno stood between Mary and the two men, his hands on his hips and glared at her.

"I'll take care of these two. They've been trouble before. I suggest you ladies make a quick exit, before the police get here."

"We haven't finished or lunch," Katie protested.

"Take it with you," Bruno said. "No charge."

They wrapped their sandwiches in paper napkins and left, noticing the open-mouthed stared of the other patrons.

Taylor

"Where is everyone?" Taylor asked Katie, the receptionist, when he entered the office, which he expected to be busy with agency personnel handling agency business, but which was now empty and quiet.

"In a staff meeting in the conference room," Katie, said, pointing down a hallway to her right. "Feel free to go in."

Taylor slipped into the room quietly, hoping to be unobserved, but at least half the room noticed him enter and turned to look at him. He slipped into an empty seat against the wall, near the door, and leaned his chair back against the wall. The chief was giving a rundown of station assignment changes, expected visitors and other agency business.

"Ah, here's one of our visitors now," he said. "Mr. Taylor Swensen just finished an assignment in Singapore and is here to help us with one of our problems." Everyone turned and looked at Taylor. A pretty lady sitting with her back to him, at the conference table, raised her hand and the chief called on her.

"Yes, Ms. Slade?" he asked.

"The toilet in the ladies' room is backed up. Is he here to help with that?" There were chuckles around the room. The chief looked aghast, but Taylor just smiled. He'd seen Ms. Slade's profile when he'd entered the room, had previously read her file and seen a photo, but had yet to meet her or get a good look at her. He could have been upset by her comment, but chose to turn the attention back on her, to see how she would handle it.

"I'll do anything for Ms. Slade," he said flirtatiously. She turned in her seat to look at him. He liked what he saw. "Show me the way," he said directly to her. Her face and neck turned red at the attention. She stuck her tongue out at him, then turned her face away. There were snickers around the room. Taylor didn't know if they were still laughing at him or if now the attention was all hers.

"Come to my office after the meeting, Mr. Swensen," the chief said, trying to ignore the banter in the room. "I have your next assignment."

"Yes, sir."

The chief finished the meeting and excused everyone. Several people stopped to shake Taylor's hand and introduce themselves. One woman seemed to be trying to convince him to meet her after work. Before Ms. Slade could leave the room, he excused himself from the woman and caught Ms. Slade by the arm.

"My apologies, Ms. Slade. I didn't mean to embarrass you," he said politely.

"Apology accepted," she said, trying not to look in his beautiful dark blue eyes. "And I apologize to you for my snarky comment."

"Apology accepted, if you'll let me buy you dinner."

"That's not necessary," she said.

"Oh, but I think it is. It's the least I can do to ensure we maintain a good working relationship. What time do I pick you up?"

"I'll be finished here about seven."

"Why so late?"

"I have to meet with the chief at six. You can go to his office or I'll meet you in the lobby."

"I see you've met Ms. Slade," Katie said when Taylor approached. He could still hear the comments from the conference room, so he wasn't surprised that the receptionist had heard their banter.

"I did," he said, trying his British accent on her. "Who is she?"

"She's been with the agency about three months. She's a courier. We see her a lot here. Be forewarned. She rubs some people wrong. She has a sharp tongue and sometimes speaks without thinking. I think she likes to keep people off-balance."

"Thanks. I already found that out."

"But she's real sweet underneath her thick shell."

"I'll keep that in mind. Can you recommend a nice place to eat nearby?"

"Are you trying to impress her or chase her off?"

"That obvious, eh? Let's try to impress her first."

She gave him the names of a couple of restaurants, then he went to see the chief.

"You certainly impressed Ms. Slade," the chief said.

"Why do you say that? It seemed to me that she was upset."

"Oh, take my word for it. The way you handled her is exactly what impresses her. Anything less direct doesn't interest her in the least. Besides, she was smiling the entire time."

"So, you think she likes me?"

"She hasn't written you off, yet. Keep her off balance and you'll be sure to win her over, if that's what you want."

"I'll keep that in mind. Thank you."

"Oh, here's your next assignment. Mr. Tanner—Ollie—said he'd send you here to get it. There's an empty office two doors down on the right that you can use to review it. Feel free to call Ollie if you have questions."

Taylor took the folder, sat in the small, private office that the chief directed him to, and looked through the file, but his mind was on Ms. Slade and the way she had responded to him. He hadn't been on a date since he'd started at the Agency. He hadn't met anyone who captured his attention and imagination the way Ms. Slade had. Maybe dinner tonight would be the start of something new.

Mary

"Who is Taylor Swensen?" Mary asked the chief when they finished their CIA business.

"I don't know much about him, Mary. I know he's a spy and assassin. He came to work for the Agency a few months ago. He works alone and rumor has it he likes it that way One agent I spoke with said he's hard to get to know and doesn't seem to have much use for people."

Mary thought about the lifestyle she'd lived since starting with the Agency. There wasn't much opportunity to get to know people, even if you wanted to, with all the travel. She had gotten to know Katie and Ricky, but only superficially, even after multiple lunch outings. It was a hazard of the job. If Mr. Swensen was an assassin, he probably didn't trust many people that he encountered, so she could understand him not getting close to people. Was he really a loner, or was he just lonely? Finding out would be a challenge. Did she want to take that on? Or, did she just want to get a free dinner out of him tonight? "So, you're saying he's not in a relationship, doesn't have a girlfriend, I shouldn't even bother trying to get to know him, is that it?"

"That's the way I hear it. Supposedly, he dumped his last girl-friend when he joined the agency. I probably shouldn't say any-thing, but rumor has it that he shot a man—killed him—on his last assignment. Not the kind of man you want to take home to meet Mom and Dad."

"Thanks for the warning," she said as she left his office, a broad smile on her lips. She found Taylor waiting for her by the recep-tionist's desk, chatting with Katie.

"You got the chief all straightened out?" He asked as she ap-proached.

"All good," she said, unable to come up with a quick comeback. The look she gave Katie said, 'I don't want to hear that you told everyone we're going on a date when I come back tomorrow'. Ka-tie's expression said, 'I want to hear all about it in the morning. "Ready to go," she said.

He took her elbow in his hand and directed her out to the street, where his rental car waited at the curb. He opened the pas-senger door and handed her in before going to the other side and getting behind the wheel.

Taylor

"Where are you taking me?" Mary asked.

"It's a surprise," Taylor said, keeping his eyes on the road and his GPS device. He didn't know his way around Sydney and didn't want to spend the evening getting 'unlost'.

"I don't like surprises," she said. "They usually mean trouble."

"Not this one, but I'll tell you if you want to know." He told her when she nodded.

"Good choice." She said. "I approve."

"Thank you. It came highly recommended." He found his way to the restaurant with only one wrong turn, which the GPS corrected by rerouting them.

The parking lot at the restaurant was small, likely because most people didn't have cars; they walked or used Taxis or uber to get around. At the restaurant, he requested a table by the wall, so he could study the people in the restaurant around them and see the front door; it was a habit he'd developed to be able to see trouble coming. Taylor sat with his back to the wall which forced her to sit with her back to the open room. He also took a quick look at the underside of the table. It was part of his training.

She looked him a question.

"Looking for listening devices," he said.

"In a restaurant? Nobody knew we were coming here until a few minutes ago."

"Habit. It gives me something to do while I'm waiting for a menu."

She wrinkled her forehead and shook her head, apparently dubious about his paranoia.

"Would you like something to drink?" he asked.

"Ice water works fine for me," she said.

"Nothing stronger?"

"I don't drink alcohol and carbonation upsets my stomach. Fruit juice if they have it."

"I'm sure they do," he said with a smile. He ordered cranberry juice for both of them. They had a nice meal—seafood for him, a salad for her—and talked quietly as they ate.

"So, you're a spy?" she asked, leaning over the table and talking quietly. He looked around to see if anyone might be listening. No one was within earshot.

"I like to think of my job as a problem solver or repairman."

"Repairman?"

"Yeah, Like in F. Paul Wilson's 'Repairman Jack' series of stories. If someone had a problem that needed fixing, he fixed it."

"I'll have to look that one up. Have you solved many problems?"

"I've only been at it for a few months, but I've solved a few."

"Anything you can talk about?"

"Not really. You're a courier?"

"I am. Most of my trips have been to Australia. A couple to London. They told me it would be that way, since I only speak English. Do you speak other languages?"

"Not many," he said, looking away shyly. "Besides English, I speak Spanish, Portuguese, French, Italian, Swedish and the language of love." He chuckled at his own joke.

She looked at him seriously. "You're joking, right?"

"Do you want to find out?" He stared into her eyes while he waited for her answer.

"Maybe," she said after a pause to study him studying her. He noticed that her eyes darkened and she looked more intense. Maybe? Did she really just say that? What would he think?

"Do you want some coffee," he asked when they'd finished their meal.

"I don't take stimulants," she said. "It's either water or fruit juice for me."

"I like that," he said, smiling.

When he took her home to her apartment, he wondered if she would give him a goodnight kiss or invite him in. She didn't do either. She held out a hand for him to shake.

"Thank you for an enjoyable evening," she said.

"It doesn't have to end yet," he said. "It's still early."

"It is," she said apologetically, "but I have a busy day tomorrow. I better get to bed."

He had thought that most women were liberated; that a goodnight kiss or even sleeping over was part of a date nowadays. Maybe he'd been out of the dating scene too long, although it had only been a few months. Maybe she just wasn't like most women. She intrigued him. Was there something special about her? Some reason to get to know her better? More reason than just to tease her?

After reading the case file he'd been given by the station chief, Taylor was concerned about his next assignment; Although he'd been on assignments in several different countries and solved several problems for the government, he still considered himself new at what he did. Each assignment was unique, posing its own set of challenges. This next one could be the most difficult yet.

Mary had brought the chief information about a series of thefts in Perth. It looked like a gang had organized and was terrorizing local minority business owners. Through sources in New Zealand, they had been tied to a gang in Auckland. The file contained names and locations.

Mary delivered the information to the station chief and was ready to leave the country. Taylor was ready to leave for Perth, to get closer to the source, when the chief called him back to the office.

"What's up, Chief?" Taylor asked.

"There was an incident at the airport involving Ms. Slade. I thought you might want to check it out."

"What happened?"

"Mary was confronted by three men with knives in the airport parking lot. No one from the office was watching out for her. She was unescorted. By the time we realized she was in trouble, it was all over."

"Tell me about it." The chief did.

Mary

"You're too pretty to be out here by yourself," one of the men said, walking between cars in the airport parking lot, approaching Mary slowly.

"I'm in a hurry, boys. I don't have time for chit-chat," she said, making a jog around a car to avoid coming face-to-face with the three men. Apparently, it was the wrong thing to say to them.

"Maybe you want to dance with us," one of them said as all three pulled knives and moved to cut off her escape.

Mary had a flashback to her childhood. She was eleven, her only sister sixteen. As she walked home from school, she could see the flashing lights of the police car in the driveway. When she arrived home, anxious and worried, her mother and dad sat in the living room with two policemen. Her dad appeared to be consoling her mom.

"What's wrong?" she had asked immediately.

"It's Shelly," her dad said. "She's had an accident." At his words, her mom moaned and bawled into a wad of tissues she held in her hands.

"Is she okay?"

"No," he said as her mom shook her head.

"What happened?"

Neither of her parents would say more and the policemen refused to say anything if the parents weren't going to.

It had taken weeks of eavesdropping on conversations and listening to gossip at school to figure out that Shelley, her only sister and the person she idolized, had been confronted in the high school parking lot after cheerleader tryouts and brutally beaten by three older boys. Six weeks after the incident, she was still in intensive care in the hospital, with little chance of full recovery. She had died two months later, never recovering from the induced coma in the hospital.

Mary had decided that would never happen to her or anyone else she cared about, if she had anything to say about it. She had already been studying gymnastics for several years. She decided to add self-defense to her schedule. She took the self-defense training offer by the school, then signed up for a Mixed Martial Arts class provided by the community. When that was done, she found a personal trainer to teach her everything she could learn.

She had followed in Shelley's footsteps, becoming a high school cheerleader, then a cheerleader at the University, where she was noticed by Ollie during a football game and recruited into the CIA.

All these thoughts flashed through her mind in a few moments. Now, here she was, confronted by three men in a parking lot, just as Shelley had been, the major differences being that these men had knives instead of fists and Mary was expecting the worst and was prepared for them.

She didn't hesitate. She reached for the closest one, pulling his knife hand toward her, the knife aimed at her midsection. The move obviously startled the man. He tried to shift the knife to his other hand. While he was off-balance, she twisted his wrist, like she had the football player months earlier, with a similar result. The man hit the ground, screaming and holding his injured hand with his good one.

"Get her," the injured man said in a gravelly voice, looking at his two associates. They both moved forward cautiously between the parked cars. She didn't wait for them to get to her. She rested her hands on the cars on either side of her, jumped and kicked the first one in the chest, knocking him into the man behind him. Then she jumped and landed with both feet on the man's chest. He tried to grab her feet, but she was too quick, or the man's reaction time had been impaired when his breath left him. She kicked his hand away and stomped on his face, knocking him unconscious.

The third man had to climb over his fallen associates to get to her. As he did, a car door opened and knocked him off balance just long enough for Mary to plant the heel of her hand into his face, knocking him to the ground.

Someone must have called in the altercation, because two airport security agents headed across the parking lot at a run about that time. They found the three men lying on the ground, helpless, with Mary standing watch to make sure they didn't go anywhere. She could have been detained, even arrested for assault, but the man who had pushed his car door open into the third man told the security people what he had witnessed. More security people showed up a few minutes later. The three men were handcuffed and taken into custody and Mary was escorted to the terminal, through the security checkpoint and right to her gate. She was bumped up to first class for the fourteen-hour flight home.

Taylor

"What do you want me to do?" Taylor asked the chief.

"Just follow up on her tomorrow to see that she arrived home safely. Give her my apology for not having someone escort her for her protection and tell her I look forward to seeing her again on her next trip."

"Of course," Taylor said, then chuckled to himself about this feisty woman who took on three bad guys and walked away without injury. She was definitely worth getting to know.

8

He flew to Perth and met with another agent who was watching the gang. The other agent had been tracking the gang and knew where to find them. They encountered the gang, wielding clubs and crowbars, as they approached the front of a minority-owned business.

"What's up, gentlemen?" Taylor asked the gang member in front, who seemed to be directing the others.

"Get out of the way, man, and you won't get hurt," the gang leader said, swinging a baseball bat around in front of him, barely missing Taylor's chest.

"I'm afraid I can't let you disrupt this business's legal operations."

"Are you going to stop us, just the two of you?" the gang leader asked. "They don't belong here. They need to go back where they came from. We're going to show them the way." The gang leader raised his baseball bat and swung it at the store front window. Before it landed, Taylor grabbed the end of the bat and pulled it from the young man's hands. His empty hands continued around him, minus the bat, and he missed the window completely.

"Not a good idea," Taylor said.

The gang leader spit out a few profanities and charged Taylor. Taylor sidestepped him and he ran right past, throwing his arm out at Taylor as he flashed past. Taylor caught his arm and yanked on it, pulling the young man up short and causing him to fall on his butt on the sidewalk. Taylor could hear his teeth clatter from the abrupt stop.

The young man grabbed Taylor's ankle and tried to pull his leg out from under him, but Taylor kicked him in the face and he went down, blood running from his face.

"Get 'em," one of the other gang members said and charged. The six remaining young men attacked as one. Taylor and the other agent took a couple of steps apart and prepared to meet them.

The first man to reach Taylor got swept to the side and slammed into the brick store front, dazed, and fell to his knees, then his face, on the sidewalk. The second got a fist in the face and fell in front of Taylor. The third one got helped along when Taylor grabbed his shoulders and pushed him in the direction he was moving. He couldn't keep his feet under him and ended up sprawled on the sidewalk on his face. The three that took on the other agent fared no better, two landing on the sidewalk in a daze and the third landing in the gutter after hitting a parked car with his head.

When one of them tried to get up, Taylor placed a foot on his back and pushed him back down.

"Stay down," he said. The young man stayed down. Someone inside the store must have called in the incident. Taylor heard sirens, then police showed up from both directions. The gang leader immediately started complaining to the police that the two men had picked a fight with them. The store employees countered their complaints with the truth. The evidence—clubs and crowbars—lay all around them.

The police had no trouble figuring out what had happened, but wanted the two men to go to the station and give testimony. When they showed their diplomatic credentials and said they had been sent by the embassy to prevent a crime, the officers agreed to take the testimony of the store employees and let the agents go on their way.

Taylor called the station chief to report what had happened, then rented a room for the night. He ate alone in the hotel restaurant, then went to bed early.

That night, using a phone number given him by the chief, Taylor called Mary to check on her. It was early morning in Virginia.

"Ms. Slade, this is Taylor Swensen. I'm calling to see if you arrived home safe and sound. I heard about your problem in the airport parking lot."

"Mr. Swensen, how kind of you. I'm fine, thank you. There was no problem. I just had to disabuse some young men who thought they had plans for my day."

"So, you got to your flight without further incident?"

"Security arrived and gave me an escort through the airport. I got bumped up to first class, with hot, moist towels, meals, a reclining seat, and entertainment, they even gave me booties, pajamas and a toothbrush. I had a wonderful trip."

"Nothing but the best for you. I'm glad you're alright"

"I'm great, thanks."

"I think so, too," Taylor said.

Mary didn't respond for a few moments, likely trying to guess what Taylor meant by that. He wasn't sure how she would take it, but hoped she was flattered by his flirting.

"When can I expect to see you again?" she asked, finally.

"Who knows? Maybe we'll have to make a date."

Once again, she couldn't think if a comeback fast enough and ended the call with a "thank you for checking up on me."

Taylor watched for her each time he stopped in Australia, New Zealand, Great Britain, Singapore, or the U.S., all of her English-speaking stops, but their paths didn't cross.

9

Mary walked through the botanical gardens near the Sydney Opera House, enjoying the cool air that wafted through the grounds. She was taking a break after delivering files to the station chief. As many times as she had been to Sydney, this was the first time she had taken time to look around. She had to get to the airport for a late flight to London, but that gave her several hours to relax.

Sudden movement and a loud noise along the walkway caught her attention. It sounded like someone was in trouble. She remembered her promise to herself after her sister's death to be proactive in protecting the innocent. This was probably nothing, but she decided to check it out, anyway. She began to jog along the path.

As she got closer, she could see that two men had dragged a woman off the path and were headed into a stand of trees. She picked up her pace to intercept them before they disappeared into the trees.

Just before she lost sight of them, she yelled to get their attention, and hopefully slow them down.

"Stop!" she called loudly.

One of the men looked up and she thought she recognized him. It looked like one of the men she had encountered six months earlier when she went to lunch with Katie and Ricky. One that she had fought off. His face registered recognition at the same time and he hurried to drag the woman into the trees.

When she reached the spot where she thought they had gone into the trees, she saw two trails where the woman must have dragged her heels. She followed the trail into the trees, looking around carefully. She noticed flashes of dark among the trees, figuring it to be the dark clothes of the men as seen through the trees.

Just as she thought she was within sight of them, someone jumped out at her from the side, hitting her on the shoulder with a rubber club. She figured it was meant to hit her head, but a sudden move on her part protected her head. Her shoulder hurt like crazy, but it didn't incapacitate her.

The man followed his strike by running into her, grabbing her around the chest with both arms, and pinning her arms to her sides. She turned her head to look at him and saw the feral grin on his lips, inches from her head. She turned her head away from him and swung her head back, hitting him in the face. Surprised, he relaxed his hold on her and she swung both arms up to break his hold on her. Then she struck out with her hand, hitting him in the throat with the side of her hand. He gagged and released her, his hands going to his throat to check the damage. She took that opportunity to stomp on his foot with her booted foot, making him dance in pain. A second-hand strike, to the side of his head, dropped him.

Mary looked around, spotted the woman and the second assailant, and rushed off to catch up to them. When she arrived, a minute later, the woman had thrown her arms around a tree trunk and held on for dear life. Mary saw the man strike the woman on the face, causing her to release her grip on the tree, then he dragged her farther away.

Mary arrived in time to note that the man was the second man she had encountered six months earlier. She wasted no time in dispatching him as well, using his preoccupation with holding onto the woman against him. He couldn't hold onto her and fight off Mary at the same time.

She helped the woman out of the trees, then called for help. While they waited for the police, she quizzed the woman. She discovered that the two men had been following her for a while and had grabbed her when she tried to escape through the garden.

"Where did you learn to fight like that?" the woman asked with awe in her voice.

"Self-defense training," Mary said. "Every woman should take some training."

"I guess so. I'll look for it as soon as I get home."

The police arrived. Mary pointed to the clump of trees and explained in what condition they would find the two men. She showed them her diplomatic credentials and asked if she could be excused. The officer agreed to get the woman's statement so Mary could leave. She figured the woman wouldn't get home anytime soon, but hoped she would remember to look up self-defense training when she did.

Mary finished her walk around the gardens a little more quickly, then caught a ride to the airport for her trip home.

10

"Hi Mary, come in," Ollie said when Mary appeared in his office door at headquarters.

"You wanted to see me?" she asked.

"I do. Please take a seat." She sat in one of the comfortable arm chairs that sat in front of his large desk.

Ollie had a file open in front of him on the desk, with a stack of other folders in a basket on the corner of the desk. Other than that, his desk was clear.

"Did you have a nice trip home?" he asked.

"It's a long flight from Sydney, but flying business class makes it less stressful. Thanks for asking. What's up?"

"You've been at this for a year now. How do you feel?"

"In general, I enjoy it. The travel to new places is interesting, as well as the people."

"You're going to the same places over and over again. Are you getting to know the people?"

"In Sydney, yes. In other places, not so much."

"Do you feel safe on your assignments?"

"Generally, but I really thought there would be more excitement, travelling the world."

"You've had a couple of adventures, in Singapore and Sydney. They didn't scare you, make you wish for less excitement?"

"On the contrary. I thought there would be more danger involved. I have the training to take care of myself."

"So, are you ready for something more exciting, a little more dangerous."

"I think I could try that. What do you have in mind?"

"We need to get a message to a woman in Rio de Janeiro. She's not part of our agency. She's a supermodel, who's boyfriend is involved in something dangerous to the United States."

"So, you want me to pass a message to this supermodel about her boyfriend's illegal activities? Is that it?"

"Exactly. The difference is that you need to memorize the message, then destroy it, so no one else will find it."

"Is that it? Sounds easy."

"The difficult part is that it's Carnival time in Rio, so there will be lots of distractions, possibly danger from the crowds of revelers. It gets crazy in Rio during Carnival."

"I'll do it."

Rio de Janeiro—February

Gaetano was an entertainer, famous in Brazil, who was laundering drug money for a Mexican drug cartel through his club in Rio, Clube Divino.

His girlfriend, Paulina, was a supermodel. Mary's assignment was to convince her that Gaetano's activities were dangerous to her and needed to be stopped before she got hurt.

Mary flew into Brasilia, the capital of Brazil to make contact with the Station Chief, to let him know she was in the country and why. She had spent the time during her travel through Atlanta and Rio de Janeiro memorizing the message for Gaetano, which she would deliver to his girlfriend, Paulina. She wondered if the trip to Brasilia was necessary since her destination was Rio and she'd had to pass through Rio to get here.

"So, you're going to Rio to contact Geatano and Paulina," the station chief confirmed. "You do realize that he is almost impossible to get close to, don't you? He is surrounded by his security team, not to mention his fans. I'm afraid I can't help you there."

"It's okay," she said. "I've been briefed on how to handle the situation. I just wanted you to know I'm here in case there's a problem."

"Thank you, and good luck."

Mary caught the next flight back to Rio. The Carnival festivities had already started, as evidenced by the crowds in the streets, all the way from the airport to her hotel, which was on Copacabana Beach. The office had made her reservations and told her how difficult it was to get reservations during Carnival. First thing she did, before even unpacking, was to place a call to Paulina.

"Allo?" a female voice said when the phone was answered.

"May I speak with Paulina?" Mary asked, expecting that she would not be the one to answer the phone for herself. Most likely her manager or an assistant.

"Nao. Ela está ocupada. Quem é?"

"This is Mary Slade, from Washington, D.C., in the United States. Will you give her a message for me?"

"Uma mensagem? O que é?"

"Ask her to please call me. Here's the number at my hotel." She left a phone number. When she hung up, she wasn't sure how well the woman understood the message, and if she did, how long it would take for Paulina to return the call, if she even would. This might drive her crazy. The entire plan depended on Paulina realizing that Mary was the messenger that the CIA had said would be in contact with her to get her cooperation. Her boyfriend was in trouble and they needed Paulina to be the one to convince him to cooperate.

Paulina

She got the message from her assistant, asking her to please call Mary Slade. Was she the contact the CIA had told her would be in touch? She understood why they would send a woman, but why during Carnival. As Gaetano's girlfriend and as a supermodel, she was expected to be visible during the festivities. In fact, she would be on one of the floats, to represent the modelling agency, during the grand parade.

She waited several hours to place the call. She had to get ready for the parade and she needed to tell Gaetano what was going on. He wouldn't be happy about her talking to the CIA, but she had to agree with their assessment. What Gaetano was doing was dangerous, for him, and by association, for her. She thought the American CIA could protect them.

"This is Paulina," she said in her limited and heavily accented English, when Mary answered.

"Oh, Paulina, thank you for calling. Can we meet, sometime soon? I have a message for Gaetano from my boss."

"Very busy tonight. In parade. Wait. tomorrow?"

"It can't wait. Can we meet tonight?"

"Ride on float in parade." What Paulina was saying was that she had to ride in the parade. Mary wondered if she was going to get a chance to talk to her tonight. After all, Carnival was a twenty-four hour a day event.

"Come now. We find you costume." Paulina gave Mary an address, then hung up.

Mary called for a cab and gave them the address. She wondered all the way there what Paulina had meant about a costume. When she arrived, she introduced herself and was ushered into a dressing room. Two women immediately began undressing her.

"What are you doing?" She asked.

"Costume." One of them said, while the other continued to undress her. Finally, standing naked in the room, one of the women pulled a hanger out of a closet and held it in front of Mary. If this was the costume, she'd have more clothes on if she wore her bikini swimming suit.

The women helped her into the skimpy outfit, then applied body paint to her arms, legs and torso, to compliment the colorful feathers that were part of the costume and covered a little of her body.

"Dance," one of the women said and started to move her body to a samba beat, apparently in her head. Mary began wondering if Paulina was expecting her to dance on the float. She mimicked the woman's movements, as best she could, standing in one place. The woman exaggerated her movements, obviously trying to get Mary to do the same. So, although she felt foolish, she copied the woman, who then smiled.

A beautiful woman entered the dressing room, then. She was nearly naked and painted similar to Mary. "I'm Paulina," she said.

"Oh, Paulina. I need to give you a message, but I'm afraid you won't understand it with your limited English language skill."

"Speak," Paulina said.

"My government is worried for your safety. They want to help you by removing you from the threat . . ."

"Stop!" Paulina said. "Gaetano speak English very good. Talk to him, not me."

"When, where?"

"After parade. Clube Divino."

"Good. Should I wait here for you?"

Paulina stepped back and looked Mary over from head to feet, turning her around once to see her from the back side. "No, you look good for parade. Come with me. We hurry"

"What are we doing?" Mary asked.

"Ride on float in parade."

"You want me to ride on the float? I don't think I can do that."

"You pretty lady. You dance on float, then we go see Gaetano."

Paulina left the room and Mary was obligated to follow, even if she wanted to argue the point.

Paulina took Mary's hand and led her out to a waiting car. They were taken to a staging area, where a ladder sat next to an enormous float, decorated beautifully with flowers and streamers. Mary resigned herself to her fate. She just hoped no one that she knew would see her in this outfit, dancing on a float during Carnival.

Paulina led Mary to a spot near the front of the float, on one side and showed her where to stand, speaking to a young woman who's been standing there and pushing her toward the back of the float. Then Paulina climbed onto a higher platform, in the middle of the float.

As the float started to move, Mary looked up at Paulina, who began to sway to music, which Mary could now hear being piped from the truck beneath the float through speakers on her level. Mary swayed to the music as the float entered the main street, lined on both sides by throngs of people cheering, chanting, and taking pictures. She was immediately self-conscious about parading in front of so many strangers in so little clothing. She looked up at Paulina again to get her reaction, but Paulina was preoccupied, dancing, her beautiful smile infectious, like she was having the time of her life. Mary looked toward the back of the float, to see how the young woman whom she had replaced, was faring. The girl danced, smiled and waved to the crowd, apparently enjoying herself.

Mary turned back to the front. There was a dance club in front of them. There must have been a hundred lovely women doing a samba as they walked slowly along, wearing nothing but short shorts and pasties, their skin painted bright colors. Ahead of the dancers, in the distance, Mary could vaguely see another float, with dancers dancing on it.

Rather than think about her situation and what she was not wearing, since there was nothing she could do about it now, she focused on the crowd. Most of the crowd wore colorful shirts and pants for the men, and dresses for the women. Some wore masks or headdresses of colorful feathers, beads or other decorations. Mixed in among the locals were people who looked like tourists or visitors, men and women in fancier or more formal dress. Everyone wore smiles. Most danced.

It seemed to Mary that the parade went on for hours. She was worn out from the stress of dancing, nearly naked, in front of thousand, if not tens of thousands, of strangers. When they finally reached the staging area at the end of the parade, Paulina descended from her perch, threw her arms around Mary and hugged her. Sometime along the parade route, Paulina had removed her top, so she was naked from the waist up. She was indeed a beautiful woman, with dark skin that glistened with perspiration and reflected the lights around the area.

"Thank you," Paulina said. "You were wonderful."

"You're welcome," Mary said. "Do we meet Gaetano now?"

"Wait. Dressing room first."

Mary liked that idea. She couldn't wait to get out of this costume and back into her clothes.

"Can I take a shower?" Mary asked when they arrived back at the dressing room.

"Not yet," Paulina said. "First dance for Gaetano."

Mary didn't like the sound of that. Was she expected to give a personal performance for Gaetano, in this outfit?

Finally, a woman came to the room and announced that Gaetano was back. Paulina held her hand up to Mary in a 'wait' gesture. Within a few minutes, Mary could hear instruments warming up; guitars, a drum and a synthesizer. When they stopped, Paulina turned to Mary again and waved her forward.

"What are we doing?" Mary asked.

"Dance for Gaetano," Paulina said, then took Mary's hand and led her out of the room into the main dance hall of Clube Divino, where hundreds of people milled about, hugging and kissing, smoking, drinking, and otherwise enjoying themselves. As Gaetano's band started to play, up on a stage to one side of the room, some of the people started dancing to the music.

Paulina led Mary to the steps leading onto the stage and climbed, urging Mary to follow. The other young women who'd been on the float with them, followed, until eight women stood, spread out across the front of the stage. Paulina was front and center, with Mary a few feet away on her right. As the band began to play their next song, the women danced, the way they'd danced on the float. Mary saw no recourse but to follow along.

Within minutes, Gaetano took Paulina by the hand and began dancing with her. He had set his guitar down so his hands were free. He held Paulina close as they swayed together, their dance sensual and lively. Suddenly, Mary found herself in the arms of a large man, Gaetano's other guitar player, who held her close. He caressed her sides with his hands and swayed in step with her. His touch was personal, hinting at the intimate. He whispered in her ear in words she didn't understand, but assumed were suggestive. She shook her head, trying to tell him she didn't understand, but he seemed to think she was turning him down and became agitated. Paulina must have noticed, since she danced Gaetano over to them and spoke to the man, Victor. Instantly, Victor became more pleasant and beamed at Mary, then tried to dance her over to the steps, likely trying to get her to go with him.

"Paulina," Mary called, trying to keep her voice down. "I can't," she said when Paulina looked her way. Victor must have realized something was wrong, since he stopped trying to drag her away. Paulina intervened again, saying something to Victor. This time, he looked agitated, but dropped Mary's hand, left her at the edge of the stage, and went back to his guitar.

Mary considered trying to find her way back to the dressing room; but when she looked toward the bottom of the steps, she was met by the grinning faces of six other men, ready to take Victor's place. She decided to stay on the stage and wait.

Eventually, Paulina stopped dancing and helped Mary get to the dressing room and her clothes. As they made their way through the crowd, Mary noticed the people around her, in their costumes. Many wore little in the way of clothes and all danced as if the world would end tomorrow. She was pinched and groped by many of the men and even some of the women.

"Now what?" she asked when they were both dressed in their street clothes.

"Vem comigo," Paulina said as she motioned Mary to the door.

"No more dancing?" Mary asked.

"Dance, não. Gaetano." Then she waved Mary again to follow.

They took a staircase to an upper floor and went to a room with a gold star on it. The name Gaetano was written in the middle of the star. A dressing room. Paulina knocked twice, then opened the door and entered. Gaetano sat on a chair pulling up his expensive black pants over his briefs. When they were fastened—he was still shirtless, his broad chest damp with sweat—he met Paulina halfway and gave her a crushing embrace and kiss. Then he acknowledged Mary.

"Quem é?" he asked.

"Mary Slade, CIA," Paulina said.

Gaetano became agitated, waving her off. "I don't want to talk to the CIA," he said in accented, but passable English.

"I've brought a message from my boss," Mary said. "I think you'll want to hear it."

"Leave it. I'll read it when I feel like it."

"It's not written down. They don't want anyone but you to hear it. I have to tell you what it is."

Even more agitated than before, he finally relented. "What is the message?"

Mary took a few moments to collect herself, distracted by Gaetano's broad chest and hard muscled arms, then began. "My government is worried for your safety. They want to help you by removing you from the threat . . ."

"There is no threat."

Mary continued as if he hadn't interrupted. "Their target is the Mexican drug cartel you are helping. They are dangerous and we fear for your safety. Let us help you get away from them before you, or someone you care about, is hurt. We can help each other."

"I'm sorry you came all this way for nothing. I don't need the help of your CIA. We're fine."

"I'm sorry you feel that way. I'll let them know. Can you call me a taxi?"

Paulina said something, which Gaetano repeated in English for Mary. "Thank you for dancing on Paulina's float. She could tell you were embarrassed. You are a beautiful, and modest, woman and she appreciated your help."

Mary turned to Paulina. "You're welcome." She said and nodded in acknowledgement.

CIA Headquarters

"Message delivered," Mary said, exhaling as though worn out.

"I take it he didn't agree to accept our help," Ollie said with a sigh. "How are you feeling after that assignment? Was it too difficult?"

"I wouldn't call it difficult, in the physical activity sense. Just exhausting."

"Embarrassing?"

"Why would you ask that?" Mary wondered how he had guessed. Could he read her thoughts?

"I saw you in the parade. It's already online."

"How did you pick me out of all those beautiful women?"

"I just looked for the woman who seemed the most uncomfortable and embarrassed. You were easy to pick out on the float. Of course, I recognized Paulina. She's quite famous, so I figured that was you on her float. Did you know her float won an award?"

"No. I left right after talking to Gaetano."

"Was that the kind of adventure you were looking for?"

"I'm not sure. It was definitely more challenging. There were both language and cultural barriers."

"I could get you into Africa, where the tribal woman walk around topless all day."

"Thank you. I'll pass on that one."

"Okay. If you change your mind, let me know. In the meantime, I have an assignment for an agent in London that you can deliver for me." He handed it to her, along with airline reservations, and she left to catch a plane.

Singapore—two years later—Mary

Mary flew into Singapore and delivered information to the Southeast Asia station chief. She'd been there dozens of times, so this was a routine assignment. She wondered if she could see something this trip that she hadn't seen before.

"Hi Mary," the chief's Executive Assistant, Kaye, said when Mary stuck her head in the office door, "Good to see you again. How are things in Utah?"

"I don't know. It's been too long since I've been home. How are things in Colorado?"

"Same story. We'll have to take a vacation and visit both places. Do you still know anyone at the U?"

Mary had attended school at the University of Utah in Salt Lake City at the same time that Kaye attended Utah State University in Logan, Utah. With Mary's frequent visits to Singapore over the last three years, they had become good friends, swapping stories about their experiences. They even discovered that they had fiends in common, back in Utah.

"I imagine there are a few professors and grad students there that I would know."

"I'm sure you're right. We'll have to check it out some day."

"Mary, you've been doing this for three years now. Level with me. Do you enjoy it, traveling around the world, meeting strange and exotic men, experiencing new things?"

"I really do, Kaye. I enjoy the travel and seldom feel threatened. I've had to resort to my self-defense training a time or two, but nothing I couldn't handle."

"I heard about your airport parking lot experience and the mugging in Sydney. I would have been scared to death. And you took down five men single-handedly."

"How do those stories get around? I certainly don't advertise."

"You're a celebrity at the Agency. People tell your stories at the drinking fountain. Someone even showed me your dance at Carnival in Rio de Janeiro. I didn't realize you were so all out there, girl."

"It wasn't my idea and it was embarrassing. It definitely wasn't something I would do willingly."

"Well, you looked fantastic. And such a good dancer. Where'd you learn to dance like that?"

"A Brazilian girl gave me a two-minute lesson about fifteen minutes before I got on the float."

"You'd never know it. You looked so natural."

"So, about your assignments, have you met any men you're really interested in?" Kaye asked

"I've run across some interesting men, but I don't stay in one place long enough to get to know anyone well, except at the stations that I come back to often, like here and Sydney."

"What do you like most about you work?"

"I really enjoy seeing exotic new places and I like meeting handsome men."

"Have you met Taylor Swensen yet?"

"I did, In Sydney, three years ago. I heard he travels a lot and has a reputation for being ruthless. Probably not the kind of man I want to get to know. What do you think?"

"That's not what I heard. I heard he had a girlfriend whose dad was rich and he was intelligent enough to attract the man's attention. He turned down a reward for rescuing the girlfriend, then turned down a job with the girl's dad to stay with the agency. And he's so good-looking. I'm sure you noticed."

Mary tried to act disinterested, but everything she heard about the mysterious Taylor Swensen intrigued her more. She determined to get to know him better the next time they met, if they ever met again.

"Kaye, if I wanted to do something different while I'm here, what would you recommend?"

"Have you been to Kuala Lumpur, Malaysia or the Angkor Wat ruins in Siem Reap, Cambodia?"

"Neither one. what's there to see?"

"If you only see one, I suggest the Angkor Wat ruins in Siem Reap. They're unbelievable."

Taylor

"What can I do for you?" Taylor asked the Southeast Asia station chief when he entered his office in Singapore.

"Thank you for coming, Mr. Swensen. I'm sorry for taking you away from what you were doing."

"Please, call me Taylor. I was just over in Indonesia, so this is no imposition at all."

"Excellent. Tell me what you've been doing since you were here last?"

"I've been doing what I've been doing since I started with the agency over three years ago. I travel the world on my assignments. I set up contacts wherever I go. Some are friendly and cooperate because it's the right thing to do; some are afraid of me and cooperate for fear of upsetting me."

"Do you know you have a reputation for being ruthless?"

"I've heard that and I actually cultivate that image with my contacts, since it helps me get the information I need, to complete my assignments. The truth is that I was a shy child."

"But you've grown out of that, right?"

"Sometimes I wonder. I think my mom worried that I'd never have a friend. It was difficult for me to talk to people. I preferred to sit at home, working jigsaw puzzles and listening to music. I was a picky eater, besides being a loner. There are still foods that most people enjoy, that I can't stand."

"Like what, if you don't mind my asking?"

"Oh, I'm past the embarrassment stage. Now I just don't buy anything I don't like, like yogurt, pickles, and sour cream. I still have trouble meeting good women."

"Really? With your exotic job, I would think you would attract them like flies."

"Oh, I meet lots of women, just not the kind I'm looking to have a relationship with, and I can't tell them what I do. I want a woman who is funny, sensitive, creative, maybe a little feisty, and who doesn't mind all my travel and secrecy, without knowing what I do for a living."

"And beautiful?"

"That's a given. But where am I going to find someone like that, with my travel schedule?"

"Only at the agency, I guess." They both laughed.

"So what do you need me to do?" Taylor asked.

"You know who Mary Slade is?"

He nodded. He could still remember how good it felt being with her the one and only time they'd been together, in the restaurant in Sydney. She met all of his criteria, but he hadn't run into her in three years.

"She was here to deliver information to me," the chief said. "She was supposed to catch a plane home today. A well-intentioned agency employee suggested that while she was here, she should see the Angkor Wat ruins in Siem Reap, Cambodia. It was a short airplane ride into Siem Reap and she could return the next day—today. But we haven't heard from her, and I'm beginning to worry."

"What do you want me to do?" Taylor asked.

"Will you go find and extract her? Hopefully, she's safe, just lost or distracted, but the agents out of Singapore, that we sent in this morning, haven't found her. They're mostly locals and lack the training and special talents you have. Will you do it?"

Taylor could imagine that a woman alone in Cambodia, could get herself into trouble, especially a beautiful, American woman. But she had been in trouble before, and handled the situation quite well. Maybe she would show up later in the day.

On the other hand, she had given him the impression that she wanted to get to know him better, so if he went after her, it would give him a chance to collect on that implied promise.

"I'm embarrassed that my team failed to keep track of Ms. Slade," the chief continued when Taylor didn't respond immediately, "but she went, on her own, outside my protective curtain. I'll do what I can to help. Just let me know what you need. Here's a five- by seven-inch photo of Ms. Slade, that I've been keeping in her file. I'll have my assistant arrange for you to fly into Siem Reap and stay in an apartment the agency has used before."

The photo was a head-and-shoulders shot, which showed her delicate features and warm coloring. "That will really help. Thanks," he said.

11

Siem Reap, Cambodia—Taylor

He flew into Cambodia and took an Uber car to his apartment. He dropped off his suitcase and wondered where he should begin to look for Mary. He'd seen an abundance of open-air carriages pulled by young men on motorbikes, but very few cars. The motorbikes must be the local mode of transportation. Maybe one of the young men pulling the carts would know where to find tourists. He walked out to the street and down to the corner where he could see one of the carts.

"What is this thing called?" Taylor asked the young driver. He had just dropped off five people who had been sitting on benches on either side of the carriage. It looked like an efficient way to transport passengers, but he wondered how the motor bike had the power to pull the weight of the carrier, loaded with people.

"It's a tuk-tuk," the young man said, proudly, in heavily accented English. He looked about sixteen, but could have been any age, up to about forty. These Cambodians didn't seem to age the way Americans did.

"This is a long shot," Taylor said, "but have you seen an American woman, tall—177 centimeters—long wavy brown hair, and gorgeous, in the last two days?"

"Tourist?" the man asked.

"Yes. She was planning to see the Angkor Wat ruins,"

"Then they would have seen her at the museum, where she would have to buy a ticket."

"Can you take me there?"

"Whenever you're ready."

"Let's go," he said, as he climbed into the back of the tuk-tuk.

"Hi there," Taylor said to the middle-aged woman behind the counter at the museum.

"Hello," she said, smiling sweetly, with a slight accent. "One adult admission?"

"Actually, I'm looking for an American woman, tall—177 centimeters—long wavy brown hair, and beautiful. Have you sold her a ticket to Siem Reap in the last two days?"

The woman hesitated, then responded in a different language, looking flustered, speaking rapidly and shrugging her shoulders. She turned to a man, a fellow employee of the museum and said something, then walked away. The man stepped over to Taylor.

"How may I help you, sir?" he asked.

"What's wrong with her?" Taylor asked.

"Sorry, sir. She doesn't speak English."

Taylor had to think about that. He figured the woman was either embarrassed that Taylor was asking about beautiful American tourists, was jealous of Ms. Slade for being the tourist in question, or upset that he didn't want to buy a ticket to visit the museum. Maybe she only knew specific phrases in English that tourists were most likely to use. He repeated his request to the man.

"Yes," the man said, "She bought a ticket this morning and caught a ride outside."

"Would she still be out there now?" he asked, looking at his watch. It was after four local time and he didn't know how long the ruins would be open, or if they ever closed.

"If she is really motivated to see everything," he said. "Most tourists tire after three or four hours. Maybe one of the drivers out front knows if she's already returned. Besides you would have trouble finding her out there. The ruins are many."

"Thanks,"Taylor said. He tried to leave a tip but the man refused.

"Local custom" he said.

Taylor walked back outside. There were five tuk-tuks in a row, the drivers gathered at the front of the queue, talking quietly. As Taylor approached, the drivers turned toward him, as a group, to see where he wanted to go.

"I need information first,"Taylor said, and repeated his question about the beautiful American woman.

One of the drivers got a huge smile on his face. "She is truly a beautiful woman," he said.

"So, you've seen her?"

"Yes, very beautiful."

"Do you know where she is?"

"I saw her leave this morning. She hired a tuk-tuk to go to the ruins."

"Did you see her come back?"

"No, but I heard her say she would want to eat when she returned."

"And you know where she wanted to eat?"

"She wanted authentic food, so she would be taken to the street where the best local food is served."

"How would she get there if she was dropped off at the ruins?"

"There are always tuk-tuks at the ruins, until everyone is gone."

"Can you take me there, to where she would have gone to eat?"

"Of course."

They negotiated a price quickly and headed out. Within a few minutes, they were travelling slowly down a street lined on both sides by eating establishments, in between gift shops, massage parlors, and other businesses. There were tables with benches set up in the street. The street was packed with pedestrians, forcing the tuk-tuk to pass slowly.

Periodically, the driver would stop and talk briefly with another driver, then continue on. Taylor wanted to ask each time what they talked about, but decided he was probably asking about the beautiful American tourist. Finally, after one such stop, the driver turned back to Taylor and grinned.

"He said she is just ahead, eating."

"Excellent," Taylor said, deciding that his driver had, on his own initiative, sought out Ms. Slade's location.

Taylor saw her when they were still fifty feet away. She was sitting on a bench with several other people, with a plate full of food in front of her. Her head was inches higher than the people around her, even leaning over her plate of food. It was definitely her.

Taylor had the driver stop immediately and gave him double what they had agreed for the fare. The driver balked at it until Taylor insisted that he had been a big help and stuffed the money in his shirt pocket.

On the way to the table, Taylor passed a stand selling pineapple smoothies and bought two of them. He stood at the end of her table, in the middle of the street, with a smoothie in each hand.

"Ms. Slade?" he asked, just loudly enough to be heard. Her head popped up quickly to see who would know her.

"I brought your smoothie," he said.

"I didn't . . ." she started to say, a surprised look on her face, then stopped. "Mr. Swensen?"

People around her looked up to see what was going on. Taylor squeezed between the benches, bumping people in the back who were eating their dinner, until he arrived at an empty spot next to

Mary. He set the smoothies on the table, and sat next to her.

"Someone in Singapore is worried about you," he said.

"Oh dear," she said. Her expression turning to worry. "I didn't call to give them an update. I feel so badly."

"Yeah, it's customary to let someone know your plans, when you're on a schedule."

"I know that. I was naughty, wasn't I?"

"Very. What should we do about that?"

"Do I need to be disciplined?"

"If I can be the one to decide on the discipline."

"What would you have me do?"

"I need to think about that. Let's eat while I decide."

"Do I need to call them right now?"

"I don't think so. As long as we get you out of here in one piece, no worries." He looked at his watch and thought for a minute. "We've missed the last flight out today. We'll leave in the morning. Where are you staying?"

"I had a place last night. I finally figured out how to get to the ruins and went today; but I failed to extend my reservation until tomorrow."

"You can stay with me, in that case."

"That's really not necessary. The places I've been staying are rather simple, but they don't require a reservation, and it's only for a night."

"I insist. I think you'll like where I'm staying. The agency arranged it," he whispered, so no one else could hear and question him. "How's the food?"

"Delicious! You should try it."

Taylor caught the attention of a worker and pointed at Mary's plate of pasta noodles and mixed, cooked vegetables.

"I'll have one of those," he said.

The worker nodded, left, then returned shortly with a large plate of food and set it in front of him. He dove into it like he hadn't eaten all day, which he hadn't.

"Thanks for the smoothie," Mary said as she slurped up the delicious, sweet pineapple.

"It's the least I could do after you accepted this date with me," he said, finishing his dinner and reaching for his drink.

"A date? Is that what this is?"

"Well, I've wanted a date with you, ever since I first met you, over three years ago, at the office. I just didn't think I'd have to wait this long and travel half way around the world to get it."

She laughed. It was a beautiful sound. They made eye contact and she winked at him.

"I think the feeling is mutual," she said. "Can we have a real date when we get home?"

"If we can work out our schedules. You don't seem to be in the office much when I'm there."

"I could say the same thing. Okay, that will be the first order of business. Find a day and time for a real date."

"You're on. Now, let's see if we can get to my apartment. I have only a vague idea which direction to go."

"The tuk-tuk drivers will know," she said.

"Okay, you're in charge of directions until we get to the airport tomorrow. Is there anything else you'd like to do before we leave?"

"Actually," she said hesitantly, "I had a foot massage near here yesterday. It felt so good, I thought I'd do it again."

"Great. Lead the way. Maybe I'll get one, too"

When they arrived at the shop a few minutes later, Taylor questioned a young woman who looked about sixteen, but could have been any age, about the massages.

"You can get a foot massage here in the shop, by one of these boys. Or, you can get a full body massage upstairs by one of the ladies." The girl said.

Taylor turned to Mary to see if she had heard. He raised his eyebrows in question.

"I've never had a full body massage," Mary said. "What do you think?"

"It's probably not like a massage back home, but it should be relaxing. Is that what you want?"

"Sure."

"Two full body massages," Taylor said, then gave the girl the requisite fee. They were led to the back of the shop, up a flight of stairs, and into a room where sheet-covered, padded benches sat in a row, filling the room, five of them. They were each handed a long, thin robe and shown to changing rooms.

"Please remove your clothes and put on the robe, then return here," an older woman said. They did as directed, carrying their piles of clothes out with them. There were two pretty, young women waiting by two of the benches. They patted the benches, indicating that Taylor and Mary should go to them.

"Please put your clothes under the bench," one girl said. "No one will touch them. Now lay on the bench on your stomach." As Taylor lay down on the bench, the girl loosened the sash on his robe and opened it. When he laid down, she pulled the robe off him and laid a sheet across his back. He turned his head to see that Mary was receiving the same treatment.

The girl poured some kind of oil into her hand, rubbed her hands together, then rubbed it onto his back. She kneaded his muscles, starting with his neck and working down his body to his feet. He noticed that Mary received similar treatment.

"Now turn over," the girl said when she'd finished his feet. He wasn't sure how he was going to do that modestly, but the girl lifted the sheet back over him while he turned over, covering him from the neck, down.

She worked his sore muscles, starting once again with his neck, working her way down to his feet. When she was done, she covered him with the sheet again while he sat up to put his clothes back on. He was so relaxed that he didn't know if he would be able to walk.

"I don't think I can walk," Mary said as she sat with her back to him, pulled the robe on, and reached under the bench to get her clothes.

"I'm glad it's not just me," Taylor said, chuckling. "Is there anything else you want to do?"

"Tell me, does your room have one or two beds?"

"I only saw one, I'm afraid."

"Then we better find me something to wear to bed."

There was a clothing store right across the narrow street, the entrance between a restaurant and a smoothie stand. They entered the store, found the women's clothes, and Mary bought a large tee-shirt with a picture of the Siem Reap ruins on it, a pair of baggy, lightweight pajamas, and a pair of modest underwear.

Back on the street, it wasn't difficult to find a vacant tuk-tuk. They seemed to be on every corner, at least wherever there were tourists. Taylor approached one, gave him the address of his apartment, and they meandered slowly down the crowded streets.

At the apartment, Taylor secured two bottles of water from a small fridge in the carport, left some change in a cup on top of it, retrieved his key from the small office, and led the way up the stairs to the door marked three. Opening the door revealed a charming, simply furnished and decorated room. It held one double bed with a single, light blanket covering it, a couch, a table with two chairs, open-air windows—It was still warm in the room, due to the tropical weather this time of year—and a small, primitive bathroom in one corner, surrounded by a plastic curtain.

"You take the bed and I'll sleep on the couch," Taylor said.

"There's no need for that," Mary said. "It's your apartment, so it's your bed."

"But I wouldn't feel right making you sleep on the couch."

"Then we'll both sleep on the bed. This is why I bought pajamas, in case we had to share. You're a gentleman, aren't you? You'll behave yourself, won't you?"

"Of course. But will you behave yourself?" It was meant as a tease, but she seemed to take his question seriously.

Mary

"I'll try to control myself," she said, with a raised eyebrow and a mischievous smile. "You still haven't told me what my discipline will be for failing to check in with the office."

Now why did she ask him about punishment just before bedtime. That was inviting him to suggest something that she couldn't agree to.

"Maybe I'll have to spank you."

Just what she was afraid of. She needed to get his mind off punishments. "You just got a massage," she said

"Then it will be an IOU, for another day."

"Okay," she said, relieved.

She went to brush her teeth and prepare for bed, pulling the shower curtain around the tiny bathroom. He removed his shirt and pants and sat on the edge of the bed. When she finished changing into her new pajamas, she opened the curtain and noticed his broad, muscular chest, flat, rock-solid stomach, and strong thighs. She imagined lying next to him in bed, both apprehensive and excited at the same time. She wondered if she could keep her hands off him after all.

"Where do you exercise?" she asked as she approached the bed. It was obvious to her that he did.

"I have a gym at home, but I also run a lot. I average a half marathon a month when I'm home. How about you?"

"I go to a local gym six mornings a week when I'm in town. I try to walk when I'm away, like now." She reached the bed, went to the opposite side and climbed into bed. She patted his side of the bed.

"Are you sure you're okay with this arrangement," he asked. "Or, would you like me to see if they have another room available?"

"Taylor, I'm fine with this. We're both mature adults. And, if something happens between us, it was probably meant to be." Maybe she was hoping something would happen?

Taylor

"I can accept that," he said. He brushed his teeth, rinsed his mouth with water from the bottle he'd bought earlier—it wasn't safe to drink the local water—then walked to the wall, turned off the overhead light, and returned to the bed. He saw that she was in bed, the thin blanket tucked under her arms. She had found two extra pillows in a closet and placed them lengthwise in the middle of the bed, separating her half of the bed from his. He wasn't sure this was such a good idea, but she had done what she could to keep them apart. He slid under the blanket and lay on his back, staring at the ceiling, thinking about Mary, lying on the other side of the pillow divider. Turning his head, he could see her profile on the other side of the pillows. He had followed her CIA career, having access to her courier file. She wouldn't have the same access to his file because of the nature of his work. Had she tried to access his file to follow his career? How badly did she want to get to know him?

He was really attracted to her. Everything about her appealed to him. She was honest, funny, and beautiful. He really wanted to take her in his arms, but he wouldn't. Instead, he decided he was glad she had placed the pillows between them, to help him keep his own counsel.

After what seemed like forever, he finally fell asleep. Suddenly, he woke, not sure what had awakened him. The first thing he noticed was that the pillows were gone and Mary had rolled over and snuggled against his side. He took a quick look at the bedside clock; it was 2:45 a.m. He was certain she was asleep and had no idea what she'd done. But who had moved the pillows, if not her?

He debated scooting away from her to avoid the feelings that the contact caused in him. Then she surprised him.

"Thank you for coming for me," she said. "Who knows what kind of trouble I could have gotten into."

He turned his head to look at her, their faces inches apart, and saw that her eyes were open. He thought he could drown in those beautiful, bright blue eyes. He wasn't sure what to say. He could try to be clever. Or seductive. In the end, he chose to be polite.

"You're welcome," he finally said and smiled. Her answering smile melted him, so that when she reached over and kissed him lightly on the lips, he found himself kissing her back. He threaded his arm beneath her neck and pulled her close. She didn't resist and they fell asleep that way, sleeping through until morning.

When the sun peeked in through the window and shined in his eyes, Mary was still lying tightly against his side. He thought he would move away from her so she didn't think he was trying to take advantage of the situation, when she stirred, threw the cover back, and got up to go to the bathroom. He watched the fluid movement of her body, the gentle sway of her hips, and her irresistible curves. The shower curtain offered little privacy, so he turned his back to her until she returned and sat on the edge of the bed.

"Your turn," she said.

"Thank you. I'll try to be quick, then we can go."

He ran his fingers across her shoulder as he rolled off the bed. She shivered, then returned his smile. He showered and dressed quickly, prepared for the day, and carried his bag downstairs,

"Do you have any luggage?" he asked when she came down to join him, the clothing store bag the only thing in her hand. He thought they might have to go somewhere to get her suitcase.

"I only planned to be here one night, so I just brought an extra pair of underwear," she said, pulling a piece of cloth out of her pocket, then dropping it into the bag.

"Oh," he said. "In that case, let's find some breakfast and head for the airport. Are you good with that?"

"Lead the way," she said, then hooked her arm in his and walked out to the street with him. A tuk-tuk driver spotted them from the street corner and hurried to meet them.

"We need breakfast," Taylor said, as they climbed into the back. The driver turned the machine around and headed out to a place that served breakfast. When he dropped them off at a likely restaurant, he asked if they wanted him to wait and take them to the airport.

"How did you know we need to go to the airport?" Taylor asked.

"You have your luggage," the driver said, "and she doesn't have luggage, so she probably doesn't have a change of clothes and needs to get to somewhere where she has clothes."

"Are you a policeman?" Taylor asked.

"No. Absolutely not," the driver said defensively, as if it were an insult. "Why do you ask?"

"That was very observant of you."

"I've been working with tourists for a long time. It was a logical conclusion."

"In that case, how's the fastest way to get to the airport?"

"It would be faster and cheaper in a taxi or Uber car, than in a tuk-tuk. I can take you to a taxi stand."

"Good. If you're willing to wait, we'll have a quick bite to eat first."

They made it to the airport without incident, found their flight to Singapore, and settled in to wait for boarding. Mary called the station chief.

12

Ashgabat, Turkmenistan, on the border with Iran
Dmitri Pavlovich

"I'm in the middle of negotiations," Dmitri Pavlovich said when he answered the phone. "Why are you bothering me?"

"You wanted to know if we saw anyone suspicious," the mercenary said.

"And you have?" Dmitri asked, quickly becoming interested in the conversation. He had told his hired help to let him know if they saw anyone who might be American CIA. "Where are you?"

"I'm in the airport in Siem Reap, Cambodia. There's an American couple here, waiting for a flight to Singapore . . ."

"So what? Probably tourists and they're nowhere near our operation. What's suspicious about them?"

"They're too good-looking. Both physically fit. I'd guess not married, but together. I'd guess going to their Southeast Asia station in Singapore."

"Not too suspicious. Take a picture with your phone and send it to me. If it looks like CIA to me, we'll share it with the team and have everyone watch for them to reappear elsewhere."

13

Siem Reap, Cambodia—Mary

"I'm sorry for not keeping in touch," Mary told the station chief when his secretary got him to the phone.

"Are you alright? Did Mr. Swensen find you?"

"We're at the airport now, waiting for our flight. Taylor was wonderful. Thank you for sending him; He was a big help. He's right here. Do you want to talk to him?"

"You're welcome. I'll see you soon. No, I don't need to . . .Yes, I do. Please," he said, changing his mind mid-sentence. As Mary handed the phone to Taylor, she noticed a camera flash and looked across the waiting area in that direction. A hard-looking young European man was just turning away with his phone up to his face. It seemed innocuous—she didn't know if he was taking their picture—so she didn't even mention it to Taylor.

"Hello, sir," Taylor said when he put Mary's phone to his ear.

"Hello, Mr. Swensen. What is your plan now? Are you headed back to the states?"

"No, sir. I'll see Ms. Slade into a taxi in Singapore, then catch the next flight out to Sydney."

"How can I help?"

"If you have someone who can make my reservation," Taylor said. "I'll be grateful."

"Absolutely," the station chief said. "You can give my secretary your document information and she'll call you back with your flight information."

"Thank you, sir."

"You're very welcome. Have a nice trip."

Walking down the concourse on their way to a drinking fountain, Mary noticed the man who'd taken the picture and pointed him out to Taylor.

"I don't know that he was taking *our* picture. I only mention it because it was unusual."

"That *is* unusual," he said. He made a quick decision to check it out and reversed direction abruptly, headed for the man. Halfway to the man, the man looked up, noticed Taylor, and took off running in the opposite direction. Taylor chased him until the man plowed through a large group of older Oriental people—it looked like a tour group—knocking down four of them in the process. Taylor considered following, then changed his mind and stopped to help the senior citizens pick themselves up. He didn't want to knock anyone down and he didn't want to step on anyone who was already on the floor. By the time he looked for the man again, he was long gone.

"Good try," Mary said in his ear as he stood looking down the concourse.

"Maybe it was nothing, but his reaction was suspicious. He definitely didn't want to wait and talk to me."

As Taylor handed Mary into the back of an Uber car in Singapore, she leaned out the door and gave him a brief kiss.

"That's to remember me by," she said.

"Oh, I won't forget you. It's been a memorable night. And we have a date."

Mary picked up her bag at the Singapore station, then returned to the airport for her flight to the states.

Ponloc

Taylor had intentionally scheduled his flight so he had time to visit Ponloc in Singapore. He hadn't seen her in several months. And although he didn't need information from her, they had become friendly and trusted each other.

"Hi Taylor," she said when she saw who was at her door. "Please come in."

He entered and gave her a kiss on the cheek. She responded by grabbing him in a bear hug and kissing him on the lips. This was their standard greeting whenever he came by, which was every few months.

"How are you doing?" he asked.

"I'm wonderful," she said.

"I know you are, but I want to know how you're doing."

"The therapist says I'm cured. No more chasing men for sex. I have you to thank for that. Now the CIA can hire me as a spy."

"I'll put in a good word for you. We could probably use a beautiful spy in Singapore."

Ponloc beamed proudly. "What can I do for you?" she asked.

"Nothing this trip," he said. "I'm on my way to Australia, and wanted to see if my money was being well spent."

"All according to our agreement. You've been so good to me; I feel like I need to do something for you. I've been studying bellydancing; can I dance for you?"

"I think I would enjoy that." She put a CD in the player, and danced for him.

"That was wonderful," he said, when she stopped.

"Can I show you another dance? One that shows you how I feel about you?"

"Ponloc, if you're trying to seduce me, please don't. I have somewhere I need to be and I can't afford to get sidetracked."

"You're always in a hurry. Maybe another time? You are a beautiful man," she said. "And honest. You've earned one free lovemaking session any time you want it."

"Sure. Another time. Let's keep that option open. Thanks." He stumbled over his words, not sure what to say that didn't give her the wrong impression. He still couldn't agree to having sex with her.

Before he left, she gave him another kiss and rubbed her body against him seductively. "To remember me by," she said.

He enjoyed a few more minutes talking to Ponloc and barely made his flight to Australia before they closed the gate.

14

Langley, Virginia—Rainbow

"You heard the debrief on Swensen's incident in Cambodia. What do you think?" Rainbow asked Ollie.

"You mean his interaction with Ms. Slade, right?" Ollie asked

"Yeah. Do we keep them apart or throw them together?"

"They work well, independently, but with the obvious attraction between them, they might do well to handle some of the missions that require a couple, rather than a single agent. By the way, I read your report. How did you get Taylor to reveal so much detail about their incident?" Ollie asked.

"I just asked the questions and he answered them. You know, sometimes, even a little detail can indicate a serious problem. Knowing about it ahead of time can sometimes prevent the problem or reduce the impact."

"Did this meeting indicate a problem?" Ollie asked.

"On the contrary," Rainbow said. "This indicated a healthy, mature, respectful relationship, one we may want to cultivate at some point."

"Would we be inviting problems by encouraging their relationship?"

"I think our main concern should be if they work well together and can trust each other. If something happens between them, of a sexual nature, they can deal with it. They're adults."

"If you're sure."

"I'm sure."

Taylor and Mary

"What's my next assignment?" Taylor asked on his return from Australia to Langley.

"We have a special assignment," Rainbow said. "A man we can't seem to get to, Dmitri Pavlovich, a Russian Siloviki who sells arms to our enemies in the middle east, is trying to buy Uranium to add to his product list. He doesn't have a routine that we can take advantage of, and has only one obvious weakness—beautiful women."

"What's the plan?" Taylor asked.

Just then Mary Slade entered the room, followed by Ollie. Ollie caught Rainbow's eye and motioned for him to wait. Ollie showed Mary where to sit, next to Taylor, and sat between her and Rainbow. Rainbow repeated his comment about Pavlovich.

"Whenever we've spotted Pavlovich with a woman," Rainbow continued, when Ollie was ready, "we've tried to follow them to their destination, but he's always too clever for us, using his bodyguards as decoys, changing routes, and other misdirection. We've actually lost two agents over the years, trying to follow him."

"By accident, Ms. Slade got close to him during one of her routine assignments," he continued, motioning toward Mary. "She wasn't even aware of his attention, as far as we could tell. We noticed his reaction to her and the seed of an idea was planted."

"Could we use Ms. Slade to get to Pavlovich, without putting her in danger?" Rainbow asked, now clearly directing his comments to Mary. "He's a dangerous man. We've used Taylor to escort couriers to dangerous meetings before, and Taylor helped rescue you from southeast Asia, which wasn't dangerous, per se, but a little tricky finding you and getting you to safety. So, we considered putting you together for this one mission. It would be dangerous for you, Mary, more dangerous than anything you've done for us in the past, but Taylor can protect you, we're sure."

"What do you think, Mary?" Rainbow concluded.

"I'll be working with Taylor?" she asked.

"If you agree, he'll take the lead and you'll take direction from him."

"I'll do it," she said without hesitation. She was breathing heavily when she looked at Taylor.

"Ollie, will you and Mary wait in the hall while I discuss this with Taylor?" Rainbow asked

"Sure," Ollie said, as he ushered Mary out of the room, giving Rainbow a dirty look.

"You realize you just coerced her into agreeing by asking her in front of me?" Taylor asked Rainbow when they were alone in the room. His expression was dangerous, his fists clenched at his sides.

"I do," Rainbow said. "I'm sorry, Taylor, but we think this is the only way to make this work."

"But you have no idea if this will work. Pavlovich is a danger-ous man and you're asking her to put herself in a compromising position with him. She doesn't have the training or skills to pro-tect herself"

"That's why we want her to go with you."

"And what if I can't protect her from him?"

"There's an element of risk with everything we do. You know that. But you're the best chance we have at getting to him."

"You know I'll go, but you need to give Mary a chance to back out. You can always have a more experienced agent go with me."

"We thought of that. Estelle would go if we asked. But we think you and Ms. Slade would have a better shot at him. I'll give her a chance to back out, but you know she won't. She really likes and trusts you."

"Regardless, I think she needs to be encouraged to back out."

"Taylor, you two are perfect for this assignment. She's beautiful. You're able to protect both of you and complete the assignment. Your physical attraction to each other will help with your cover story."

Before leaving for Budapest, Taylor confirmed that Rainbow had spoken with Mary again. They both knew she wouldn't back out, and she didn't.

15

Mary knew what Pavlovich looked like, so she knew when he approached her that he was the target. She danced with him, playing up to his reputation as a ladies' man and hanging on him for show. It worked. He took her hand and led her to the elevator, followed by three of his men. In the elevator, she continued to hang on his shoulder, her small handbag dangling from the crook of one arm. He had one arm around her waist and nuzzled her neck with his lips. She felt a chill, but couldn't tell if it was from excitement or disgust.

Entering the suite, the three bodyguards watched as Dmitri led Mary to the bedroom, lecherous smiles on their faces. Then they went to sit at the small table. They were soon sharing a drink.

Pavlovich led Mary into the bedroom and closed the door behind them. He took her small purse and rifled through it. Taylor had told her he might do that, so she acted surprised rather than alarmed. Pavlovich had stayed alive as long as he had because he was paranoid about his safety. Not finding anything of interest, like a gun, he threw the purse on a chair. She went to reach for it, but he held her arm and turned her toward the bed.

His eyes wandered down the front of her lowcut dress.

"Хороший вид!", *nice view,* he said. He reached up and moved one spaghetti strap off her shoulder and let it fall, revealing more of her. He did the same with the other strap and the dress fell to her waist,

"Очень хороший вид !", *very nice view,* he said. "Let's get rid of that," he added, switching to flawless English.

She hesitated, thinking about Taylor and where he might be right now. Maybe she should try to stall him, but he didn't give her a chance. He pulled her to him and stroked her neck, pushing her hair over one shoulder. She raised her arms out to either side, indicating that she would not resist him. She just hoped Taylor was close by.

Pavlovich placed his thumbs inside the elastic of her waist band and pushed the dress over her narrow hips, letting it fall to the floor. A mischievous smile played across her lips as she stepped out of the dress, and past him, to the bed.

Her back was to him as she turned the bedding down. Before she could lie down, he was behind her, bent over, resting his head on her back, his arms reaching around her midsection.

"Soft and smooth," he said, rubbing his hands up and down her stomach. "You're CIA, aren't you, Ms. Slade? Both you and Mr. Swensen."

She froze for only an instant, but probably gave herself away, if Pavlovich was as smart as she thought he was. She slipped out of his embrace and crawled between the sheets without answering.

If he suspected they were CIA, he might kill her, outright. He pulled a handgun out of the back of his belt, pointed it at her and went 'click' with his mouth, implying that he had just shot her, or that he could shoot her anytime he wanted. He set the gun carefully on the dresser, undressed, then crawled in after her, taking her in his arms. She stiffened at his touch, thinking about her training and how to defend herself. She might have to use it now.

"Don't try anything, Ms. Slade. May I call you Mary? No?" he asked when she shook her head a fraction. "Why not? We're going to get to know each other quite well in the next while. Sorry about

Mr. Swensen," he added, "but my men are expecting him to try to rescue you. They're ready for him."

There was noise in the suite, which was loud enough for both of them to hear through the closed door. "Aw, that's probably him now." Pavlovich's mouth turned up at the edges, making Mary wince and steal herself for action.

Taylor

The meeting was a global conference on agriculture. Taylor's cover story was that he was the head of an agricultural consortium from Ohio, there to pick up on the latest farming techniques and equipment. Mary was his bored and beautiful wife who was looking for some excitement. The conference was held in the ballroom of a large hotel in downtown Budapest. In their roles as husband and wife, they were supposed to be affectionate in public, saving their true reservations for private. It would require some acting skills to pull it off.

He was listed in the program, along with the other delegates, so anyone wondering about them would be able to see his cover and, hopefully, believe it.

"Do you have any questions about your role?" Taylor asked Mary, in their hotel room, before the conference started.

"I think it's pretty straight-forward," Mary said. "I'm your beautiful, affectionate, but bored wife. I'm to make sure Pavlovich tries to take me to bed. You're going to rescue me and kill him in the process."

"Perfect," he said. "Do we need to practice our roles?"

"Do you mean, do we need to practice being affectionate?" she asked.

He waved her over to where he was sitting on a couch and patted his leg. She sat on his lap and leaned into him, laying her head on his shoulder, her face against his neck. They sat that way for a minute.

"I guess we should kiss," she said, then wrapped her arms around his neck and kissed his neck. She kissed him again as he turned his face toward her, her next kiss landing on the curve of his jaw, then the corner of his mouth, then his lips. He held the kiss long enough that she came away breathless.

"Nice!" he said. "Anything else we should practice?" He wrapped his arms around her waist and hugged her to him. "Should we practice the bedroom part?"

"If we do, who's going to rescue me and shoot you?"

"You don't need to be rescued. You're my wife, remember?"

"If you want a bedroom scene, you'll have to make me your wife for real."

"Is that a proposal?" he asked.

"It sounded like one, didn't it? We'll have to think about that."

"I'm still thinking about how to discipline you for making the southeast Asia station chief worry."

"Taylor, that was three years ago."

"And we still haven't settled it."

"Is it time to go to the reception?" she asked, looking at her watch.

"I guess so. We'll have to continue practicing later."

Mary held Taylor's arm as they left the room. When they entered the elevator, two burly eastern European men stood at the back of the car and watched them. Mary leaned into Taylor and gave him a kiss on the cheek.

"What was that for?" Taylor whispered.

"For our audience," she whispered back, pointing her thumb

toward the two men, holding her thumb in front of her where they wouldn't see it. Taylor nodded. She was being cautious, not knowing who the two men were and wanting to play her role correctly.

They exited the car at the main floor and walked across a wide hallway into the ballroom. Taylor noticed that the two men followed them, passing and heading across the room.

"Why don't you mingle with the guests here, while I see what's going on in the rest of the room?" he asked. Taking her lead from him, she stood near a refreshment table, looking around casually. While Taylor mingled with the other farmers in the room, introducing himself, using his alias. He had studied enough about the farming techniques that would be addressed at the conference to carry on a short conversation, if needed. Mary picked up bottled drinks and set them down again. She shifted from foot to foot, awkwardly, trying to appear bored. After a while, she wandered, staring and smiling at some of the men who weren't mingling, of which Pavlovich was one.

She had moved on, beyond Pavlovich, when she heard someone behind her.

"Will you dance with me?" the voice asked.

She turned to see that it was Pavlovich. She gave him an amused smile without answering, then raised her eyebrows in question.

"You look bored," he said in flawless American English. "I thought I would make your evening more interesting." He must have been watching her for a while and her acting must have been convincing.

Taylor had told her not to speak to him unless absolutely necessary. He would remember her voice, which could cause problems later. She lowered her eyes and nodded shyly. He took her hand, then her arm, and led her to the dance floor. He took her in his arms and she rested her head on his shoulder, playing her part perfectly. She placed one arm around his neck, as he held her close and snuggled against her neck.

"Let's go somewhere more private and get to know each other better," he said after a couple of dances. She looked down shyly. He smiled at her, the corners of his mouth lifting; but the smile never reached his eyes. He led her off the dance floor and into the hallway, toward a bank of elevators.

Taylor watched them from across the room. He saw them leave the dance floor and exit the ballroom. He turned on the tracking device she wore as a toe ring and followed casually into the hallway.

Two large men stood at one of the elevators, possibly the two men who had ridden down with them. They looked like they were running interference for Pavlovich. Taylor went to a different elevator, entered, and hit the button for the top floor. When the two men tried to follow him into the elevator, he raised a foot and kicked the first one in the chest, hard. The man fell backward into his associate, knocking them both down. They pulled guns and pointed them at Taylor, but the doors closed before they could get a shot off.

Taylor split his attention between watching the tracking signal from Mary on his wrist and worrying what the two men would do and who else they might contact. He expected that they knew where Pavlovich was staying, so he watched the elevators. When he reached the floor where Mary's signal moved away from the bank of elevators, he hit the emergency stop button, exited his elevator, and followed the signal around a corner, until he knew he was at the correct room. He studied the empty hallway, drew his gun, attached the silencer and put his ear to the door. He heard nothing.

Just then, he heard an elevator door open and the two men he'd hit, turned the corner, headed his direction at a run, bringing their guns out and trying to aim them at him. He shot the first in the head and he fell backwards, into the second. The second bounced off and moved around the first, bringing his gun to bear on Taylor, but Taylor got his shot off first, hitting the man in the chest. He fell on top of his associate. Taylor didn't bother to check to see if they were dead.

Taylor worried that the noise of the men hitting the floor would alert Pavlovich, but there was no noise from the hotel room and the door remained closed. He pulled a set of lock picks out of his jacket pocket and began working on the lock. He worried the entire time that he was taking too long and Mary was at the mercy of a dangerous man, one he knew was responsible for the deaths of at least five people, two of them agents.

Prepared for anything, Taylor leaned to the right of the door, using the door frame to protect his body. When he cracked open the door, he heard the unmistakable sound of a silenced gunshot and felt a sting in his left bicep. He looked down to see blood running from a gunshot wound on his arm. It stung, but must not have hit a bone. He pulled the door closed, removed his jacket and tied the sleeve around his arm above the wound, pulling it as tight as he could, letting the rest hang to his side.

He fully expected the armed men, one or more, to attack, so he had to be prepared when the door opened. When it didn't, he realized he had to take the initiative, in order to save Mary

He moved to his left, so he could shoot with his right hand, then opened the door again with his left hand, stretched across the door. He fired through the crack in the door, without looking, the gun making a soft, popping sound, and heard one man fall. He peaked in and fired again, hitting another who was approaching from the right. A third man began to rise from his seat at a table a few feet away. He shot him as well, then opened the door wider to see who else was in the room.

The first man was only wounded, lying on the floor in front of him. Taylor took a quick look at Mary's tracker and saw that it placed her in another room to the left. He debated what to do about the man on the floor in front of him, but the man took the decision out of his hands when he raised his silenced handgun and pointed it at Taylor. Taylor shot him in the head.

None of the three men called out or made a noise that would have alerted Pavlovich; but Taylor knew the sounds of shooting could have alerted him anyway. He entered the room in a crouch and looked around. No one else was in the room.

He quickly checked the balcony as a possible escape route, then approached the door to the left, which he guessed was the bedroom, where he figured Mary and Pavlovich would be.

The bedroom door was unlocked. Taylor turned the knob slowly and looked in. He took careful aim at the back of Pavlovich's head, then realized that his high velocity bullets could penetrate him and hit Mary, effectively killing both of them with one shot. He held off, waiting for a better shot; but after several moments, it still hadn't come. He finally made a small, purposeful noise in his throat and Pavlovich rolled away from Mary, looking at the door, possibly thinking that one of his men had interrupted them to give him a status on Taylor.

As he turned, Pavlovich started to say something in Russian, then stopped when he saw the gun pointed at him.

Taylor took his shot. Unfortunately, Pavlovich kept rolling away from Mary. His movement caused the bullet to miss, hitting the mattress between them. Pavlovich rolled off the bed, onto the floor, as Taylor fired three more shots into the bed, each one barely missing, and scrambled toward the bathroom on hands and knees. Mary jumped off the other side of the bed, grabbed her dress and purse and ran past Taylor into the other room. Taylor backed out of the room and closed the door, keeping his gun aimed at it. He didn't expect Pavlovich to follow: he was smart enough to know Taylor could be waiting for him to stick his head out of the door.

Taylor wondered if he should have continued shooting at Pavlovich, but was more concerned about Mary's safety. When he turned, Mary was just pulling her straps onto her shoulders. As she turned toward the door to the hallway, she must have noticed the three dead men, two lying in a pile on the floor and the third leaning back in his chair, all three with holes in their head or chest. She started to shake, either from fear or relief, Taylor wasn't sure. He held both her arms and pulled her to him, trying to lend her support and warmth, then went to the door.

He opened the door to the hallway and looked both ways. It was clear all the way to the corner by the elevator. He grabbed Mary's hand and rushed her out of the room, into an open elevator. It moved frustratingly slow, but was faster than taking the stairs from twelve stories up. They stopped at the fourth floor to get their luggage, checking the hallway before leaving the elevator. A burly man turned a corner a few yards away and raised a gun toward them. Taylor shot him in the chest. They entered their room and packed haphazardly, but quickly. Taylor pulled out his phone and pressed a button.

"Extraction, front entrance, three minutes," he said, then hung up. "Let's go," he said to Mary as he took her hand and led her back to the door.

"You're bleeding," Mary said, noticing his arm and the coat wrapped around it, reaching for it.

"I'm okay," he said. "We need to get out of here." He looked out the door, then led her quickly back to the elevator.

They continued to the lobby. When the doors opened, Taylor looked out, then ducked back in, as gunshots rang out in the hallway. He reached his gun hand out of the door and fired without looking. Then he looked, confirming he'd hit one man, firing again to take out another. He rushed her out of the building, watching for more threats and seeing none, and into an agency car that was now parked at the curb with the doors open. The driver saw them coming and popped open the trunk, then helped them load their suitcases and settle into the car.

"Airport?" the driver asked, as he pulled into traffic, his heavy accent making him difficult to understand.

"Airport!" Taylor said, then leaned back in the seat, still holding Mary's hand in his.

"Are you alright?" Taylor asked. "You're shaking and have goosebumps. You're not injured, are you?" He rubbed her arms until she felt warm to his touch and she'd calmed a little.

"No," she said, quietly. "But you are. Do you have a first-aid kit?" she asked the driver.

He reached over and popped the glove box. Handed a small first-aid kit over the seat to her. She opened it and began working on his arm.

"I don't feel a bullet," she said, as she palpated the tissue around the wound, making him wince from the pain. "It looks like a clean in-and-out."

"It hurts," he said as he rolled his eyes and leaned his head into the seat back. He'd been shot before, during his training, and agreed with her assessment. As gunshots went, this one was minor. "And you're okay?" He asked.

"Only embarrassed," she said. "That was close. He accused me of being CIA and knew my name. Yours, too. Why would he know that? Did we give ourselves away somehow?"

"I don't see how. What did he say, specifically?"

She told him.

"I don't know," he said again. He placed a call, explained that Pavlovich knew who they were, and asked Ollie to look into it. When he hung up, she was looking at him intently.

"Did you shoot those men?"

"Yeah. I'm sorry about that. He didn't . . . ?" he started to ask.

"He tried," she said, nervously, "but someone interrupted him. Thank you."

Taylor wanted to smack himself for not arriving sooner. He had cut it too close, finding them in close quarters. He also wanted to hurt Pavlovich in the worst way. "I'm sorry," he said again. "I cut that too close."

"That's sweet," she said. "You're sweet. Don't worry about it. I knew the risks going in. He was a little more determined than I expected, but I wasn't surprised by his intentions."

Taylor watched traffic as they were driven to the airport. He could tell she was really disturbed by the experience. She was still shaking and she clung to him tightly. He placed his arm across her shoulders and pulled her head against him. She left it there and seemed to relax a little from the close personal contact.

Normally, he would check in with the local station chief, give a report, and call or send a report to Virginia. Not today. Pavlovich was still alive and suspected he'd been targeted by the CIA. He would be as mad as a wet hornet. Taylor would have to keep his eyes and ears open for the fallout from this failed mission.

Mary placed her hand flat on Taylor's chest. He was sure she could feel his pounding heart. She laid her head against his chest, as though to listen to his heartbeat. She closed her eyes and a smile spread across her lips. He wondered if she'd fallen asleep or if she was just reassuring herself that he was real.

"We're here," Taylor said softly, when the car stopped at the departures curb at the airport. Mary opened her eyes, looked up at him, and smiled. She was so close. He wanted to kiss her again.

She sat up straighter, until her mouth was even with his, and kissed him, long and hard. "Thank you," she said, then sat all the way up. He pulled away from her, reluctantly, and got out of the car, He met the driver at the trunk, got their luggage and carried it to the ticket counter, wincing as he lifted her heavy bag. He purchased tickets—there were still two seats together in business class on the next flight to New York—then they checked their bags, got their boarding passes, and went to their gate. They sat side-by-side in the nearly empty waiting area. Mary closed her eyes again and leaned her head against his shoulder, while Taylor looked around. His dark glasses hid most of his eye movement. He went to place an arm around her shoulders until he winced at the pain and realized it was his injured arm.

In his peripheral vision, he caught a sudden movement. A quick glance revealed an eastern European man reaching into his overcoat inside pocket and removing what looked like a gun. As the silenced gun swung toward them, it snagged on an inside seam of the coat. Taylor grabbed Mary's arm and pulled her to the floor. Almost immediately, he heard the little *phutt-phutt* of the silenced weapon and felt the brush of air pass his head. If the man followed up with another shot, while they were still on the floor, one or both of them were dead. But, when he looked up, the man was running away. He dropped the gun in a trash receptacle as he ran down the near-empty hall.

"Are you alright?" Taylor asked, helping Mary up while holding her elbow with one hand, the other arm wrapped around her waist, ignoring the pain in his arm.

"What was that?" she asked as she sat back in her seat. But just before she sat down, Taylor noticed the two bullet holes, one in each seat back, at chest level.

"Someone shot at us. If we hadn't moved, we'd both be dead."

Mary looked around. "I didn't see a thing. Where is he? And how did he get a gun in here?"

"He's gone. He didn't even wait to see if he hit us. I suspect the shots were a warning from Pavlovich."

"What now? Will he follow us, trying to kill us?"

"I don't think so. He knows we missed. He has a business to run. He'll watch for an opportunity for payback, but he's a practical man. He'll think we've gone to ground to plan our next attack, and he'll be better prepared next time."

First Date

Back in Virginia, after giving their reports, they were both given time off to recuperate.

"I'll have to think about what your meeting with Pavlovich means and what we have to do to protect you two," Rainbow said to Taylor after debriefing him. "Why don't you take some time off? Be back here in a week."

"Did he just imply that we should spend time together?" Mary asked Taylor, as he met her in the lobby. She had been debriefed first, and could have left the building, but had waited for him.

"I don't know," Taylor said. "I don't think Rainbow has a dating service. but I kind of like the idea. What do you think?"

"What do you want to do?" Mary asked, nodding her head in approval of the idea.

"We're going on that date," Taylor said. "Do you like NBA basketball? The Wizards are playing the Bulls this week. Maybe we can get tickets."

"I used to follow the Jazz, when Stockton and Malone played, but that was years ago. I don't even know who plays anymore."

"Okay, Let's go to the Smithsonian instead." He hailed a cab and took her into Washington, D.C. They spent the day walking and visiting Smithsonian buildings on both sides of the reflection pool. They talked about anything and everything, finding that they had similar backgrounds, interests and ambitions. When they got hungry, they hailed a cab and asked the driver to take them to his favorite restaurant for lunch, which he did. When they got tired of walking and sightseeing, they took another cab to her apartment, where she made him dinner. They sat on the couch to eat and talk and ended up in each other's arms, kissing and hugging. They made plans to meet for breakfast the next morning and continue their tour of Washington. They had made a small dent in the number of things to see, so they planned to spend a couple more days in Washington.

Taylor learned that Mary was interested in the Revolutionary and Civil Wars, but had never toured the Northeast, so they agreed to take a grand tour. He also learned that they liked the same kinds of food, especially seafood, that neither drank alcohol or coffee, and neither believed in pre-marital sex.

For the next two days, they shared breakfast, toured historical sites— more Smithsonian exhibits, the Lincoln Memorial, the Washington Monument, the Vietnam Memorial, the Holocaust Museum and a few other sights in between—and ended each day the same way, in her apartment, making out on her couch.

The fourth day, they drove to New York to visit ground zero, Ellis Island, and the Statue of Liberty. They ate Philly Cheesesteak sandwiches at a little hole-in-the-wall restaurant downtown, then visited the Empire State Building and other sites around the city. Intrigued by the subway system, Mary wanted to ride it from one end of town to the other. They ended up in Central Park and ate hotdogs purchased from a street vendor. Before it got too late, Taylor made reservations at a Hilton hotel, where they had adjoining rooms on the twenty-fourth floor, with a view of most of the city and access to an all-day buffet on the twenty-second floor. They ended the day in the exercise room, then the hot tub, then Mary's room, watching a romance on cable TV and making out.

Taylor bought tickets online for a Broadway show for the next night, planned one more day in New York, then a trip to Boston. They ended the day in each other's arms, watching the city lights.

On their way to Boston, Taylor broached the subject that he suspected was foremost on both their minds—love and marriage.

"Are you enjoying yourself?" Taylor asked.

"Absolutely," Mary said, holding his hand in both of hers. "Are you? Do you want to do something else instead?"

"What I want to do is get married. I love you."

"You hardly know me. We've only been together for a few days."

"But we've had lots of time to talk and share experiences in those days."

"We have, Taylor, and I love you, too."

"We have to report back to work in a couple of days. They'll send us our separate ways. We may not have another chance like we do now to do something about it. Besides, I worried I might lose you on our last assignment. I don't want to lose you before we have a chance to know each other better, if you know what I mean."

Mary

"You mean have sex, don't you?" she asked bluntly. She loved him so much that she had been considering ignoring her own goal of being a virgin when she married. Now, Taylor was putting the question to her. What did she want? Was she willing to have sex with him before marriage?

"No," Taylor finally said, "I mean make love. There's a difference."

"Only in your attitude while engaged."

"Let's go home. I have a camping trailer. Go camping with me for the time we have left. Then decide what you want to do."

She agreed, so they went home, spent the rest of that day packing and left the next morning. They didn't have a campground reservation, so they dry-camped in a wooded area near a campground in Western Virginia.

On their campout, she showed him her yoga exercises. He showed her his collection of sixties and seventies rock music. He sang along with his favorite artists and she laughed when he squeaked out the high notes. They talked some more about marriage, about where they should live, how many children they wanted and how their careers would be affected by their decision. They agreed to get married, but she wanted a big wedding and he just wanted to go to the courthouse and be married by a judge.

When they reported back to work two days later, they still hadn't agreed on how to proceed. They were sent their separate ways. She went to Australia with information for the station chief and he went to Columbia, to resolve a political problem. They were both distracted by their feelings for each other and questioned whether or not they could be effective at their jobs or if the distraction would result in one or both of them becoming careless and getting hurt.

Venezuela

A few weeks later, having successfully protected a political candidate from assassination in Columbia, Taylor was sent to join Mary for an assignment in Venezuela. He met her at the airport and they drove to their hotel.

"So, what are we doing here?" Mary asked.

"Our target is a general who has managed to steal a million dollars' worth of diamonds from the government. Our information is that he's planning to sell them and use the money to finance a government overthrow. All we have to go on is a photograph of the general and some information on his military organization."

"What information?"

"He's always surrounded by soldiers. The agency has a mole in his organization. He was finally able to tell us when and where to catch him without all of his men around him."

"How do we get close to him?" Mary asked.

"He's attending the reception of a niece who is marrying one of his men. The reception is on the main floor of the hotel where the general is staying. Our mole got an invitation, which the agency doctored, for us to get in to the reception. Once we're inside, we need to get you close to him so you can get to the jewels."

"How do I do that?"

"Be creative. He's a powerful man with a big ego. Use it against him."

"You mean, seduce him." It was a statement. He nodded.

They were stopped at the door to the reception.

"I don't see your names on the guest list," a soldier guarding the entrance said.

"We have an invitation," Taylor said. "Maybe whoever prepared the guest list made a mistake."

"Possible," the soldier said. "Friends of the bride or groom?"

"Friends of the bride's father. I did him a favor a few months ago." Part of Taylor's briefing for the assignment was background on the bride's father's illegal investments. If necessary, Taylor had information about specific investments in Florida that he could use to cover his story. It wasn't necessary. Maybe the soldier knew about the man's illegal investments.

"I'm sure it's just a mistake," the soldier finally said. "Go ahead in."

They bypassed the guest sign-in table and wandered around the reception room. They checked the location of the reception line, the refreshment table, the gift table with its multitude of expensive gifts, and emergency exits. Mary spotted the general at the refreshment table, alone, and worked her way slowly over, standing casually across the table from him.

"What a lovely lady," the general said a few moments later.

Mary set the fork holding her chunk of pineapple onto her small plate. "Thank you." She said, sneaking a peak at him. "You're a handsome man. Look at all those ribbons on your large chest. You must be an important man."

"I'm General Gonsalvez," he said. "The most powerful general in the Venezuelan Army. And you are?"

"I'm Mary. I'm here with a friend."

"I'm glad you came." He stared at her, unashamedly, his eyes wandering over her for a few moments. "Would you like to get away from this crowd?"

"What do you have in mind?" she asked, smiling encouragingly.

"I have some pretty trinkets in my room."

"Trinkets, huh? That sounds interesting," she said as she worked her way around the table to him. She laid a delicate hand on his arm. He placed his other hand on hers and led her to an elevator, then up to his suite. He kissed the back of her hand, then left her standing in the middle of the room. He removed a painting from the wall, opened a hidden wall safe, and withdrew a small leather pouch. After closing the safe, he opened the draw strings and held the pouch under an overhead light to show her the glittery gems.

"Ooh, can I hold them?" She asked.

"Of course," he said, holding the pouch out to her with one hand while he played with the strap on her evening dress with the other.

She poured the stones into the palm of one hand and studied them, the light reflecting onto her face from the facets of the cut gems.

"What are they worth?" she asked, "in dollars."

"At least a million dollars," he said.

"They're beautiful."

"Almost as beautiful as you." He slipped first one strap, then the other off her shoulders watching her dress fall to her waist, then looked into her eyes. He took the pouch by the two leather straps, closed it over the diamonds, then tied the pouch around her neck by its leather straps, so that the pouch rested between her breasts.

"Beauty, for the beauty," he said. She giggled, then leaned over and kissed his rough, whiskered cheek. He took her by the hand and led her to the bed, soon lying beside her between the sheets.

Suddenly, the bedroom door opened and Taylor stood majestically in the doorframe, his silenced weapon in both hands. He placed one bullet between the general's eyes, splattering Mary with gore.

"Ewww," she squealed. "Now I need a shower."

"Make it quick," Taylor said, then watched as she ran to the bathroom, crouched over to cover herself with her arms, wearing only the pouch containing the diamonds.

"Do you need some help?" He asked through the door a few moments later.

"I think I can do this," she said. "Thanks, anyway."

"Just trying to be helpful," he said.

"Maybe another time," she said.

"I'll remind you that you said that."

When she came out of the bathroom with a towel wrapped around her body, up to her armpits, he could see the leather strap of the pouch, still around her neck, wet from the shower. He could also see her curves wrapped in the towel.

"Would you like to see these?" she asked.

"Sure," he said. She lifted the leather strap over her head, pulling the pouch out of the towel, causing it to slip. She handed him the pouch, which he opened, to get a look at the gems, then stuffed the pouch in his pocket. She placed her arms around his neck and kissed him. He placed his arms around her waist and pulled her to him.

"I think we better go," she finally said when he started moving his hands around on her back.

"Okay," he said. "We can continue this discussion another time."

"We seem to be putting off a lot of discussions until later."

"You mean your marriage proposal and discipline for not following instructions?" He asked.

"Yes, and your request for a bedroom scene and to help me shower."

"Okay, next time we're in Virginia, we'll pick up where we left off." He winked at her and she nodded.

"I'm afraid if we work together any more, we're going to have to start keeping better track of our debts to each other," she said.

"Or, just follow through on them."

They returned to Virginia directly from Venezuela, and filed their reports.

16

New Home and Family—Taylor

"We need a vacation," Taylor told Rainbow.

"Both of you?" Rainbow asked, a mischievous look in his eyes. "At the same time?"

"We're both here, so now's a good time for both of us."

"Fine. Nothing pressing right now. Check with me in a week."

"Thanks, Rainbow." While Taylor prepared his travel trailer, Mary called a justice of the peace. She scheduled the wedding, then called her parents to invite them. They dropped everything to fly to Virginia for the wedding. They would be the witnesses. Taylor and Mary thanked them for coming and being their witnesses, then he carried Mary to the truck and helped her into the passenger seat. That was as close as she would get to being carried over a threshold.

They found a campground that had full hookups and could be reserved for an entire week. They spent the entire week inside the trailer, cooking their own meals and getting to know each other better. They followed through on all of their delayed promises, including the shower. Then they went back to work.

Mary

Six weeks later, with morning sickness, Mary told Taylor that she wanted to take maternity leave to keep herself healthy and have her baby. Rainbow wanted her to keep working for a few more months, but Taylor insisted, so she took a leave of absence of indefinite length from the agency. She delivered a boy, who they named Drew, a few months later. Mary loved being a mother and enjoyed this new stage in her life. She had no desire to go back to work. They bought a house in Virginia, close to the office, and she stayed home, anxiously waiting for Taylor to come home between assignments.

On a vacation to the west the following winter, to snow ski in the Utah mountains, Mary fell in love with Utah. Taylor agreed they could move—it didn't matter where he lived for his work—so they bought a house in Provo, Utah and Mary set up housekeeping there.

Two years later, still not working, she had another boy, Michael. Two years after that, she gave birth to a girl, who they named Lynne.

Rainbow

"Mary, I need to talk to you," Rainbow said shortly after Lynne was born. "Will you come in to talk with me?"

"I don't want to work," Mary said. "Nothing has changed since the last two times we talked."

"Just hear me out, okay?"

Back in Virginia for a short visit, Rainbow pointed out all the successes Mary had experienced while working with Taylor.

"Did Taylor put you up to this?" She asked.

"No. No. I just wanted you to realize how valuable you are to your country and how much you've learned over the years working with him."

Mary *had* learned to work with Taylor over time; learned his habits, his tricks, his preferred actions and tactics. She got better at surveillance and tracking, neither of which were a big part of her training.

Rainbow promised her that the mission he had for them was an easy one, one that they were uniquely qualified to handle for him. She reluctantly agreed to one mission.

17

Costa Rica

He sent them to follow two guys into the Costa Rican rain forest. The two guys they were following split up, one going with a guide on ATVs through jungle trails, while the other went with a different guide on a zipline course through the tree-tops. Taylor followed the one on the ATV, while Mary followed the one on the ziplines, which she'd never been on before.

Taylor may have been too obvious with his attention to the guy on the ATV. He figured out quickly that Taylor was after him. The guy tried to run Taylor off the trail, into the trees. When that didn't work, he took out a gun and tried shooting him. He got distracted, trying to shoot at Taylor and drive at the same time, and rolled the ATV, crushing his legs underneath it.

Their guide was worried that he would be blamed for the accident, even though the guy didn't follow safety instructions. Taylor gave the guide fifty dollars and told him to forget it. Taylor called ahead to tell authorities where to meet them, then handcuffed the man to the ATV and stayed with him until the guide got them back to the event office. A police van was waiting to take him into custody.

Mary followed the guy on the ziplines. Climbing ladders to elevated platforms, then being buckled into harnesses to slide down ziplines for hundreds of feet, hundreds of feet above the forest floor, made Mary nauseous. As Mary relaxed more with each run on a zipline, and the guy became more nervous, he tried to stay ahead of her; but they were in the same tour group.

He tried to quit the tour, part-way through, but the guide told him there was no way until they got to the end Then he volunteered to be the first to take the ride each time. He got so nervous, trying to keep ahead of Mary, that he jumped off one of the platforms before he had his harness buckled completely, trying to get his gun out of his belt.

He ended up dangling from the harness, several hundred feet above the ground, for about ten minutes. He finally lost his grip and fell, just before he got to the next platform. The guide had to climb down and retrieve him from the bushes, where he'd landed on a branch that went through his neck. He was still alive, so Mary handcuffed him and stayed with him until they met up with Taylor and the police van at the tour office.

Rio Negro River, Brazil—Mary

"I have another mission that only you two can handle," Rainbow told Mary when she called to say they were coming home. "Since you're already almost there now, go to Manaus, Brazil, and I'll send you the case file electronically" Mary had told Taylor in confidence that the last mission hadn't been as much trouble as she had expected—she had actually enjoyed the ziplines—and that she might try another one some time. She suspected he had shared that comment with Rainbow, but couldn't be sure.

"Rainbow, you agreed this was our last mission," Mary said, clenching her jaw and biting back what she really wanted to say to him.

"I know. I know. This one will be the last one. You're already half-way there and this is an important case. With Taylor's language skills and your close relationship, you are uniquely qualified for this."

She reluctantly agreed, told Taylor, and they flew to Manaus, in the middle of the Brazilian rainforest, on the Amazon River. In the case file, they found information on their reservations to stay in a jungle tree house on the Rio Negro River, a tributary of the Amazon. They also found reservations for a boat ride up the river to the tree house.

When they arrived at the boat dock in Manaus, their target was there, waiting. They boarded the boat—a barge, really—and their target boarded with them. Taylor tried to relax in a hammock tied between two poles on the deck. After being bitten multiple times by fleas, he gave up on the hammock and sat with Mary on a bench, looking out over the river.

"Do you know anything about our lodgings?" she asked.

"All I know is that it's the tree house that was featured in the movie, Anaconda."

"Are we going to have to deal with giant snakes?"

"No, I don't believe the snakes in the movie really exist."

"But you don't know?"

"Tell you what. If they suggest we take a ride up the Rio Negro River, I'll turn it down."

Their cover was that they were rich Americans, on vacation. When the boat arrived at the dock, they stepped out onto a plank platform, up wooden stairs to an octagon-shaped lodge with wire screens for windows, with tables and benches inside like a school cafeteria. A clothes tree to one side was filled with stems of bananas and one side of the room sported a kitchen. On the side opposite the entrance was an exit that led to the guest rooms. They exited the lodge, walked along an elevated boardwalk through the jungle to a three-story tree house. There were two rooms on the main floor of the tree house and a staircase curving up the right-hand wall to the upper floors.

In their welcome and orientation, they were warned to eat only in the lodge. The monkeys would take away from them any food they removed from the lodge. And the monkeys were clever enough to open the doors on occasion.

They were given a schedule that included a piranha fishing demonstration and a ride up the river to a native farm the next day. Since nothing was scheduled until the next morning, they spent the afternoon walking on the elevated boardwalks, through the jungle, between the guest tree houses. At the far end of the boardwalk was a large elevated platform marked as a helicopter pad. They watched the beautiful Macaws, and played keep-away with a monkey who wanted Taylor's banana. The monkey won. They returned to the lodge, ate sandwiches with tropical fruit juice, then retired to their room. They noted that their target had one of the upper rooms in their building.

There was no hot water in the shower, but it wasn't necessary. The air was warm enough that they didn't chill. The bed was barely wide enough for both of them to lay side by side if they pressed their bodies together. The mattress was comfortable enough that they slept soundly.

The next morning, early, their guide took them piranha fishing in a small boat; it was crowded with four of them in it. The guide was showing them how to fish by wiggling the end of their stick—no hook, just bait—in the water. The movement attracted a piranha to the bait and the guide pulled it out of the water to show them. They each tried it, without success. There must be a trick to it, or maybe the guide caught the only piranha in the vicinity. Mary pulled her handcuffs out of her purse and told the target he was under arrest.

He had nowhere to go. He jumped in the water and swam toward shore, almost tipping them all into the river. By the time they rescued him, halfway to shore, and pulled him back into the boat, all his fingers and toes had been chewed to the bone, his left arm was chewed up from his wrist to his elbow, and he had a fish hanging on his nose. The guide pulled the fish off, taking a huge chunk of flesh with it.

"Gross," Mary said. "I think I've had enough. Take me home, Taylor."

The rest of the morning was a blur for Mary; she couldn't wait to get out of the jungle and back to civilization. When the guide headed upstream, she complained to Taylor, who questioned the guide.

"It's only a little way up the river," the guide said. "There's no danger."

"No snakes?" Mary asked.

"No giant Anaconda," the guide said, smiling. "That movie hurt our business."

They stopped at a small farm, with chickens and mostly-naked children running around. A small vegetable garden looked pathetic. When Taylor asked the guide how the family was able to survive in these conditions, he confessed that they relied on handouts from tourists who stopped by. Then he gave Taylor an opportunity to give them some money, which he did.

While they talked, quietly, a storm cloud came over and dumped a flood of rain on the farm. Since the storm was a daily occurrence, they were forewarned and able to step under a shelter to wait out the twenty-minute deluge. Then they returned to the lodge.

The police arrived a few hours later from Manaus and took the target off their hands. The hotel host was disappointed when Mary insisted that they leave the next morning, instead of taking a ride up the Rio Negro River. When Mary heard that was the plan for the next day, she couldn't wait to get on the barge to return to Manaus.

Perth, Australia—Mary

It was more difficult to get her to agree to the next mission, but Taylor told her how much he liked the seafood in Perth, Australia. So, she agreed to go if Rainbow would promise this was absolutely their last mission. Taylor took her to the seafood restaurant on the wharf, where she eventually agreed that the food was great. They got on a tour of a centuries old prison, dating back to when Australia was a penal colony for England and they sent all their criminals there. Even small violations resulted in a trip down under. Mary was reminded of the Broadway play, Les Misérables, which she loved.

When the tour group reached the basement of the prison, where prisoners were chained to the wall and left to die, centuries earlier, Mary was tempted to chain their target up and leave him there. The chains were still attached to the walls.

Taylor would have let her, but decided the chains were so old and rusted, the guy could probably have broken out without help. So, they handcuffed him and took him outside, where a police car waited, having responded to Taylor's call.

"I think I'm done," Mary told Taylor. "The travel and stress are getting to me, and I hate leaving the kids alone for so long at a time."

"Okay. I'll tell Rainbow we're done for a while. I'm sure he'll understand. I'll tell him you're losing your edge and you're afraid of getting hurt."

"You know that's not true," she said and slugged him in the arm. It actually hurt.

"What do you want me to tell him?"

"Just what I said. I need time to watch my children grow up. I need to be a mother to them, not just a visitor when it's convenient for him."

"Rainbow said that was fine," Taylor told her later. "He doesn't have any more missions right now that require our specific talents. Besides, they've got new recruits that they want to get out in the field."

"Didn't you escort a new recruit on a recent mission?" she asked.

"I've actually trained several new recruits in the last four years while you were on leave. Now, he's letting both of us rest for a while."

Several months later, Rainbow called Taylor and asked if they would handle another case for him. The target was a Guatemalan billionaire who was buying and supplying weapons to a terrorist group in Columbia.

18

Guatemala City—Mary

In Guatemala City, Mary reluctantly connected with the billionaire, in her usual style. But as they were leaving the room, she made eye contact with Dmitri Pavlovich, who they didn't know would be there. She looked around quickly for Taylor, spotted him, and gave him a signal for an immediate extraction. He got to her in moments and tried to take her away from the billionaire, whose bodyguards intervened. By the time he had fought them, knocking out two and possibly killing a third, the confusion had drawn the attention of a great crowd, including Pavlovich. Before they could leave the room, Pavlovich gave Taylor a two-finger salute of recognition.

They left the ballroom, took the stairs to their room on the third floor, then escaped out the window after calling for an extraction and shooting their way out of the alley behind the building.

Taylor reported the contact with Pavlovich, the first in several years. Rainbow wondered if it meant a new escalation in Russian KGB activity. He also worried about the safety of his two favorite agents, if Pavlovich had become active again.

Taylor also wondered about their safety. Russian spies held grudges and this one was particularly mean, especially since Taylor had interrupted his attack on Mary years earlier. He told Rainbow they were ready to retire. Rainbow asked them to handle one more mission, a sensitive one requiring both of them, the most complex and possibly the most dangerous for Mary.

Taylor tried to talk his way out of the assignment, but Rainbow reminded him that he had signed an agreement that was effective for life. Taylor and Mary could go voluntarily, or he could force them to go, against their will. If they went under duress, it would go in their files as a black mark.

19

She was going back to Brazil to try, once again, to get Gaetano to stop working with the Mexican drug cartel. This time with Taylor to help her. They knew they couldn't get Gaetano alone, without Paulina's help, because of his bodyguards and fans.

Paulina agreed to meet with the CIA agents and stipulated it had to be a couple, on Copacabana Beach, where she would pass along information on when and where to get him alone.

Rainbow handed Mary a small bag, telling her that this was what they needed for the meeting with Paulina. Her mouth dropped open when she reached in the bag and pulled out a pile of string and cloth. She sorted it out into a skimpy bikini for her and a speedo for Taylor.

"What's this?" Mary asked.

"That's what you need to wear when you meet with Paulina. She said she'll only give you the information if she sees you wearing these."

"But why?"

"No place to hide weapons?" Rainbow guessed.

"And this is for real, right?"

"You'll fly into Galeão International Airport on Governador Island, take a taxi to your hotel on Copacabana beach, then meet her on the beach, wearing just these the next morning. She'll give you the information on where and when to find Gaetano. Then you go from there. Stop him any way you have to. You're authorized to use deadly force if necessary."

They flew into Rio, settled into their hotel, then walked across the street to check out the beach that evening, a Friday. Taylor told Mary he understood Paulina's insistence on the costumes after seeing what the men and women wore on the beach. They wouldn't stand out at all. Everyone dressed that way. Mary, with her long, shapely legs and tan, would fit right in. Taylor with his muscular build and tan, would fit in, as well.

They went to bed early so they would be refreshed for what they expected to be a long day, Saturday. At breakfast, Mary pointed out three small red spots on her shoulder, all in a row, and asked Taylor what he thought they were, some kind of a rash. Taylor showed her one he had on his ankle, chuckled, and told her they were flea bites. Even staying at one of the best hotels in Rio, they still had fleas in the beds.

Just before the appointed meeting time, they changed into their costumes. Taylor whistled when he saw Mary's outfit. Even after giving birth to three children, Mary was in great physical shape. Covered by beach wraps, they left the hotel. Where the night before, the traffic on the street had been light, that morning, all of the traffic lanes were full, and some cars had squeezed between other cars, straddling the lane markers. When the light changed, cars and busses sped through the intersection at high speed. There was no pedestrian light, so they waited until traffic backed up at the light again, then crossed between the stopped cars.

The sidewalks were made of small, black and white, flat-faced stones, arranged in patterns to show the creativity of the builders and the gaiety of the city. They crossed over onto the sand and walked along the beach. Taylor didn't know that Mary had met Paulina once before and knew what she looked like. So, while Taylor tried to identify the most beautiful woman on the beach,

Mary made eye contact with Paulina, who was walking in their general direction, wearing a black micro-bikini. She elbowed Taylor, as much to stop him from staring at Paulina's beautiful body, as much as to let him know that she had spotted her. He saw where Mary was looking and nodded his agreement. That must be her. They continued walking, adjusting their direction to intersect her path.

Paulina wore a wide-brim hat to protect her face, her only other article of clothing besides the black micro-bikini, which was little more than two small scraps of black cloth held in place by a string that circled her back and around her neck. The bottom consisted of a small strip of cloth between her legs tied by string to a string around her waist. Her bronzed skin begged to be worshipped and hugged. Mary jabbed Taylor again in the side with her elbow when he continued to stare at her.

They slowed as they approached Paulina, stopping just two feet away from her. Mary wondered if she would be recognized. Suddenly, Paulina stepped forward and threw her arms around Mary.

"Mary!" she exclaimed. "Um prazer!"

Taylor, who had been to Brazil before and knew a little Portuguese, looked surprised, knowing Mary knew only English. "Tu es Paulina?" he asked.

"Sim. Voces são do CIA?"

"Sim. Voce tem informação?"

Without speaking, Paulina turned her back to them and raised her hair to reveal a message written in marker on her neck. It read: "Gaetano, 1600 horas, Clube Divino."

Taylor leaned in close to read the message, close enough to be distracted by the smell of lotion and perspiration, then backed up a step. "Obrigado," he said and turned to Mary. Mary nodded to Paulina and turned away. Taylor joined her and they walked back the way they had come. Before crossing the road again, Mary looked back, saw that Paulina was still watching them, and waved. Paulina returned the gesture.

Back in their hotel, they changed into street clothes, called a cab and considered what to do between then and four p.m., the time they were supposed to be at the club.

"What was that?" he asked, referring to the obvious recognition between the two women.

"We've met before." Mary said. Taylor just stared at her, inviting an explanation.

"On a previous assignment I was sent to meet with Paulina and Gaetano to gain their cooperation. It didn't work then, so we're coming to try again."

"And when were you going to tell me about this prior assignment?"

"I just did. Don't make too big a deal about it. You've been here before. What do you want to do to kill some time?"

They decided to go to Corcovado, since Mary hadn't been to Rio before and the Christus statue on Corcovado Mountain was the single most tourist-worthy site in the city. They stopped at a panificadora and bought some sweet rolls and a 'vitamina abacate'.

"What is it?" Mary asked as she stared at the thick green liquid in her cup.

"It's an avocado shake."

Mary wrinkled her nose, not sure what to think.

"Try it," he said.

"Mmm" she said when she did, surprised at how sweet it was.

He pointed to the large, round fruit on the counter, that was so different from the small, somewhat bitter avocados in the United States.

"It's made with that, milk and sugar. Isn't it great?"

"It's surprisingly good," she answered.

Next, he stopped at a fruit stand on the street and bought a small branch of baby bananas to eat on the way. It was a peaceful trip up the backside of the mountain in a taxi, through dense jungle on either side of the narrow road. Mary was so impressed with the statue, when it came into view, that she took several pictures, then asked another tourist to take more pictures of the two of them in front of it, so she could be in them.

They spent a leisurely day walking around the statue, then walked down the staircase on the other side of the mountain, catching a cab once they had reentered a neighborhood at the bottom of the mountain.

They arrived at the club fifteen minutes early, paid a cover charge and entered a large hall, where a band played on a stage on the far side, drinks and food could be purchased at booths around the walls, and chairs were arranged in front of the stage for those who just wanted to sit and listen. They recognized Gaetano as the lead singer, holding a guitar and singing into a microphone while his band played behind him. They sat on the back row of chairs and looked around at the milling crowd, applauded with the crowd at the end of the current song, and waited; for what, they didn't know.

A few minutes later, a beautiful brunette sat next to Taylor, who he recognized from the beach, now dressed in a lovely pale green, backless gown that matched her eyes. It dipped low in the front, and barely covered her backside when she sat.

"Paulina, um prazer," Taylor said.

"Vem comigo," Paulina said without preamble and without smiling, as she stood. Taylor, then Mary followed as Paulina led them to a side door out of the hall, past a bouncer, and up a set of stairs to the next level. They entered a room with a large gold star on it. 'Gaetano' was embossed on the star—his dressing room, which Mary had been in before.

"Sente-se, por favor," Paulina said, pointing to chairs at one side of the room. She leaned against a counter attached to the opposite wall. A large mirror showed Taylor and Mary how low her dress was cut in back, clear to her waist.

The door opened and Gaetano entered, hurriedly. "O que é isto?" he asked, looking at Paulina.

"Elles são do CIA," she said. "Ouvi-los, por favor." Listen to them, please.

"You speak English," Taylor said.

"I do," Gaetano agreed, his accent barely distorting his words. "What do you want?"

"We want to help you stay alive."

"What do you mean?"

"You're dealing with some nasty people in Mexico. If you ever cross them, or fail to do exactly what they say, they'll kill you and Paulina. We want to help you get away from them."

"I don't know what you're talking about."

"Sure you do. And I'm sure you agree that your life and the lives of anyone you care about are subject to the whim of the drug lord you're dealing with. He's a violent man."

Gaetano thought about that for a few moments. He must have recognized the truth in Taylor's words.

"What do you want me to do about it?" he asked.

"Two things. One: stop taking money from them."

"They'll kill me for sure," Gaetano complained.

"Not if you do number two: Let us hide you for one month. We think that's all it will take for the drug lord's operations to be in trouble and start a civil war within his organization."

"Then he'll kill me."

"We don't think so. He may want to, but he'll have so much in-fighting to contend with that he won't be able to trust anyone to do what he wants. Either way, we'll be there to watch and protect you."

"You're asking me to hide, when I'm at the peak of my success as an entertainer?"

"We believe the drug lord is in financial trouble and is about to approach you to change the terms of your agreement. He'll probably want to increase his percentage of the take, maybe by as much as double."

"I won't do it."

"Then you'll die, and you know it. Let's do this. When he comes to you, or calls for you to go to him, agree. Agree to his terms, then let us remove you to a safe place. Put your career on hold for a month, then hire a publicist to kick off a new career."

"I have a publicist."

"Great. Will you do it?"

"If all of those things occur as you say, then I'll agree." Paulina went to him and took his hand. He explained briefly what Taylor had said and what he had agreed to do about it. Paulina smiled and hugged his hand to her chest.

"Good," Taylor said. "We'll be in touch. Paulina knows where we're staying in Copacabana."

It was two days later that Paulina appeared at their hotel room door.

"Vem comigo, por favor," she said. Taylor and Mary got their coats and guns, and followed her to a cab that waited outside. The cab took them to the club, to a side entrance. Paulina led them up to Gaetano's dressing room.

"What's up?" Taylor asked.

"The drug lord sent a committee of three armed men to tell me I now owe him three times as much as before. One of them stood threateningly behind Paulina while they told me. I'm ready to do as you say; but I have a major performance in two weeks that will cost a lot to cancel. Can we do this after that performance, or can I perform that one night?"

"Is it worth your life? Or the life of your girlfriend?"

"I have bodyguards and security people."

"And can you trust them that none of them have been threatened by the drug lord?"

"Could they do that? Turn my own people against me?"

"They could and they would. What we're doing could cause a blood bath within the drug lord's operations. He might do anything to save himself. Your best bet is to just disappear, you and Paulina and anyone else you care about."

Gaetano turned to Paulina and exchanged a few words with her in Portuguese. "She has her mother and younger sister who she worries about. She's already told them that we all have to hide They are willing, even though it will disrupt Paulina's promising modeling career."

"Okay, let's meet back here, the four of you and no more than one small suitcase each, at nine, tonight, and we'll all disappear."

There were two black SUVs across the street from the club when Taylor and Mary returned just before nine. Taylor suspected these were the drug lord's men, keeping an eye on Gaetano. It was already dark, so it was impossible to tell how many people were in the SUVs; but from past experience, Taylor guessed at least three in each, a driver and two gunmen.

"Do we try to avoid them, or confront them?" Taylor asked Mary.

"You're assuming the worst, aren't you?" she asked.

"I have to. We can assume it's not what we think, and try to just drive away; but if I'm right, they'll chase us, maybe even shoot at us."

"Can Rainbow help?"

"I've already alerted him. He'll help if he can; but that means he has to get people here and get set up to help. I think we should try to get out of this on our own."

"How are we going to do that, Taylor. Now I'm scared. I've never been this scared before, not even in Budapest."

"Okay," he said, patting her hand affectionately, "Let's make sure they're ready to leave. I have an idea."

They found everyone anxiously waiting and ready to go. They loaded the luggage and the four people into the armored embassy SUV that they had borrowed for this little trip, then Taylor left the alley and pulled into the street. As soon as he did, the two SUVs pulled away from the curb, their headlights on, and followed, staying close behind them.

From Taylor's prior trips to Rio, he knew the streets were winding and narrow and he wasn't familiar enough with them to try to outrun the SUVs. He *did* know where the police station was, from a prior visit when he needed to coordinate with them. He drove to the station, which wasn't too far from the club and stopped in the street in front, double-parked. The two SUVs pulled up behind him. He gave them a few moments to see how close they were to the station, then laid on the horn, attracting attention from drivers and pedestrians all around them, besides blocking traffic.

Taylor watched in his mirror to see what the SUVs would do. When arms holding guns appeared out of the windows of the first one, he warned his passengers.

"Everyone down," he said, then looked back to see that everyone obeyed. Several bullets hit the back of their SUV. Then policemen appeared in the doorway of the station to see what the commotion was about.

Taylor was sure the police could tell shots were fired, from the sound, and he wasn't too worried about the bullets that were hitting the SUV. He would be patient. Suddenly, policemen swarmed out of the station, taking cover behind cars, and calling to the shooters to lay down their weapons. The two SUVs pulled around Taylor and sped away, with two police cars in pursuit moments later.

A policeman came to Taylor's window, still holding his gun in front of him. Taylor rolled down his window and spoke to the policeman in Portuguese, for a few moments. He showed the officer his diplomatic credentials and his driver's license. They spoke for another few moments, then shook hands and the officer waved Taylor away.

"What was that about?" Mary asked.

"I told him we were from the embassy, transporting important guests, and the SUVs attacked us. He remembered me from my last visit and wished me a good day."

Taylor wasn't sure they could get to the airport without at least one of the SUVs spotting them again, especially if the shooters guessed that they might head there. He decided to chance it. They had reservations for a flight out of the country, that the embassy had made for them. He took the shortest route to the Ilha do Governador in Guanabara Bay, watching his mirrors and looking around constantly.

Partway there, a passenger car behind them slid sideways off the road and hit a tree. Taylor looked closely at the traffic around the car and saw the black SUV. It must have sideswiped the car. Suddenly, another car was swept sideways into the median, hitting a concrete barrier at low speed. The engine caught fire as the passengers bailed out of the car. The SUV weaved between cars, gaining on them, pushing cars out of the way. When a third car went nose-first off the road and down an embankment, Taylor picked up his speed and began racing through traffic himself.

"Hang on everyone," he said. "I'm going to try to outrun them."

When the SUV was right behind them, Taylor noticed a man standing in the sunroof opening with an automatic weapon in his hands, aimed at them. Taylor thought that the automatic weapon could lay down enough fire power to breach the car's protective armor, so he accelerated again.

The SUV bumped them from behind doing 180 kph, then hit them again and stayed with them, pushing them faster, probably hoping to force them off the road or cause them to roll. Mary surprised Taylor by pulling what looked like a grenade from her purse.

"What's that?" he asked.

"A flash-bang."

"What are you doing with it in your purse?"

"I'll explain later," she said as she reached up and pushed the button to open the sunroof. Taylor heard the sirens immediately as emergency vehicles approached. Mary looked back at the SUV and started to stand. Taylor grabbed her hand and pulled her back down.

"Don't," he said. "That guy with the automatic would hit you without a doubt."

"Okay," she said, then looked back again. She bounced the flash-bang in her hand a few times, getting a feel for the weight of it, then tossed it straight up in the air. The movement of the cars made it appear that the flash-bang arced behind them as it flew through the air. The gunman in the SUV took a swing at it as it approached him, arcing back down, He missed it and it entered it

SUV through the open sunroof and exploded.

There was a sudden brilliant flash of light and ear-piercing noise. The SUV swerved erratically back and forth as the blinded and deafened driver tried to maintain control. He took his foot off the gas, allowing other traffic to catch up, and pass, swerving around the SUV. Taylor sped ahead, putting distance between them. He noticed when the SUV hit one car head-on, a glancing blow, then went off the road and down the embankment. The explosion as it hit something down the hill sent a fireball into the air. Drivers who had slowed to put distance between them and the altercation, stared, pointed and gawked as they passed.

"Okay, put the guns away," Taylor said when he noticed both Mary and Paulina had pulled handguns from their purses. We'll be at the airport in minutes. He dropped everyone off at the curb, with their luggage, drove to a far corner of the parking lot to leave the car and the guns, then called the embassy to tell them where to find it and to apologize for its condition. Inside the airport, they got their boarding passes quickly and went through airport security as soon as possible. Taylor relaxed then, having put a layer of security between them and those following them, in case they made it to the airport and located them.

"Where are we going?" Gaetano asked as Taylor sat next to him in the waiting area, with Paulina on his other side of Gaetano.

"What does your ticket say?" Taylor asked.

"Miami, Florida. Is that our destination or an intermediate stop?"

"Destination. We'll put you all in a CIA safe house for a while. You'll find it has everything you need to be comfortable."

When they boarded, they found that they had all been placed in first class seats, where they had more personal space, food and other conveniences. Taylor and Mary studied each of the boarding passengers as they passed them in the cabin to make sure no one paid undue attention to them. They were met in Miami by an Agency car and taken directly to a safe house, located in a remote wooded area.

20

Rome—Taylor

A few months later, Rainbow contacted Taylor again.

"I need you to go to Rome," he said.

"We told you we were retiring after Rio de Janeiro," Taylor said.

"You have to do this for us, Rainbow pleaded. We have no one else who can pull this off."

"Then you better start training someone."

"Please?"

"You know, Rainbow, it's only a matter of time before one of us gets hurt, maybe killed. We'd rather stop while we still have our good health."

"I know what you mean, but what's so bad about dying in the line of duty?"

"Save the speech. We'll do this, then it's over."

"Okay."

"I mean it."

"Alright."

"Put it in writing and I'll believe you."

"I'll do it today."

"And send it to me."

"Okay."

"What's my role on this trip again?" Mary asked her husband of nine years. She knew this was his mission and she was along to assist him. That had been her condition for participating, that and the letter from Rainbow retiring them. They had arrived at the Fiumicino airport a few hours earlier and gone directly to their hotel. Now they were hiding out until the start of the reception.

"You're my cover," Taylor said. "I'm going to meet a man, who will handoff information that will help us bring down the largest Mafia family in Italy. You are my excuse for being here."

"You mean, I'm supposed to distract anyone who appears interested in you, is that it?"

"In that outfit, you should be able to distract anyone with male genes. You're distracting me now and I already know your hidden assets." She wore a long, silk dress, slit up the middle to the top of her thighs, that showed off her tanned legs whenever she moved. The plunging neckline, spaghetti straps and no back left little of her hourglass figure to the imagination. She wore little makeup—she didn't need much, with her dark, Mediterranean features. She was, in a word, gorgeous.

"So, why are we staying in our room until the reception?"

"I don't want us to run into someone who will remember our faces. This is a quick in-and-out. We get the information, then we leave. Leo is waiting for our call to pick us up and return us to the airport."

"Can we order room service?"

"What do you want? There will be food and drinks at the reception."

"Will there be time to eat anything?"

"There should be. I don't expect too much pressure."

"So, I just mingle with the other guests and watch your back, is that it?"

"Basically. Is that alright with you?"

"As long as I can enjoy myself as well."

"As long as your fun doesn't distract from the mission."

"Got it, boss."

Taylor sensed some unease in his wife. This wasn't her assignment; it was his. She had been involved in many of his missions and was more than ready to quit. She could vividly remember Copacabana Beach in Rio de Janeiro. The prison in Perth, Australia, the rain forest in Costa Rica, and several other missions with Taylor. None of them had scared her like this one did.

Taylor walked over and placed an arm around her shoulders, noticing her goosebumps. He gave her a hug, then helped place the faux-mink warmer around her shoulders. He gave her a light kiss on the lips.

"No one in Rome should know us," Taylor said. "We've never been to Italy and have never participated in operations that involved Italians." However, with modern international travel, he knew that didn't mean anything, anymore.

At the appropriate time, they left the room and made their way to the ballroom on the main floor of the hotel, where Taylor expected the reception to be held. He was right. They found the room, filled with men and women in their finest dress—lots of tuxes and gowns, and other dress not quite so formal. Most of the people milled around, talking to others. Some sat on chairs around the walls, while others sat in groups at small tables set around the perimeter. Gaming tables, at the far end of the room, were surrounded by men and women trying their luck.

Almost immediately, a server passed them, carrying a tray of drinks. Taylor snagged two of them as he passed and handed one to Mary. Neither of them drank alcohol as a rule, so Taylor sipped his, nodded to Mary, then set his drink down on a small table. Mary set hers down without tasting it, having been warned by

Taylor that it was alcoholic.

Mary sat with her back against a wall and greeted those who stopped or spoke to her in passing. Her dress was distracting, but it wasn't so unusual in this crowd of well-dressed, international party-goers.

"And who might you be?" A well-dressed man asked Mary, taking her hand and lifting it to his lips for a quick kiss.

"I'm Mary," she said. "Who are you?"

"Sir Leland de Forest," he said. "I haven't seen you at one of our receptions before and I know just about everyone. Are you here alone? Would you like some company?"

"Thank you. I'm here with my husband."

"Oh. Well, enjoy yourself." He walked away, greeting people that he seemed to know. Perhaps most of these people knew each other from other receptions.

Two women in lovely gowns had been standing close by Mary, apparently listening to the conversation.

"You're apparently not a regular," one said, "Is that your husband down by the roulette table?"

"The one with the black bowtie. Yes."

"What a gorgeous man," the second one said. "Are you staying for the dance at the end of the reception? We'd like to get to know you both better, maybe get one dance with him."

Mary thought quickly. Taylor had said not to be too chatty with anyone. "I'm not sure," she finally said. "We have another engagement later this evening."

"That's a lovely gown you're wearing," the first one said.

"Thank you. Both of you look marvelous in your gowns. I'll have to remember to look for one similar to those for another time."

"Thank you," both women said at the same time. That seemed

to turn them off to her. They stepped away and went back to talking to each other.

Taylor stood at the roulette table and placed a small wager, which he lost immediately. He placed another wager, which he also lost, then he wandered away from the gaming tables, searching for Mary. They made eye contact and he winked. He assumed that her appreciative smile meant that he looked good in his tux.

He walked over and stood by her. The two women who had tried to chat her up watched him appreciatively. He hardly noticed them.

"You're being watched," Mary said, making a thumb motion toward the two women.

Taylor looked at them, nodded an acknowledgement, then returned his attention to Mary.

"Why don't you sit?" she asked.

"I don't want to sit. It would be too easy to get surprised and I don't want to be at a disadvantage by being stuck in a chair. I need to be on my feet so I can move quickly and respond to conditions changing around us." He looked around the room, trying not to appear too interested in anyone in particular. Seeing nothing that bothered him, he turned back to Mary.

Mary made a subtle motion with her head to the far wall, where a man in a thigh-length black suitcoat leaned against the wall. His dark glasses hid his eyes and prevented Taylor from knowing where the man was looking. Taylor nodded to Mary and moved slowly in that direction, guessing that the man was his contact. He was about fifteen feet away, walking obliquely, so it wasn't obvious where he was going, when the man pushed off from the wall and walked in a direction that would intersect Taylor's path at an angle. They were within five feet of each other when the man turned his head abruptly toward a table about ten feet away, that he had just passed, then changed direction and walked quickly to the nearest exit, cutting through the crowd hastily and drawing attention to himself.

Taylor cursed under his breath and scanned the area where his contact had looked moments before. There were four men in tuxedos and a woman in revealing evening wear, sitting at a table. All of them looked Eastern European. Taylor recognized one of the men from their prior encounters. He was a Russian, former KGB operative, turned Mafia, now industrialist and reorganized KGB, Dmitri Pavlovich. No wonder Taylor's contact had broken off and left. If the Russian KGB was involved, that complicated this mission and seriously jeopardized his and Mary's safety if they were identified.

They needed to leave, quickly. But, instead of changing direction abruptly, like his contact had done, Taylor turned at an angle so that his path did not bring him into contact with the Russians, but wove his way through the crowded room, back toward Mary. As he passed within six feet of the Russians' table, however, he noticed in his peripheral vision that Pavlovich looked right at him, holding up a hand to stop his associates in the middle of their conversation and stared for a few moments. When Taylor looked in Pavlovich's direction, Pavlovich gave a two-finger salute of acknowledgement. Then Pavlovich looked around the room and saluted Mary against the far wall.

They'd been sent to accept a handoff; critical information from a mole in the Italian mafia, who was trying to help bring down the family. They were not prepared to get mixed up with the Russian KGB, He returned to Mary, took her hand and led her toward the exit that led to the elevators.

"I was so close," Taylor whispered so only Mary could hear.

"So, the guy against the wall was your contact?" Mary whispered back.

"I'm certain he was. Now his cover has been blown and we've been seen by Pavlovich."

"How did he recognize me," she asked, "We only met that one time."

"It was a close encounter," Taylor reminded her, "and he's a trained spy. Now, anyone with undercover training will recognize what happened, a failed handoff, and realize that I'm a spy, too. We need to leave, quickly," he continued, as they left the conference room.

Out in the hallway, Taylor noticed someone lying on the floor, spread-eagled, the back of his head a bloody mess. The thigh-length coat was a give-away. Taylor's contact had been taken out by a head-shot, assassination style. Taylor looked down the hall in both directions, debating the best course of action, and reached behind his back, pulling his nine-millimeter Beretta handgun from his belt.

"We'll take the stairs," he said as they passed an open elevator and continued to the stair well. A man exited the open elevator and turned a silenced handgun in their direction. Taylor turned and shot him in one smooth move. Taylor removed his hard-soled shoes and held them in one hand while he cracked the stair door open. Assassins could be anywhere by now. They entered the stairwell and began to climb, quietly. A man appeared above them; his gun pointed generally in their direction. Taylor shot him, too, and waited while the man tumbled down a flight of stairs, breaking his neck in the process. If the bullet in the chest hadn't killed him, the fall down the stairs surely had. Taylor helped Mary climb over him, then followed him to the third floor, quickly but quietly.

He took a quick look at Mary, to see how well she was handling this. Her face had bleached of color and she was shaking.

He knew he had to get her to their room before she went into shock, He would take care of her there.

He stopped at their landing. "Let me take a quick look," he said, then peered into the hallway, looking in both directions. Seeing no one, he led Mary out of the stairwell. That's when another man appeared from around a corner, in the direction of the elevators. Taylor shot this one in the forehead. He led Mary to their room, entered the door key, watched for the light to turn green, and pushed the door open. Inside, he closed the door behind them and double-locked it.

"You pack while I check the alley," he said, keeping his voice down and his words to a minimum. She didn't move. He went to the freezer and got an ice pack. He wrapped it in a towel and took it to her.

"Sit down and place this on your forehead," he said. She sat on the couch and leaned her head back, resting the ice on her forehead. Without turning on lights, he punched a number into his mobile phone, listened briefly, then said, "lagoon", the preselected keyword for an immediate extraction.

They didn't have much to pack. They were only in Rome for this reception and handoff, and they would be returning directly home. Taylor took a quick look out the patio door, checking the fire escape above and below and the alleyway in both directions. Satisfied that no one was there to observe their departure, he returned to her and asked how she was feeling.

"Much better, thank you," she said and smiled. He loved her smile.

"How about you pack our bags while I watch for Leo?"

Mary nodded and stood from the couch, dropping the towel and ice pack on the couch where she had been sitting. When she went to the bedroom, he closed the patio door, pulled the drapes, and pushed the couch against the patio door. When he turned around, Mary stood by the door to the hallway with her coat on, their two rolling suitcases at her feet, and his coat over her arm. Even as stressed out as she was, she was as efficient as she was beautiful and charming.

"Do we have time to make phone calls?" Mary asked, holding her phone in a shaking hand.

"Once we're in the car and moving." Taylor said.

"Why is my hand shaking?"

"You're exhausted. Why don't you sit down again and rest?"

"You moved the couch."

"It's okay. You can sit on it until we leave."

Suddenly, the sound of automatic weapons fire and shattering glass put them both on high alert.

"Down!" Taylor said. He reached for Mary's arm and pulled her onto the floor with him, landing on top of her as a shield, just as the glass patio door shattered and bullets tore through the curtain, streaked across the room, and stitched a line across the wall above their heads. From the angle of their trajectory, Taylor guessed they came from a room across the alley. He would have to take out a sniper's nest before they used the fire escape.

"Take a position by the bedroom door while I check the hallway," Taylor said, hoping her training would kick in and help her follow him without questions. He watched as she crawled to the bedroom and stood in the doorway. He really needed to make sure she was okay.

"Be careful," she said.

Taylor crawled across the room. When he reached the door to the hallway, he checked to see that Mary had hidden herself behind the door frame before reaching for the door handle. Satisfied that she was as safe as she could be, he turned the knob and opened the door a crack. He quickly shut it again as bullets passed through the small opening where he would have been standing, if he'd been standing, and the door frame around it.

"I called for an extraction," he said, "but I think we need to hold out for a couple more minutes. How are you doing?"

"I'm fine," she said. He wasn't sure; she might be in shock.

21

Extraction—Taylor

"Our ride should come to the alley, the quickest way to extract us. Why don't you go lay down?" He moved toward the kitchen after he confirmed that she had moved away from the bedroom door. When he was in a protected position, behind the fridge, he checked on Mary again. She was partially hidden behind the bedroom door frame, holding her gun pointed at the door to the hallway, the direction an assault would come from if their enemies attacked now. Smart girl.

The lock on the door to the hallway was blown apart by gunfire and the door opened inward. Three men rushed through the door with automatic rifles spraying bullets all around the room. Taylor pulled back as bullets hit the fridge protecting him, then peeked out and fired two rounds at the nearest shooter with his left hand. The shooter fell, his gun clattering away from him against the couch. A fusillade of bullets in his direction made him duck back again. He reached his left hand around the corner again and fired off several more shots, until his gun was empty. He popped out the empty cartridge and pushed in a full one from his pocket.

Suddenly, the shooting stopped, so he took a quick look in Mary's direction. A second shooter was down on the floor and he couldn't see Mary. He hoped she had found shelter in the bedroom, but thought the only place to hide would be on the other side or under the bed. The third shooter reloaded and headed toward the bedroom.

Taylor fired off several more shots in the shooter's general direction, just trying to get the shooter to focus on him instead of Mary. It worked; the shooter turned and fired off another series of rounds at the kitchen, walking in that direction. If Taylor could hold out until the shooter had to reload again, he had a chance to take him.

The shooting stopped again, so Taylor looked out. The third man was down and Mary stood in the bedroom doorway holding a smoking gun to her side. The first shooter, the one he had shot but must have only wounded, had crawled to the couch and was reloading his automatic. Taylor rushed to the man, trying to catch him off-balance, but the man pointed his gun at Taylor. Taylor kicked the man's wrist with his stockinged foot, heard bone crunch in the assailant's hand, and possibly his foot, and the gun went flying. The man grabbed his wrist and grimaced, then braced himself for Taylor, who was on him immediately.

Taylor grabbed the injured man, one fist on the nape of his neck and the other in his belt, and threw him backwards over the back of the couch and into the drapes covering the sliding door. He crashed through the drapes and the glass door panel, which had been weakened by the earlier bullets, and landed on the fire escape deck on his back, struggling to untangle himself from the drapes.

Taylor pushed the couch out of the way far enough to get to the door, ducked through the broken glass panel and caught the man, just standing up. With his shoulder in the man's stomach, he pushed him into the railing. The man landed with the top of the railing against his butt, balanced there for a few moments, then toppled over backwards, his thick chest making him top heavy. He made no sound as he fell; but a loud thud let Taylor know the man had landed. It sounded like he had hit the roof of a car, then bounced off, onto the ground.

Taylor knew he was risking being shot by someone in the alley, or the building across the alley; but hoped he was sheltered somewhat by the man he struggled with. When he heard gunfire below him in the alley, he believed it was from Leo, with their getaway car, clearing a path for them.

Taylor ducked back through the door knocking the largest pieces of remaining glass out of the way, just in time to see a fourth man, standing in the doorway, raising a gun in Mary's direction. Suddenly, the man toppled over, a bullet hole in his chest. Taylor looked toward the bedroom, where Mary stood, holding her gun in both hands, pointed at the man, smoke drifting up from the end of the barrel. He went to Mary, took the gun from her shaking hands and led her to the couch. He forced her to sit while he went to the kitchen and got her a cup of water. He told her to drink the water. She did and seemed calmer because of it. The shooting in the alley stopped as abruptly as it had started. He waited a few moments, then opened the patio door. There was no more shooting, so he preceded her out the door onto the fire escape and looked down to see Leo standing at the back of an SUV, looking up at him.

"Throw down your luggage," Leo said, holding out his arms. Mary handed Taylor one of their soft-sided suitcases which he dropped over the railing, then the other. Leo caught each one and set them in the trunk of the car.

"Go on, I'll cover you," Taylor said, pointing down the fire escape. Mary handed Taylor his coat, then hiked her gown up her thighs and draped the long train over her arm. She hurried down the fire escape, with Taylor following a few steps behind, all the while looking around for potential threats.

Taylor saw movement from the corner of his eye and looked

at the building across the alley. A man stood in an open balcony door, one floor above him, raising a gun in their direction. Taylor took quick aim and shot the man, who fell back into the room. Taylor looked around again for any other signs of attack, and fired a shot up the fire escape toward the next landing. A body dropped with a thud and toppled down the stairs toward him, landing at his feet.

"Nice shots Taylor," Leo said from below.

"Lucky I spotted them," Taylor said. Seeing nothing else, he looked down to where Mary had lifted one bare leg over the metal railing and slid the rest of the way down the fire escape, on her butt, sliding off the end of the railing and falling into Leo's arms. Leo hugged her to him for a moment before setting her on her feet. Taylor hurried down the steps and joined them by the SUV, which had been waiting with its engine running. Taylor slapped Leo on the shoulder.

"Thanks for coming for us," he said, as Mary opened the back door and climbed into the SUV. Taylor noticed the large dent in the roof of the car, from the man falling on it, as he followed Mary into the back seat.

"You damaged my car," the driver, an agency employee from the Rome station, said, pointing to the ceiling. Everyone ignored him. Leo got in the passenger seat and the driver left in a hurry, before the doors were fully closed.

"You were great!" Taylor said to Mary as he gave her a kiss.

"What about all the bodies?" she asked. "The one on the ground, the one on the fire escape, and the ones in the room?" This was the first time she had shot someone or seen Taylor shoot someone with intent to kill, and she had lost count of how many they'd shot in the last hour.

"A team will be along shortly to clean up," Leo said. "If not, the

Italian Policia will ask questions and we'll try to satisfy them. This happens occasionally. What happened Taylor?"

"Our contact spotted a table full of Russian Mafia and panicked," Taylor said while rubbing Mary's shoulders in an effort to help her relax. "He broke off, so I had no option but to do the same."

"Why the emergency extraction?"

"I made eye contact with one of the Russians. I think his name is Pavlovich."

"Dmitri?" Leo asked, surprised. "I wonder what he's doing in Italy. We don't want him here. He's trouble."

"Well, he's here. He may have guessed that we'd be here. He has unfinished business with us. I didn't hear any of his conversation and wouldn't have understood it if I had. Anyway, I got the impression he figured out what we were doing."

"He's former KGB, and part of the new KGB, so he very well could have figured it out, having done the same thing himself over the years. This is not good. We'll get you home, then you can figure out your next steps. We'll try to do damage control here."

"Can't you move a little faster?" Taylor asked the driver, who drove carefully between cars parked on both sides of the narrow street.

"Moving through Rome, even in the middle of the night, is a slow process for a car," the driver said, lecturing Taylor, "because of the narrow streets, parked cars, and heavy traffic. It's off-season for tourists, and late in the evening, but that doesn't mean the streets are easy to navigate. And no one seems to be in a hurry, except us. Just sit back and relax. We'll get there when we get there."

Taylor drummed his fingers against the top of the seat in front of him, trying to plan, while Mary made two calls, one local and one long-distance.

"The plane is ready and waiting," she told Taylor when she hung up the first call. "We're booked through to Salt Lake City."

"Good." Taylor nodded. He expected nothing less. The CIA took care of their own.

"The kids are fine. The sitter put them to bed and she's sleeping in the guest bedroom. My call woke her. I reminded her what time the kids need to be up and dressed and told her we're on our way home."

"Fine," Taylor said. "We still have a long flight ahead of us, so let's relax if we can. How are you feeling now?"

"I'm fine. Really."

"Alright. Then I need to think."

As they turned onto a four-lane highway, leaving the narrower streets, a compact car ran a red-light and T-boned their car on the passenger side.

"Whoa!" Mary squealed, as the side airbag exploded, pushing Taylor into her. He pulled a knife out of his boot and stuck it in the airbag, deflating it and sending powder flying all over them.

"Did you have to do that?" Mary complained, coughing.

"Sorry," Taylor said. "It was distracting."

The driver backed away from the compact, pulled around it, and continued, but not before the windows of the compact powered down and two people started shooting at them.

Several bullets penetrated the side of the car, but were stopped by the armor plating. Several more hit the windows, first scarring the bullet-proof glass, then causing it to crack.

"Oh no!" Mary said, panicked.

"Not to worry," Leo said. He opened his window—it only lowered three inches before it stopped against the damage to the door—aimed his silenced gun and fired back at the compact as they sped away. The compact followed them.

Apparently, the compact had a more powerful engine. Try as he might, Leo's driver could not pull away. In fact, the compact gained on them, hitting them from behind, jarring their teeth and causing the car to swerve.

"Can we lose them?" Taylor asked, with concern, looking through the rear window, which was now spiderwebbed with cracks,

"I don't want to get back on the smaller streets," the driver said. We'd be sitting ducks.

Taylor could see that the driver watched his rear-view mirror as much as the road ahead. Suddenly, the driver swerved around the right side of a truck that was turning in front of them, running up onto the sidewalk, passing between a light pole and a street sign, knocking a side-view mirror off the car in the process and narrowly avoiding a collision with the truck. The truck's horn blared at them, but they continued. The compact wasn't so lucky. Taylor heard the impact of the compact car with the truck- screeching metal and breaking glass. The men in the compact must have jumped out and run around the truck, because several shots were fired from that direction, two of them hitting the rear window of Leo's car.

The rest of the way to the Fiumicino airport, they watched out the windows for any other attempt to detain them, knowing that the Russian KGB, and Pavlovich in particular, had tentacles all over the world. At the airport, they were directed to terminal three, since the other terminals were closed for renovation. Leo led them to the international flight desk, where there was a long line of waiting passengers, but he waved a laminated pass in the air and an employee waved them to the front of the line, attracting stares and glares from the other passengers who were waiting in line. Leo showed the clerk their tickets and passports, and placed their bags on the scale. Shortly, Mary and Taylor had their boarding passes and directions to a gate where they would be shuttled to their private plane.

"Was that fair to all the people waiting in line?" Mary asked.

"Don't worry about it," Leo said. "Our diplomatic status allows us to do that and most people know it or will be told if they ask."

At the gate, a man stepped in front of them, looking grim.

"Oh no," Taylor said. "What now?"

"Fermare. Passaporti per favore," the man said. Taylor reached for his gun, then remembered that they'd left their guns with the agency driver. It wouldn't do to try to pass airport security with a loaded gun. Then he realized that this man wore the uniform of an airport employee. Relieved that this wasn't another bad guy, Taylor showed the man their passports and boarding passes. The man looked them over, smiled, and moved out of their way. With a smile, he motioned for them to proceed out the door.

At the bottom of the stairs they caught an airport shuttle. In a matter of minutes, they were climbing the stairs onto a private jet. Their luggage followed them on board. A military steward stored their luggage in the back, helped them get settled with a drink and a snack, then rattled off the preflight safety instructions from memory. As the plane rolled down the runway, Taylor stared out his window at the terminal, until the plane left the ground and departed without further incident.

"What were you looking at?" Mary asked.

"Just making sure we didn't get any more interference," Taylor said. "I expected the worst, hoping for the best. I'm satisfied that the entire process was quick and efficient. That was too close."

"I understand this is an unscheduled departure," the steward said, having completed his spiel and prepared the plane for take-off. Taylor turned to look at him.

"Yes. A change of plans," Taylor agreed. "Thank you for accommodating us."

"No problem, whatsoever. We're on call, so we're ready whenever our passengers are. When we stop in Madrid, please stay on the plane. We need to refuel and change crews for the overseas leg of your flight, so you'll have a short wait; but you're safer on the plane than on the ground."

"Safer sounds good to me," Mary said. The steward smiled.

In Madrid, they refueled and changed flight crews, then flew directly to JFK in New York. In the luxury of reclining chairs, Mary slept, but Taylor thought back on everything that had happened over the last two days, trying to understand what they had missed. He was good at dissecting operations and getting to the root of problems. He was grateful they weren't required to enter the terminal in Madrid; He fully expected that there would be another attempt to intercept them. The KGB had eyes all over the world.

Having thought through the entire operation, Taylor called Ollie in Virginia on his satellite phone and gave his report.

"Have you analyzed the operation to see if you could have done something differently?" Ollie asked Taylor.

"Ollie, I've reviewed every aspect of the operation and how it went wrong, I'm satisfied that we couldn't have done anything differently. There was no way we could have predicted the Russian's presence. However, in the future, we should spend a little more time on reconnaissance before attempting to make a pass. Now we need to worry about fallout from the operation."

"Okay. We know the Russians are good at tracking people. And Pavlovich is KGB, so I'm sure he's extremely well trained. Since you've been seen, that makes it imperative for you to disappear for a while, if possible."

"That's our second encounter with him, Ollie," Taylor said. "In fact, if I didn't know better, I'd say that he anticipated our being there."

"From all the bodies you left behind, I'd say you may be right. That's even more reason for you to disappear. How's Mary holding up?"

"She's pretty shaken up. I thought I might lose her—fainting—a couple of times."

"But no injuries?"

"Amazingly, no injuries."

"How's your arm?"

"It's healed nicely and wasn't any trouble."

Taylor's conversation with Ollie woke Mary. So, while Taylor spoke with Ollie, Mary called the sitter to let her know they were in the air and to confirm that the sitter had no trouble getting Drew to and from school and Michael to and from preschool.

"All's well," she reported to Taylor when she hung up. "They're playing with Legos in their room." He nodded.

"Rainbow wants to hear your report," Ollie said, transferring the call. Taylor repeated his report for Rainbow. "I think our cover was blown, Rainbow." he said into the phone. "Pavlovich spotted us in Rome. He may have been expecting us to be there."

"Why do you say that?"

"You know we had a run-in with him once before. This time, he had people spread out all over the building, that I had to remove before we could get away. It was almost like an ambush. They even tried to intercept us on the way to the airport. If he's decided to take us out, he won't stop until he follows us home."

"Understood," Rainbow said. "Let's get you to a more secure location. What do you suggest?"

"We're planning a campout in the Diamond Fork Campground in Spanish Fork Canyon. We'll call you from there and you can set up a link from the NSA listening post near Camp Williams."

"Fine. I'll be waiting for your call."

"How do we protect our children and neighbors?"

"Do any of your neighbors know or suspect what you do for a living?"

"I don't think there's any way they would know. Not even our children know."

"Let's get you taken care of, then evaluate the situation with the children."

"Fine. We'll give you a call."

22

The Crimea—Pavlovich

"Where is the interference coming from?" Pavlovich asked the leader of his team of mercenaries.

"A small boat followed our contacts into the harbor. When we arrived, they started shooting at us."

"You took care of them?"

"My team is cleaning up right now." Pavlovich could see the rest of the team, four young ruffians, prodding a group of six people along the dock at gunpoint. They got within a few yards of Pavlovich before they were stopped. They were all dressed in heavy coats and hats, against the cold coming off the water. One of the mercenaries, a young man with a scar on his left cheek, running from his ear to the corner of his mouth, walked along the line, from one to the other, pulling open their coats and ripping the hats off their heads, throwing the hats on the ground. It was then that Pavlovich could tell that four of them were young men, one was a young woman and one looked like a teenage boy. The mercenary, himself young, walked over to his leader, who was still standing with Pavlovich, and spoke.

"What do you want us to do with them?"

The leader looked to Pavlovich for direction. "We don't take prisoners," he said. The young mercenary pulled out his handgun and shot each of the six in the head, then pushed each one off the dock into the water. The woman squealed and looked at Pavlovich just before she was shot, but he didn't say anything; just watched without emotion.

When it was over, he walked up to the young man. "What is your name?" he asked.

"Vladamir." The young man said. "Vladamir Pachenko."

"Come with me, Pachenko" Pavlovich said, turning and walking away. The young man followed him to his car, a bright blue Mustang Shelby GT500 convertible.

"Have you ever been to the United States?" Pavlovich asked.

"Nyet," he replied.

"I have a problem in the United States that I want you to take care of for me. I need to set some things up, then I'll let you know. Tell me how to get in touch with you." He did.

23

Home—Taylor

At home, Taylor retrieved their car from long-term parking in Salt Lake City, returning to the arrivals island at the terminal after checking the engine compartment and undercarriage for explosives and tracking devices and finding none. He loaded the luggage and his wife into the car and left for their fifty-five-minute ride home.

Family

"Mom, did you put a pin in the map to show us where you went this time?" six-year-old Mick asked.

"I did, Mick. See, it's right here," she said, pointing to Italy. "Doesn't Italy look like a woman's high boot?"

"It does. What part of the boot did you go to, the heel or the toe?"

"It's more like the ankle."

"What's Italy like, Mom?"

"Well, English isn't their native language, for one thing."

"So, how did you talk to them?"

"Even though Italian is the national language, the people we interacted with mostly spoke English with us. A lot of the people know more than one language. As you know, your dad knows six languages, but I can't carry on a conversation in anything but English."

"You're not going to leave us alone again, are you?" Mick asked.

"No dear," Mary said, brushing Mick's hair out of his eyes. "I love your hair, Mick, but you need a haircut."

"No, I don't. I like it like this."

"Okay, we'll talk about it tomorrow. Now, it's time to go to bed. I love you, honey."

"I love you, too, Mommy. I'm glad you're not leaving again. Drew will be glad, too. We miss you when you're gone."

"I miss you, too. So does Daddy. We love you so much."

Eight-year-old Drew waited until he got his mother alone before asking his question. "Mom, don't you worry about your safety when you travel so much? You know air travel isn't safe, right?"

"We're very careful, Drew. We don't take any chances we don't have to. Air travel has some risks, but so does riding in a car, or walking on the sidewalk. And now, we're both taking a vacation, so there won't be any air travel for a while." Maybe never again. Drew always amazed her with his mature questions.

"I know Mom. It's just that I woke up in the middle of the night thinking that you guys were in some kind of trouble. I worried until you got home."

"That's sweet, dear," Mary said, pulling her oldest son close and giving him a hug. "Thanks for worrying about us."

24

Two months later—Mary

"Mom, the door's for you," Drew said.

"Who is it, dear?"

"I don't know, Some man."

Mary approached the entry and saw Dmitri Pavlovich standing inside the house. She put a hand to her throat and looked around, to see if there was some place to hide if he drew a gun. But she couldn't see that he had a weapon. His white tee-shirt was snug against his impressive chest and his black chinos looked like they were painted on. He was a good-looking man and it troubled her to notice that.

"Hi, Mary," Pavlovich said in his flawless English. "Are you going to invite me in? That's the American custom, isn't it?"

"What are you doing here, Mr. Pavlovich?" she asked, her voice choked and barely loud enough for her to hear herself.

"Please, call me Dmitri. I think we're past the formalities. I was in the neighborhood and thought I'd drop by. That's the polite thing to do, isn't it?"

She nodded. She didn't know why she was acknowledging him. She was scared speechless.

He looked around the room, then took a seat in a recliner, without being invited. "Do you mind if I sit?" he asked, after the fact.

She didn't respond. She willed Taylor to show up. "Taylor," she finally called.

"Coming, love," she heard his voice coming from the back of the house.

"You have handsome children, Mary. Drew looks like his father. And this must be Michael, who you call Mick, and Lynne. She's pretty; She takes after her mother. She's going to be a beautiful woman."

"You leave my children alone," Mary said, venom in her voice.

"I have no interest in your children, Mary. It's you I have unfinished business with."

A blush crept up Mary's neck and burned her ears. She knew exactly what unfinished business he referred to. When they were together in Budapest, she had been naked, lying in his hotel room bed, with him lying naked next to her. Taylor had tried to shoot Pavlovich, but had missed and Mary had escaped without being raped. She remembered the feel of his very masculine body on hers, aroused by his musky smell. It was as clear in her mind as if it had happened yesterday and had the same effect on her now.

Taylor entered the room from the hallway. "You kids go clean up ..." he started to say, then saw Pavlovich, sitting across from Mary, totally focused on her face.

"What are you doing here? How did you get here?" he asked.

"I think it's obvious that I'm visiting with Mary," Pavlovich said. "I got here like anyone else would, in a car." He waved toward the front door as he said it.

Taylor looked out the still open door at the bright blue Mustang Shelby GT500 parked at the curb, with six neighborhood children crowded around it, looking in through the windows. When the passenger door opened, the children ran away and Taylor could see a scar-faced, ugly man sitting in the passenger seat. He waved at Taylor, then closed his door again, but not before Taylor got the feeling of menace that exuded from him.

Pavlovich obviously didn't drive the car across the ocean, but he may have had it shipped over to use here.

"What do you want?"

"I wanted to meet the family."

"Okay, you've met them. Now what?"

"Why the hostility, Taylor? I came in peace. I'm not threatening anyone."

"Your being here is threat enough. I'd like you to leave."

"Taylor?" Mary said, to get his attention. He made eye contact with her and a message passed between them. Flies and sugar.

"I'm sorry," Taylor said, his tone of voice softening immediately. "Where are my manners? Would you like something to drink?"

"No, thank you."

"Something to eat?"

"No, thank you."

"D . . .Dmitri," Mary choked out in a soft breath. "I don't know how you got here . . ." his picture was posted on security bulletin boards at all the major airports, "or why you've come, but . . ." She looked around to see that the children had left the room before finishing. "I hope it's an indication that we can begin to normalize our relationship and be more agreeable" instead of trying to kill each other.

Dmitri smiled at her, the smile not reaching his dark and angry eyes. "I would like that," he said, his eyes darkening, almost smoldering with passion. She didn't like it; it told her he was still thinking about taking her to bed.

Mary stood abruptly and moved to the front door. "Well, Dmitri, in case we don't see each other again, have a safe trip home."

Dmitri looked flustered for a moment, then his eyes cleared. He stood and went to the door. He took her outstretched hand, raised it to his lips and kissed it. "Good-bye, Mary," he said, then winked and left.

"I hope that's the last we see of him," Taylor said.

"His good-bye sounded final to me.," Mary said. "I don't think we'll see him again."

"What was with the first names?"

"Before you came in, he asked me to call him Dmitri and said we were past the formalities."

"Meaning what, exactly?"

"He said we had unfinished business, so I'm sure he was talking about the hotel room incident in Budapest."

Taylor became defensive. "I'll kill him," he said. "I'll get my gun and go out there right now, before he can get away."

"You tried that already. He's like a cat, with nine lives."

"Then I'll have to try eight more times."

Goose bumps appeared on Mary's arms. "I hope we don't have to see him one more time, let alone eight times."

They watched him until he got in his car and drove away. Taylor noticed that the young man with a scar on his left cheek watched the front of the house, his eyes empty of emotion.

25

The Squaw Peak Trail—Taylor

He threw their suitcases into the back seat and climbed into the driver's seat next to Mary. He backed out of the garage and pulled into the street, unaware of the man standing in a copse of aspen trees in the vacant lot across the street. The man looked at the device in his hands to confirm that the signal from Taylor's car was being received. It had been nearly impossible to place the tracking device, since Taylor never left the car outside where he could get to it. Even when Taylor went shopping, he always checked under the car if it had been left out for any length of time. The man had finally resorted to breaking into the garage, a risky decision where CIA agents were involved. He figured the only reason Taylor hadn't found it was because the car had been locked in the garage.

Instead of going to Spanish Fork Canyon, Taylor drove Hobble Creek Canyon to get to the camping spot they had selected a week earlier. Their thirty-foot Coleman camper was set up, the fresh water tank was full, and the batteries were fully charged. It would stay there for two weeks, the most they were allowed in one spot, then they would relocate to another dry camp in the same canyon. They had set up their listening post on a tree—It was camouflaged to look like a growth on the tree trunk—with a relay to the trailer. They could park anywhere within a thirty-mile radius of the listening post without losing reception quality, as long as they had line-of-sight to it. Someone would have to know what to look for and what it looked like, in order to find it.

Taylor had confirmed with Rainbow that the listening post was working, receiving messages for them. If they were within range, they would respond immediately. If not, the message would be forwarded to Taylor's voice mailbox for later handling.

They had already been camping for close to a week, so Taylor was confident that they hadn't been followed or located; but he didn't relax his vigilance where his family's safety was concerned. Pavlovich had tracked them to their home, but he didn't think Pavlovich could track them to the campground.

It was Friday morning and Taylor wanted to get out and do some fishing on the weekend. He'd heard the fishing was good on the Spanish Fork River and wanted to check it out. With no hookups in the campground, they would be using the water in their fifty-gallon fresh water tank and the generator and solar panels for power. The fridge was full of food and Walmart was just down the canyon if they ran out of anything.

They had discussed bringing the children. Drew loved being with his dad, whether fishing, hunting or just sitting around a campfire. They loved to sing campfire songs and play games on the picnic table. Drew also liked hiking and investigating new places, and this campground was new for him. He also liked listening to his dad's collection of sixties and seventies rock music. Four-tear-old Lynne just liked being with her mom, whatever they were doing. Unfortunately, Taylor and Mary were not yet ready to relax enough to bring the children. They would give it another week.

Taylor had performed his usual surveillance before leaving town, to make sure they weren't being followed. They had even decided to take the long way to the campground, going over the mountain road from Hobble Creek Canyon instead of up Spanish Fork Canyon. That should throw anyone off who might try to follow them.

"He said he thought we were in trouble," Mary said, telling Taylor about Drew's nightmare.

"Did he have any specifics? Do you think he really had an idea about our problems in Rome?"

"No specifics. And no, I don't think he knew anything, although you know that I believe in visions and premonitions."

"Yes dear. I've been the recipient of several of your impressions. I trust your intuition and always follow your suggestions."

"I know you do and I appreciate your trust in my intuition. Now, slow down!" she said as their Hyundai Elantra slipped across the yellow line in the middle of the mountain road on the Squaw Peak Trail. Taylor slowed, quickly corrected, and returned to his lane. It was the second time he had crossed the median on the winding mountain road and Mary was becoming concerned. It wasn't like Taylor to be so distracted.

"What's distracting you?" she asked. He was driving too fast for existing conditions. He needed to pay closer attention. She loved this man and this was the first time she had complained about anything he did, for as long as she could remember. They'd been all over the world on assignments, without a problem and without a serious argument, so she could overlook this one thing, as long as they stayed safe.

"I'm still thinking about that Rome assignment," he said distractedly. "Maybe we could have stayed in the room until we were sure we'd been seen. Maybe I should have gone after my contact and gotten the information he had. Maybe, if I'd been there, he wouldn't have been shot."

"Or maybe you would have been in danger, as well."

"We sure need the information he was going to give me. I don't know when the Agency is going to get another chance like that one."

"They're already trying to set something up," Mary said. "Maybe it can be simpler next time. Send a courier alone, without the big guns."

"I don't think that's a good idea, especially if you're the courier. I don't think it's safe."

A few minutes later, Taylor took another bend too fast and slipped over the median . . . again. Suddenly, a sports car appeared behind them, moving fast, and slid between them and the hillside on their right, bumping them toward the left. Already struggling to control the Elantra, Taylor was distracted by the sportscar, a Mustang Shelby GT500, just like the one Pavlovich was driving, worth a small fortune. The driver looked like the one Taylor had seen in Pavlovich's car in front of their house. He must be crazy to push the Shelby so hard that it would get scraped up in a fender bender. Taylor took pity on the stupid driver and allowed his Elantra to move farther to the left—there was no oncoming traffic. He figured he still had time to correct after the Mustang passed.

Bumping up against the guardrail at the left side of the road startled him into realizing that he had no more room to give. He tried to correct, taking his foot off the gas and turning the steering wheel to the right, but the Mustang stayed on his fender and his car trailed along the curving horizontal barrier. Worried about going off the road when the barrier ended, he turned the wheel harder, bumping the mustang and driving it into the hillside. It climbed the hillside a couple of feet, its right-side tires climbing onto rocks, then rebounded into Taylor's Elantra, driving him left. For several seconds, the two cars battled for position on the road, the Mustang advancing until it was even with the Elantra. The Mustang was forced up the hillside again, going up on two wheels until it looked like it would tip over. Then it came back down, pushing the Elantra to the left again. It became a battle of which car had more power, and they stayed even for a few seconds, long enough for Mary to dial 9-1-1 and state their location and the problem.

Taylor told Mary to get his gun out of the glove box, which she did immediately, without question.

"When I say three, shoot him," Taylor said.

"What? I can't do that," Mary said.

"You don't have to hit him, just distract him."

"Oh, Okay."

"One . . . two . . . three."

While Taylor counted, Mary aimed the gun out the window. On three, she fired. The bullet shattered the driver side window, just as Taylor slammed on the brakes. The Shelby shot ahead of them, still pushing to the left. It brushed up against the guardrail and hit a bolted joint in the barrier, which separated.

The Shelby broke through the guardrail and left the pavement, going airborne. It plowed through the tops of several trees, then dropped and bounced down the steep hillside. The car began to roll sideways. The top caved in, then the sides, crushing the car despite all the safety features. By the time the car stopped rolling, up against a large tree at the bottom of the hill, it was in flames and looked more like a giant hotdog than a car.

Back on the road, Taylor pulled to the left side of the road to see what had happened to the Shelby, then continued on, driving slowly to their campsite, wishing that Pavlovich had been the one driving, but knowing he wasn't.

A family, just disconnecting their RV from their truck in the campground below, noticed the smoke billowing from the car, and guessed correctly what they were seeing. One member of the family drove down the canyon until he had cell service and called 9-1-1, while the rest of the family ran to the scene to see if there was anything they could do to help. The flames were so hot that they couldn't approach the car, and it was clear to them that anyone trapped inside the car could not survive the heat, fumes and any injuries they might have suffered, for long.

The family member who'd gone to make the call, heard the sirens and flagged down the police car. After a brief discussion, he led the police and fire department back to the scene. The rest of the family sat and watched the car burn until the fire truck arrived. By the time the paramedics arrived, the fire was nearly out, the damage done. The fire engine had soaked the car with water and chemicals, to cool the metal and allow the police to try a rescue, in case anyone might still be alive. The police had to cut the car open using their jaws-of-life tools, only to find the driver crushed and burned, almost beyond recognition. They were, however, able to recover some paperwork in the glove box, to identify the car and driver.

Because there were no witnesses to the accident, it was ruled suspicious and the Provo police opened an investigation. They searched the scene, in the campground and on the road above it, likely finding evidence of the Mustang's excursions up the hillside and the broken railing. They interviewed the family camping near the accident, the one that had called it in, as well as other campers in the canyon. When the police spoke to Mary, she told them that she and her husband had been in the campground for a week already and hadn't seen or heard a thing.

26

"Do you have the cash?" Pavlovich asked his contact, in Spanish, to show that he had bothered to learn his contact's language.

"I have," the Venezuelan said, also in Spanish "and you'll get it as soon as we confirm the merchandise is what we agreed to pay for." He said it belligerently, as though questioning Pavlovich's integrity, something that seldom happened and always made him furious. This was his first dealing with this Venezuelan contact and he only agreed to travel to South America because he had been assured that the Venezuelan understood that his weapons and information were the best, but wanted to meet his business partner The Venezuelan's behavior so far flew in the face of good-will.

"Good. The merchandise is in the back of the truck. You can take a look for yourself."

"No. I'll have my people look at it and tell me if it meets our needs."

"I'm sure it does. I've been selling these weapons all over the Middle East and North Africa."

"If my people agree, I'll send you the money."

"Wait. You agreed to cash on delivery and insisted that I come here personally to ensure that everything went according to out agreement. I'm here, and you won't even bother to check for yourself? That sounds one-sided, like you don't trust me, but you expect me to trust you."

"I know I'm trustworthy," the Venezuelan said. "I've never dealt with you before."

Pavlovich didn't normally allow himself to get angry, but his clenched fists should have sent a message to his contact. As he turned away and walked back to his truck, followed by his men and his contact's people, he mumbled under his breath, to one of his men.

Suddenly, Pavlovich's guards raised their guns and opened fire on the Venezuelan's entourage. Several fell before the others could get their guns out and aimed at the Russians. Everyone dove for cover as bullets flew in both directions. Pavlovich managed to duck into his armored vehicle before being shot. The Venezuelan did the same. When most of their men were dead or injured and laying on the ground, the two men used their own weapons to reach out of their respective vehicles and fire at each other.

Ollie

A report from the NSA stating that a satellite observed fighting in Maracaibo reached Ollie's desk a few hours later. Concerned about rumors that the KGB was trying to negotiate with drug cartels in Central America, Ollie called Taylor and asked him to take a team and check it out. Reluctant to go on another mission after Rainbow had allowed him to retire, he argued against it. Ollie would not be swayed. Taylor was one of the best agents they had and they needed him.

Ollie gave him three young agents to go with him, Rader Jay, Isaac Jensen and Grant Petersen. Taylor read the personnel files on each of them and approved; they were all proficient with weapons, electronics and stealth. Agent Jay was also fluent in Spanish. Jensen and Petersen could get by in Spanish, if required. All those skills would be needed.

Ollie arranged for them to take a private jet, one registered to a corporation in the Bahamas, from a small airstrip near Arlington, Virginia, that the Agency used sometimes. They dressed casually and each took a small backpack containing their weapons, electronics and night-time assault clothes. Taylor worried about getting into Venezuela with their packs.

Taylor

At the Maracaibo airport, Jay approached the security checkpoint first. He chatted up the guard, then told him he didn't need to check their packs—they just contained clothes—as he palmed him a hundred-dollar bill. The money disappeared and they were allowed to pass. The guard put a hand up to stop Taylor, being the last to pass through, and being several years older than the other agents. In fluent Spanish, Taylor complimented the guard on his immaculate, pressed uniform and told the guard he was the chaperone for the three younger men. Petersen gave him a dirty look, likely offended at the thought that he might need a chaperone, but the ruse worked and Taylor was allowed to pass.

Taylor had found a small motel in an old part of town, where he rented one room for one night. He worried all the way there that the taxi they had secured at the airport, would fall apart before they got to the motel. It rattled, squeaked and rumbled all the way. After attaching small microphones to collars, placing receivers in their ears and hiding knives in their clothes, they split up to see what they could learn.

Taylor sent each agent to a different bar on a different street, to buy drinks for all and to see who they could get to talk about rumors of Russians, arms deals, or gun fights. They met back at the motel several hours later to compare notes.

"What did you learn?" he asked as they sat on the edge of the single bed or sat on the floor.

"Russians were definitely here two days ago," Jay said.

"They met with a representative of a drug cartel," Petersen said. "It didn't go well. Big egos and little trust. It ended in a shootout. Most of the soldiers on both sides died or were seriously injured."

"What's left of the Russian contingent are still here. I couldn't find out where they're holed up. It sounds like they still want to make a deal."

"What kind of deal are they looking for?" Taylor asked.

"Gun for access to drug routes into the states, best I can tell," Jensen said.

"Do we know when or where they'll meet again?" Taylor asked.

"I know where the cartel hangs out," Jensen said, "It's in an industrial area northeast of town. Would they invite the Russians there, to their stronghold? Should we stake it out?"

"We should definitely do that. Is there anywhere else they would go?" Taylor asked.

No one had a suggestion.

"Okay, here's what we'll do." Taylor said. "While you were all out buying drinks, I located a shop to rent motorcycles. We'll have Jay and Jensen use them to stake out the cartel. Petersen, you and I will wander around town, looking for anything that stands out to us. If we see anything that looks like a meeting is about to take place, whoever notices it will call the rest and we'll converge on the meeting."

"You mean, if the cartel leaves for a meeting," Jensen asked. "Or if you see the Russians?"

"Exactly. The bikes are out front. Here are the keys." They left together, figured out which keys went to which bikes, and left for their assignments.

"I don't expect anything to happen before dark," Taylor told Petersen, "so feel free to hang out here or drive around to get a lay of the land."

"We're at the cartel's hangout," Tylor heard over his earpiece a while later. *"We're selecting hiding places that give us line-of-sight to the exits."*

"Good," Taylor said. "I'm not expecting anything to happen before dark, so we're just hanging out. Can you see a way to get inside without being seen?"

"It looks like there's a second story window that we can access from the attached lean-to roof of the back. I'll go check it out."

"If it's too noisy, then wait."

"I'm inside the warehouse, on a walkway above the open room. I can see people milling around, waiting." He heard a short time later. *"I'm going back out so I don't get spotted."*

A half hour after dark, a van arrived at the cartel's warehouse and four men exited the van. A cartel guard appeared from the shadows and met them at a door to the warehouse. Jensen notified the team.

"Okay," Taylor said. "Now get inside and watch. We're on our way."

"We're here," Taylor said a short time later. "What's the situation?"

"They're all sitting around, talking," Jensen said. "The leader of the Russians appears agitated by the indifference of the Venezuelans."

"Are you both inside?"

"No, just me. Jay is on the lake side of the building, in a tree. Oh oh, the discussion seems to be deteriorating. The Russian is standing. He pulled a gun. He's threatening. Now everyone has guns out. The Russians are outnumbered. Shooting started. Everyone is down; dead or wounded."

"We're coming in from the west. Cover us." Taylor slammed

into the door and it crashed open and against the wall. The noise attracted the attention of those in the floor who could turn their heads, but no one was standing. Taylor and Petersen panned their handguns around the room, looking for anyone dumb enough to resist. No one did.

Jay entered the room from a doorway on the far side of the room, looked around and waved to Taylor. The three men approached the middle of the room, where all the bodies lay on the floor. While Jay and Petersen checked each downed man for a pulse and breathing, Taylor went directly to the two men who had been negotiating.

Using the toe of his boot he turned the Venezuelan over. Seeing the hole in his forehead and his glassy eyes, Taylor went to the Russian. Turning him over the same way, he was face-to-face with Dmitri Pavlovich. There was blood on his stomach where he'd been shot, but he was alive. He grimaced at Taylor, then struggled to speak.

"Here to rescue me . . . or kill me?" Pavlovich asked.

"I think you would survive if I got you to a hospital right away," Taylor said. "But I don't know what you would do with your miserable life if I helped you. You might just come after my family again and we can't have that."

"You survived the car crash in Utah."

"Unlike your hit man. Maybe you should have come yourself."

"Would I have been able to kill you?"

"We'll never know, will we?"

Pavlovich coughed up blood. It spilled down his chin and dripped onto the concrete floor.

"I'm dying," he said. "Don't let me died like this, in this godforsaken place. Shoot me and throw my body into the lake. I'd much rather have a burial at sea, like my father."

"I can't shoot an unarmed man."

Pavlovich pulled a handgun from under his leg and tried to point it at Taylor. His hand shook. Three guns fired simultaneously and three bullets hit Pavlovich in the head, making it splatter like a melon. Taylor looked up to see his three agents standing close, their guns out, lowered to their sides. He looked back at Pavlovich and thought the look on his face was the most peaceful expression he could imagine. Pavlovich had welcomed death.

Headquarters

"That's it, then," Taylor said to Ollie. "I'm done here."

"Okay," Ollie agreed, "I have permission to retire you and Mary for real now. Thank you for your service. You realize there won't be a ceremony or public recognition, right?"

"Yeah. I get it. We were never here. Never did that. I'm okay with that. I just want our kids to be safe now—no pushback from any of the enemies we've made."

"I don't think any of them are alive anymore, now that Pavlovich is gone. So, you're in good shape. Any chance you want to become an analyst for the NSA out there in Utah? You know they have a building there in Utah, by Camp Williams."

"They can contact me in a few days if they want. In the meantime, I'm going camping."

They shook hands and Taylor got a ride to the airport to catch the flight Ollie had arranged for him. While he waited for his flight, he called Mary to let her know he was coming home.

Three months later

Taylor and Mary were both hired by the NSA to work as analysts at their Lehi, Utah, facility a month after leaving the CIA. Within two months, Taylor was bored and wanted something more exciting to do. Mary was happy to go home at the end of her work day and play with her children.

"How about a vacation?" Mary asked when they discussed it. "Maybe that's what you need to help you settle down."

"We can try that," Taylor said. "If that doesn't work, I'm going to have to consider going back to work for Ollie. I need the adrenaline rush."

"You don't think raising vegetables will give you the same rush as chasing bad guys around the world?"

"Where would you like to go?" He asked after giving her a look. "How about Singapore? I'll introduce you to Ponloc and show you the Merlion on Sentosa Island."

"Who's Ponloc?"

"She's a contact I made when I first started travelling for the Agency. She's a lovely lady who gave me information to help solve problems in that part of the world."

"Am I going to be jealous of her?"

"There's no reason you should. I married you. You're my whole life."

"Okay. You make the travel arrangements and I'll set up the babysitter."

A week later, they were packed and on their way to the airport. They figured to spend three days in Singapore, two days in Siem Reap, Cambodia and two days in Kuala Lumpur, Malaysia. They flew to Malaysia first, visited the Petronas towers, the Batu caves and China town. Mary discovered that she didn't like heights when they stood on the glass enclosed walkway on the fifty fourth floor between the twin towers.

In Cambodia, Mary wanted to show Taylor the Angkor Wat ruins in Siem Reap, which she had visited the day she had to be rescued by him. He had been there as well, but he let her be the knowledgeable one and show him around. They took pictures next to the massive tress growing out of the seams in the stones that made up the ancient buildings. They ate on the street where they'd eaten that day and got a massage while they were there. In Singapore, they went to Sentosa Island to see the Merlion, the giant light trees and the massive hotel. Then Taylor took Mary to Ponloc's apartment. When Ponloc cracked open the door and saw Taylor standing there, she rushed into the hallway to give him a hug and kiss on the lips. In the process, she noticed Mary and froze, looking to Taylor for an explanation.

"Ponloc," Taylor said, "This is my wife, Mary. We worked together for years and recently retired from field work. I wanted her to meet you, as one of my favorite people in the whole world."

As he spoke, Ponloc relaxed. Then she invited them in. Mary, seeing her greeting to Taylor, entered reluctantly, not knowing what to expect from this beautiful, exotic woman. The women watched each other warily while Taylor sat casually on the comfortable couch.

"This is new," Taylor said, patting the arm of the couch.

"I bought it with my first paycheck from the station chief," Ponloc said.

"You've gone to work for the Agency?" he asked.

"Three months ago. They hired me on your recommendation."

"What do they have you doing?"

She looked at Mary before speaking. Taylor noticed and anticipated her concern about revealing confidential information.

"It's okay, Ponloc. Mary was a courier for several years. She even helped me on some of my missions. You can speak freely in front of her."

Ponloc smiled. "I'm a courier. I travel between here, Tokyo, and Sydney. They said my responsibilities would increase with time if

I met their expectations."

"That's wonderful. Do you enjoy it?"

"It seems glamourous now." She addressed her next question to Mary "Does it get old or boring?"

"It never did for me," Mary said, "but the assignments got more complex over time. The best ones were the ones I shared with Taylor."

"I bet," Ponloc said, looking at Taylor with affection. "I love this man and everything he did for me."

Mary looked startled at her declaration of love for Taylor. Taylor decided he better explain.

"Ponloc was having a difficult time of it when we met," Taylor said. "I was able to get her some professional help that resolved some of her issues. We became good friends and helped each other when we could."

"I'm glad it has worked out so well for you," he said to Ponloc. "Is there anything we can do for you while we're here?"

"You're on vacation, I take it?"

"We are, and this is our last stop before going home."

"Are you hungry? Can I fix you something to eat?"

"We're good. We'll pick something up at the airport. I'm sure you have things to do, so we'll get out of your hair."

"That must be an American colloquialism, 'get out of your hair'," she said. "I'll have to remember that."

Taylor nodded.

"Being your friend is enough for me," she added. "Come and see me again sometime."

"We will."

"Yes, definitely," Mary added.

Ponloc gave both Taylor and Mary a hug and kiss on the cheek, then saw them to the door.

They had a long wait at the airport because they arrived hours before their flight was scheduled to leave. They found a place to eat, then Taylor bought a novel to read while Mary watched people. Then their flight was delayed for mechanical reasons. When they finally boarded the plane, they found their seats in Business Class and promptly fell asleep. While they slept peacefully, their plane had engine problems and crashed down in the Indian Ocean, disintegrating on impact. Everyone on board died.

When neither Taylor or Mary called Mary's dad to let him know they were coming home, Ralph Slade called the airline company and found out their plane had crashed. They were presumed dead, pending the recovery of their bodies. So far, only twenty-seven of the over two hundred passengers had been recovered and identified. Ralph left his name, address and phone number for them to contact him when they knew more.

Two Salt Lake City police officers, Representing the National Transportation Safety Board, came to Ralph's house in Salt Lake City to let him know that Taylor's and Mary's bodies had been recovered and were being sent home. When the bodies arrived, they were in sealed coffins. Ralph suspected that was to prevent the family from seeing the condition of the bodies, so Ralph had the coffins rerouted directly to the funeral home listed in their family trust.

27

The Aftermath—Grandpa Ralph

It was left to Grandpa Ralph to give the children the bad news about their parents' deaths. Eight-year-old Drew, who his four-year-old sister Lynne called Dee until she was old enough to pronounce his name, was stoic. He didn't accept the deaths as real. Drew idolized his dad, who took him camping, fishing, and rabbit-hunting, and had taught him to shoot a gun. It would take time for him to adjust.

"Why, grandpa?" Drew asked.

"I don't know why, Drew," Grandpa said, taking Drew in his arms and hugging him.

"Dad always takes me shooting and fishing. Who's going to do that now?"

"I can take you shooting and fishing."

"Thank you, but it won't be the same without Dad."

"I know, son, but we'll try to manage."

Six-year-old Michael, who Lynne called Mick, cried for days. He was inconsolable.

"Grandpa," Mick said. "Are you sure they're really dead and not just lost in the ruins?"

"You saw the coffins that arrived last week, right? We couldn't open them, but I was told they were in there. The funeral home will confirm that for us."

"Thanks, Grandpa," Mick said through his tears. "What if they're not in the coffins?"

"The police say they are. But if they're not, we'll have to figure out what to do to find them."

Ralph tried his best to comfort his three grandchildren, singly and together; but other than providing for physical needs, like food, clothes and transportation, he was at a loss to explain to the children why this had to happen to good people like their parents.

Rather than disrupt the children more, by moving them out of their home, Grandpa put his house up for sale and moved into Taylor's house in Provo with the children.

Retired, on Social Security, Grandpa didn't know how he was going to take care of the kids. He believed they needed interests to keep their young minds off their parents' deaths. He needed to give them a way to explore their interests and develop hobbies.

He had a few investments which he considered liquidating to pay for things the kids needed. Then he learned there was a million-dollar life insurance policy on Taylor and Mary, each. The policy also had a clause which doubled the payout in the case of accidental death. They would receive the payout upon confirmation that their deaths were accidental, as stipulated in the policy

"I suggest we don't hold a viewing," the funeral director told grandpa after examining the bodies. In fact, I'd recommend cremation.

"What do you think, boys," Grandpa asked Drew and Mick. Your mom and dad got pretty messed up in that accident.

"Yeah," Drew said.

"We don't want to scare anybody," Mick added, obviously thinking about scary movies with walking dead and other scary things.

"I don't think we need a funeral, either, since I don't know any

of their friends and there's no family close by to plan it or participate."

"If you want to write an obituary and give it to me," the funeral director said, "I'll place it on the funeral home website. We can also schedule an open house at the funeral home for anyone who sees it, to pay their respects to the children."

Grandpa agreed with each of the suggestions. The open house was surprisingly well attended and several people gave grandpa money or offered to help with the children when needed. He took their names and contact information, placing a note under each name to identify what they thought they could do to help. Neighbors, friends and church members brought enough food to the house to fill the fridge and freezer and feed them for several days.

They held a graveside service, which Drew, Mick and Grandpa agreed would honor the couple sufficiently.

Grandpa knew few of the guests, but was impressed by all the well wishes of friends, neighbors and work associates.

Oliver Tanner

One man approached Drew while he was alone, off to the side of the crowd. He was a little rough around the edges, with his long, shaggy grey hair and an ear stud, but Drew wasn't afraid of him.

"You must be Drew," the man said.

"That's me," Drew answered. "Who are you?"

"I'm a friend of your parents. You could say I worked with them. Can you help me?"

"I'll try."

"Has anyone approach you or one of your siblings, who seemed strange or out of place?"

"You mean, besides you?"

"Yeah, besides me."

"No . . . Yes. A man came to the house a few weeks ago, before the accident, and upset Mom, why?"

"Did you get his name?"

"It was funny. Dimmy. Dim Tree, Something like that."

"Dmitri?" the man asked.

"Yeah, that might be it."

The man looked pensive for a moment. "Can you tell me what they said to each other?"

Drew tried to recall what was said, by whom, including his dad's comments, although he was too inexperienced to catch the deeper meaning behind the words.

"I wonder if you would let me know if anyone else comes around asking questions?" the man asked, holding out a business card to Drew. "I think your parents' accident may not have been an accident, so I need to know if anyone is paying unusual attention to you."

"Really. Are you saying you think their plane was sabotaged? Was it bombed?" Struck by a missile?

"I don't know, but I need to find out. Did you notice if anyone unusual was at the graveside service?" the man asked.

"No, but there were a lot of people I didn't know."

"Thank you. You'll call me?"

"Sure. Why not?" Drew looked at the business card again. It read, 'Oliver Tanner, Global Services, Inc., Richmond, Virginia' above a phone number. There was nothing else on the card. "You can leave a voice message, too," Mr. Tanner said, "if I don't pick up. Thanks."

A few days later, Ralph commented on Drew's boredom and restlessness. It was obvious from his lack of interest in anything at home or any desire to go do things with friends. He had trouble concentrating or sticking with anything for more than a few minutes. He mostly stayed in his bedroom and looked glum whenever Ralph saw him.

"Drew," he said, "What do you need, to keep your mind off your parent's accident? Do you have a hobby?"

"No . . .I don't know, Grandpa. I've always thought I'd like to learn photography, but never even bought a camera. I don't even know if I'd be any good."

"There's only one way to find out. Let's get you a camera. I think that's a great idea. What about you Michael? Do you have a hobby?"

"No, Grandpa. And I don't know what I would want to do."

"All he does all day," Drew said, "is work on jigsaw puzzles, listen to music, and read."

"Reading is good," Ralph said. "Do you have a computer, Mick? You can do a lot of different things with a computer."

"No."

"Would you like one?"

"Sure. Why not? That might be fun."

"What about me, Grandpa?" Lynne asked, not to be left out. "Who's going to teach me girl stuff?" She was the most sensitive to the loss of her mother, since she relied on her mother for most everything.

"What do you need to know that I can't teach you?" Grandpa asked.

"Do you know about makeup? And girl clothes? And . . .stuff?"

"How old are you? Sixteen?"

"Grandpa, I'm four."

"Then why do you need to know about that stuff?"

"I don't need to know today, grandpa, but Mom said we would

talk about girl stuff."

"Then, we'll find someone to talk to," grandpa said with a wink. He had his notes from the viewing, so maybe he could contact someone who had offered to help.

Eventually, three months after the accident, the NTSB ruled the crash the result of a mechanical malfunction, an accident, and the insurance company sent Ralph a check for four million dollars. Ralph invested it in stocks, index funds, preferred stock and CDs. With over four thousand dollars per month in interest, plus the proceeds from the sale of his home, when it sold, he could cover the family's usual expenses.

Drew thought about the man who'd approached him at the graveside service and pulled the business card out of his top dresser drawer, where he kept all his important odds and ends. 'Oliver Tanner,' he read again. He considered telling Grandpa about the man's concern, then decided not to say anything. He still wasn't convinced Mr. Tanner was on the level. He needed to tell someone, so he told Mick.

"Are you going to call him?" Mick asked, sitting on the edge of Drew's bed.

"And tell him what? He's the one who told me it might not have been an accident."

"What would you guys like for dinner?" Ralph asked from the doorway.

"Grandpa," Lynne called from the kitchen, "I thought we were making Mac and Cheese, then you disappeared."

"It's okay, Lynne. I'm coming right back."

"Why did you leave?"

"I had to talk to your brothers."

"Grandpa!" Lynne whined.

"Coming."

"What should we do, Drew?" Grandpa asked, clearly baffled and flustered by Lynne's temper tantrum. "I'd like to use up the food the neighbors brought, so I was thinking of heating up some lasagna."

"Well, I'd rather have the lasagna," Drew said, "so if you'll cook the lasagna, I'll make Lynne some Mac and Cheese."

"It's a deal. Thanks."

28

Mick, two years younger, noticed the girls, but he was more serious and put priority on his education. He excelled in math, the sciences and drama, but didn't want to be in the spotlight. So, he never volunteered and seldom raised his hand in class. He just wanted to be left alone. He sulked a lot.

Lynne was pretty and intelligent, but moody and temperamental. Her stubbornness showed whenever anyone tried to get her to cooperate, with anything, even when it was her own idea. By the time she reached junior high school, she had a reputation for doing anything she wasn't supposed to and nothing that she was asked to do. Her grades showed it.

Growing up without parents—Drew

Ralph tried his best to give the kids a normal routine, but it was difficult at the best of times. Drew had a few friends from school, so his life experienced the least disruption. Grandpa knew Drew cried himself to sleep sometimes, and didn't know how to make life easier for him; but he took Drew fishing and to the shooting range often—at least weekly—since that is what Drew wanted, and the two became close. Not quite parent-child close, but it was better than nothing.

For months after the death of their parents, Drew or Mick would enter their parents' bedroom. about to ask a question, before remembering that it was now Grandpa's room and their parents wouldn't be returning.

On his ninth birthday Grandpa bought Drew his own .22 caliber hand gun and rifle and taught him how to shoot, clean and care for them. He learned how to break down and reassemble his hand gun in minutes.

"Are you ready to go, Drew?" Grandpa asked each weekend.

"Are we going fishing or shooting today?" Drew asked.

"We can do either one. What do you want to do?"

"Well, we went fishing last week, so let's go shooting."

"Okay. We went shooting the four weeks before that, but that's okay. You prefer shooting, obviously."

"I do. Okay. I'm ready," he said as he carried his rifle, hand-gun and ammo box out to the car.

Drew also took an interest in cars and girls and started walking girls home after school. In third grade, Drew joined a group of children playing kissing tag at recess. He was the fastest runner in his class, and easily caught a cute, blond-haired girl. The other kids said he had to kiss her, which he was reluctant to do—he'd never kissed a girl—but he said he would do it if everyone turned their backs. The other students formed a big circle around them and turned their backs; but when he went to kiss her, some of them turned and watched. Later in the day, the principal came over the school PA system and said there would be no more playing kissing tag on school grounds. Apparently, he was the first boy to actually catch a girl and kiss her.

Grandpa worried about him taking an interest in girls at such an early age, so he checked up on him. He called the parents of the two girls he was walking home regularly and discovered that they were mostly sitting and talking, sometimes playing on yard toys or climbing trees—nothing personal.

In ninth grade Drew told Grandpa that he had decided he liked the attention from the girls and asked his advice on how to get one special girl to like him in return. They were camping in the Uinta mountains, eating tinfoil dinners they cooked in the coals from the campfire.

"I bet you like the attention," Grandpa had said, laughing. He had a deep voice that rumbled in his chest when he laughed. "Just remember who you are and don't get carried away."

"You mean, don't get too personal with the girls?" Drew had asked

"You're still young," Grandpa said. "There's plenty of time for girls."

"But how do I get her to like me?"

"Be yourself." Grandpa said. "Don't try to be too cool, or something you're not. Girls like honesty and humility. They also like boys who are sure of who they are and what they want. So, don't be afraid to do the things you like to do. Don't do things just to impress."

Drew became interested in photography, so Grandpa bought him a nice thirty-millimeter digital camera with telephoto and wide-angle lens attachments. He also bought Drew a book of instructions and ideas for photo projects. Drew was creative and took to photography with a passion.

He got more clever and creative with his photography over time and enjoyed his hobby. The girls liked having their pictures taken, so he mounted pictures of the cute girls in scrapbooks and had a different book for each of the prettiest ones. But what he wanted to do was fish and shoot his guns.

Over the next few years, Drew received an increased amount of attention at school, from the teachers and the students. One day he asked Grandpa about it.

Grandpa said he was sure it was out of sympathy because of the death of his parents. "They're well meaning," Grandpa said "but you need to forgive them if they seem morbid or overly interested." Drew had to agree, that the initial attention was sympathy over the death of his parents. Each school year someone—well-meaning—let it be known that he was orphaned, and the attention increased; talking behind his back, sudden and unexpected sympathy. He resented the sympathy, until gradually, it seemed, the attention was because of who he was, not out of sympathy for his situation. Drew noticed it first, being the oldest, but Mick saw it, too.

Drew was handsome and always had money to spend on his friends. There was a candy shop by the junior high, where he would go with friends during lunch, to buy treats. There was a fast-food restaurant by the high school, where he would often buy lunch for anyone who went with him, usually a girl.

He really began to enjoy the attention in high school, especially when it was from certain girls. He took advantage of it, going to all the dances and performances where he could be seen.

Grandpa took Drew camping, fishing and shooting as often as he could, taking Lynne and Mick with them as often as they were willing. He didn't force them and had to make arrangements for them to be watched when they stayed home.

Watching Drew target shoot was always impressive because of his accuracy. He could make all the bullets hit so close together in the bull's eye. He tried to teach Mick how to shoot, but Mick could never bunch them together the way he did. Sometimes, he missed the target altogether.

Drew finally decided he liked Sheila the most and began spending a lot of his time with her. She was a cheerleader in junior high, then again in high school, attractive, and best of all, a good kisser, he told Mick. They were exclusive for his entire senior year and he believed they were becoming very close, maybe falling in love. When he went to the University, majoring in Art, she was excited that he wanted her to be his model. Everywhere they went—hiking in the mountains, boating on the lake, sitting on the swings in the park—he took her photo, in all sorts of poses. She seemed to love the attention and he was becoming an excellent photographer. His bedroom became plastered with pictures of her.

He studied all sorts of art forms and tried them all. He tried different art styles and mediums. His favorite project was hand coloring a twelve by sixteen inch, black and white photo of Sheila. It was beautiful, bringing out her natural skin tones and hair color. He gave it to her as a high school graduation present. Then she met a young man in an ROTC uniform at a college football game and broke off the relationship with Drew. She kept the picture and they never dated again after that.

As word of his breakup spread, girls flocked to him, to get a chance to date the good-looking photographer. He dated for a while, but got little enjoyment from it. He missed Sheila. Then, having no other plans, and soured on relationships, not interested in starting a new one so soon after his failed one, Drew joined the Airforce. He attended basic training, then volunteered to go to Afghanistan as part of a photojournalism team, filming the war effort.

Sheila married the ROTC guy. He got shot during a training exercise and died, making her a childless widow. Drew told Mick that she wrote to him, wanting to get back together, but he told her he wasn't interested.

Lynne

Lynne was too little to understand what had happened to her parents, and felt abandoned. Grandpa couldn't help and neither could the boys. None of them understood Lynne's problem and she seemed to resent them for it, although she couldn't explain her issues to them. The result of her resentment was to rebel, to try to get attention by doing unusual things, naughty things, like running out of the house naked. If either of the boys tried to correct her, all she had to do was cry and Grandpa would come to her rescue, telling the boys to be good to their sister. Lynne learned quickly that she could have anything and do anything she wanted, without punishment or consequences.

She was always pretty, even as a little girl. She was dark complected like her mother. After her mom died, she got the idea that wearing dark makeup would give her an exotic look. She got a friend's older sister to show her how to apply her own makeup and started making up her face at about age six. She started dressing up for fun, but it wasn't just a temporary interest; her clothes got more radical every year. It seemed like she was picking up the styles of the girls several years older than her. Whenever Drew or Mick had the nerve to question or correct her behavior, she would throw a tantrum, often stripping off the offending clothes and running outside naked, so one of them had to go tackle her and carry her back inside. Her behavior became more radical over time and Mick took it upon himself to watch and help her, but he was frustrated.

When she went through puberty, which she did early, she kept her slim figure. She was gorgeous, and it seemed like she knew it and wanted attention for it. Older boys were always around her. The first time Mick really noticed, she was in sixth grade and he spotted her behind the junior high, which was close to their house, making out with a ninth grader. He didn't say anything to her—he didn't know what to say—but he told Grandpa, thinking he would know what to do about it. When he didn't say anything to her either, Mick asked him about it. Grandpa thought she would get tired of her strange behavior and settle down eventually, but she didn't.

When Grandpa tried to find out what hobby Lynne wanted to develop, that he could pay for, she couldn't tell him; she didn't know what she wanted. She seemed totally unfocused. Unlike Drew and Mick, who focused their energy toward a specific goal, like education and work, she was always trying new and strange things, anything her friends wanted her to do. They decided that, with Mom's death, Lynne lacked the example of a normal, mature female to guide her.

Consequently, she got involved with other girls at school who had little direction in their lives and went along with the group. She finally told grandpa she wanted piercings and tattoos. Although grandpa didn't approve of her choices, he decided that maybe she would grow out of this rebellious stage at some point and have a normal life like her brothers. So, he indulged her. Her first tattoo was a butterfly on her bicep. Then she got a flower on her shoulder blade. Then it was flower vines down both arms and across her shoulders. Then there were other tattoos on the small of her back, stomach, legs, and arms. She got multiple piercings in her ears, one in her nose and two in her lower lip. With each tattoo and piercing, she showed Drew and Mick, to see their reaction; their negative reactions seemed to please her. The more dramatic the reaction, the more pleased she seemed. She was especially pleased with Grandpa's reactions; although it was apparent that he objected, he kept his thoughts to himself, hoping she would realize her behavior was ridiculous.

Deciding that these weren't naughty enough, and enjoying the negative reactions of her family, her friends convinced her to get tattoos in places that were normally covered by clothing which clothing she had to remove to be tattooed. Then came the piercings in private places. Her girlfriends approved and openly praised and admired her for her courage, wanting to be like her; but each rebellious act alienated her a bit more from her family.

The neighbor women who tried to help, were kind, but lacked the motivation and constancy a mother would have. Lynne must have felt it; she didn't get close to any of them. They gave her pointers on wearing makeup sparingly, how to dress stylishly, but modestly, and how to get boys to treat her respectfully. It seems like most of it didn't sink in, either because she didn't want to be modest and respected, or because she didn't respect herself.

Lynne was spoiled, twisting the men in her life around her finger. She got into gothic clothes, colored her hair strange colors and enjoyed embarrassing her brothers by showing them her piercings and tattoos. She started going to parties where there was drinking, and she started smoking and taking recreational drags. When Drew and Mick tried to get her to stop the drinking, smoking and drugs, she quit talking to them, for several months, deciding that they didn't understand or appreciate her.

She convinced Grandpa that she needed to be on the pill. 'For protection from rape,' she said. Mick thought it was just an excuse to start being promiscuous. Anyway, Grandpa sent her to a female doctor, who agreed to give her the prescription, just one more step down the road she had chosen for herself.

For her high school graduation, Mick was so proud of her for sticking with it and graduating, that I told her he'd give her anything she wanted, within reason, as a graduation present.

"What would you like?" he asked.

"I want to see you naked," she said.

"Lynne, why would you even think that was okay?" he asked

"Cut it out, Mick," she said. "You said you'd give me anything

I wanted and that's what I want."

"I said 'within reason' and that's not reasonable."

Lynne pouted.

"I'm sorry, Lynne. I can't do that."

"I thought you might have trouble with it, but I've loved you all of my life—longer than anyone—and I really would like to have a relationship with you. If you change your mind, please let me know."

When she turned eighteen, she moved to Wendover, Nevada and became a cocktail waitress and dealer, wearing the short skirt, lowcut top, and heels that were their uniform. Grandpa asked Drew and Mick to watch over her; he must have finally realized what had happened to her. She was no longer under his influence and he had botched it up, anyway. They could all see problems in her future, except her. The boys tried to tell Grandpa that his protecting her from reality was part of her problem, but Grandpa either didn't understand or didn't want to hear it. They still cared about her, but had to go out of their way to visit her in Wendover. Since Drew was generally out of the country with his military job, this responsibility fell primarily to Mick.

29

Mick

Michael spent a lot of time alone, learning to use the computer Ralph bought him, and playing with jigsaw puzzles and other games that strengthened his mind and memory skills.

He had a friend who lived nearby, so Grandpa had a talk with his parents, to see if they could encourage the relationship. Although they had very different personalities and interests, after not many days, Mick and Ken could be seen together regularly. Everywhere one of them went, the other would always be nearby. Ken liked model car racing and drones. He had his own remote-controlled car and drone and eventually found neighbor boys with the same interests. As Ken grew, he became fearless when it came to girls and could be counted on to be in a lip lock with almost any girl, an hour after meeting her.

Mick watched, but couldn't force himself to follow Ken's lead. He was happy to sit in his room with the radio going, working on a puzzle on the card table he'd set up for that purpose.

They would often sleep over at each other's house, in a bedroom or back yard. They would watch the night sky for shooting stars or satellites, and learned the names of all of the major constellations and brightest stars, a fascination that would stay with Mick for a lifetime. Mick would sometimes burst into tears for no apparent reason. Ken, at a loss to know how to console his friend, patiently helped him carry his gear home in the middle of the night when staying out was too difficult for him.

When Ken's mother died from cancer, his dad remarried; a divorcee with a teenage daughter a year younger than Ken. Debi added a dynamic to Mick's relationship with Ken that neither had anticipated. Over time, becoming more at ease around each other, Debi became Mick's first secret crush. He eventually found the courage to get her alone and kiss her one night at a party. Nothing ever became of the relationship, probably because of Mick's reluctance to pursue it.

Ken liked playing games on Mick's computer, so they found games that they could play together and compete. Mick found he didn't enjoy the competition like Ken did, so that activity petered out after a while.

Mick experienced a phenomenon in school similar to Drew. Being more reserved, even shy, he resisted the urge to get too close to any of the girls who paid attention to him. He dated a little in high school, went to the school dances, finding that he liked to dance, but seldom dated the same girl twice.

He saw how unhappy Drew was as a result of his breakup with Sheila, so he determined to avoid that kind of heartache. He, too, was popular with the girls, but decided to not get serious with anyone while he was in high school.

30

Friday night—Lydia Hancock

When Mick started at the university, two years behind Drew, everything changed for him. He joined a fraternity and spent a lot of time dating. The fraternity scheduled two socials a week, usually dances, one during the week and one on the weekend. They traded lists of names and phone numbers with sororities, then called enough girls to match up with the frat members one-on-one.

A lot of the girls were really fun and cute and Mick enjoyed being with them, although he didn't get to know any of them well. He enjoyed dancing, but he had to put himself out, which sometimes made him wonder how badly he wanted to be involved. He sometimes thought he would have preferred to sit at home.

Then one young woman changed his attitude, almost overnight. Lydia Hancock, was a knockout, with all the qualities he wanted in a partner, even though he had never before thought about what that meant. When he arrived at the address he'd been given, a petite—five foot two to his five foot eleven—young woman opened the door. She looked about seventeen, but was dressed and made up like a sophisticated woman.

"Lydia?" he asked. She nodded, not speaking. "Hi. I'm Michael Swensen. Call me Mick. Are you ready?"

"Yes," she said, in a sweet, southern accent. He was bowled over by how sexy she sounded. She handed him a light sweater and turned her back to him. He got the hint immediately and draped the sweater over her shoulders. He held out his elbow and she threaded her arm through his.

"Where are you from?" he asked, when he was seated behind the wheel, but before he started the car, finally working up the nerve to talk to her.

"Atlanta."

"How long have you lived here?"

"I don't live here. I'm staying with an aunt and uncle. I've been here about a month."

"How do you like it so far?"

"Everyone is friendly and kind. I think a lot of people like my accent. It seems to open doors for me."

"I bet it does. It's beautiful, like you," Mick said, then wondered if he was being too forward.

"Thank you," she said. "I think I'm just normal—a plain Jane."

"You're anything but plain." He started the car and pulled away from the house, a bit too abruptly, causing her head to jerk back against the headrest.

"How did you get invited to this party? I don't suppose you belong to a sorority; that's usually where they get the names of young women they want to invite."

"A couple of girls from church mentioned it and asked if I wanted to go. When I said it sounded like fun, they said they would tell someone and get me invited. Now here you are." She reached over and patted his arm affectionately. He felt sparks from her touch. They ran up his arm and hit him hard in the chest. He glanced over at her to see her beautiful, friendly smile.

"How often do you have these parties and are they always dances?" she asked.

"Usually twice a week, unless sporting events or finals interfere. And they're almost always dances; that's what the guys like. Do you like to dance?"

"I love to dance. How about you?"

"I like dancing, too," he said, although he hadn't been to many dances before becoming involved with the fraternity. "This should be a lot of fun."

They arrived on campus and parked next to a building that looked like a student dorm. They descended steps to a basement door and were admitted by a good-looking young man

"Hi Mick," the man said. "Who's your date.?"

"Lydia, this is Brady Fairchild," Mick said. "He's the fraternity president. Brady, this is Lydia Hancock, from Atlanta."

"It's a pleasure to meet you," Brady said. "So, you're the young lady who asked to be invited. I'm glad we could accommodate you."

"Ooo, a young lady. I like that," Lydia said, her accent as silky and warm as molasses. "Thank you for inviting me,"

Brady pretended to swoon, smiled broadly while taking Lydia's hand in both of his, and kissed the back of her hand.

"You look so lovely," Brady gushed over Lydia. "Welcome to our party. I hope you have a good time. These parties are always so fun."

"Thank you. I'm sure I will," she said, smiling her sweet smile, first at Brady, then at Mick. Mick wondered if Lydia affected every male this way, or if Brady was falling in love with her or, he hoped not, making fun of her.

Mick and Lydia milled around the refreshment table while they waited for the dance to begin. They exchanged introductions with a couple of men Mick knew and liked, and each picked up a cookie and a drink of orange punch.

"Welcome, everyone," Brady said into a microphone, once the majority of the guests had arrived, filling the large room "I apologize for taking a few minutes to conduct some frat business before we start. You'll remember that we cancelled next Wednesday's dance due to the mid-week basketball game. So, our next dance will be next Friday night at the usual time."

"Let me introduce Everett Kahn," he continued, motioning to a large man standing next to him. "Everett is the president of the theta-chi frat. We've agreed to an exchange, on a date yet to be scheduled. Be nice to him tonight, so we can get concessions from his frat when the time comes." Brady laughed self-consciously as he looked at Everett. There were chuckles among the nearest members, although Mick didn't understand what Brady meant, exactly, or what was funny about it. It probably just meant that Brady would get invited to a theta-chi social sometime. "Before the night is over, we'll introduce our newest inductees. I'll also remind the young ladies, in case you don't know or remember, we have a 'last dance' rule; whoever you dance with for the last dance is who will take you home—your choice—it doesn't have to be the guy who brought you. Now, enjoy the dance." Brady looked around the room before turning off the mic and moving it out of the way. Mick thought he noticed Brady focus on Lydia again before he finished.

Music started to play, a Waltz. They set their empty drink cups on the nearest table and Mick took Lydia in his arms. As they started to move, Mick realized that Lydia was not just a good dancer, she was a great dancer.

"You're so smooth on your feet," he said. "Have you taken dance lessons?"

"Only about twelve years of lessons, both private and in public school," she said with a delicious smile.

"Well, it shows. You're a natural." As the dance progressed, Mick tried several different dance steps that he'd learned at prior dances; mostly ballroom steps; fox trot, cha-cha, waltz, swing, tango. She followed his lead as though they had practiced ahead of time. She even threw in a few moves that he hadn't seen before and showed him how to keep up with her. It was fun.

After a few dances, Brady cut in, to dance with Lydia. Then others cut in one after another. It seemed that everyone wanted to dance with the sweet southern belle. At first standing off to the side, Mick finally took the opportunity to dance with several other girls that he was attracted to, then eventually made his way back to Lydia. Late in the evening, near the end of the activity, Brady approached Mick, who was waiting with Lydia for the next dance to start.

"Everett would like the last dance with Lydia so he can take her home. You'll let him do that, won't you?"

Mick didn't know Everett. He didn't know if Everett would treat Lydia respectfully, but worried that he might try to take advantage of her, which Mick wouldn't tolerate or condone. He knew he had to be polite to his president and guest, so he would encourage Lydia to agree.

"I'll suggest it." Mick said, as diplomatically as he could. "girl's choice, you know." Brady frowned as Mick turned to Lydia and spoke quietly to her.

Mick realized that he had yet to be accepted as a member of the frat, so a denial of this request could hurt his chances of joining. And, the look Brady gave him added to his dilemma. Brady really wanted this to happen. Why? What was more important here? How important was the frat to him?

At the same time, there seemed to be no limit to the number of girls who wanted to dance with Mick; the smooth, charming, good-looking, soon-to-be engineer. Several of the girls he had danced with had been clearly interested in him. So, he should have no trouble finding another young woman who would allow him to take her home. Nevertheless, when the next dance started and Mick was dancing with Lydia again, he asked if she was okay with Everett taking her home.

"He's that large man over by the punch bowl, right?" Lydia asked. "The one who was introduced to us at the start, the one with roaming hands?"

"He has roaming hands?" Mick asked, beginning to see how Lydia's decision would go. She was implying that Everett might try to take advantage of her if he took her home.

"He was all over me," she said. "I practically had to peel him off me after one dance."

"Okay," Mick chuckled, "who would you like to take you home?"

"You, of course," she said, matter-of-factly.

"Out of all the men you danced with tonight?" There were several good-looking, intelligent, men in the room and most of them had danced with her. Maybe she was choosing him because she had danced with him most often and they'd had a few minutes to talk on the way to the dance. Maybe she just thought he was safe, in his reserved, shy way. Regardless of the reason, he was flattered that she had chosen him. He wanted to take her home.

"Absolutely."

Mick

Just before the last dance, Brady announced that three pledges would be inducted into the fraternity the following Friday and introduced them. Mick was one of them.

"Congratulations!" Lydia said. She turned and gave him a spontaneous kiss on the cheek, then acted embarrassed. "I'm sorry, Mick. Was that too forward?"

"The kiss was wonderful. Thank you," Mick replied, "and I'm

still not sure I want to join the frat."

"What's the matter?"

"I'm beginning to see some things that I don't like, so I'm un-decided."

"What don't you like?"

"Let's talk about it after we leave, okay?"

"Sure."

"This is the last dance, ladies," Brady said into the microphone, interrupting their conversation, "so get with the man you want to take you home."

There was movement around the room as young women lined up with the young men they wanted to dance with. Mick noticed that both Brady and Everett were staring at him and Lydia, approaching them within a few feet. He wondered if one or both of them would have the nerve to walk over and pressure them. He also noticed that two or three girls were looking at him expectantly, but didn't approach him, probably because Lydia held his arm captive in hers.

Lydia surprised him by taking his hand, turning into him and dancing him out onto the dance floor. He put his arms around her and danced, reassured by her choice. After the dance, on the way to the car, Lydia asked Mick about his earlier comment.

"Mick, why did you say you weren't sure you wanted to join the fraternity?" she asked.

He thought for a moment about how to explain his reasoning.

"Brady put a lot of pressure on me tonight. I think he's more concerned with his image and satisfying his own needs, than he is with the welfare of the fraternity or its members."

"That would be unfortunate. I hope that's not the case."

"No problem. I have a life outside this fraternity."

Mick opened the car door and helped Lydia into the passenger seat. He started the car and pulled into traffic.

"Would you like to come to my induction party?" he asked, suddenly.

"Are you still going to go through the induction," she asked, "if you're not sure you want to belong to it?"

"It wouldn't hurt. I can always drop out. And it gives me an excuse to go dancing with you again."

"We don't have to go there to go dancing," she said.

"I know, but I'm curious about the induction ceremony. Have you ever been to one?"

"No, and I'm curious, too. What happens at an induction party? I've heard about initiation ceremonies where the initiates have to get naked and do stupid things. Is it going to be like that?"

"I can't imagine it," he said. "But I've never seen one, so I don't know. Would you like it to be like that?"

"Do you mean, would I like to see you get naked?" she asked, then apologized again for being too forward.

He stared ahead at the road, unwilling to make eye contact with her, but he nodded in response. She blushed. He knew he was good looking and physically fit. Maybe she was thinking that she would.

"Maybe," she said quietly, looking out the window, her accent making her answer almost musical. Her response made him smile. He thought he would like to see her naked, too, but that wasn't what this was about.

"May I ask why you're staying with your aunt," Mick asked next, to keep the conversation going.

"My parents are having marriage issues and thought I should spend some time away from them. I'll be here for another two weeks, then I'm headed back."

"Is there anything I can do?"

"Just take me to your induction party and we can have some fun before I go home."

"What kind of fun would you like to have before you go home?" he asked, emboldened by her earlier comments.

"I haven't seen much of your city or state since I've been here. Maybe I'd like to see the highlights. I hear there are five national parks in Utah. Can you take me to one of them?"

"The national parks are several hours away. Maybe we could see one next weekend, after the induction ceremony. In the meantime, I can show you some things closer to town. Would you like that?"

"I'd love it," she said, taking his arm with both hands. "I'd like to spend as much time with you as possible this week, if you're not too busy."

"I just have school, and I'm finished early every day. Can I call you in the morning?" he asked. He wracked his mind for just the right things to show her.

"Please do."

"I will. Thank you for a wonderful time."

"Thank you for a fun evening. You're a great dancer."

She looked down shyly for a moment, then seemed to come to a decision. She looked at him mischievously, then leaned in and kissed him on the lips, tentatively, like she wasn't sure how he would feel about it. Then she reached for the door handle.

Emboldened by her touch, he placed a hand on her arm and held it. She turned back to him just as he leaned into her for another kiss. She placed her arms around his neck and drew him to her, holding the kiss. When they broke the kiss, she sighed, opened the car door and went inside, turning to give him a finger wave before closing the door. He breathed heavily, trying to get his pulse back to normal, as he sat in the car.

31

Saturday morning

He called her early.

"How did you sleep, pretty lady?" he asked carefully, not sure he should be so bold.

"I slept wonderfully, thank you. I dreamt about you."

"Was it a good dream?"

"It was great. We went dancing. Then we were in your car for a long time. We were hugging and kissing."

"Sounds like something I would enjoy," he said, not sure where these comments came from. He was normally very modest, but she was so easy to talk to. He felt like he could open up to her and not be judged. And he really liked her kisses. "Do you have any preference on what you would like to do today?"

"Not specifically. I'd like to see your mountains."

"Okay. Mountains, it is. When would you like to go?"

"I'm ready now. I got up early, hoping you would call."

"Good. Grab a jacket or coat. It can be chilly in the mountains this time of year. I'll be there in thirty minutes."

When she answered the door, she wore new jeans, sneakers and a pretty sweater. She had a parka draped over one arm. He wore worn jeans, a flannel shirt and hiking boots.

"Ready?" he asked.

She stepped out onto the porch and leaned into him. She kissed him lightly on the lips. Then he backed up a step to give her room to exit.

"Was that too forward?" she asked.

In answer, he leaned into her and kissed her back.

"I've missed you," he said, smiling. "Is that weird?"

She smiled back at him. "We were together last night. You haven't had much time to miss me."

"Just the same. I was anxious to get back to you." He took her hand and led her to the car, making sure she was in and belted before driving away.

He drove up Big Cottonwood Canyon, explaining the year-round activities in the canyons; the 150 inches of snowfall at the ski resorts, avalanche dangers in the winter, snowmobiling, hiking, campgrounds, hotels and vacation rentals. He pointed out Solitude ski resort, where he and some friends had sat in a hot tub on top of a hotel, while it snowed on them.

He parked at the trailhead to Cecret Lake and they hiked the mile to the lake, where families played at the edge of the water and teenagers wandered around the other side of the lake or sat on rocks, talking or skipping stones on the cool water.

"Would you like to sit for a few minutes?" he asked, leading her to a flat rock on the side of the trail,

"That would be good. I need to catch my breath after that last steep stretch of the trail."

The size of the rock forced them to sit with hips touching. She placed a hand on his thigh and looked into his eyes.

"This is beautiful," she said, then looked around the lake, the rugged mountains and the forest. "Thank you for bringing me here."

"Thank you for suggesting it. I hope the trail wasn't too strenuous."

"I appreciated your help in a couple of places. But no, it wasn't too difficult. It's beautiful up here."

"I wish you were going to be here in June. At this higher elevation, the flowers bloom late. Those fields we passed through are a riot of color when they're in bloom."

"Maybe I can come back," she said, then frowned, "But I doubt I'll make it. It's expensive to fly and coming out here was only possible because my uncle paid for it, as a favor to my mom. I don't know if he'd be willing to do it again. I'll ask, if I get a chance."

They shared a bottle of water and each ate a trail bar that Mick had brought along. They walked partway around the lake and skipped a few rocks across the water, before heading back to the car.

They drove over Guardsman Pass into the Heber Valley and down past the Wasatch Mountain State Park campground. He stopped to see if they were allowing overnight camping yet. They were, and reservations were not required for a few more weeks.

"We'll keep that in mind," he said. "Do you like camping?"

"You mean, in a tent?" she asked.

"Yeah. Have you done that before?"

"Yes. My memory of camping is of the heat and bugs, but that's Georgia. The last time was several years ago."

"Well, here the only problem will be the cold. Would you like to do that?"

"Maybe. I'm not a real fan of the cold, either."

Mick drove into Heber City. There was a chick flick playing at the local theater. It was a couple of years old, but Lydia said she hadn't seen it and would like to. The timing was right, so he parked and they went in to watch the movie. The theater was old, but relatively clean.

Near the end of the movie, when the boy and girl broke up, Lydia turned her head and cried into Mick's shoulder, leaving a wet spot. When the boy and girl got together again at the end of the movie and made love, Lydia cried again, this time holding Mick's shirt in her fists and crying against his chest. Mick placed his arms around her and hugged her to him until she stopped crying. As they left the theatre, she apologized.

"I'm sorry for ruining your shirt," she said as she tried to rub the wet creases out of it

"It's not ruined," he laughed, as he pulled each of her knotted hands out of his shirt and kissed her palms, then her lips. He pulled on the bottom of his shirt to straighten it as much as possible, then smiled at her.

They walked across the street to the Dairy Keen, home of the train, where Mick said he always ate when he came to Heber City. It was a fast-food restaurant, a popular one, that had a model train mounted near the ceiling that wound around the seating area on a continuous loop. They ordered burgers, fries, drinks and one shake to share, then found a seat and waited for their order to be called. The food was good, the atmosphere fun and the company great.

While they waited, they talked about the movie then planned their next day.

"Anything else you would like to see while we're here?" Mick asked.

"I don't know what else is here. What do you suggest?"

It was already late in the afternoon. "What time do you need to be back tonight?" he asked. "We could drive into Park City, then home from there."

"I don't have to be home tonight. My aunt and Uncle have gone to Wendover on one of those senior busses and won't be home until morning."

"In that case, we could drive around Jordanelle Dam, then camp overnight at the campground we stopped at this morning." It was a bold suggestion; he didn't think she would agree to camping overnight. Lydia thought about that for several moments, trying to decide what she wanted to do. She studied Mick's face, like she was trying to decide if she could trust him.

"Can we do the drive and camping?" she finally asked.

"Absolutely," he said, surprised. "Will your aunt and uncle worry about you?"

"I don't think so. I told them I would be with you and that you're trustworthy."

"We can call them if you change your mind."

They walked back to the car and drove north out of Heber, past Jordanelle reservoir, then turned up the highway toward Kamas. At Kamas, they turned south and finished the loop around the reservoir, stopping at an overlook to see the big, beautiful reservoir. Mick pointed out the Jordanelle Campground near the water.

"Can we stay there, instead," Lydia asked. "That looks pretty."

"I've never camped there and I don't know if they're open yet. We can go ask."

"No. That's okay. We already know we can stay at the other one."

They left the overlook and drove west to the campground. They had no trouble finding an available tent site in the upper loop, this early in the year. When Mick opened the trunk and pulled out a tent, two sleeping bags, and a couple of blankets. Lydia was surprised.

"I didn't realize you had the equipment already. I don't think I know anyone who carries camping gear in their trunk. Were you planning this ahead of time?"

"No. Absolutely not. Just prepared, like a good boy scout."

The air outside was already starting to cool, so they put on their coats. He set up the tent, laid out the bags, side by side, then folded a blanket and stuffed it in each bag for extra warmth. There was a pile of wood next to the fire pit, that someone else had left, so he built a fire. They cuddled together in front of it.

"Do they always provide wood for their campers?" she asked.

"Only for me," he laughed. "No. Really. Someone else must have left it. That was the reason I picked this camp site."

Mick removed a cooler from his trunk and set it on the picnic table. "Do you like hotdogs?" he asked.

"Sure," she said, so he opened a package of hot dogs from the cooler, along with buns and condiments. She roasted and ate one and he ate three. He took every opportunity to touch her; her hand, as he poked the hotdog on her stick, her arm, as he suggested how to hold the hotdog over the coals instead of the open flames, her neck and face, as he stood beside her preparing their hotdogs to eat, and her hair, as they sat together at the picnic table, eating. They roasted marshmallows and made S'mores for dessert. They sat in front of the fire, sitting close together, talking and holding hands, until the cold drove them into the tent. Mick put the fire out and turned on a catalytic heater to warm the space. He would turn it off before they went to sleep. She stripped down to her underwear and crawled into her bag, between the layers of the blanket.

"Are you cold?" he asked.

"A little," she admitted.

He pulled a spare flannel shirt and pair of wool socks out of his bag and handed them to her.

"Here," he said. "These will help."

She got back out of the bag, put on the shirt and socks and got back into bed, between the layers of the blanket.

"Much better," she said. "Thank you."

He removed his shoes and jeans, then replaced his shirt with a warm pullover and climbed into his bag.

"If you're still not warm enough, there's one other thing we can do."

"You mean, sleep in the same bag?"

"That would work, but it's a little personal. These bags zip together, making one large bag. We could share body heat without really touching."

"Let's do it," she said, after thinking about it for a few moments.

They both climbed out again. She threw a blanket over her shoulders to keep warm while she waited for him to zip the bags together. He laid both blankets out flat inside the combined bag, then they climbed in, between the blankets.

"How's that?" he asked. "Am I crowding you?"

"This is perfect," she said, then rubbed her stockinged foot along his leg, from his ankle to his knee, several times. "How does that feel?"

"Fantastic," he said, then did the same to her.

She searched for his hands under the blanket, found them, then held them with hers, between their faces.

"I like that," he said, trying not to move too much, so he wouldn't let cold air inside the bag. Within a few minutes, she had moved closer to him, rolling onto her side and pressing herself against him. It felt good and wasn't even that personal. He thought that maybe she had fallen asleep and didn't realize what she had done. He decided to lay as still as he could so he didn't wake her.

What would it feel like if he got closer to her? Put his arms around her? Pulled her to him? He didn't dare.

Suddenly, she moved her hands, laying them over his body, resting one hand on his ribs and the other on his thigh. Then she lay still again. Her hands were cool against his warm skin. He thought he might fall asleep now, but a few minutes later, her hand moved up under his shirt. Her hand was cool against his stomach, then his chest. She curled her fingers in his chest hair. Then she lay still again, maybe asleep, but he was wide awake. How could he sleep with her touching him like this?

He must have dozed off. Next thing he knew, light was peeking in under the window flap. He was still lying on his back, but she had rolled closer and lay against him, one shoulder on top of him. He turned his head to look at her and saw her face inches from his.

Her eyes opened slowly, looking into his eyes from inches away.

"How did you sleep?" he asked. He worried that their sleeping position had been a little too intimate for her liking.

"It was perfect," she said. "You kept me warm all night."

"I thought it was perfect, too," he said.

Her eyes shifted to focus on his lips. Then she closed the distance and pressed her lips to his.

"It wasn't too personal?" he asked when she broke the kiss.

"Not at all. It felt good. I would have been too cold otherwise."

They lay there, neither of them wanting to move from the warmth of the other, alternately watching each other and the steam from their breathing in the cold morning air.

"I guess we should get up," he finally said, when he had to go to the bathroom. He didn't want to put on his cold clothes, so he pulled them into the sleeping bag to warm them. She followed his example.

They dressed, used the outhouse, then washed using a gallon jug of water that Mick had brought. He had a bar of soap in the end of a nylon, tied to the jug. The nylon allowed the soap to lather and soak through to their hands and faces.

"It's a little cold, but it works," she said, drying her hands and face on a towel.

"You're a good sport," he said, giving her a hug.

"You're fun to be with. Thank you for bringing me," she said as she hugged him back.

"What would you like to do today? Do you want to go straight home?"

"Is there more to do up here? It's Sunday. Can we go to Church?"

"There are churches everywhere. It's a very religious area. We can find a church or we can do more travelling." He looked up local churches on his Google App and showed her where they were with respect to the campground. Then he showed her a map of the area and suggested they drive to Evanston, Wyoming, then to Bear Lake, then home. So that's what they planned to do.

First, they took a walk around the campground, taking a few pictures to remember the trip. Then they went to the nearest church building. They didn't have dressier clothes to wear to church, but no one seemed to mind. They sat in the back of the room and left as soon as the closing prayer was said, so they didn't have to feel like socializing. But, instead of driving to Evanston, he drove east toward Duchesne. They stopped at Starvation Lake along the way and spent the afternoon hiking around the lake and the state park. When they got back to the car, it was near dusk, so they decided to call it a day.

When they got back to her aunt's house, Lydia seemed reluctant to get out of the car. They sat in the car talking about her plans to return home in a few days. He asked if he could show her more things during the week, after classes. They made a date for the basketball game on Wednesday. Then, he said he would call her after classes on Monday to see if she wanted to do anything.

Monday afternoon, he called to say he was done with school for the day and did she want to get together.

"Absolutely. What can we do in the time we have left today?"

"I'll pick you up in a half hour and we can decide."

Lydia said they had several hours before she needed to be home, so Mick drove to the north end of the Great Salt Lake and they walked out to the Spiral Jetty, a manmade structure made from rocks in the form of a conch shell spiral, that had been buried in the salt water of the lake for forty years and was now encrusted in salt crystals, only visible because of multiple draught years that lowered the lake level. They walked in the shallow water along the spiral, looking at the crystals which formed interesting patterns on the rocks. The lake was beautiful from this direction. They took a few pictures to remember the event.

Mick drove to the Golden Spike Museum, not far away, the site of the driving of the last spike in the trans-continental railroad. There was a small museum and a short walk out to the track. They read about the annual reenactment to commemorate the event.

On the return trip, they drove out to Antelope Island, from the east side of the lake. They drove across the causeway, to the beach, and floated in the salt-water. Mick kept extra clothes in his trunk, just for this kind of emergency, so he found a pair of shorts and shirt for each of them to wear in the water. They used the outdoor shower to wash off the salt water, then changed back to their clothes in the car. They drove to the south end of the lake, to the beaches at Saltaire and read about the history of the site, a large building that had been a dancehall for many years, before it burned down. Now it had been rebuilt at the historic location, hosting small events and selling saltwater taffy. By the time they finished looking through the building, it was dark, so Mick took her home.

Once again, she had trouble leaving him. They hugged and kissed until the porch light came on, letting Lydia know that her aunt or uncle had noticed how long they had been in the driveway and that it was time for her to call it a night and come in.

Tuesday afternoon, when Mick called, Lydia said she wanted to see the downtown. He picked her up and drove to temple square, in the heart of Salt Lake City. They found parking; after driving around the block for twenty minutes—until they caught someone backing out of a parking space so they could pull in. It was that busy with tourists. They walked around the square, stopping in the museum and visitors' center to watch videos and see the giant Christus statue. They signed up for a tour of the Conference Center roof, on the next block. While they waited for their tour, they walked around looking at the beautiful flowers that lined the patios and walkways

The Conference Center was like a theatre for twenty-six thousand guests—huge—with a free-span ceiling. The beam holding up the roof was the largest Mick had heard of, with a built-in arch, called camber, to support the weight of the roof. On top of the roof, and the reason he wanted to show it to her, was a garden, complete with flower beds and small trees. The tour was fascinating, especially for Mick, who was studying engineering. This was an engineering marvel.

They went back to the car and drove up to the state capital building. They walked around the grounds, looking at the massive old trees, some of them a hundred years old, then went into the building to see what was going on. Mick knew that there were sometimes exhibits in the rotunda and he wasn't disappointed this time. On display were twenty hand-woven native American rugs, all of them for sale and all of them expensive. They found a tour already started, so they joined the group and saw some of the government building—the senate and house chambers, the governor's offices, and so on. After the tour, they drove up memory grove and into the avenues and looked at the old mansions along North Temple Street, including the governor's mansion. They drove through the University of Utah campus on their way back to Lydia's aunt's house. Once again, they ended up in front of the house, kissing and hugging until the porch light went on.

Wednesday, Mick picked up Lydia for the basketball game and drove to the University of Utah campus. Traffic was crazy, but they had no trouble figuring out where the game would be held. They were directed into a parking lot across the street from the venue and walked over with the crowds. Mick stopped to buy popcorn and drinks before going into the seating area. Lydia turned out to be an enthusiastic fan, cheering for the Utes all the way. They beat USC in overtime, an exciting ending with a buzzer-beating three-point shot to win. Instead of going directly home, they stopped for ice-cream at Fendall's, Mick's favorite ice cream store, not far from campus. They sat in a booth, enjoying their treat and staring into each other's eyes.

"Hey, get a room," a voice said, catching Mick's attention. He looked up to see who was talking.

"Jerry," Mick said, "what are you doing?"

"Just giving advice to a love-sick friend. Introduce me."

"Lydia, this is Jerry Draper. We went to school together."

"High school?" Lydia asked.

"We've known each other since seventh grade," Mick said. "Jerry, this is Lydia Hancock, my girlfriend."

"Nice to meet you, Lydia. Watch this guy. He has powerful hormones, but he's totally trustworthy. Later, Mick." Then Jerry walked off, his arm around a girl who was turned away from them, talking to someone else.

"Girlfriend?" Lydia asked.

"How should I have introduced you, if not as my girlfriend?"

"That's okay. I like the sound of that. In fact, I really like it. I'll be your girlfriend."

"Good, cause that's how I think of you."

Thursday, they drove over to Butterfield Canyon and drove to the overlook above the Kennecott Copper Mine.

"It's the largest open pit mine in the world," he told her, as they stared into the huge hole in the ground that was originally a mountain range. "It's so large that it can be seen from outer space, just like the Great Salt Lake, that we saw yesterday," Mick said, standing on the edge of the overlook, peering into the pit.

"Wow." Lydia said. "That's impressive."

32

Lydia

It had been a wonderful week. She thought she loved Mick. She loved his caring manner, his ambition, his energy, his enthusiasm for adventure and the outdoors. He was respectful, in a personal way. He was everything she thought she wanted in a man. And he had called her his girlfriend. That meant something to her.

They sat quietly in his car, each lost in their own thoughts.

I want to get closer to him, she thought, but this darn console is in the way.

"Can we sit in the back?" she asked suddenly.

"Sure. Whatever you want. Is there a specific reason?"

"I just want to be closer to you," she said, pointing to the center console and rolling her eyes.

"No problem," he chuckled, as he opened his door and got out.

She did the same and they settled into the back seat next to each other. She looked around and noticed there was only one other car in the overlook parking lot, with two boys standing on the edge, looking down at the mine.

She scooted onto Mick's lap and kissed him. She twisted her hands in his shirt, holding him to her. After they'd been kissing for several minutes, she unbuttoned his top button. He didn't seem to notice, or didn't care. Maybe this was what he wanted.

They were soon so engrossed in each other that she didn't notice the two teenage boys come up to the car, until one of them tapped on the window. Lydia broke her passionate kiss and backed a few inches away from Mick, looking out the window at the boys. They were laughing and pointing at Mick. He looked down to see that Lydia had pulled his shirt out of his jeans, totally unbuttoned, and was rubbing his exposed chest. He looked from her to the laughing boys, then back at her.

He rolled his window down a few inches. "Can I help you?" he asked the boys.

"We had a question about the mine," one boy said, "but we can see you're busy."

"What was your question?"

"I don't remember now," the boy said as they walked away, still laughing. She looked around the darkening overlook parking lot. If the boys hadn't interrupted them, where would this have gone? She wondered.

Lydia looked at Mick. His cheeks were pink, like he was embarrassed. She realized that her ears burned, like she was embarrassed, too.

"What did you have in mind?" Mick asked, a silly look on his face. She shrugged and looked away from him.

"Lydia, I think I love you," he said. "I want to get to know you better."

"I feel the same way, Mick. I thought that's what we were doing."

"Are we taking things too fast," he asked, watching her closely. When she didn't answer, he changed the subject. "We have the frat party tomorrow night. Are you still good to go? Or, would you like to do something else?"

"Yes. I'm looking forward to dancing with you again."

"Good. I called Brady and told him that I would bring you to the induction party as my date. He said that was fine and to make sure you wear your nicest clothes. He said you'll get a chance to be in the spotlight."

"I don't think I want to be the center of attention," Lydia said.

"I told him that," Mick said. "I told him I thought you were a little too bashful to enjoy the attention of strangers. He said we're not strangers to you now and that you would need to get over that. He said you're going to get some attention, but wouldn't say more. We don't have to go; we can do something else."

"No. This is your induction ceremony."

"I told you I'm not so sure I want to join the frat now."

"Well, we've committed now. Let's go."

"You're sure."

"Yes."

Mick

When Lydia came to the front door Friday night, she wore a tight, black dress that hugged her curves. It was sleeveless, deep cut in front and back, and barely long enough to cover her backside. With her high heels and her hair made up, she looked like a supermodel, right off the runway. She was gorgeous and Mick knew he was in love ... or lust. He used his hand to close his mouth. She smiled at his obvious discomfort, likely flattered that she had affected him so. She handed him her light sweater, leaned over and gave him a quick kiss on the cheek, then took his arm as he led her to his car.

At the dance, Lydia wouldn't dance with anyone except Mick, not even Brady. That concerned Mick; he didn't know if Brady would feel insulted and take it out on him. He'd known Brady for a few months, not enough for Mick to feel secure in their relationship.

"Can't you get her to dance with me?" Brady whispered in Mick's ear.

"Sorry, Brady. She does her own thing. I don't think I could get her to do anything she didn't want to."

"I hope that's not a problem during the induction ceremony."

"What do you mean?"

"If she doesn't do her part, you don't get inducted. That's what I mean."

"What does she have to do?"

"You'll find out, when the time comes." Mick thought he noticed a smirk on Brady's face as he turned away.

Mick was apprehensive at Brady's reluctance to say more. During an intermission, Mick took Lydia outside to look at the stars. He placed his arm around her waist and pulled her to his side. She turned her head toward him, coming face-to-face with him. She was a few inches shorter than him, so she had to look up slightly to meet his eyes. His lips were inches from hers. She leaned into him and they kissed.

"Thank you for bringing me," Lydia said as she put her arms around Mick's waist and hugged him tightly to her. He liked how she felt against him, the thin fabric of her dress making him all too aware of the heat from her body pressed against him.

"I'm worried about what Brady has in mind for the induction ceremony," he said.

"Why."

"He's being secretive, but suggestive at the same time. If you don't want to participate, you don't have to."

"What does he expect me to do?"

"That's just it. I don't know and I worry about what it might be."

"I'm sure it's nothing. Maybe a little prank. I'll let you know if it's a real problem."

"You promise?"

"I promise."

Brady was just calling the three inductees to come forward

when Mick and Lydia returned to the room. He and the other two took their dates by the hand and led them to the front, to stand in front of Brady.

"We're about ready to start the last dance. Remember our 'last dance' rule. For the three inductees and their dates, we have a special requirement. With the agreement of the presidency, we've modified the induction ceremony a little. Your initiation," he said, looking at each of the three inductees, then pointedly at Lydia, as though his words were meant for her especially, "will consist of undressing your date, or in lieu of your date any other willing young woman at this party, and dancing the last dance with her, naked."

All three women, the dates of the inductees, backed up a couple of steps and gasped. Mick turned to Lydia, waiting for a verdict from her. Now Mick knew what Brady meant when he said that Lydia's response would determine his ability to join the fraternity. Lydia just stared at him, expressionless, like she was trying to decide how she felt about the requirement.

"We'll do this alphabetically," Brady continued. "Logan, you first. Bring your date out here. By the way, anyone who doesn't want to watch is welcome to move toward the other end of the room." Several of the couples drifted toward the refreshment table.

Logan was in his late twenties, but his date was young, probably right out of high school. He held her hand, trying to coax her, but she backed away from him. Then she turned and ran to the door, then outside. He ran after her.

"Okay," Brady said, laughing. "Let's have Nicholas come forward with his date."

Nicholas looked at his date, a question in his expression. She looked around at all the faces, likely seeing no one that she knew, then moved forward slowly. She was a good-looking woman in her mid-twenties.

"You need to undress each other," Brady said, stopping the date who had started to unzip her own dress. As they undressed each other, there were appreciative noises from some of the men in the group, even some of the women. It was hard to watch, very personal, and Mick turned to see how Lydia would respond. She studied the couple closely, watching their movements and physical response to each other.

Mick noticed Lydia's movements, as if she were removing her own clothes . . . or his.

"Are you going to be okay?" he asked her. "Do you want to leave, instead?"

"I'm good," she said and inched closer to him.

"All right," Brady said, when Nicholas and his date stood in their underwear, side-by-side, on the dance floor. "Your turn Mick."

Mick took Lydia's hand.

"That's good enough?" Lydia asked, pointing to the couple standing near them, half undressed, and looking at Brady for his reaction.

Brady nodded.

Lydia turned her back, so Mick could see the full-length zipper down her back. He ran the zipper down her back, then stood in front of her and pushed her straps off her shoulders. Her little black dress fell to the floor. She was even more beautiful than he had imagined through her clothes. He had seen her in her underwear at the campground, but in her sheer, black, lacy underwear, that left nothing to his imagination, she looked captivating; he couldn't have drawn his eyes away from her if he'd wanted to, which he didn't. What he saw was all her. He knelt in front of her, lifted her feet, one at a time and removed her heels, then she stepped out of her dress. Mick picked it up and draped it over his arm.

Lydia took hold of Mick's upper arms and encouraged him to stand. She unbuttoned his dress shirt and removed it. She knelt in front of him, unbuckled his belt and dropped his pants. He stepped out of them. He wore boxers with a smiley face on them.

"Okay," Brady said, as a slow song started to play "this is the last dance. Nicholas and Mick, start us out."

The two couples moved to the center of the room and began dancing. Mick held Lydia close, one hand on the small of her back, the other holding her hand between them. He realized his hand was pressed against her breast and tried to move it, but Lydia trapped it there, holding his hand in place with her own.

"You're a smooth dancer," Lydia said, looking up into his blue eyes. They had become dark and intense.

"I could do this all night with you," Mick said.

"Let's go to my place and we can continue."

The dance ended and Mick went to collect their clothes. They helped each other dress, then started to leave, passing Brady on the way.

"Thank you," Lydia said to Brady.

"Yes, thank you," Mick said. "Was there anything else I needed to do for the induction ceremony?" he asked Brady.

"No, not really. All we'll do is give you a ceremonial key to the fraternity, and Lydia, you are now an honorary member and welcome to come to any of our future activities, with or without Mick. In fact, if you want, I'll call you before each activity and remind you. I'll even puck you up."

"Thanks, Brady, but I'm going home next week, so I won't be able to attend any more activities, as much as I may want to."

"I'm sorry to hear that. Home is Atlanta?"

"That's right. Hence the southern accent."

"I get it. Well, if I'm ever passing through Atlanta, I'll give you a call. Maybe we can get together."

"I'll make sure Mick has my phone number and email address."

"Great. Thank you for coming. You were a good sport." And I got some great pictures, he didn't say.

"Thanks. Good bye." Lydia said.

"Send me a copy of all the pictures," Mick said quietly to Brady, letting him know that he had noticed.

"Sure thing," Brady said, looking surprised.

In Mick's car, Lydia held his arm in one hand, while rubbing up and down his arm with her other hand.

"Mick, thank you for holding me so close. I felt safe and protected."

"You're welcome. It was my pleasure. Can we see more of each other before you leave?" He meant that he'd like to get together again in the next few days, but she may have misinterpreted his remark.

33

"You want to see more of me?" she asked. "You want to see me naked?"

"That's not . . . I meant . . . I'd like to see you again before you leave," Mick said, choking on his words. His face felt flushed with embarrassment. His ears burned. Images of dancing with her earlier filled his head.

"I thought that's what you meant, Mick," she said thoughtfully. "I'm not sure this is appropriate—we've known each other such a short time—but I'm leaving in a few days and I really like you. I feel so safe with you that I want to be naked with you. Do you feel the same way?" her voice lowered and became husky with emotion.

"I really like you, too," Mick said, "but we don't need to go that far. I'd be satisfied holding you and dancing some more."

"Would you like to come in?" she asked, when he parked in her aunt's driveway.

"Are you sure it's alright? Your aunt won't mind?"

"I don't think my aunt or uncle are home. They were going out for the evening—dinner and drinking—which usually means drinking into the early hours of the morning."

"Okay, if you're sure it's alright." He wasn't sure it was a good idea to be alone with her in the house, particularly with her in this mood.

He followed her into the house and she took him to her bedroom, stopping in the kitchen on the way, to get a drink of water for Mick's dry throat. He hesitated at her bedroom door before she pulled on his hand to get him to follow her. The room was simply furnished; a double bed, dresser, and a couple of family pictures hanging on one wall. Her pretty bedspread looked homemade.

"Is the bedspread handmade?" he asked.

"My aunt loves to sew. She made the spread, the pillow cases, and some of the clothes I've worn since I got here."

"Anything that I've seen?"

"I don't think so, but I'll show you some of them." She opened her closet and pulled three dresses out to show him. They were all different colors and styles, all pretty, and well made.

"Would you like to see them on me?" she asked.

"I'd like that, if you want to show me." He expected her to go into the bathroom that was just off the bedroom, but she laid them on the bed and started undressing in front of him. He turned his head to give her some privacy. She didn't hesitate. She kicked off her heels and removed her little black dress. She picked up one dress and started climbing into it.

"This one is my favorite," she said. It was a simple, yellow, high-waisted dress with a large flower pattern. "Please zip it up in the back for me." He did, trying unsuccessfully not to focus on her exposed skin. She stepped back and twirled for him. The skirt flew up as she twirled, exposing a lot of leg.

"I like it," he said.

"So do I." She removed it and pulled the second one on. He turned away belatedly, and felt embarrassed by what he saw. It was a slim, dark green sheath dress, slit up the middle, to her upper thighs. As she twirled for him, he caught glimpses of her tanned thighs in the slit.

"I like that one, too," he said.

She exchanged it for the third one, this one a bright blue jumper with cut-away sides. From just above her ankles to just below her hips. Even standing still, the sides flared out to expose much of her legs.

He was embarrassed watching her change back into her black dress, so he looked around again. A suitcase lay open on a chair with clothes folded neatly and stacked in it.

"So, you really are leaving next week?" he asked. "That wasn't just an excuse?"

"If I hadn't had a legitimate excuse, I would have made one up. That Brady gives me the creeps."

"How so? I've always thought of him as a nice guy. He told me the FBI has invited him to come and talk to them when he graduates in a few weeks."

"It just feels like he's hiding his true self, like what you see on the outside isn't who he really is."

"Really? I'll have to give that some thought and pay better attention." She had returned to the black dress and stood looking at him expectantly. "What do you want to do?" he asked.

She hesitated, looking down, before answering. "Can we dance?"

"I'd love to." She turned on her radio and he took her in his arms.

"You're a wonderful dancer," he said.

"Were you serious about wanting to see more of me?" she asked.

"I was serious about wanting to see you again."

"But you don't want to see me naked, is that it?"

He stopped dancing and looked her in the eyes. "Lydia, you're a beautiful woman," he said seriously. "Everything I've learned about you in the last week makes me think we would be good together. But we don't have much more time together. If you trust me enough to be naked with me . . . It's your call."

She thought about that for a minute. "I'd like to dance naked, if it's alright with you," she finally said.

"Do you like to dance naked?"

"I do like to dance naked. Sometimes," she looked down shyly again, "I like to watch myself in the mirror while I dance naked. I like the way it feels."

He thought about that. So, this was something she did. It was probably no big deal to her, like it would be for him.

She interrupted his thoughts. "I used to skinny-dip with friends in the stream near my home."

"Mixed company?" he asked, the words escaping before he thought about how she might take his question.

"It wasn't sexual, just a bunch or friends enjoying the cool water on a hot day. But maybe the others thought differently about it."

Maybe his first impression of her was wrong. Maybe she was not the bashful southern belle he imagined originally. But she had let him know ahead of time what she wanted. He was physically attracted to her and enjoyed holding her, so maybe this was alright. His standards precluded having pre-marital sex, but he got excited thinking about seeing her naked.

Without waiting for an answer, she looked him in the eyes and slowly unzipped her dress again, letting it drop to the floor, while she swayed back and forth sensually. She gradually removed all of her clothes, still looking deeply into his eyes.

"Your turn," she finally said.

"And you really want me to get naked, too?" he asked. She nodded.

Did he really want to do this? She said this is what she wanted. He was kind of committed, since she had gone first. He tried to undress while dancing, but couldn't manage it. It was awkward and embarrassing. She helped him. When he was finally naked, she stepped into his arms and started dancing, again. He held her close. She hugged him tightly to her. He rubbed her back, up and down, with one hand while the other held her hand to his chest. "You're amazing," he said.

"Does that mean you like me?"

"I think I love you."

"I think I love you, too. Is that possible when we've known each other for so short a time?"

"I don't know. I only know how I feel. Will we feel the same way after you've gone back to Atlanta?"

She stopped dancing, held his hand, and walked to the bed. She turned down the bedding and climbed in, patting the space next to her. He climbed in next to her and pulled the bedding over them He didn't know what she wanted to do, so he wrapped his arms around her and held her to him. He would let her decide.

Around two o'clock, he slipped out of her embrace and dressed.

"Thank you," she said, quietly from the bed. "I've had a lovely week. Will I see you tomorrow?"

"If you want to."

"I do." She got up and peeked out her window, confirming that her aunt and uncle had yet to arrive home. He left her room and drove home to his apartment to spend the rest of the night alone, remembering the feeling of Lydia in his arms and dreaming about her body and the things they had done that night.

He called her when he was awake again. "How do you feel?" he asked. "Are you up for a little trip?"

"I'm a little tired, but I'd love to do something. What do you have in mind?"

"I want to drive to Jackson Hole, Wyoming and show you how cool it is, a real Western atmosphere." He was thinking this might be the last time they saw each other, with her leaving in a couple of days and living so far away. He would see if she wanted to sleep with him again.

"Sounds wonderful. I can be ready by the time you get here."

She wore jeans, a man's flannel shirt and sneakers and carried an overnight bag—she said she enjoyed sleeping with him and wanted to do it again. They drove to Jackson and found a motel. It was expensive, but they didn't have a lot of choices; everything cost more in Jackson. After leaving their overnight bags at the motel, they drove to the center of town and found a parking space. They walked around the park, where the arched entrances on each corner were bordered with antlers, hundreds of them. They window-shopped at the little shops along the streets, entering a few of them to look at the souvenirs and merchandise.

In one shop, a woman sat at an embroidery machine, embroidering sayings on shirts, then putting them up for sale. Lydia fell in love with a shirt that read, 'Home is where your heart is'.

"I love that," she said, so Mick bought it for her. She pulled it on over her clothes and wore it the rest of the day.

"You know why I love this?" Lydia asked over dinner, when Mick didn't ask her first.

"Why?" he finally asked.

"Because it means that it doesn't matter if I have to return to Atlanta; my home will always be wherever you are."

Mick didn't know what to say to that. He was amazed that she felt so strongly about their relationship. He took her in his arms and kissed her. "I love you, too," he finally said, thinking that was the right thing to say under the circumstances. Maybe he even believed it. He definitely liked everything he knew about her. That night, in the motel, they shared a bed and made love most of the night, before heading home in the morning.

Two days later he rode in her uncle's car with them, to the airport to see her off. They had to leave her at the TSA security checkpoint, where he kissed her good-bye, promising they would see each other again and thinking that he would definitely try.

34

Pachenko's brother

"I think we have someone on the inside we can use," Victor Pachenko said into his burner phone. Pavlovich had recruited Victor when his brother, Vladamir had died in the auto accident in Utah. Pavlovich had hired Victor thinking that he would have incentive to take revenge on the Swenson's "and he can be influenced. I'll keep watch and let you know as things develop."

"It would be poetic justice to use one of the Swensen's own children to get to their government," Pavlovich said. "The oldest son, Drew, now serves in the military. It's not a key position; not one that can supply what we need, but that could change. And, we still don't know what his brother will end up doing with his engineering degree. Keep me informed."

"Yes, sir."

Mick

Mick found that he had no interest in dating or in attending fraternity dances. Without Lydia, there was nothing that attracted him. He spent all of his time thinking about her. He wrote to her regularly, even though he didn't see how they would ever get to see each other again. His letters became less and less frequent and her replies got further and further apart, until they stopped altogether.

His grades the first year of college, in chemistry, calculus and physics, were poor enough that he worried about not being able to graduate. He asked his counselor if he needed to take any of the classes over again and was told he had two options; he could take the classes over again for a chance at a better grade, or he could dedicate himself to his remaining classes and bring his GPA up enough to graduate. He decided to quit the fraternity and concentrate on bringing his grades up. Brady was not understanding of his decision. Mick dated little, and none of the girls compared to Lydia in his mind. What few dances he went to, no longer got in the way of study.

Ollie

Oliver Tanner finally called Mick. It had been years since they'd last spoken and Mick hardly remembered who Ollie was.

"Oliver Tanner—Ollie—a friend of your parents," Ollie said, when Mick questioned him. "We spoke shortly after they died and you sent me a message that a Russian had come to your home."

"Sorry, now I remember," Mick said. "What can I do for you? That was a long time ago."

"It has been a long time. Sorry it took so long for me to get back to you. But we've finally figured out what to do with the information you gave us."

"You want me to do something, is that it?"

"Actually, we can do something for you, then you can do something for us in return. Can we meet to talk about it?"

"Sure. What do you have in mind?"

"If you can meet tonight—I'm in Provo right now—I'll buy you dinner."

"Sounds good." They agreed where to meet and Mick left right away for the meeting. When they were seated in the restaurant and had ordered, Mick looked at Ollie, inviting him to speak.

"What?" Mick asked.

"You're studying Engineering, right?" Ollie asked.

"Yes. I want to be a project manager."

"Perfect. We want to help you with that. Our offer to you is to pay for the rest of your education, pay for you to take the Project Management Professional Certification exam, then help you get a job managing one of the nuclear power plant projects starting up."

"That would be fantastic, Mr. Tanner . . ."

"Ollie, please."

"That would be fantastic, Ollie. But what's the catch? What do I have to do for you in return?"

"Let me tell you about your parents. You were what, six, when they died?"

"Yeah."

Ollie looked around to make sure no one was within hearing before he spoke. "What I'm about to tell you is government classified. You can't tell anyone, not even your family, do you understand and agree?"

"If you can tell me why my parents died, I'll agree to your condition."

"Great. What you don't know is that we recruited them to work for the CIA while they were still single. Your mom worked as a courier and your dad as a field agent—a spy and assassin."

"Assass . . ." Mick said before Ollie shushed him.

"Eventually," Ollie continued, "they worked a few missions together and fell in love. They married, then your mom became pregnant with Drew. She took a leave of absence and wanted to retire to raise her family. But she had signed an agreement that was binding for life, so she agreed to a few more missions before we finally let both of them retire."

"One of their missions was to stop a Russian KGB mob boss, who was very dangerous and difficult to catch. They ran into him a couple of times. After your mom retired, he even went to your house in Provo.”

“I think I remember him. He didn't have an accent, but he scared Mom really bad.”

“That would be him. Anyway, we think he tried to have your parents killed, using a hitman that worked for him. His name was Pachenko. He died in an accident, trying to kill your parents. Anyway, one of the reasons we wanted to stop this Russian was because he was selling weapons in the Middle East, contributing to the wars there. Since the government has started building nuclear power plants again, we've learned that he wants to get his hands on Uranium, for making bombs, to sell to his customers. We can't allow that.”

“So, you want me to do something. What?” Mick asked when Ollie stopped talking and stared at him.

“We want to set up a sting operation to catch him.”

“What, and use me as bait?”

“The Russians have long memories. We believe that when he learns that the son of his old enemies is a project manager at one of power plants, he'll try to trick you, or force you, to get him some uranium.”

“Doesn't the government keep strict control and inventory of uranium?”

“They do, but this Russian doesn't let things like laws and rules get in his way. He has no conscience and he'll try to find a way to force it to happen.”

“Won't it be dangerous?”

“It could be very dangerous. That's why we'll keep a close eye on you the entire time. Are you willing to help?”

“Will it be dangerous for Drew and Lynne? Would this Russian use them as leverage to get me to help him?”

“He could, and we need to think about how to protect them

and anyone else close to you. We've been keeping track of you, Drew and Lynne and know what each of you have been up to over the years. We know that your grandfather came to live with you and to help raise you. Your first love, Lydia Hancock went home without making a commitment to each other, didn't she?"

"She went home to Atlanta before we could really test the relationship," Mick said, "but I think it would have ended in marriage if she'd stuck around a little longer."

"And you never got back together with her."

"I've thought about her a lot, but there hasn't been a way to get back together."

"And now you have a girlfriend, Raquel Austin. How is that going?"

"That relationship could end in marriage, if she'll accept my proposal."

"You've proposed to her?"

"Not yet, but we're close to talking about it."

"You think she'll accept?"

"Not sure. That's why I haven't proposed yet. She really likes her job and may not want to interfere with her climb up the corporate ladder. She's very motivated, ambitious and dedicated to what she does."

"Thanks Mick. I'll let you go now. I just wanted to tell you how I knew your parents." Then, as an afterthought, he added, "Drew is nearly twenty-five, so your grandpa will share a surprise with you soon, that will impact your decisions going forward."

The will

When Drew came home for his twenty-fifth birthday celebration, Ralph wanted to have a serious talk with him. It was a small party, just the four of them, with ice cream, cake and presents. After opening the small gifts from Mick md Lynne, Drew looked at Grandpa to see what he would do.

"Drew, we need to talk," Grandpa said, "You must be aware that your parents prepared a trust and will. They were very thorough and conscientious about planning for the future. There is a stipulation in their trust that states when you turn twenty-five, you qualify to receive your inheritance, one third of your parent's estate. What you probably don't know and couldn't guess, is that they had a significant life insurance policy. A million dollars each, double if they died in an accident, which they did. That's four million dollars, in addition to their savings and investments. If you'll come with me to the office, I'll show you where I've invested it all."

"Can we see?" Lynne asked.

"You can see where it is, but you can't get your share until you turn twenty-five." Grandpa said.

"That's not fair," Lynne said.

"Boo-hoo," Mick said, looking at Lynne.

"Mick!" Ralph said, "the sarcasm is not helpful."

Drew followed Grandpa to the office, where Grandpa booted up the computer, and showed Drew a spreadsheet that listed each investment and its initial or current value. The funds were diversified between several companies, with most of the money invested in dividend stocks, exchange-traded funds, index funds, preferred stocks, and time certificates.

"Grandpa," Drew said, "I have a good salary with the government, and I spend almost nothing. I eat free on the base and my medical and dental are provided, I don't need money."

"Then I suggest," Grandpa said, "that we leave the money where it is. I'm currently the custodian of all the funds. I've written my own will to make you the executor in the case of my death."

"You'll probably outlive all of us."

"Just in case, I've left the clause in my will that neither Mick nor Lynne can touch their portion until they turn twenty-five."

"Maybe we should make Lynne be forty?"

"I'll leave that up to you," Ralph said with a sigh. "Anyway, we're currently earning over four thousand dollars a month in interest, which, so far, has been enough for the incidentals the family needs. Lynne has asked for specific amounts of money a couple of times, which I've given her, but that's it."

Mick

Ollie paid for the remainder of Mick's education as he'd promised. He finally graduated with a bachelor's degree in Civil Engineering and got a job as a project manager at the power company, managing the construction of electric substations and expanding transmission power lines to rapidly expanding service areas, where the population was growing. A year later, Ollie contacted him again.

"Are you ready to take the Project Manager exam now?" Ollie asked.

"I am. I've been studying for it. It comes up in a few weeks."

"I know. I've been keeping track. Remember our agreement? I said I'd help you get a job managing a power plant if you would help us stop the Russian."

"I remember and I'm still willing, although I'd like to have some details about how you're going to keep me safe."

"Great. I'm sending you the contact information for the recruiter who has a project manager position available at the power plant in Central Utah, on the Green River. Send him your resume—he already has your name—and let's see where this goes."

"I'll do that as soon as I get your information, and thanks."

"You're welcome, and thank you. We'll talk again soon."

Mick submitted his resume to the personnel manager in Green River, Utah, got an interview and was hired three weeks later, working for a government contractor, helping to manage the newly-constructed nuclear power plant. It was part of a nation-wide effort to decrease dependence on fossil fuels by increasing the availability of nuclear power. There were power plants being built in a handful of locations across the country. The small town of Green River, Utah, was one of those locations. He moved to Green River, sent Ollie his new address, and began watching for Ollie to show up and talk to him.

35

Five months later—Drew

"Mick and Lynne," Drew said, "we need to talk after the graveside service."

"I can't believe Grandpa's dead," Lynne said. "He was in such good health on your birthday. Then, all of a sudden, he was in the hospital and died the next day."

"That's what happens with heart attacks," Drew said.

"I thought he would outlive all of us," Mick said. "So, what do you want to talk about?" he asked as they walked from the grave toward Mick's car.

"Five months ago, when I was here for my birthday party, Grandpa told me about Mom's and Dad's wills."

"I remember," Lynne said. "You were both mean to me."

"Quit being a fathead. Let's hear what Drew has to say," Mick said to Lynne. Lynne pouted and sat back in her seat.

Drew told them what he and Grandpa had discussed and offered to show them how the money was invested.

"How much money are we talking about?" Lynne asked.

"When I checked the numbers yesterday, the total was almost 4.4 million."

"Dollars?" Lynne asked? Drew nodded. "That's over a million dollars apiece. I want it, now."

"Unfortunately, Lynne, you can't touch it until you turn twenty-five."

"Why not, if it's mine?"

"That was a condition of Mom and Dad's will, which Grandpa put in his will as well."

"That's not fair. So, you can have your share, but Mick and I can't have ours?"

"Actually, I don't need it," Drew said. "It's earning great interest where it is. I've left mine where Grandpa invested it."

"Well, I want mine," Lynne said. "I have expenses."

"What expenses?"

"I'm planning to get some medical work done."

"In other words, you don't have expenses. You just want to spend it. That's exactly why that requirement is there, so maybe you'll be mature enough to not spend it on frivolous things."

"They're not frivolous. They're important."

"What are they?"

"None of your business, if you're not going to help me."

"I'm helping you by not giving you the money now. Talk to me again when you turn twenty-five."

"I may not talk to you until then," Lynne said in anger.

"Mick, are you okay with that arrangement?" Drew asked, then showed them the spreadsheet grandpa had shown him months earlier.

"Yeah. I have a good job, that pays well. With the amount Grandpa was giving us each month, I've been fine. You're planning to continue giving us the earnings monthly, aren't you?"

"Yeah, that's all set up automatically to distribute to your checking accounts."

"Do you have a will?" Mick asked Drew.

"I do, and it leaves everything to you and Lynne if I die first. If I get married, I'll change it to leave my share to my wife. Do you have a will?"

"If you'll give me a copy of yours, I'll get mine updated to match, so we keep it all straight."

"I already made you a copy. It's in this envelope, along with the name of my attorney, in case you need one," Drew said.

"Thanks," Mick said as he took the envelope from Drew.

"What about me?" Lynne asked.

"Do you have a will?"

"No, but I want one."

"Then I'll make a copy for you as well."

"Thank you."

"I thought you weren't talking to me."

"I'm not. Not again after today."

"Promise or threat?"

"Take it any way you like," she said and stormed away.

36

Wendover, Nevada

Mick drove the three hundred miles to Wendover and parked his car in the casino parking lot, then texted Lynne to tell her he was there. "Pick me up at the front door," Lynne texted back. "We'll go to my place to talk."

He pulled up to the door and Lynne, dressed in her work clothes, pranced out of the casino and climbed into the passenger seat.

"Hi!" she said and immediately pulled her top off over her head, shaking her hair out so that it fell back into place. She set her top between them on the console.

"What are you doing?" Mick asked.

"I hate wearing clothes. If I had my way, I'd be naked all the time." This was said as she lifted her hips and slid her short skirt down her legs and off.

"Turn left," she said as Mick stopped at the edge of the parking lot. He turned onto the main street and headed west, slowly.

The strappy heels came off next, then the panty hose, then the underwear.

"Doesn't it embarrass you to be sitting naked in my car?" he asked, trying not to look at her, or to focus only on her face. It was impossible. She really did have a nice body.

"Turn left here," she said, so he slowed for the turn.

"It's the first driveway on the left," she said as she pushed a button on a console she'd pulled from her purse and the garage door started to rise.

"Where's your car?"

"Back at the casino. I'll walk back and pick it up later."

Mick drove the car into the garage and stopped. Lynne slipped her feet back into her heels and climbed out of the car as she pushed the button to close the overhead door.

"This way," she said and walked toward the house door.

"I don't think I can walk that way," Mick said out his window, watching her hips move in a way she must have had to practice to execute. He had a good view of most of her piercings and tattoos.

She turned her head and grinned at him. "You like what you see?"

"That's quite a wiggle you have there." The tail wagging the dog, was the thought that came to mind. He followed her into a small, but functional living area, with a two-person table in the middle of the room, a couch against the wall to the right and a small kitchen beyond the dining table. Lynne shook out her top and skirt and laid them over the arm of the couch, then sprawled onto the couch in an un-lady-like position. Mick pulled out one of the two chairs from the small table and sat, facing her.

Mick looked around to get a feel for how she lived.

"Why only two chairs?" he asked.

"I never have more than one person in the house at a time," she said.

"Lots of large windows, but no blinds."

"I like to see out. And I don't care who sees in."

"Do your neighbors ever bother you?" He was thinking about what a neighbor might see if she ran around the house naked all the time.

"You mean, do they ever come over to borrow a cup of sugar?" she asked.

"Something like that." Maybe she just didn't get it.

"No. No bother. But one guy across the fence has a telescope that's usually pointed at the sky, but sometimes pointed at my window." Mick couldn't resist looking out the back window.

"Not the one right behind me," she said. "The one to the right. If you look closely, you can see the telescope."

"I see it. That doesn't bother you?"

"Not really. He can pay to see it at the casino, or he can see it here for free."

Mick could tell that Lynne really didn't care about her privacy, and it wasn't his place to lecture her about modesty; they'd had that discussion years earlier. He struggled at first to look away from her, then gave up and studied her instead.

"Do you like what you do here?" he asked.

"I do. The pay isn't great. There are other things I could do to make more. But it pays the bills and I enjoy it. I get attention from all sorts of men, but don't take much of the attention seriously."

"What is your objective here? I mean, do you have a long-term goal in mind?"

"Yeah. Find a sugar-daddy and live off him for the rest of my life."

"Any candidates in mind," he asked, amused.

"A couple," Lynne said seriously. "One old guy comes in and spends everything in his wallet each week. I think he's on social security, so he doesn't have a lot. But he's friendly. When I bring him a drink, he'll run his hand up the inside of my thigh and pinches me. I can usually still see the welt when I get home. But he always leaves me a tip, his last twenty-dollar chip."

"And the other one?"

"He looks like he really does have money. He comes in about once a month, spends a lot, then leaves while he still has a pile of chips. More self-control. He's expressed interest in getting to know me, but hasn't done more than talk. If he gets serious, maybe I'll take a chance on him."

"There are a couple that I've brought home a time or two. Either one would like to make it more permanent, they say, but I don't buy it and don't encourage it. Then there are the ones who just want sex, a one-night stand. I figure they're not getting enough at home, so they come sniffing around the casino, to see if any of the bitches are in heat."

"Do you encourage that?"

"Not at all, but sometimes I want it, too. I don't discourage it."

Mick decided this line of discussion was also unproductive, so he changed the subject again. "Do you need anything, Lynne?"

"I have an itch that needs scratching. Do you want to scratch it?"

"An itch?" Mick asked innocently, thinking that, being his sister, Lynne couldn't mean what he thought she meant; but she had propositioned him once before.

"Yeah, between my legs. Are you interested?"

"Lynne, I'm your brother."

"We're both healthy, good-looking and have normal sex drives. At least I do. I assume you do, too, unless you're gay. So, why not?"

"I'm not gay. Do you need anything that I can provide?" Mick asked, frustrated.

"Will you get naked, at least, so I know what I'm missing?"

Mick shook his head. "I don't think that's a good idea, Lynne."

"Why not? You always give me what I want, except that one time. And that's what I want."

"That was when Grandpa made me feel guilty for not taking care of you. Now you don't need me and Grandpa is gone. And this is the same subject as the last time I said 'no'."

"Then, can you get Drew to give me my share of the insurance money?"

"You know what Drew would say to that. Anyway, what would you do with all that money?"

"New boobs," she said, placing her hands under her breasts and bouncing them a few times.

Mick shook his head in disbelief.

"Liposuction," she said, slapping her bare thighs with her hands.

Another head shake.

"New clothes."

"You don't wear the ones you have now," Mick said.

"Jewelry," she said, holding up both hands so he could see the simple, small band on her right ring finger.

"Sorry, sis. I don't think Drew would see any of those things as a good reason to give you money before it's scheduled."

"Then there's nothing you can offer me that I need," Lynne pouted.

"I better get going, then."

As he stood to leave, Lynne went to him and rubbed her naked body against him.

"Are you sure you don't have time to play around a little," she asked in a sultry voice that she must have cultivated for her job.

"Lynne, I have all the time I need for the things I'm interested in. I'm just not interested."

"Your body says otherwise," she said, touching him where she got her clue.

He moved away from her hand. "My body doesn't control me like some people," he said.

"Spoil sport!" Lynne cried and gave Mick a kiss on the lips that surprised him with its intensity and passion. He could tell his body was responding then.

"What is it you really want, Lynne?"

"I want your body."

"Sorry, Lynne. I can't accommodate you there." As he turned to leave, he spanked Lynne's bare bottom and laughed. "You almost make me want it," he said and went into the garage to get his car.

Victor Pachenko

"Do we have a plan now?" Pachenko asked.

"We do. We kidnap the sister and force the brother to cooperate."

"What if he doesn't cooperate? Do we kill the sister?"

"That isn't the first choice, but it is an option. And we've never backed away from doing what was necessary to get what we want."

"When do you want it done?"

"You have a place to stash her, right?"

"We do."

"Then do it."

Lynne

Two weeks later, as Mick parked his car in the casino parking lot, he texted Lynne to tell her he was there. She texted right back that she was by the front entrance and would come out to meet him. They could find a place to sit and talk. Mick remembered his last visit and was glad she had offered to go somewhere else besides her apartment.

As he turned toward the entrance, Lynne stepped outside, dressed in her work uniform, about fifty feet away. Before Mick could tell what was happening, a sports car pulled up to the door, two men jumped out, threw a dark hood over Lynne's head and threw her into the back seat of the car. She didn't put up much of a fight. They jumped back into the car and sped away while Mick was trying to decide if this was a real emergency or if Lynne had staged it to get his attention. By the time he got to the edge of the parking lot, the car had vanished, with Lynne inside.

Mick gave the police a report, a bright blue Mustang Shelby GT500, headed west, two men, white, late twenties or early thirties, longish hair, facial hair, not close enough to get a plate or better description of the kidnappers. Mick promised to be in touch if he got a ransom note or any other information, and they excused him. He immediately texted Drew, who agreed to take time off and fly in from Europe. After all, this was Lynne.

"How do you know it was a Mustang Shelby GT500?" Drew asked, when they sat together in the living room of the Provo house, which they still owned.

"Hey man," Mick replied. "Have you ever seen one up close? You'd never forget it. It's good looking and one of the fastest machines on wheels. I've seen the one Mr. Shelby modified for himself. It's been sold or auctioned several times since it was built in 1966. It went for 5.5 million last time and is estimated to be worth as much as eight million now. It was called the 'super snake' and there was only one other one built like it. The owner of that one drove it off a cliff in California a few years ago. They never found it or him."

"Interesting," Drew said. "I *have* seen a GT500 before, when that guy came to the house in Provo, a few weeks before Mom and Dad died, and upset Mom."

"What? Details, man."

Drew explained the visit from the Russian who had upset their mom and who had let himself in the house like he owned it.

"What did he want?"

"He said he had unfinished business with Mom, but I never figured out what he meant." Dad tried to kick him out, but he only left when he wanted to. It was right after their collision near the campground.

Mick looked amused for a moment, then got serious. "Suppose that guy thought Mom and Dad had died in that crash," he said. "Why?"

"Good question. Why?"

They both thought about that for a few moments, eyeing each other.

"That would only make sense," Mick said, "if Mom and Dad were supposed to go off that cliff instead of the other car. Is that possible?"

Drew told him about his conversation with Oliver Tanner and his thinking that their parents' plane crash wasn't really an accident. "But why would anyone want to kill Mom and Dad?"

Mick thought about *his* discussion with Ollie and decided not to share what he thought it meant and had agreed to do. Ollie had said that the less anyone knew about their parents' jobs at the CIA or their relationship with the Russian KGB, the safer they would be. "Why would anyone want to kidnap Lynne?" Mick asked instead.

"Both good questions"

"Any ideas"

"None whatsoever."

"Who can we ask?" Mick asked, deciding that he would ask Ollie after he spoke to Drew.

"Have you received a ransom note?" Drew asked.

"I thought I saw a piece of paper flutter to the ground after Lynne was kidnapped, so I went to look," Mick said. "A couple, just leaving the casino, got to it before me. When I stopped near them and got out of the car, the woman asked if I was Michael. When I said I was, she said, 'Then this must be for you,' and handed it to me. Then they hurried away, before I could read it and ask questions." Mick pulled a note from his pocket and let Drew read it. It read:

Tell Michael that we'll trade straight across, him for your sister. If we don't hear from you soon, your sister will disappear, forever. No police.

There was a phone number at the bottom.

"Why would they want a trade?" Mick asked. Drew and Mick studied each other.

"Does it have something to do with what you do for a living?" Drew asked.

"Maybe," Mick said. He had good reason to suspect that this was the first push by the Russians, to get him to give them some uranium.

"Are you going to tell the police about the note?"

"I better, but it will raise questions I don't think I can answer."

"Well, you better figure it out or Lynne could die."

"I think they're bluffing. They're using Lynne as leverage to get me, for some reason. If they kill her, they lose that leverage. They won't do anything to her until they try to talk to us again. So, we have some time to figure out what to do. Is it possible this has something to do with your job with the air force?" Mick asked.

"They mentioned you, specifically," Drew said, "but I'll look through my photos and videos to see if there's anything that would attract the attention of kidnappers or murderers. I'll also call Mr. Tanner and let him know what's happened, if he's still around."

He was still around, Mick knew, but he didn't tell Drew how he knew.

Cold case

Mick went to the police station in Wendover and told the investigator what had happened. The investigator wanted the note, so Mick agreed to give it to him if he could have a copy. When Mick mentioned the car, the investigator asked if Mick had ever seen the car before. Mick told him what Drew had said about the Russian that came by the house nineteen years earlier.

"That was a long time ago," the investigator said, "I don't know what to make of that. Do you?"

"Drew and I wondered if our parents were meant to die in a car accident that occurred three months before the plane crash, like maybe the plane crash was a second attempt on their lives." The investigator laughed at that.

"Are you going to ask us to reopen a nineteen-year-old cold case on a theory that somebody in a Shelby tried to murder them, then shot down a plane to make sure, then kidnapped your sister?"

"Only if you're not positive that they weren't murdered."

"Get out of here and let me get some work done," the investigator said and laughed. "Get back to me if you get anything else."

Raquel

Friday evening, Mick drove to Provo after work and met Raquel for their usual Friday date at their usual restaurant.

"Are you sure you want to eat here?" Mick asked. "Would you like to go somewhere different for a change?" Ollie had suggested that he change his routine regularly and watch for cars following him, just in case the Russians were involved. He wasn't comfortable with the suggestion, only because it made everything real, but he tried to comply.

"I'm good here, Mick," Raquel said. "The food is good, with good variety, and the company is fabulous." She leaned into him for a quick kiss before sitting down at the table.

"I love you, too," Mick said, as he held the kiss longer than she had intended. It was their standard joke. He liked the food, too.

Mick had met Raquel at church in Provo and they had been dating ever since, eight months now.

She had a degree in accounting, with a specialization in Finance. She worked as an analyst in a brokerage house and was up for a promotion. She was intelligent. She loved pitting wits with Mick in card games and jigsaw puzzles. She was better at the games and he excelled with the puzzles, having grown up with them.

They were getting close to talking about marriage. They were affectionate with one another. When they began kissing, whether at his apartment or hers, they got so involved in each other that it was difficult to stop. On more than one occasion, they had only been able to stop when the alarm had gone off that Raquel had set for herself. Raquel wanted to get to marriage as a virgin, so it was important to her that Mick respect her and stop before they went too far.

Mick was sure Raquel was his one true love and was close to asking her to marry him. He didn't know what he was waiting for, but he had thought he loved Lydia a few years earlier and it made him wonder if he was capable of making a decision as important as who to spend the rest of his life with. They were both so special to him.

"A man came into my office today, looking for you," she said. "Why would anyone look for you at my office?"

"What did he look like?" Mick asked, worried that because he hadn't called the number the Russians had given him, they were now tracking him down. Except that they hadn't approached him in Green River, where he was living, so maybe this was something else.

"Nothing unusual. Caucasian, late twenties or early thirties, facial hair. He had an accent. European, I think."

"If he shows up again, call security and have them hold him while they get the police."

"Why? Who is he?"

"I don't know, but some funny stuff is going on. I told you my sister, Lynne was kidnapped. Now I'm worried about you. I don't think this is a coincidence."

"You think that man who came into the office wants to kidnap me?"

"I don't know what he wants, but I don't want to see you hurt."

"Have you figured out who took Lynne and what they want?"

"They seem to want me, for some reason. Drew thinks it's related to my job at the power plant." He couldn't tell her that Ollie said he should expect to be pressured into giving them uranium

"Could it be? Related to your job, I mean."

"It could. I asked Drew to consider his job, too."

"What do you think it means?"

"I don't know," he said. As much as he wanted to tell her, he wouldn't. "But I worry about the safety of the people around me, especially you right now."

"You don't have to worry about me."

"But I do. Can you take some time off? Leave the area for a few days?"

"No. Not if I want to keep my job."

"Then, will you move in with me for a few days?"

"Oh, you'd like that, wouldn't you? Would I be sleeping with you or in Grandpa's old room?"

"You can sleep anywhere you want. I just want you to be safe."

"But I still have to go to work each day. You couldn't be with me all the time."

"What if I drove you to and from work?"

"You still wouldn't be with me all day."

"Okay. What do you suggest?"

"I suggest you don't worry about me. I'm a big girl. I can take care of myself."

"But if we're right, they killed Mom and Dad and have now kidnapped Lynne. They're dangerous."

"I have pepper spray in my purse."

"Have you ever used it?"

"No."

"How long have you had it?"

"Let's see. About six years."

"So, you don't know if it even works, do you?"

"It's okay, Mick. I'll be fine."

Mick finished the last bite of his food, then continued to watch Raquel eat until she finished. When she looked up, Mick was staring at her.

"What?" she asked.

"I love you. Marry me."

"I love you, too, but I'm not quite ready to give up my independence and ambition to own the company. You need to be patient and let me come around, in my own time."

"Are you still interested in going back to my place for a little alone time?" Mick asked.

"How about we go to my place this time? We can still be alone and do anything we can do at your place."

"I'd like that," he said. "So, who's turn is it to pick the activity? Yours or mine."

"It's mine. And I want to play cards."

"You always win when we play cards."

"That's because I make up the rules as we play," she joked and laughed at his expression.

"Alright."

Three days later, two men entered the building where Raquel worked, one of them hanging back by the door, while the other approached the receptionist.

"Where can I find Ms. Raquel Austin," the man asked the receptionist.

"She's down that hall, second door on the right," she said, without looking up from her movie magazine. Then she did look up. She wanted to see what package went with the sexy accent. "Is there something wrong?" she asked.

"No. Thanks." He said and headed in the direction indicated. The other man, who had been holding back, hurried to catch up with him. Raquel's office door was open a crack, so the men pushed the door open and entered.

"Raquel Austin?" he asked, looking between the two women in front of him, then he must have noticed the name plaque on the desk, since he directed his next remark to Raquel.

"Ms. Austin, you need to come with us. Michael has been injured and asked for you."

Raquel was on her feet in an instant, grabbed her purse and jacket and headed for the door.

"What happened?" she asked.

"He's been in an auto accident. He's headed for the hospital and asked us to bring you to him."

"Amy, please tell Mr. Clarke where I've gone. I don't know when I'll be back."

"Sure thing," Amy, her office mate, said.

"Wait," Raquel said. "You called him Michael, not Mick," she said as she passed both men on her way out the door. "Who are you?"

"We were witnesses to the accident."

"You didn't witness Mick in an accident, did you?" Her thoughts drifted to her conversation with Mick, over dinner. Were these men dangerous? She reached into her purse, trying to find her mace.

By then, all three of them were in the hallway. One man grabbed her arm and tried to propel her toward the lobby and the front door. She resisted, so he slapped her face, hard enough to turn her head, then grabbed both her arms and tried to drag her forward. The other man got behind her and pushed.

Raquel dug her heels into the carpet and tried to break free, twisting, turning, jerking her arms and body, and yelling for help.

Amy stuck her head out the door, likely attracted by the commotion, and saw what was happening. She started yelling, too.

"Help! Help!" She yelled.

The receptionist got up and looked down the hallway, seeing the struggle. She hurried back to her desk and got on the phone.

"Get her legs," the first man said, looking around to see the attention they were attracting. At least half a dozen people were watching. A large man started walking quickly toward them from across the lobby.

The second man captured her kicking legs while the first grabbed her under both arms. When they had s firm hold on her, they carried her out the front door.

A security guard appeared in the lobby a few moments later.

"Two men just kidnapped Raquel," Amy said, frantically. "Get out there and rescue her."

The guard seemed at a momentary loss, then left the building, drawing his gun as he reached the door. He was followed by the large man who had hurried across the lobby, looking intently past the guard to see where they were taking Raquel.

An older man entered the lobby from the hallway and Amy

ran up to him. "Mr. Clarke, Raquel just got kidnapped by two men who said her boyfriend was in an auto accident and needed her. They lied to get her out of the office, then picked her up and carried her away."

Mr. Clarke was still trying to process Amy's comments when the security guard returned. His gun was back in his holster and he looked a little disappointed. Mr. Clarke met him halfway.

"Well?" he asked.

"They were double-parked in front of the door. By the time I got out there, they were just pulling away. I could see someone through the back window, struggling, so I figured that was them."

"Did you get . . . ?" Mr. Clarke started to ask, but the guard spoke over him.

"I got a plate number and a description of the car. I'll call it in."

"Thank you." Mr. Clarke said. "Let me know if you need anything." Then Clarke walked away, back toward his office, apparently dismissing the episode from his mind.

"Mr. Clarke!" Amy yelled. He turned back to her.

"Yes, Amy?" he asked.

"Aren't you going to do something? Raquel's been kidnapped."

"What would you like me to do? Stand here and wring my hands with worry. This is a police matter." Then he walked away.

Amy threw her hands in the air, in frustration, but knew Mr. Clarke was right. There was little that they could do besides call the police.

Amy answered Raquel's phone when it rang just before the end of the workday, thinking it might be the police, with news. In her hurry, Raquel had left it on her desk.

"Is Raquel there?" Mick asked, recognizing that Raquel had not answered the phone.

"Is this Mick?" Amy asked.

"It is. Is this Amy?"

"It is. I'm so sorry, Mick."

"Wh . . . ?" Mick started to ask.

"Raquel was kidnapped this morning."

"What?"

"I'm so sorry." Amy told Mick everything she knew, including the name of the guard who tried to help and the name of the police officer who had questioned her earlier. Amy transferred the call to the receptionist and Mick asked to speak to the guard. When he finally had him on the line, he asked the guard to tell him everything he knew. He discovered that the two men had European accents, drove a Shelby GT500, the plate number and the name of the detective the guard had spoken to at the police station.

Mick called the police and spoke to the detective. He explained his interest in the case and gave the detective the name of the investigator in Wendover who was in charge of Lynne's investigation, so they could share and consolidate information. He was certain the two kidnappings were related.

"Why?" the detective asked.

"Why do I think they're related?"

"Yes. That's what I mean."

He had to be careful here. Ollie said he couldn't tell anyone that he was working with the CIA on a case relating to Russian gangsters. So, what could he say?

"I don't know what to say. Give me ten minutes, then call this number and talk to the man who answers." He gave the detective Ollie's number, then called Ollie to prepare him for the call.

"I'm sorry, Ollie," Mick said, after he explained. "I didn't know how much I could say."

"I'll handle it," Ollie said. "Thanks for letting me know."

"What can we do about the two kidnappings?"

"Let me think about that and I'll get back to you."

Mick called Wendover and gave that investigator the name of the Lehi, Utah detective. Mick had just decided to call Drew and bring him up to speed when his phone rang. It was Amy.

"Mick, have your learned anything new?" Amy asked.

"No Amy. What can I do for you?"

"As I was cleaning up the office to go home, I saw a note on Raquel's desk. I don't know how it got there, but it must have been left by the kidnappers. Do you want me to read it to you?"

"Please read it."

"It says: *'We'll trade Ms. Austin for Michael. You'd be wise to accept or you won't see her again.'* There's a phone number at the bottom."

She read it to him. It was the same phone number that was left at the scene of Lynne's kidnapping. Mick called both investigators and gave them the additional information. The Wendover investigator said he was taking the lead on the investigation, so Mick didn't need to call both of them every time something new came up. Mick thanked him and said he would get the note to him in the next few days. The Provo investigator confirmed what the Wendover investigator had told him.

Victor Pachenko

"We now have the sister and the girlfriend." Pachenko said.

"Has he called you?"

"No."

"Then escalate it. Get a tail on him. See if you can get him alone and kidnap him, too. Or do I have to come over there and do this myself?"

"I don't think it's safe for you over here. Your name and face are known. I'll get it done."

"See that you do."

37

Mick drove up from Green River to meet with Drew, two days later, in Provo, as planned.

Mick wanted to meet sooner, but Drew was out of the country and unable to get back. Mick let Drew read the note, then asked what Drew could tell him about what he did for a living that could be related to the kidnappings.

"I can tell you that I'm on a photojournalism team that records what's going on at the front line of military conflicts. I've gone through all of my recent photos and videos and can't see anything that would explain the kidnappings. But I'm willing to entertain ideas. Since both notes refer to you, and it was Raquel who got kidnapped, I'd guess that this is related to what you do at the power plant, Mick."

"I can tell you that I work with uranium," Mick said, "which could be the target of terrorists or other bad guys. However, kidnapping me won't get them the uranium. It's government controlled, and the government would never let it out of their control. They'd swarm the job site and arrest everyone who came on site, but they wouldn't give up the uranium."

"Do you know who these people are?" Drew asked.

"How would I know?" Mick asked. "All I have is a phone number to call when I'm ready to give myself up for whatever they have in mind." He still didn't feel right telling Drew what Ollie had told him. He would have to see how this played out. "I supposed that giving myself up is no guarantee that the women will be released. What do you think?"

"I think that since we have no idea who these people are or what they want, I don't know what to suggest." Drew said.

"Here's something else," Mick said. "I think I'm being followed."

"How can you tell?" Drew asked.

"You met that old widow lady, Mrs. Sloan, who lives two doors down from the Provo house?"

"Yeah. The one who's only son has been trying to get her into a rest home so he can sell her house and spend his inheritance?"

"That's the one. I've been staying at the house for the last three days, since Raquel was kidnapped. There have been cars parked outside her house every night. I noticed that it looked like the same three cars, taking turns. And I've seen them elsewhere as well. In a city this size, you wouldn't think you'd run into the same people so often, Now I've got plate numbers and descriptions. Maybe we can trap them and get information from them."

"That would take too long, time that we may not have." Drew said.

"Alright. I'll give the information to the police. I need to go to Wendover, so I'll bring the investigator up to speed."

"Here's an idea. I've got a work associate in the CIA," Drew said.. "I'll see if there's anything he can do."

"Who is he? I've been wondering who this mysterious man is that offered help. Could it be the same man?"

"It is the same man. His name is Oliver Tanner."

"That's the one."

Brady

"Mick, this is Brady Fairchild," the voice on the phone said.

"Brady! What's up, man? Working for the FBI now?"

"Can't say, bro."

"How is it?"

"Exciting. Challenging. Lots of travel."

"What can I do for you?"

"What ever happened between you and Lydia Hancock?"

"She went home to Atlanta. I've spoken with her, but haven't seen her since."

"Well, hey. I'm travelling later this week. I'll be passing through Atlanta and remembered that Lydia lived there. If you still have her phone number, do you mind if I give her a call to see how she's doing?"

Mick remembered that Lydia thought there was something off with Brady, but it wasn't for him to control who talked to her. If she didn't want to talk to him, he was sure she would just tell him to leave her alone.

"Sure, Brady. It's been a long time since I've spoken with her, so I don't know if it's still a good number."

"If her number has changed, I'll try to find a good number for her." Mick suspected Brady was saying that as a police officer, he could trace Lydia through the Atlanta police. The thought troubled him for a moment—that could be good or bad—but Brady was an FBI agent, so he thought he could be trusted. "I'll let you know if anything's changed."

"Thanks."

Lydia

"Is this Lydia?" Brady asked. Hearing the sweet, howbeit stressed, voice on the phone, he suspected it was. Lydia didn't recognize the phone number, so she hesitated to answer. Brady continued. "This is Brady Fairchild. How are you?"

"I'm very busy, Brady. If you'll excuse me . . ."

"Lydia, I'm passing through Atlanta in a few days and would like to see you."

"I really don't have time, Brady."

"I know you're busy, raising two boys as a single mom. I just want to stop by and say 'hi', see if you need anything."

"How do you know I'm single and have two children?" she asked, becoming concerned. "Are you stalking me?"

"I'm a cop, Lydia. We have access to information."

"You're creeping me out. Leave me alone. I have to go."

"I'll see you in . . ." he said before she disconnected to call.

Ollie

When Mick and Drew met again, three days later, in Provo, Drew had Oliver Tanner with him.

"Mick, this is Ollie. I think he can help us." Drew said. Ollie was a handsome man in his fifties, with shoulder-length hair, a scruffy beard and a pierced ear with a diamond stud in it.

"Oliver Tanner, the man said, holding out his hand for Mick to shake." When he smiled a dimple appeared in one cheek. Neither Ollie nor Mick let on that they had already spoken to each other.

"Pleasure to meet you," Mick said. "What can you do to help?"

"Ollie works for Airforce internal affairs as an investigator. Internal affairs is the team that investigates internal problems."

Mick already knew that Ollie worked for the CIA, so maybe this Air Force thing was a cover for what he really did.

"You mean, like crimes committed by Airforce personnel against Airforce personnel?" Mick asked.

"That's close enough," Ollie said with a wink.

"The point here," Drew said, "is that Ollie is a professional investigator. In this case, what little time he has available to help us will be spent investigating our clues. Can you show him the notes?"

Ollie laid the notes out, side-by-side, then bent over them for a few minutes without commenting. When he looked up, he was smiling.

"What?" Drew asked. "What does that grin mean?"

"There are a couple of things I can do with this information," Ollie said seriously, the corners of his mouth lifting a bit. "One: We need to know what Mick does at the power plant. I agree that is the key to solving the mystery. Two: We need to check that phone number. I suspect that will be a dead-end, but we should check to make sure. Three: We need to check the connection with the cars. If you don't know, the GT500 is a limited-edition car. There are a couple of variations on the Shelby, like the 'super snake', but there were so few of them manufactured, that we can consider them at the same time. Besides, they're just variations of the Shelby. My point is that the Shelby is traceable. If we had a little more of a description, I might be able to identify an owner."

"How about a plate number?" Mick asked.

"That would help."

Mick gave Ollie the plate number of the car used to kidnap Raquel. "What about the cars following me?" Mick asked.

"That one's easy," Ollie said. "Drew showed me the descriptions and I ran them through our database. All three are rentals, the renters are fictitious. They don't exist."

"If they don't exist, how did they rent cars? Isn't photo ID required to rent a car?"

"It is, but ID's can be faked. In this case, we already have two of the fake IDs in the system. We don't know who owns them, yet, but we've seen them before and we have photos. That may help us track them down."

"Are you going to arrest and question them?" Mick asked.

"Sorry Mick. The CIA doesn't operate domestically," Ollie said. "That's a job for local police or, maybe the FBI, if a federal crime has been committed. I can't do anything about them."

"Is kidnapping two women considered a federal crime?"

"If they're linked, it could be considered a serial kidnapping, which is a federal crime."

"Then we could get the FBI involved, right?"

"Yes, you could, if you want to go that way."

"How can we help?" Drew asked, becoming excited that they had a new way forward.

"Mick, what is there at your construction site that a criminal might want?" Ollie asked.

"You mean, besides uranium?" Mick asked. "I can't think of anything. There are tools and supplies, welding equipment, that sort of thing; but nothing special or valuable."

"The uranium, then. I'll see if I can find any leads on uranium or the Shelby. Give me two days to see what I can find, then we'll decide if we need to go another direction."

The next day, Mick went to Wendover to give the original note from the kidnappers to the police investigator and to see what they had learned, if anything. They had nothing new, but had spoken with Mick's security manager and several others that he interfaced with at the plant. They had also interviewed the people who worked with Raquel. They had also spoken with Ollie and he had shared what he had found thus far.

At least he's being thorough, Mick thought, even if he hasn't made much progress. As Mick was leaving the police station, sometime later, he noticed a box on the hood of his car that someone must have placed there and forgot to take with them when they left. He debated just setting the closed box on the ground and leaving. Then he thought maybe he should take it into the station.

In the end, he took a quick look inside and saw that it contained the outfit of a cocktail waitress from the casino, like the clothes Lynne would have been wearing when she was kidnapped. Suspicious now, he looked further and confirmed that it was women's clothes, the kind the workers at the casinos wore, including underwear and shoes, just like Lynne's favorite shoes and monogrammed panties. It could be a coincidence, but he didn't think so. These were Lynne's clothes. Which meant that the kidnappers had taken them from her. Or, she had given them up voluntarily.

Mick took the box of clothes into the station and reported what he thought he had found. The police investigator put the new evidence into evidence bags and tagged them, then excused Mick.

Mick and Drew met with Ollie the next day, before Drew left for Europe again. Mick told them what he had found and how the police had dismissed him without so much as a 'thank you'. He was still upset about it. They listened politely, then Ollie asked if they were ready for what he had found.

38

"Yes?" Lydia asked the man standing outside her front door.

"Hi Lydia. Remember me?" A pause, while Lydia considered how to answer Brady. She knew who he was, but she remembered that she didn't trust him.

"Brady Fairchild?" Another pause. "From Utah?" Pause. "I spoke to you the other day?"

"I remember you, Brady," Lydia finally said. "Why are you here? I thought I told you I didn't want to talk to you"

"I told you if I was ever passing through, I'd stop and see how you're doing. Well, here I am."

"I see. I'm doing fine. Was that all?" She made to close the door in his face, knowing it wasn't polite, but not particularly caring.

"Wait!" Brady said, placing his hand on the door to prevent Lydia from closing it. "Can I come in for a visit?"

"This isn't a good time. I'm just putting the baby down for a nap. I need to go check on him."

"I can wait while you check on him."

Frustrated, but feeling at a loss for how to deal with Brady, Lydia left the door open and walked away from it, toward the back of the small house. Brady stepped inside and closed the door behind him. When he turned back around, he saw how small the house was. He was standing in a small entry, which opened immediately into a small living room. To the right was a small kitchen-dining room. Straight ahead was a short, narrow hallway that led to the back of the house.

Brady could see two doorways off of the hall, one on each side, presumably bedrooms, one of which Lydia had entered. At the end of the hall was a third doorway, which was most likely a bathroom. He hadn't noticed basement windows as he approached the house, so what he saw was most likely the entire house.

"When will your husband be home?" Brady asked when Lydia returned a few minutes later and stood in the entry, rather than sitting down.

"There is no husband," Lydia said, reluctantly, after a pregnant pause. Why was that the first thing he wanted to know?

"The baby's father?" Brady continued, awkwardly.

"Not around." Lydia said, having already committed herself to answering his questions.

"Are you doing okay? Do you need anything?"

Nothing you can give me, she thought. Or rather, nothing I want from you. "No," she said.

"You sound hostile," Brady said, obviously noticing her reluctance to open up to him. "Have I offended you?"

Lydia didn't know what to say. She just wanted him to leave and let her get back to her life, as simple and unfulfilling as it was.

"I'm sorry, Brady. It's nothing you've done. I'm just struggling right now."

"Is there something I can do to help?" Brady said as he stood from the couch to stand next to her.

Too close, she thought. I don't want him that close, but I need to be nice.

"Let me do something to help," Brady said as he reached an arm around Lydia and tried to kiss her.

Lydia put both her hands on his chest and tried to force him away. He was too strong for her.

"What are you doing Brady?" she asked, alarmed. "Leave me alone."

"Give me a kiss."

"Get away from me."

"One little kiss?"

"Get away!" She was starting to panic. "I don't want your attention."

"Waaahhh!" came a tiny, angry voice from down the hall. Brady stopped moving, but didn't let go.

"Let me go, Brady!" Lydia insisted. "Ike needs me. My baby needs me."

"Ike?" Brady asked.

"His name is Isaac. Named after his father, good riddance."

"He left you?"

"Uh huh. A year ago."

She pushed away from him and went to the bedroom. She returned, cradling her baby in her arms and holding the hand of a boy a little older. "This is Ike," she said, turning her head towards the baby. "And this is Micky," turning her head the other way, toward the toddler.

"As in, Mick Swensen is the father?"

Lydia stared at him, wondering if she shouldn't have given Brady the boy's name. She didn't answer him.

"They're cute," Brady said. "I can see the resemblance to you, but not to Mick."

"It's in his eyes and ears; the shape of his head," she said.

"Now about that kiss."

"Brady," Lydia said angrily, "I didn't want to let you in. I didn't want your attention. I thought you worked for the FBI; so why are you harassing me."

"I'm not . . ." Brady started to say, taken back by her accusation.

"Please leave."

"Alright. I'm going. I'm glad you're doing well. Call me if you need anything." He pulled a business card out of his shirt pocket and dropped it on the couch where he'd been sitting.

Like that's going to happen, she thought, not bothering to pick up the card. He let himself out and she locked the door behind him, then went to the kitchen to prepare food for her family.

39

Ollie started his report with an explanation that he couldn't reveal his sources and that his information was only as good as the sources, which made him about eighty percent confident in the information. Drew smiled knowingly, Mick's lips formed a straight line across his face, his expression bland.

"What?" Mick asked Drew.

"What Ollie's not saying is that his information is at least eighty percent accurate. More likely one hundred percent."

It was Ollie's turn to smile.

"Here's a list of known Shelby owners," Ollie said. "This list accounts for about seventy-five percent of all Shelby's known to still be in operation. Notice the two names I've underlined. This one is a technology company in Italy that has a fleet of seventeen Shelby's, all owed by the owner of the company, a flamboyant billionaire who likes to show off his wealth. This one is a Russian industrialist, part of the new Russian KGB."

"I thought the KGB was dissolved when the Soviet Union disintegrated," Mick said.

"We thought so, too, but they just reorganized under new leadership. The former KGB became the Russian Mafia, then industrialists, who were treated like royalty because of their role in the former establishment. They were given favored treatment in the transition to a market economy. The Russian, Dmitri Pavlovich, has seven of the cars. No one else on the list owns more than three, and some of those are in collections or travelling shows."

"So, are you saying one of those two, the Italian or the Russian, are responsible for the kidnappings?" Mick asked.

"No!" Ollie said, but his wink to Mick let Mick know this was the information they had talked about—this was the Russian they were after. "This is just the first step in the search. Now we have a possible link to a motive. Now we look into those two to see what else we can learn about them."

"How do we do that?"

"Already started. I'm waiting for background checks on the Italian billionaire and Pavlovich, as well as two others on the list who I have dealt with before on other criminal investigations. I should have that information in the next day or two, three at the outside. By the way, the plate number you gave me for the car that kidnapped your girlfriend does not match any of the Shelbys on the list. It belongs to a car that was reported stolen a few weeks ago in Denver."

"So, we can't trace the kidnapping to any of the owners?"

"I'm afraid not. Sorry. What did your father do for a living?"

"He and our mother worked together for a wholesale conglomerate, mostly managing global markets, why?"

"What if I told you that was a cover story for what they really did?"

"What do you mean?" Drew asked.

"Drew, what I'm about to tell you is government classified. You have to promise me that you will tell no one, not even family. Will you agree to that?"

"Yes," both men said, even though Mick had already been sworn to secrecy. He wondered if Ollie was going to repeat the things he had already heard, or share something new. "Okay, that was their cover story. I knew both of them. They worked for the

CIA. Your dad flew recon flights over eastern Europe and the Mediterranean, including southern Russia. He also participated in several missions around the world, the nature of which I can't share with you, since the details of the missions are classified. Your mother was a courier of messages to CIA posts around the world. I can't share any of the information in her mission files either. Some of them are classified Top Secret and sealed. I think there's a good chance what's going on with you now is related to your parents."

"Wow, that's heavy," Drew said. "You really think so?"

"Your parents were CIA agents with deep cover. The Russians have long memories. Some of their missions cross generations. If they're involved, this could be one of them."

"What would our parents have been doing that would make the Russians interested in us?" Drew asked.

"Not sure," Ollie said. "We know that this particular Russian sells weapons to our enemies in the Middle East. It's possible they think one of you has access to something that they want."

"You mean, like, Uranium?" Drew guessed, looking at Mick.

"Maybe. That gives me another idea. The NTSB would have handled the investigation into the plane crash, but who had jurisdiction over the auto accident your parents were involved in just before the plane crash?"

"The Utah County sheriff's office, why?"

"Did they ever figure out what caused the accident?"

"They thought Dad had run the other guy off the road, but couldn't prove it, so it was dropped. No one ever filed a complaint against him. And the damage to Dad's car showed that the cars had collided, possibly competed for space on the road, before the one went off the cliff," Drew said. "I asked the investigator if the other car could have instigated it. He squirmed, like he thought it was a possibility, but they couldn't find enough evidence to pursue it. It was easier for them to call it a no-fault accident."

"I'll see what I can find out about that, too."

"Thanks Ollie. Are you free for dinner tonight or tomorrow?"

"Sure. Tomorrow would be great. Where are you staying, in case I need to get in touch with you?"

"We're both staying at the Provo house for now, until we get this settled," Drew said.

Mick looked frazzled when he arrived at the restaurant twenty minutes late the next evening.

"What took you?" Drew asked. "Ollie is on a timeline."

"Sorry about that. I ran into a problem."

"A girl problem?"

"I wish. No, I think I was being followed. I had to ditch the tail."

"Why do you think that?"

"One of the same three cars pulled out behind me as I left the house. I took several turns through the city, including illegal turns, running stop signs and speeding. He stayed with me until I ran in front of a semi-truck on University Avenue that honked and almost hit me. The tail had to stop for it or run into it. By the time the truck passed and he was able to continue, I was long gone."

"You didn't get stopped by the Provo police?" Drew asked as Ollie smiled, likely at Mick's confession.

"I was surprised I didn't get stopped by the police. They always seem to be there when you don't want them, but now, when I would have welcomed one, I didn't see any."

"But you lost the tail." Ollie said, confirming.

"Yeah. Drew, I'm being sent to Florida on a fact-finding mission for the NRC. I'll be gone two or three days. I have to leave in the morning."

"Okay. Call me when you're back in town. We'll compare notes and see where we are," Drew said.

"What about the phone number on the notes?" Mick asked Ollie.

"Thanks for reminding me, Mick," Ollie said. "Another dead-end. It's a burner phone that will disappear as soon as we try to track it. Sorry."

"Fine. What else do we have?"

"I'm still trying to identify the drivers of the three cars. I also want to talk to your security manager about the situation at the site."

"Keep us informed?" Drew asked.

"Naturally."

40

He caught his flight, a Delta 767 through Atlanta to Miami. During his layover in Atlanta, he thought about Lydia Hancock. He had thought at one time that he might love her and have a long-term relationship with her. She seemed willing and interested, too. Before she told him she had to go home to Atlanta, he had planned to pursue that. Unfortunately, her parents had resolved their issues, at least as far as he knew, and wanted her home. Now, he wondered what she was up to. A lot of time had passed; about four years, so he wondered if he would still have the same feelings for her. He wondered if they could pick up where they had left off, or if one or both of them had moved on. If so, there would be no emotional draw between them.

Considering everything going on at home, especially his feeling that everyone around him was at risk, he thought it would be a bad idea to get mixed up with her right now. Brady Fairchild had said he would look her up, but he hadn't called back to tell Mick whether or not he saw her, or how they had made out. He wandered around the airport, found the gate for his flight to Miami, then wandered some more. In the end, he called her.

"Lydia," he said when she answered. Her voice was as soft and velvety as he remembered. "It's Mick." From her initial hesitation, he wondered if he would have to explain who he was.

"Oh Mick," she said. "It's so good to hear your voice. Where are you?"

"I'm at the airport." He didn't know what else to say. Getting together needed to be her idea, if she was even interested and available.

"Do you have time to come and see me?" She asked.

"I'm on a short layover, on my way to a meeting in Florida."

"Oh." She sounded disappointed.

"But I'll be coming back through day after tomorrow and have a bigger layover. In fact, I can arrange to stay in town overnight if I need to."

"That would be wonderful Mick. Let me give you my address. Just come over when you can. I'll have the house cleaned up by then so you're not embarrassed to see me."

"Not possible," Mick said. "See you in two days."

Mick met with representatives of Florida Power, who were building another one of the new nuclear power plants. The conference went well. He was able to get a tour of the power plant and compare notes with their project manager. They were impressed that Mick's plant was finished and in operation and had lots of questions for him about the start-up and operation. He spent several hours with them, then returned to Atlanta.

He rented a car with GPS and headed for Lydia's house, still wondering if this was such a good idea.

Her house was a small rambler, sandwiched between two similar houses, on a small neighborhood street. He guessed it to be about nine hundred square feet, a two-bedroom bungalow. He parked in the driveway, where the concrete was cracked and spalling, the tiny yard boasted two flower beds and not much grass. The screen on the door had a fist-sized hole in it.

He pressed the doorbell and heard it ring in the house. The front door must have a hollow core, not well insulated. The rest of the house may be as poorly insulated.

He wasn't sure what to expect, it had been so long since they'd last spoken to each other. He could see a shadow pass by the peephole, then Lydia threw open the door.

"Mick!" she said excitedly. She looked as beautiful as he remembered, in a simple white blouse and red skirt. But her face looked careworn and tired. She fussed with her hair and patted down her skirt self-consciously. "Would you like to come in?" she asked as she opened the screen door.

"I'm sorry it's taken me so long to come and see you," he said as he stepped inside.

He looked around, seeing the poor condition of everything in the house. It was clean, but looked old and run down, worn out. When he looked back at Lydia, he could see the dark lines under her eyes, the sag of her shoulders. She looked worn out too.

"Are you okay?" Mick asked.

"Just tired."

"Are you here by yourself?" Better to find out right away if there was a husband or boyfriend.

"Just me and my two boys."

"No husband?"

"He's been gone for almost a year. Decided he didn't want a family."

"I'm sorry."

"Don't be." Just then, Mick heard the sound of children playing.

"Sounds like they're not asleep, like they're supposed to be," she said. "Why don't you come and meet them?"

"Do you own the house," he asked as they walked toward the back bedrooms, "or are you renting?"

"You remember that my parents were dealing with marriage issues?"

"Yes. You said they resolved them."

"Well, it didn't last. They divorced a few months later. Dad left first, then Mom turned the house over to me and moved to Mississippi to live with her sister. She wrote me recently and said she was in the process of deeding it to me. I don't work, so I have no way to pay rent. Keeping us fed is a full-time effort."

"I'm sorry, Lydia. How can to help?" Mick asked as they entered a bedroom where two small boys bounced on a twin bed in one corner of the small room. A crib sat in another corner of the room. A colorful mobile twisted lazily above the crib.

"Don't worry about us, Mick," Lydia said as she grinned at the boys, lovingly. The older boy collapsed on the bed and began to laugh. The younger one watched his brother for a moment, then did the same. "We get help from the local churches and food bank. We don't have other expenses."

"You're supposed to be asleep," she said, mock anger in her voice. Then her face split into a wide grin, love obvious in her expression. "Let me introduce you to Mick."

She turned on a light and two small boys covered their eyes with their arms to block the sudden light.

She pointed at each in turn. "Ike is two and Micky is three."

"Micky?" Mick asked.

"Named after you. I'm pretty sure he's yours."

"How is that possible?"

"The timing is perfect for the week of your induction ceremony."

"I'm so sorry, Lydia. I would never have intentionally done that to you."

"It's alright, Mick. We were both inexperienced back then. I love my little Micky. He reminds me of my first time and the love you made me feel. You were the perfect gentleman; the perfect first time."

"Micky," Mick heard a small voice say, He turned to look and saw that Micky was pointing to his chest. "Micky," he said again.

Mick walked over to the bed where Micky sat with his legs tucked under him, smiling beautifully. He ruffled Micky's hair and pointed to Micky's chest, then at his own. "Micky . . .Mick," he said. Micky's smile widened to stretch all the way across his face.

"I like you," Mick said.

"I love you," Micky said.

"You look like you're struggling," Mick said to Lydia. "Is there anything you need?" He was ready to give her money if she asked. He reached for the wallet in his back pocket.

"We're doing fine. Really." She must have noticed him reaching for his wallet and figured out his intent, as she shook her head vigorously and waved her hand at him. "The house was given to me. My ex sends money every month. We don't have many expenses. Please don't feel guilty or that you owe me anything."

"How can I not feel responsible?"

"It takes two, Mick. But, since you're here, there is something you can do for me."

"What is it? I'll do anything."

"Stay with me tonight. Make love to me. No strings attached. No regrets."

Mick studied her for a long time, trying to understand her thinking. His thoughts went immediately to Raquel, whom he thought he loved and wanted to marry. Would that be fair to Raquel?

"Seriously, Mick. I haven't felt truly loved since that week with you. All I want from you is your love, this one time, then we can forget each other."

"I'll never forget you, Lydia, and I'll always feel responsible. I'll do what I can to help."

"Are you hungry?" she asked, as they left the boys' room. "Do you want me to fix you something to eat?"

"I ate on the plane. I'm fine."

Lydia got the boys ready for bed, with Mick's help. She lay between them on the bed and read them a story from a children's Bible story book, then knelt by the bed with them to pray.

"Thank you, Father, for bringing Mick to visit us and protect him as he travels home," she said as part of the prayer. The boys repeated her words, as much as they were able. She put them into their respective beds, kissed each one good-night and moved to the bedroom door. Micky sat up and held his arms out to Mick.

"Good-night kiss?" he asked. Mick gave each of the boys a hug and kiss on the forehead, then helped them lay down again, covering them with their blankets. He joined a smiling Lydia at the door, where she turned out the light and closed the door most of the way. She led Mick to the front room couch, where they sat side-by-side.

"Lydia?" he started to say, wondering how he could tell her about Raquel.

"It's okay Mick. We don't have to," she said, as though reading his mind. "I just thought it would be a nice memory. Our last time together."

He realized he didn't want this to be their last time together. "Lydia, I think I still love you."

"I know I love you."

"I just don't know what to do about it."

"It's okay."

He took her in his arms and kissed her passionately. She returned the kiss, then stood and took his hand. She led him to her bedroom, where they spent the night together. The next morning, Lydia made him breakfast, then kissed him one last time before he got in his rental car and drove back to the airport.

41

Provo, Utah

Back in Utah, Mick called Drew.

"Ollie's in the hospital," Drew said immediately. "Meet me there."

"Are you okay?" Drew asked Ollie, who lay on a hospital bed with one leg in a cast and elevated. He had one hand wrapped, an IV in the other arm, and bruises on his face and arms.

"Broken leg, busted hand, bruises and cuts. Nothing wrong with my head. I was T-boned by an SUV on my way back from the County Sheriff's office. They say I'm lucky to be alive. Although I'm not tickled to be in the hospital, I think it means we're on the right track."

"So, what did you find?"

"There was evidence, which didn't come out in the inquest, of bright blue paint on the right side of your parents' car. They recovered a paint sample, which they traced to a Shelby-exclusive paint. The Shelby was so badly burned that the investigators decided they couldn't be positive that's what it was, that they had the color pegged, or that it wasn't from a prior accident. They didn't pursue it since no one came forward to claim damage to their Shelby, and they had evidence that the car was doing forty-five miles per hour in a thirty-five-mile zone." The investigator thought that maybe the two cars had a drag race—running side-by-side down the road—and the Shelby lost.

"I'll be in here for a couple more days, then I need to check in at the office, so it will take me some time to get back to you on the Shelby owners, but don't fret. We're on the right track."

"Did you find anything on the car that kidnapped Raquel?" Mick asked.

Stolen plates. Sorry.

"You get some rest," Drew said to Ollie. "I'll check on you tomorrow."

Mick and Drew walked to the parking lot together. There was a box on the hood of Mick's car. He groaned, suspecting and dreading what he would find in it. Sure enough, it contained a complete woman's outfit, including underwear, shoes and thigh-high stockings and garter belt—Mick knew Raquel didn't like panty-hose—and a handkerchief like Raquel always carried. There was another note, which read;

You're running out of time, Michael. Call me before we start taking it out on your sister and girlfriend. The same phone number was at the end of the note.

"What do we do?" Mick groaned.

"Can we trace the phone number?" Drew asked.

"Ollie already said it was a burner phone. If we want to pursue it, I don't know how, but I have a frat brother who's an agent with the FBI. Ollie said this could be considered a serial kidnapping, so the FBI should help. He may not be able to do anything, but maybe he can point us in the right direction. I'll talk to him and let you know."

Brady

The next day, Mick called Drew to tell him his FBI friend, Brady Fairchild, had checked the phone number.

"He confirmed that it's a prepaid, burner phone, one that someone buys, uses once, then throws away, so it can't be traced.

It's a dead-end," Mick told Drew, "unless we want to spend a lot of money or try to talk the FBI into opening a case file to investigate it."

"You are the FBI, aren't you?" Mick had asked Brady, knowing he was kicking a dead horse. The FBI wasn't interested in pursuing this cold case and wouldn't voluntarily dedicate resources and time to it.

"Feel free to call again when you have another question," Brady said without answering Mick's question.

"Sorry, Brady. That wasn't fair. How about this? Both my sister and my girlfriend have been kidnapped in the last few weeks, and I'm being followed."

"And why are you just telling me?"

"I didn't think you could help."

"I can't help if you don't tell me what's going on."

"Let me buy you lunch and I'll give you all the details."

"You're on," Brady said, so they met for lunch.

Mick showed Brady the kidnappers' messages and the description of the three tail cars.

"Our investigator has already checked the cars and confirmed that's a dead-end. He's also trying to figure out the source of the messages."

"What has he discovered about the messages?"

"There's nothing in the messages that give us any clue," Mick said, "and we can't think of anyone who has a grudge against me or my family, who would do such a thing." Mick told Brady about the Mustang Shelby tie-in, the Russian and the Italian Tech firm. He also mentioned what Ollie had learned about the accident nineteen years earlier that his parents had been in. He also mentioned the plane crash and his question about whether or not it was shot down. Brady listened intently, made a few notes on his phone, and promised to see what else he could find out. Since the NTSB had ruled the plane crash an accident, he didn't think there was anything he could find out there.

"So, who is the investigator you hired to get all this information?" Brady asked.

Mick told him about Ollie, the internal investigator from Air force internal affairs, who was doing it as a favor. He purposely didn't tell Brady that Ollie was CIA. "He's currently in the Utah County Regional Hospital, recovering from an auto accident. I'm going to see him again tomorrow, to see when he'll be released."

"Is his accident tied in, in some way?"

"Unknown, but I wouldn't be surprised. This thing just gets crazier all the time."

When Drew and Mick met at the hospital to visit Ollie, Brady had already been to see him.

"Your FBI friend was here," Ollie said. "We don't normally share information between the two agencies, but I don't think he knew who I work for."

"I didn't tell him," Mick said.

"Thanks for that. I want to keep it that way."

"I'm sorry," Mick said. "I should have asked you if it was okay to share with him."

"I'm not angry, but I couldn't share everything I know, just as he hasn't shared everything he knows with you."

"What did he say?" Drew asked.

"He said he was suspicious of the way the investigation was handled nineteen years earlier and is going to check into it," Ollie said. "I told him I have an associate checking our files on the Russian, the Italian tech firm and your parents, to see if there are any links between them, or any other information that is relevant."

"Oh, and I added the police investigators to the list I gave Agent Fairchild, both those who investigated my accident and those who investigated your parents' accident, just for good measure. I'm becoming paranoid because of all the coincidences."

"How about adding everyone who's involved in any of the investigations?" Mick asked.

"What about your friend, Brady?" Ollie asked.

"He didn't know anything when I spoke to him, so I don't see how he could be involved. But he won't investigate himself. You'd have to do that."

"So, you don't want me to investigate him? Or, you want to leave it up to me to decide?"

"I don't know. He's FBI. He's got to be clean. But you decide."

"Okay."

Ollie was out of the hospital two days later and flew back to Virginia. The same day, Mick was stopped by the police and he was threatened with arrest.

"Get out of the car," the officer said when he approached the car window after he'd pulled Mick over.

"Have I done something wrong?" Mick asked.

A second police car pulled up in front of Mick and two more officers approached from that car. Mick started to open his door and the first officer jerked it out of his hand, pulled Mick out of the car by his arm, and threw him up against his car.

"Put your hands on top of the car," he told Mick, sternly, and kicked his feet apart, roughly. Then he frisked him. Mick tried to talk to the officer, turning slightly to look at him, but the officer shoved him in the midsection, knocking the wind out of him.

"Did you see him resisting?" the first officer asked the approaching officers.

One of them started to say something, when the first officer slugged Mick in the kidney. Mick started to double over in pain, but the officer wouldn't let him. He pulled him back up and slugged him in the other kidney. Mick collapsed to the ground and the officer was on him immediately, kneeling on his back.

"Can't breathe," Mick gasped. The officer slapped him across the back of the head, then stood, yanking Mick up by one arm and pushing him toward the waiting police car.

"Do you have to be so rough?" one of the other officers asked.

"He resisted arrest," the first officer said.

"What did he do? Why are you arresting him?"

"Routine traffic stop, suspicion of drugs and alcohol."

"Did you find any?"

"I didn't finish my search. I'll have his car impounded and finish. Meanwhile, this guy needs to spend some time in lockup."

"Wait a sec, Jim," the third officer said, pulling the first officer off to the side, out of earshot. "I recognize this guy. His picture has been in the papers. He's the project manager at the nuclear power plant in Green River."

"Then he should know better than to have drugs and alcohol in his car, or to resist arrest."

"I think you're being a little hasty here, Jim. Let's work together to complete the search, before we arrest him. I'd hate to see you hit with a false arrest charge."

Officer Jim scowled, looked over at Mick, then back to his fellow officer, finally relenting.

"Okay, let's get this over quick, so I can get this guy to lockup. I just know there's something off with him."

Officer Jim told Mick to stand where he was while he searched the inside of the car. Another officer got a flashlight and looked under the car, while the third popped the trunk. The trunk was not only empty, but vacuumed clean. The underside was clean. Jim checked.in all the nooks and crannies inside the car, then pulled the back bench seat out and left it for Mick to figure out how to put it back together. They found nothing wrong; no alcohol, no drugs, nothing for which Mick could be arrested, or even scolded.

As a final affront, Officer Jim gave Mick a breathalyzer test. He was clean. He let Mick go, but he didn't apologize. "Stay out of trouble," he said.

"You're welcome, officer," Mick said, fully expecting Officer Jim to arrest him for talking back. He didn't, but he scowled at Mick before getting back in his patrol car.

42

"For this exercise," the trainer said to the four men, agents-in-training, standing in front of him in a row, "our team, the Blue team, will be kidnappers and the other team, the Red team, will be the rescuers. We'll be kidnapping a female agent from her home in Atlanta and taking her to a secret location to wait. The Red team will use any and all resources to find you and rescue the hostage. For this exercise, you will be Able, Baker, Charlie and Delta," he added, pointing at each of them in turn. "Able will be the lead and the decision-maker. The rest of you will do what he says without question. I will be monitoring your progress periodically through the lapel mic that Able will wear."

"A question," Able said, raising his hand in the air. When the instructor acknowledged him, he continued. "Does the hostage know what's going on?"

"She has been fully briefed on the exercise. However, since this is training, she will pretend like she would in a real hostage situation. So don't treat her like another agent. Do not break character. This exercise will go much smoother if you treat it like a true hostage situation."

"Another question?" Charlie asked. "What if someone gets hurt?"

"I don't want anyone hurt. In fact, empty your guns and leave all the ammo here. No knives or other weapons that could accidentally get in the way."

"Is that realistic?" Charlie asked.

"It doesn't matter if it's realistic. This early in your training, I don't want anyone in harm's way. You can take your guns for appearances, but no ammo." All four men emptied their weapons and set the ammo aside.

"Here's the address of the hostage and here's the address of the apartment where you will hold her until the rescue team shows up," the instructor said as he handed Able a slip of paper. "This was set up by someone else, so I haven't checked the locations. Check them out on your GPS before you start, so you don't have trouble finding them."

"How long is the exercise?" Delta asked.

"Do you have a hot date or something, Delta? Just stay put until they get there, whether it's an hour, a day, or longer. The apartment is fully stocked with food and drink, so you shouldn't run out of anything."

Drew

Mick told Drew about being stopped by the police.

"Could that be involved somehow?" Drew asked, then called Ollie and put him on speaker phone. He told Ollie what Mick had said. "Do you think you can check it out?"

"I'll see what I can find out," Ollie said, "While I have you on the phone, let me tell you that your father, Mick, crossed paths with Pavlovich a couple of times during his career, most recently the year before the accident. I was warned at the office not to pursue the connection with Pavlovich. I wasn't told why, It's a sealed file."

"So, what can we do?" Drew asked Ollie.

"I think we should tell the media," Mick said. "If there's a conspiracy involving the CIA, I want to blow the lid off of it. This is our parents we're talking about"

"I don't think that's a good idea," Ollie said, thinking about the advice to leave it alone. "However, maybe there's something we can do to bring this to a head. It could backfire on us and become dangerous for you, but if you're willing, it might be worth a try. Something else. I got a call from an agent I know in our Atlanta office. He said they got a call from someone and mentioned your name, Mick."

"Really? What did he say?" Mick asked

"A lady by the name of Lydia Hancock has been kidnapped and they want to meet with you to discuss it."

"Lydia? How did they even know that I know her?"

"Have you been to see her lately?" Ollie asked.

"Actually, I saw her last week, for the first time in four years. On my way home from Florida. Someone must be following me cross-country."

"You think it's related?"

"I'm convinced it is. The three most important women in my life have all been kidnapped because of me. What do you think this does to my self-image?"

"Relax, Mick," Drew said. "What can we do, Ollie?"

"We've already got a team in Atlanta looking for her. I'll keep in touch with them and let you know how they're doing."

"What about her kids?" Mick asked.

"I didn't hear anything about kids," Ollie said. "She has kids at home?"

"Two boys, ages two and three. They can't be left home alone. Can you send someone over there to check on them? Stay with them?"

"We're not a babysitting service," Ollie said, "but let me see what I can do."

"I'll reimburse you for any expenses," Mick said, having already thought about what he wanted to do when he got access to his inheritance on his birthday, which was coming up in a few weeks.

Another Kidnapping

"Mommy," little Micky said, "there are men at the door."

"Who are . . .," Lydia started to ask as she came up behind Micky and the open front door. She didn't get to complete the sentence. Three men in dark clothes, dark glasses and ball caps, pushed into the house and grabbed her. Before she had even formed a protest, they were dragging her outside and toward a black SUV that sat, running, at the curb. She was thrown into the back seat, her arms flailing and dragging her feet, then the three men climbed into the SUV to join another who was behind the wheel. Then the SUV pulled away quickly. Lydia tried to look back at the front door where she suspected Micky was standing, looking through the screen and crying.

"Who are you and what are you doing?" Lydia asked angrily.

"You don't need to know who we are and I think it's obvious what we're doing," the driver said. He seemed to be the one in charge. "We're kidnapping you."

"I don't have any money and I don't know anyone who does, if that's what you're looking for."

"No more talking. Just sit back and enjoy the ride."

"I can't. You've kidnapped me and left my children home alone to fend for themselves. Let me go. I won't tell anyone what you've done."

"Sorry, but we only need you."

Maria

Maria Smith watched through her front window as three men dragged her across-the-street neighbor, Lydia Hancock, out her front door and pushed her into an SUV waiting at the curb. Maria could see Lydia's son standing inside the screen door, crying. When the SUV was gone, she went across the street and let herself in.

"Micky," he said. "Where's Ike?"

"In the bedroom."

"Let's go check on him, okay?"

"Okay," He said, sniffling.

Maria convinced the boys to go with her to her house, where she sat them at the kitchen table, with a slice of white bread each, then called 9-1-1.

"9-1-1. What's your emergency?"

"I think my neighbor has been kidnapped."

"What is your name and address?"

"Maria Smith, 468 Centennial."

"Is that the same address as the kidnapping?"

"No, it's across the street, at 477 Centennial."

"I have dispatched officers to the scene. Please stay on the line until they arrive."

"Yes, mam."

A few minutes later, two police cars arrive in front of Lydia's house and four officer stepped out. One headed toward Maria's house while the other three went to Lydia's front door, which was still standing open.

Maria met the female officer in the street and they walked together back toward Lydia's.

"I was told she has two small children," the officer said.

"I took both of them to my house for now."

"So, you've been in the house?"

"Just to get the boys. I didn't touch anything, but I did walk back to the bedroom to get the younger one."

"Fine. Can you keep the children until we can get back to you?"

"No problem."

Back at her own house, Maria thought about who else she should call. She knew Lydia was estranged from her parents, who were divorced. Maria didn't know how to contact either of them. The only other person she knew in Atlanta was her own father-in-law, Wren Smith, who she thought worked for the CIA.

43

Twenty years earlier—Maria

When Taylor and Mary Swensen had convinced Gaetano de Sousa and his girlfriend, Paulina, to accept CIA protection and travel to a safehouse in Florida, Paulina's mother and little sister had gone with them to avoid any fallout from the civil war that they expected within the Mexican drug cartel. Two months after their departure from Rio de Janeiro, the drug cartel had disintegrated from within and the drug lord was dead, by the hands of his own men, along with about ninety percent of the others in the cartel. Most of them were either dead or defected to other cartels.

Gaetano and Paulina returned to Rio to go back to work, Gaetano as an entertainer and owner of the Clube Divino, Paulina as a super model. Their popularity had suffered little by their two-month disappearance. In fact, media and fans were intrigued by the disappearance and flocked to see them and try to learn anything about it.

Paulina's mother, Maria Penha da Costa and her sister, Maria de Jesus da Costa chose to remain in Florida, where they were protected by the CIA agent, Wren Smith.

Agent Smith, out of the Atlanta field office, convinced mother and daughter to move to Atlanta, so he could continue to watch and help them integrate into society. The daughter fell in love with and married Agent Smith's son. They moved into a small home at 468 Centennial. It was the same Maria who had witnessed Lydia's kidnapping.

44

Present day—Maria

Maria called her father-in-law and told him about the kidnapping. Agent Smith told his boss about it, then looked up the case file on Gaetano and Paulina, to see if there was anything else he should do. In the case file he saw the names, Taylor Swensen and Oliver Tanner. He knew Tanner was once a trainer and handler of field agents. He confirmed that Ollie was still active, so he called and let him know what had happened.

Lydia

The FBI agents-in-training took Lydia to a three-story apartment building and dragged her into the basement apartment. It was simply furnished; very little furniture. They pushed her toward a couch, then pushed her onto the couch.

"Stay there!" one man said.

Lydia looked around, trying to figure out a way to get away, but the men were aware of her every glance and movement.

"Don't try anything stupid. I wouldn't want to hurt you."

Maria

The Atlanta station chief sent a female agent to Maria's home to check on Lydia's two boys.

"You must be Maria," the agent said. "I was sent by your father-in-law to check on the boys. How are they doing?"

"I've fed and changed them. They're ready for bed. I have a

spare room I can put them in for tonight. Is Wren working to get their mother back?"

"He is. I'll check back tomorrow to see how you're doing with them."

"Thank you. And please thank Wren for me."

"I will. Good night."

Lydia

"Are you hungry?" Able asked Lydia, who was watching TV and had been all day, except when Able had brought her a slice of pizza and a drink of water. She didn't answer, so Able went back to the kitchen and continued preparing a meal of spaghetti and garlic bread. When it was ready, he called the other agents and encouraged Lydia to join them for dinner.

"How do I know you won't poison me?" Lydia asked.

"Listen lady, if we'd wanted to off you, you'd be dead already. Besides, we're all dipping from the same pan, so we're as much at risk as you."

Lydia couldn't fault that reasoning, so she dished up some food and took it to the couch, where she didn't have to see the way they looked at her, like she was desert. Able found some alcohol in a cupboard—whiskey—so he poured each agent and the hostage a small glass. No one spoke as they ate, but after Lydia sipped the alcohol, gagging on it, she set it aside and asked for water. It was after ten when they finished and cleaned up, so after taking Lydia's dishes to the kitchen, Able spoke to his team.

"It looks like they're not coming before bedtime. So, here's what we'll do. One of us will stay with her at a time, through the night. I'll take the eleven o'clock shift for two hours; Baker, one o'clock; Charlie, three o'clock; and Delta, five o'clock. I'll check in at seven to see how we're doing."

"How do we keep her from trying to escape when there's only one of us watching her?" Baker asked.

"If we pay attention, I don't think she can escape," Able said.

"Maybe we should tie her to the bed," Charlie said. "Then she couldn't get away unless she's better at knots than we are."

"Maybe we should take her clothes," Delta said. "She doesn't appear to be the type to run out of the house naked. Although, being an agent, she may be willing to do that. We don't know how resourceful she is."

"Or, we could take longer shifts and two of us watch her at a time." Able said.

Able thought about the options. Taking her clothes was too personal and could be embarrassing, for her and for him; but she was a real good-looking woman, so it was tempting. "Okay, set your alarms, so you don't forget your shift time."

Able went to the bedroom where Lydia lay on top of the covers with her eyes closed. He poured some whiskey into a glass and handed it to her. She took a sip and set it aside, He had thought that if she got drunk, maybe she would be less inclined to give them problems Now, he was more inclined to take her clothes to keep her in place.

"Lady," Able said. "I need to make sure you don't try to get away during the night."

"I won't try," Lydia said, staring at him angrily. "I'm just worried about my boys."

"Just to make sure you don't try," Able said, ignoring Lydia's comments, "I need you to get undressed and give me your clothes."

"You're not serious," Lydia said, indignantly.

"Deadly serious."

"No."

"You can do it, or I can get you some help. Which will it be?"

Lydia thought about that for a few moments, then decided she had better comply. She undressed down to her underwear and laid her clothes on the bed between them.

"The rest."

"No."

Able decided it wasn't worth a fight and he was already embarrassed enough. He picked up the pile of clothes and carried them out to the living room, setting them on the couch. When he returned to the bedroom, Lydia was under the covers, with the covers pulled up under her chin.

"We're going to have to do one more thing," he said, holding several short lengths of rope in his hands. He walked to the head of the bed.

"Give me your hand," he said. She hesitated, so he reached under the cover and grabbed her arm, his hand touching her side in the process. The heat from her body seemed to sear his skin. She brought her hand out and he took it. He tied her hand to the post of the headboard. He walked calmly around to the other side of the bed and repeated the process with her other hand.

"Do I need to tie your feet, too?" he asked.

"What do you want from me?" She asked. "I haven't done anything wrong and don't deserve your attention." The way she was tied up now, he could really do just about anything he wanted to her without her having the ability to resist.

"We're just holding you until we get further instructions." He thought that was a pretty good ad lib, since he'd been told to make this as realistic as possible and he had instructions not to reveal that he knew she was an agent. She was playing her part very well. If he didn't know better, he would think she was just a woman on the street who he had kidnapped for no reason.

He'd gotten a good look at her body. For a mother of two, she was in great physical shape. He could feel his body responding to being near her.

"Go to sleep," he told her, then lay down next to her on the bed. He thought he could feel her body heat through the bedding, and he was certainly hot.

He finally got up and pulled his sweatshirt over his head, hoping that would cool him down a little, and dropped it on the bed. He made eye contact with her when he turned back around.

"What do you want from me?" she asked again. "Do you want sex? Is that why you trussed me up? So I couldn't resist you? Huh?"

Able was speechless. He could see what she meant. He had made her vulnerable to assault. Would he do that to her? Why had she mentioned it? Did she want it? Did he? If this were a real hostage situation and they wanted a ransom for her, he would be stupid to touch her. Since she was a fellow agent, was she trying to get him into a compromising position where she could turn the table on him. He was just an agent-in-training, so she was probably better trained in self-defense than he was.

But she was so gorgeous and hot—literally and figuratively. He wanted her. If he got started and could tell she didn't want it, could he stop himself? He decided it wasn't worth a try. He sat in a chair by the door and closed his eyes.

When Baker entered the room, Able woke immediately, stretched and stood.

"Is everything okay?" Baker asked.

"Yeah. See you in the morning." Then Able left and Baker sat in the chair he had just vacated. He was asleep in moments.

Agent Smith

"What have you found?" the station chief asked his head of security.

"We started with a video from the neighbor across the street. We hacked into their home security system. That told us when she was kidnapped, what the kidnappers look like and a plate number. Then we followed them out of the neighborhood, using the traffic cams at intersections. Whenever we lost them, we spread the search out in all directions until we spotted them again. They finally pulled into a driveway on West Digital Ave. We got an angle on them from a home three doors down and watched them drag her into the basement apartment. No one has left the apartment since and it's been over twelve hours."

The security chief turned to one of his agents. "Can you confirm?" he asked.

As you know, chief, we have bugged every FBI asset we could find over the years; vehicles, phones, and buildings. Our listening post can monitor each asset so we can both see and hear what's going on. Today, when you asked, we did a quick check to see which buildings, if any, were occupied. We weren't listening to conversations, just verifying occupancy. We found four occupied, including the one on West Digital Ave.

"That's got to be it. Let's take six agents and leave as soon as possible," the chief said to Agent Wren Smith. "You'll lead the rescue."

"Yes, sir." Smith said.

Lydia

The FBI instructor used his pass key to enter the apartment and went directly to the room where his agents should be holding the hostage. He pushed open the door and saw Delta lying on the bed with the hostage, partially undressed.

"What are you doing?" he shouted, causing Delta to jump to his feet and grab for his pants. "And who's she?" He continued when he got a look at Lydia.

Delta was flustered and didn't know what to say. "Who is she?" He finally croaked out. "She's our hostage. Are you here to rescue her? Where's the Red team?"

"Your intended hostage is at her home having breakfast with the Red team. You never picked her up," the instructor said as the other three agents scrambled into the room, like The Keystone Cops, to see about the commotion. "Where are your instructions?"

Able pulled a slip of paper out of his pants pocket and handed it to the instructor. "Here it is," he said "477 Centennial Ave," he read off the paper.

"That should have said 747 Centennial. Someone transposed the numbers. You went to the wrong house."

"We went to the house in our instructions," Able said defensively. "Who wrote the instructions?"

"One of our agents. Oh my. This is bad."

"Will someone explain what's going on?" Lydia asked angrily, figuring out immediately that she had been kidnapped and assaulted by mistake, but for real.

Smith

A white van and a black SUV parked a half block from the apartment on West Digital and six CIA agents exited. They had a floor plan of the FBI apartment, so they knew there were two entrances, one in front and one in back. Agent Smith sent two agents to cover the rear entrance, while he led the others to the front. They listened briefly, then tried the door, finding it unlocked.

Smith cracked the door and yelled, "Police." Then the four agents entered the apartment, guns out and ready. They saw five men standing casually in the hallway, a woman behind them. She looked like she was missing her clothes. All eyes turned to the front door and the armed men standing there.

"What . . . ?" the instructor said. He had the presence of mind to leave his gun in its holster. Delta, lacking the experience of the older man, drew his gun and was shot in the chest, three times. He fell to the floor.

"Stop! Wait!" the instructor said. "We're FBI agents-in-training, on a training exercise . . . gone bad. Can I get my credentials to show you?"

"Stand down," Smith said and allowed the instructor to reach into his jacket and pull out his FBI creds.

"Okay, we're here to take Ms. Hancock home." Smith said. "And you have a lot of explaining to do."

"We can't tell you anything," the instructor said. "You'll have to talk to my supervisor."

"Then that's what we'll do," Smith said as he took the instructor's ID and placed a call to CIA headquarters.

"Can I get dressed?" Lydia asked angrily. Smith could tell she was upset, rightfully so. She was shaking, too, like she had been under a lot of stress.

"Sure. Where are your clothes?"

"I think they brought them in here when they took them from me," she said, looking around and scowling at the agents. "There they are." She pulled away from Charlie, who held her arm, and went to her pile of clothes.

"Hey boss?" an agent said. He was kneeling next to Delta.

"What is it?" Agent Smith was still on the phone with the office, but interrupted his report to listen to his agent.

"He's dead. What should we do?"

"Great. Well, we knew this was an FBI apartment. But why is the FBI Involved in this?"

"What do you mean?" the FBI instructor asked.

"I was told this kidnapping could be part of a bigger operation out in Utah. I need to call this in." He got back on his phone and asked to be transferred to Rainbow.

"Rainbow," the agent said, "this is Agent Smith, Atlanta Field office." Then he proceeded to explain what they'd found.

45

Provo, Utah—Mick

"I'll try anything," Mick said after Ollie explained his idea for how to proceed. "That's as good as anything I can think of."

"It sounds dangerous. Maybe we shouldn't," Drew said.

"It's your call," Ollie said, but I'd like to try it.

"Let's do it!" Mick said.

"It's your skin," Drew said, shaking his head.

The next morning, Mick called the local CIA office.

"Central intelligence Agency," the operator said. "How may I direct your call?"

"This is Michael Swensen. You need to have agent Rainbow"—that was the code name Ollie had given him for the agent who had access to most of the classified files and had told Ollie to back off— "contact me by three p.m. today or I'm going to the media with a CIA conspiracy, a coverup involving the death of my parents nineteen years ago, the near-death of an air force internal investigator last week and the kidnapping of three women in the last month, involving a Russian KGB officer, Dmitri Pavlovich."

"I'm sorry sir, but there is no one here named agent Rainbow, and I have no knowledge of the things of which you're speaking."

"That's fine," Mick said, "just have him contact me today."

"I'm sor . . ." the operator started to say, but Mick had already disconnected.

At 1:14, Mick was driving home from the grocery store when two unmarked cars with exempt plates cut him off, forced him to stop and kidnapped him at gunpoint. He tried to protest, but was told to shut up. He was handcuffed, a dark hood was thrown over his head and he was shoved into the back of one of the cars. He was taken to a nondescript abandoned warehouse a few minutes away and pushed onto a chair under bright lights.

"Okay, Michael Swensen, you need to tell us everything you know about this supposed conspiracy."

Mick thought he had figured out what was going on. They wouldn't hurt him. They were probably FBI or CIA, trying to find out what he knew without telling him what they knew. Although he was nervous—he wasn't positive they wouldn't hurt him—he decided to risk it and call their bluff.

"Or what?" Mick asked through the hood.

"Don't make this difficult. It's an easy question."

"But I don't know who you are or why you think I should tell you what I know."

"We can make you disappear where no one will ever find you."

"Can you? Then you're either CIA, FBI, or part of the kidnapping ring. Which is it?"

"We'll ask the questions. You'll answer them."

"Or what? I want my lawyer."

"Get real, Michael. That only works on TV. Now answer the question."

"You answer mine. Who are you and why should I say anything to you?"

"Let's start with a simpler question. What do you know about the kidnappings?"

"I don't know what you're talking about," he said. The air in the hood was getting stale and he wanted it off.

"You claim to know something about a CIA conspiracy," the voice said.

"I'm not saying anything until I'm speaking to Agent Rainbow and until this hood is removed so I can breathe," Mick said, trying to express confidence that he didn't really feel.

The kidnappers stepped away and spoke quietly, then the hood was removed and he could breathe freely again.

"I'm agent Rainbow," one of the men said.

"CIA?"

"Yes."

"May I see some ID?"

The agent showed Mick his CIA ID. His name was Ren Bloosey.

"Okay, Agent Ren Bloosey," Mick said as the handcuffs were also removed. "You already know my parents died nineteen years ago. We were told it was a mechanical problem with the airplane engines. We now believe it was murder, they were murdered at the direction of a Russian KGB officer, Dmitri Pavlovich. Then the murders were covered up for some reason by the CIA and NTSB, possibly to protect some CIA operation in Russia."

"The KGB was dissolved years ago," Bloosey said, sounding annoyed and impatient.

"According to our sources, it's been reorganized and revitalized."

"Your sources?" Bloosey snorted, but fell silent.

"Then, a few weeks ago," Mick continued, "my sister, Lynne, was kidnapped and I was told I could trade myself for her life. When I didn't bite, they kidnapped my girlfriend, with the same outcome. I now believe the kidnappers were hoping to convince me to give them uranium from the nuclear power plant in Green

River, Utah. They obviously don't understand the restrictions that protect uranium from being stolen. The government would rather see me die than give up a few ounces of something that could be used to make a bomb."

"Now," Mick continued, "our CIA investigator has been hospitalized trying to help."

"Call me Rainbow, okay?" Bloosey asked, with a grunt. "We're sorry about Ollie. We tried to protect him, but we didn't identify the danger soon enough." Just then, Ollie limped into the warehouse and waved to Mick.

"Hi Ollie," Mick said.

"Mick," Ollie replied. "Are you alright?"

"I'm good. Thanks."

"Why didn't you come to the CIA to begin with?" Rainbow asked Mick. Ollie frowned at Rainbow, knowing the answer, but let Mick speak.

"You would have blown me off if I'd come any sooner, just like you did when I came to you with the facts we uncovered on our own. I think we accidentally came across something that someone is embarrassed about. Maybe it's a career buster." He studied Rainbow to see if that got a rise out of him. It didn't. "Maybe it's an inside job." That didn't get a reaction either. "If the Russians hadn't gotten greedy and returned after nineteen years, it would have stayed buried forever. Now, a woman I care a lot about in Atlanta has disappeared. That's the three most important women in my life. I want answers."

From the look on Rainbow's face, Mick knew he had hit a nerve with that comment. Ollie smiled at the exchange.

Rainbow

"I'll say this much," Rainbow said. "You're right that your parents' deaths were not an accident. Over two hundred people died in that plane crash. It was murder, and the person responsible will be held accountable."

"When?"

"Eventually. As soon as we can get our hands on him. That doesn't make your loss any easier, but you can rest assured that your parents died serving their country; serving it well."

"I'll also tell you that the kidnappings and your job are related," Rainbow continued. "We're working on those and expect that situation to come to a head shortly. One other thing . . . we just got a report from our Atlanta office. They said they rescued Ms. Hancock and took her home to her children today."

Mick sighed. "Good," he said. "Is Lydia's kidnapping related?"

"We're not sure, but we're looking into that, too."

"How would they know about her?" Mick asked. "I haven't seen her in four years, until last week. They must have followed me."

"All the way to Atlanta?" Ollie asked.

"And I was just passing through on my way home from Florida."

"Wow, these guys are serious," Ollie said, noticing Rainbow's sour expression "assuming they *are* related incidents."

"Okay, so Lydia's probably safe. What are you doing for the other two?"

Rainbow looked constipated, and didn't speak.

"What?" Mick asked.

"While Ms. Hancock was captive, she was assaulted by at least one FBI agent-in-training."

Mick was so angry he sputtered. He took a step toward Rainbow, both hands fisted in front of him. "I want his head," he said.

"Sorry. Too late. He was shot by a CIA agent sent to rescue her."

Mick was speechless. He took another step toward Rainbow.

Ollie stopped him with a word.

"Mick," Ollie said. Mick stopped and looked at Ollie. He could see the warning in Ollie's eyes. He tried to calm himself. How did that kind of thing happen in America? "Who's responsible?" he finally asked the only thing he could think of.

"The FBI has agreed to find out who gave erroneous instructions to the agents who kidnapped her. Regarding the other two women, we're working on it. We'll get them back."

"Before either of them dies?" Mick asked angrily. He wanted to punch Rainbow for taking this so lightly.

"Calm down, Michael. The women are fine."

"You know where they are?"

"We know where they are," Rainbow said. "Your sister and Ms. Austin. We're working on getting them released now. I think we're done here. We'll let Ollie get you home."

As the CIA agents headed for the door, Mick took another step toward Rainbow.

"Rainbow," Ollie said, "tell him more."

"I don't think that's a good idea, Ollie," Rainbow said. "Most of it is classified."

"He deserves to know whatever you can tell him."

46

Revelations—Mary Slade

"Alright," Rainbow said after a few moments looking at Ollie, then the ceiling. "Sit down Michael."

"Please, call me Mick."

"Okay Mick. You need to understand that what I'm about to tell you . . ."

"I've already signed a non-disclosure agreement," Mick said, cutting Rainbow off and looking at Ollie. Rainbow also looked at Ollie, getting a nod from him.

"Okay. We recruited your parents while they were still both single, in college. Mary Slade was studying political science and criminal justice We saw Mary at a college football game. She was a cheerleader, athletic and beautiful. She caught Ollie's attention because she appeared so self-confident and able to handle herself."

"What do you mean by 'handle herself'?" Mick asked.

"Two very large football players got in her face, and she took them both down. They were carried to the locker room and didn't return to the game."

"My mom did that?" Mick asked, grinning despite the seriousness of the discussion.

"It was pretty impressive. I invited Mary and her parents to come to Virginia for a talk. Her parents were reluctant to let her train with us because they wanted her to finish school and become a nurse. We tested her anyway and showed them her scores. She had the aptitude to become an excellent agent. Despite her parents' misgivings, Mary agreed to become a courier, delivering messages to CIA stations around the world. She enjoyed the travel, the mystery, and the exotic nature of the job. And there was seldom danger to her."

"The first trip that caused me concern was three months after beginning her job. We flew her into Sydney, Australia to deliver information to the station chief. Mary gave the station chief the information and was ready to leave the country when she was confronted by three men with knives in the airport parking lot. We had no one watching her. She was on her own. By the time we realized she was in trouble, it was all over. She had disabled all three of them by the time airport security arrived. They escorted her to her flight, bumped her up to first class, and she enjoyed the amenities of first-class travel for the first time."

Taylor Swensen

"Taylor Swensen, your dad, was a different story. He was an excellent marksman, fearless. He was dating the daughter of a wealthy businessman. The daughter was careless. Growing up with money, she liked to wear expensive clothes and jewelry. They were on a date when she was kidnapped, wearing at least a quarter of a million dollars in jewelry at the time."

"Taylor was taken along with her. He was tied up tightly and dropped in a corner of the warehouse where they were being held. One of the kidnappers was assigned to watch him. They had taken her jewelry, then stripped her; Looking for more, they said. One of the men had apparently decided he couldn't resist her charms. Then a shot rang out and the man dropped to the ground with a bullet hole in his forehead. Looking around, they realized that Taylor had not only untied himself, but had overcome his guard, stolen his gun, taken aim from over fifty feet away and hit the guy between the eyes without hurting the girl that was inches away from him."

"When we arrived, Taylor had the girl by his side and the other two kidnappers in a standoff, which we quickly resolved. Taylor was easy to convince to join us. He became one of our most successful and trusted assassins. His missions, like Mary's, took him to exotic places, but they were search and destroy missions, sanctioned killings of enemies the government couldn't get to any other way."

"What about the girlfriend?" Mick asked.

"Taylor told us he was never really interested in the girl. He was dating her to get her dad's attention. He thought he could convince her dad to set him up in business. After we spoke to him, he postponed that ambition for future consideration. The father tried to give Taylor a reward, but he turned it down. Then he turned down the offer of a job working for one of her dad's companies in lieu of working for us."

Rainbow turned toward his men, most of whom had walked away toward their cars. He started to follow, when Mick stopped him.

"Rainbow," Mick said, "Is there anything else you can tell me? What about some of their missions?"

"All of their missions are classified. What I can tell you is that they worked separately for about three years, then we got the idea of using them together. Some of our missions require a man/woman team and they got along so well, we thought we'd take a chance on sending them out together. Mary became the bait, to reel in the targets, many of whom were womanizers, and Taylor would capture or kill the target while the target was distracted."

"Did my mom use sex to distract the targets?"

"She used the possibility of having sex as a distraction. Your mother was a beautiful woman. Men were drawn to her."

"Was she ever in real danger?"

"Once or twice, we thought she was in trouble, but we sent your dad in to rescue her and everything turned out just fine."

"I think they fell in love on one of those missions. She got side-tracked, looking at the ruins in Cambodia. When he found her, she was fine, just distracted. They got to know each other on that trip and realized they liked each other a lot. They agreed to start dating, when they could find time in their busy travel schedules."

Rainbow became pensive, a smile playing on his lips, as though he were enjoying reminiscing about their missions. Then he spoke again. "We sent them after terrorists, thieves, murderers and a Russian KGB officer, a man who had been a thorn in our side for years. Each mission was a success, with the exception of the Russian. He alluded us, even when we thought we had him cornered. We heard, over the next few years, that he had asked about them all over Europe and had mercenaries looking for them, even in the United States. I understand he even visited them at their home in Provo after they retired to raise three children."

"Us?" Mick asked.

"Yes, you. This was a short time before their deaths. We know now that the Russian sent an assassin after them, but the assassin died instead of them. That was the car crash. Then a plane they were travelling home in, from Southeast Asia was blown out of the sky. Over two hundred people died, including your parents. We couldn't prove it was an explosion, so the NTSB called it a mechanical malfunction, to hide the fact that we were still looking for the murderers."

"Have you seen the news?" Ollie asked Rainbow, when he thought

Rainbow had finished his story.

"One more story," Rainbow said. "This is my favorite assignment."

"Your favorite?"

"Well, the assignment I like thinking about the most. It was the most complex and possibly the most dangerous for Mary. We sent them to Rio de Janeiro to stop a famous entertainer who was laundering drug money for a Mexican drug cartel through his club in Rio."

"Over a period of months, we convinced his girlfriend, that his activities were dangerous to her and needed to be stopped before she got hurt. She agreed to help us meet with him to try to convince him to stop, without involving violence. We couldn't get him alone because he was always surrounded by his bodyguards and fans."

"She agreed to meet with your parents and got their meeting with him. They convinced him to go into hiding. We placed the entertainer, his girlfriend and her family in a safe house in Florida and the drug cartel blew itself apart."

"That's a fascinating story," Mick said. "I wouldn't have believed Mom and Dad had that in them. They seemed so mellow and normal at home. This is a side of them we would never have seen if you hadn't known them all this time. Thank you."

"You're welcome," Rainbow said. "I'm happy to tell you about them; but I need to say that most of what I've told you cannot be repeated to others. If these stories became public, it would be not only embarrassing, but criminal. We could all go to prison. Do you understand what I'm saying?"

"I do and promise not to share anything you've told me, except maybe with Drew."

Rainbow looked at Ollie again.

"Drew's been sworn to secrecy, too," Ollie said.

"Okay, that would be okay, as long as he understands the restrictions as well."

"Are you ready to see this news report?" Ollie asked. He had set up a TV and DVD player on a table and turned it on. He slipped a DVD into a slot on the front of the machine.

"This was the headline story for the noon news," he said as the TV came to life.

"We have breaking news," the TV anchor said excitedly. *"We have an exclusive report from an unknown source, that swears there is a government conspiracy to cover up a close relationship between our intelligence services and a Russian industrialist who was responsible for the murder of a US couple nineteen years ago. A CIA source, who refused to be named, said the CIA is looking into who is responsible for giving the Russian the information on the couple, who were trying to stop him from stealing uranium to sell to terrorists.* A picture of Pavlovich appeared on the screen. *In a related story, a Russian KGB officer, Dmitri Pavlovich, possibly the same person, has been found floating in Lake Maracaibo in Venezuela, dead from at least one bullet to the head. The rumor is that he was involved in an arms deal that went bad. No one could be reached who knew anything about the incident."*

Rainbow swore. He looked at Mick, then Ollie, then turned back to the other agents. "Let's go. Nothing more to do here."

The agents moved to leave with Rainbow, leaving Mick, Drew and Ollie.

"Thank you, Ollie," Mick said. "Were you the CIA source?"

"Can't say. Let's just be happy that Pavlovich can't trouble anyone anymore."

"Fine. I'm happy about that. But have we determined if he had a source of information inside the intelligence services?"

"That's more troubling. Our guess is that there's someone in the clandestine services who was, or still is, on the take, for reasons unknown, probably for money."

"Okay," Mick said. "That's one pin down. One more to go."

Uranium

"How good of an actor are you, Mick?" Ollie asked when they met at the restaurant for lunch. Drew was there with Mick and Ollie had a woman with him who he introduced as Estelle.

"I did some acting in high school, but I'm afraid I'm not the best judge of how well I did," Mick said.

"He's a lousy liar," Drew said, "if that's any indication."

"It may well be," Ollie said, chuckling. "It's also what I would expect, knowing you. So, let's try to make this as realistic as possible so you don't have to pretend."

"Do you want Drew to be part of it?" Mick asked.

"I don't think Drew is the right kind of bait," Ollie said. "We'll have to make the bait something we know the Russians want, like the uranium."

"But we can't . . ."

"I know we can't, so it has to be something we can pass off as Uranium or something that would be as attractive to him. Now, think what that might be."

"How about the shipping container the Uranium arrived in?"

"Do you still have one around?"

"Actually, we do. Your comment is what made me think of it. The team that delivered the last shipment neglected to take it with them, so we've had it in locked storage for several months. It can probably still set off a Geiger counter. That stuff has a really long half-life."

"Fine. We'll use agents as much as possible. It needs to look realistic, so we'll let you coach them. We'll need to announce the delivery a couple of days ahead of time, to allow word to leak out. We want the bad egg to be there and I think he'll want to be."

"But if your bad guy is an agent, he'll recognize the other agents and see the trap."

"Good point, Mick. We'll have to bring in outside help. Let me see what I can set up."

They worked out how far in the future they had to conduct their charade, then Mick coordinated with the site security manager, letting him know that they were participating in a CIA sting operation

"It still needs to look real," Ollie said, when they touched base the next day.

"We have an actual delivery in a few days," Mick said. We can receive the Uranium, then give the kidnappers the empty box. Or, we can move the Uranium to the empty box and let the kidnappers take the new box. It will read louder on the Geiger counter anyway.

"Okay," Ollie said. "You decide how to do it."

"And you need to talk to the security manager so he understands what we're doing and why. He'll be more cooperative if it comes from you."

"I better have a conversation with the agents," the security manager told Ollie. Ollie set it up and the security manager included the safety manager, to make sure he was on board with the plan and to get his input and cooperation. It was difficult to make specific plans when Ollie was trying to keep the facts to as few people as possible. The security manager said he would have men ready to intervene as soon as Ollie pointed out the bad guys to him.

"Do we tell the FBI about the sting?" Mick asked Ollie.

"To what purpose?" Ollie asked. "I think we can handle this ourselves. I'm sure we'll have to tell them at some point, but let's wait a while. We need to keep the number of people who know as small as possible."

Three days later, Mick met at an office near the site with a team of agents. Mick was surprised when Ollie showed up with the agents.

"I thought you said the CIA couldn't operate domestically and that this should be an FBI operation." Mick said.

"Technically true," Ollie agreed.

"So these are FBI agents?"

"Let's just say they're volunteers, vetted volunteers," Ollie said, "Mick, I need to be up front with you," Ollie added after some thought. "The line has been obscured here and the CIA needs to take this one to completion,"

"Well, thanks, in that case."

"You're welcome."

"Okay everyone," Ollie said to get everyone's attention. "Mick is going to explain what we need to do, then we're answer your questions. When we've finished that, you're all welcome to take off until Friday, when we receive the Uranium for real. Thanks for being here. All yours, Mick." Most of the agents had reserved space in the local campground, so they would be close at hand on Friday morning.

Mick explained the process of delivering fresh Uranium to the site and exchanging it for the used Uranium. The agents picked their roles and practiced, accepting Mick's suggestions on how to treat the Uranium, how to move in hazmat suits, what to say and not to say to each other, and so on. He also answered questions that the agents had about possible, unexpected situations.

"What else should we do?" Mick wondered.

"Can't think of anything," Ollie said.

"Maybe I'll call Brady and let him know we're receiving a new shipment and ask if he wants to send some men to watch the site."

"Fine. It won't hurt to have more eyes on the site during the delivery."

"Brady, Uranium is being delivered on Friday morning," Mick said, when he had Brady on the line. "If the uranium is the target of the kidnappers, it wouldn't hurt to have more eyes watching the delivery."

"I'll have some agents waiting offsite to watch for a theft," Brady said. "If we see anything, we'll intercept."

"That sounds good," Mick said. He had agreed with Ollie that everyone would play their parts better if they thought it was real, so he decided not to say anything about it being a sting operation or about the CIA being involved.

Mick was surprised when the security manager told him the delivery of the Uranium was announced on the morning news.

"Has that happened before?" Mick asked.

"Not that I've ever heard."

"Maybe the CIA leaked it to ensure the thieves make a try for it. But making a public announcement could attract other bad guys. This could get complicated."

Friday morning, early, Mick was nervous. So was the security manager. Several of Ollie's volunteers showed up early, dressed like workers and carrying concealed weapons. Mick introduced them to the security manager. The security manager, in turn, placed them in strategic locations around the building and showed them how to look like regular workers.

Late in the morning, a delivery truck arrived on site. Mick was notified by the front gate. He dressed in his hazmat suit and met the truck at the dock. He talked to the driver for a few moments, giving him instructions on where the delivery should go. He moved away and the driver backed up to the loading dock. His two helpers jumped up on the dock and unloaded the single box inside that was strapped to a hand truck and moved it to the dock.

This was when Mick expected the attack to occur. It was the easiest and simplest point in the process for stealing the delivery. But it didn't happen. Mick worried that maybe the thieves didn't take the bait. He led the delivery team to the storage location for the Uranium, and had them move the Uranium, which was in a shielded box inside the shipping container, to the empty box in the store room, then they returned to the truck, stored their hand truck and drove off.

The security manager approached Mick, who could see the disappointment on his face. He had thought they could help the agents capture known thieves, but it hadn't worked. Suddenly, the security man's expression turned sour as he looked over Mick's shoulder. He drew his gun just as Mick heard a whisper in his ear.

"Tell him to drop the gun, if you want to see the sunrise," the voice said.

"Did you hear him?" Mick asked the security manager.

"Yeah." He set his gun on the floor at his feet.

"Now kick it over here." He did. Mick tried to read the security manager's eye movements, but they were beyond him. Some code that other security people would probably understand.

"How did you get in here?" Mick asked.

"We told them we forgot to pick up the used uranium," the voice said, "and they bought it. Now let's get that box back out to the loading dock." Mick was dying to turn around and see which agent was the traitor. He had studied all of their faces over the previous days and thought he would recognize him. In fact, he had already judged them and thought he knew which ones were most likely to be the traitor.

As he moved back toward the storage unit, the person behind him leaned over to pick up the security manager's gun. Mick thought that would have been a good time to resist, but he couldn't see the man and movement was awkward in a hazmat suit. Then his opportunity was gone and he was opening the store room door.

He pulled back on the hand truck, backing the empty box out of the store room and turned toward the dock. That's when he got his first look at the thief. He wasn't any of the ones Mick thought it would be. He was a young, freckle-faced agent who looked like a new recruit.

"Why?" Mick asked.

"Why not?" the young man asked.

"It's criminal. You have a long life ahead of you. You can spend it protecting your country or you can spend it in prison. Are you sure you're making the right choice?"

"Shut up and get moving. I'm going to be rich."

"If they let you live, that is."

"Okay. Shut up."

"You'll never get this off the site. You realize that, don't you?"

"That's where you're wrong. You're coming with us to make sure we get off site. Then we'll drop you off when we're safely away. You'll be dead, of course."

"You don't know how to handle this material. You'll all die horrible deaths," he said, stretching the truth; they would possibly get sick over time and die early from cancer. It was a long-term medical problem rather than an acute problem. He counted on the possibility that this agent was naïve about the possible dangers.

"Good try, Swensen. We've studied all about handling the uranium and radiation exposure. But since the boss has a surprise for you, I'll let you live to see it."

Mick was scrambling for what to do as he loaded the box into a truck similar to the one that had delivered the box to the site. If he didn't figure it out soon, there was a good chance the young man would uncover their ruse. Either way, there was a good chance he would die.

As he wheeled the box into the back of the truck, he heard the door close and lock behind him. He turned to see that the young agent had locked himself inside. Not good. He heard the door to the cab open, then close. Then the engine started and the truck began to move. The best thing that could happen now would be if the security manager shot the driver and caused the truck to crash, even if he were injured in the process.

Mick could tell when the truck passed the site security perimeter and hit the highway, increasing in speed. He kept waiting for the security team or Brady's FBI agents to stop the truck or run it off the road, but it didn't happen. He tried to get the agent talking; maybe he would get a chance to overpower him and escape.

"Why are you doing this?" Mick asked.

"For the money," the agent said.

"Tell me about it."

"You've heard enough. Now shut up."

"Can I remove the hazmat suit?"

"Aren't you worried about radiation?"

Mick realized his mistake. By announcing that he wasn't worried about radiation, the agent would figure out that there was no risk to him or his associates. He could either leave the bulky and awkward suit on, or he could explain.

"It's not dangerous as long as it stays in the box," Mick said When the agent nodded, Mick removed the suit and set it aside.

As the truck sped up, he started counting in his head. He was good at this; it's how he kept track of his morning exercise, counting to sixty, then holding up a finger. He had successfully counted for ten minutes with almost perfect accuracy, he figured. They drove this way for a long time. He thought they were headed South, into the desert on a dirt road, but couldn't be sure, so he had no idea where they were or where they were going. He lost track of time, being distracted from his counting by his concern over what was happening. He hoped someone was following. Finally, after what seemed like hours, but may have been less than an hour, the truck slowed and turned off onto a side road that was rough and rutted. They drove for another few minutes, the tires crunching on gravel, then pulled to a stop. After a few minutes, a voice from outside called to him.

"Mick, it's Brady. I'm going to open the door, then you and I will go rescue Lynne and your girlfriend. Okay?"

Mick got excited, realizing that Brady must have followed them. He didn't hear a scuffle or shots fired, so he wasn't sure how Brady had taken control of the situation. He must have a bunch of agents with him.

The rear door was cracked open and diffused sunlight entered, lighting up the trailer so he could see. He noticed that the agent had stood and pointed his gun at him, so he didn't dare make any sudden moves. The door opened further, and Brady's face appeared in the open doorway.

"Hi Mick. Are you okay?" Brady asked.

Mick motioned to the young agent, holding a gun on him, with his head.

"Hey Blake," Brady said to the agent. "Everything cool?"

"Yeah," Blake said. "He hasn't been a problem."

"Brady, he's one of them," Mick said quietly, not sure what he wanted Brady to do. He worried that the young agent might shoot first and ask questions later.

Suddenly, Brady had a gun in his hand and shot Blake in the chest. Blake flew backwards, hitting the wall and collapsing to the floor of the truck.

"Come on, Mick," Brady said. "Bring the box."

Brady lowered the tailgate while Mick pulled back on the handles of the hand truck and moved it to the tailgate. Brady lowered the tailgate to the ground and motioned for Mick to follow him with the hand truck. Looking around, he noticed the barren landscape, interrupted by low hills and a periodic bush or stunted tree. They were at an old, abandoned farmhouse somewhere south of Green River.

"Where are Lynne and Raquel?" he asked.

"Inside. We need to rescue them. They're being held by agents who've been turned by Pavlovich." Brady explained. That sounded right to Mick.

Two of Brady's agents stood by the door to the large, dilapidated barn, as Brady and Mick approached. One of them opened the passage door, then Brady, Mick pushing the hand truck, and the two agents entered. The barn floor was hard-packed with straw strewn around. There was a little light coming in through holes in the roof, that illuminated the dust motes floating in the air. A raised platform stood in the middle of the room, with three vertical poles mounted on it. It looked like Lynne and Raquel were tied to two of the poles. Two men, likely other agents, stood next to them, partially hiding them from Mick's view. One of the men looked like the guy they had seen at the house with Pavlovich.

"What's going on?" Mick asked quietly.

"The best I can tell," Brady said, also talking quietly, "The kidnappers have been holding the women here. Let's go untie them."

"What about the kidnappers?"

"They think I'm with them. But we're going to shatter that idea right now." Brady walked boldly over to the platform, Mick and the other two agents following. They climbed the four steps to the platform. Now Mick could see that Lynne and Raquel wore thin robes and slippers.

The two men standing next to the women, each with a hand on one of the women's shoulders, possessively, turned to acknowledge Brady.

"Pachenko," Brady said and one of the men raised a hand in acknowledgement, his eyebrows raised. Brady raised the gun he still held at his side and shot each of the two men in the head. They dropped to the floor of the platform, dead. Raquel screamed and both women cringed.

Mick took a step toward Raquel, when the two agents with Brady grabbed him by the arms and dragged him to the third pole. He struggled to break free, but the well-trained agents held him until they could get him to the post and bind his hands behind him with duct tape.

"Brady!" he yelled. "Tell them to stop."

Brady looked at him, but said nothing.

"What's going on, Brady?" he continued. Brady walked over to Mick and looked him in the eye from a foot away.

"I'm trying to protect the Uranium. I'm guessing this box is empty, but I know you have access to the real thing. You're going to bring it to me, so I can keep you from giving it to terrorists."

"You want to keep *me* from giving it away? *I'm* trying to keep it away from them. Whose side are you on, Brady."

"That's a stupid question, Mick. I'm FBI; We're the good guys, so you must be the traitor. You're going to give the Uranium to me so I can protect it. As I said, you will now bring me the real thing. I want it in FBI control and safe."

"I can't . . ." Mick started to protest.

"You will." Brady said, or your women will suffer. "Just so you know where things stand, I've been monitoring everything. I know you and your Air Force investigator friend, Tanner, are in with the kidnappers. I also know Tanner is on his way here, with the Uranium, on the pretext of rescuing all of you. But we're going to stop him and anyone else who gets in our way. Then we'll have the Uranium to turn over to the authorities."

"You know I'm not one of the kidnappers. That's not even logical. Why would I kidnap Lynne and Raquel, then threaten myself?"

"Tell me" Brady said. "I'd be interested in why and how you did it. You have a twisted mind, I'll agree. But we'll have the Uranium that Tanner stole from the plant and you'll all be dead anyway. No one will question me."

One of the agents slapped duct tape on Mick's mouth, ending the conversation.

47

Rescue—Ollie

Ollie turned onto the rough road leading to the barn and stopped. Drew and two of Ollie's agents stepped down from the Ram 1500 Crew Cab, leaving the other two agents with Ollie. Drew and the two agents moved away from the truck and hid in a ditch away from the barn. Ollie pulled right up to the door before stopping again.

Ollie and his two men stepped into the barn, but stayed by the door. He could see the platform and the people on and around it.

"Fairchild," he yelled, "It's over. Drop your weapons and give yourselves up."

"You drop your weapons, Tanner," Brady called back. "I know you're part of the kidnapping ring. This can only end one way. Give it up."

"You're deluded, Fairchild. I didn't expect you to be part of this, but I'm not totally surprised. You knew where Ms. Hancock was, had seen her just before her kidnapping, and was the one who prepared the instructions for the FBI kidnapping team. You're in this up to your eyeballs."

At Ollie's explanation, Mick turned to Brady and tried to talk through the duct tape. When nothing intelligible came out, he cursed a streak, twisted his bound hands behind his back, trying to break free, then settled back down when nothing worked. He would have to wait for an opportunity to escape.

Brady raised his gun and fired off three shots, killing Ollie's two men and hitting Ollie in the arm. He, too, would have died if he hadn't turned sideways at the last moment. All three fell to the ground. Brady turned to one of the two men with him.

"Set the charge for fifteen minutes, then we'll get out of here."

The man brought a briefcase around in front of him, opened it and removed what looked like dynamite, attached to a timer. He set it up near Mick and pushed a button. The timer started to tick.

"Mick, I'm afraid this is where it ends. There's enough explosive there to bring down the barn on top of you, but you won't feel it because you'll already be dead."

One of the men cut the tape binding Raquel's hands. Brady grabbed her arm and started dragging her away.

"I'll take Ms. Austin with me. She should provide entertainment for us for a few hours, before we have to get rid of her, too. I'll make sure no one finds her body. They'll assume she died in the explosion."

Raquel tried to resist, so the two men picked her up, one holding her shoulders and neck, the other capturing her calves and holding them. She continued to struggle, making the thin robe fall open, revealing that she wore nothing underneath. Brady and the two men looked at her for a few moments before Brady lifted the two halves of the robe and covered her again. He looked at Mick, almost apologetically, before leading his men toward the door.

Suddenly, shots rang out again. Brady, his two men, and Raquel, all fell to the ground. Mick looked toward the sound, near the door, and saw Drew, holding a smoking gun to his side. Drew ran to Ollie and raised his head.

"What can I do for you?" he asked.

"I'm good for now. It's just a flesh wound. I've had worse. Go help your brother." Ollie said in a rush. Drew took off his coat, folded it under Ollie's head, then ran to the platform. When he had Mick unbound, he started working on Lynne. Mick jumped off the platform and ran to Raquel.

"Wetzel and Van Buren," Ollie said in a soft voice, to the men who had entered with Drew, "get over there and defuse that bomb."

"We need to get you to a doctor," Mick said to Ollie as they sat in the cab of the truck. Mick was in the driver's seat, with Raquel next to him. Drew and Lynne were in the back seat with Ollie between them. Wetzel and Van Buren, Ollie's remaining two agents were inside the building, cleaning up the massacre, and had called in reinforcements to help.

"I'm fine," Ollie said, holding a bandage on his left arm to slow the bleeding. "It's just a scratch. There are things I need to tell you first." Blood seeped between his fingers and ran slowly down his arm.

"What's more important than getting you fixed up?"

"I need to tell you what we found just before following you to the farm."

"How did you know where to find us by the way?"

"A tracking device on the truck, placed while they were backed up to the dock. Do you want to know what we found out, or not?"

"Of course, I do."

"Then shut up and listen."

"Okay."

"Fairchild is the one who wrote the misleading instructions to the FBI agents-in-training, that caused them to kidnap Ms. Hancock in Atlanta. A former contact of mine lived across the street from her and witnessed the kidnapping. She notified the Atlanta

CIA office immediately, which helped us locate her quicker."

"I sent a request for information to our eastern European office a few days ago. I just got the response today. Pachenko, the brother of the guy who tried to kill your parents in the auto accident, had a deal with Pavlovich to get a million dollars for the Uranium. But someone within the clandestine services, who we now believe was Fairchild, had a deal to get five million for it."

"Pachenko is what Brady called the man holding Raquel, just before he shot him. That would explain why Brady shot Pachenko. He was not only not needed, he was competition."

"You're probably right about that."

"Brady said you stole the Uranium."

"I had to convince the security manager that we needed the real uranium and agreed to take responsibility for it. I have an authorization from the NRC to take it, as long as I accept responsibility for its safety."

While they were talking, four black SUVs arrived, stopping near the door to the barn, and over a dozen agents in dark clothes, glasses and ball caps got out of the SUVs. Most of them entered the barn. A couple looked around. They all looked alike.

"Roll down the window," Ollie told Drew. He did.

"Rainbow!" Ollie called out the window. One of the men looking around turned toward the truck, walked over, and looked in the open window.

"Did you get careless cleaning your gun?" Rainbow asked Ollie, obviously teasing him about being shot.

"Funny," Ollie said. "If you've got this, I'm going to have these nice folks take me to a doctor."

"I can handle it," Rainbow said. "Tell me what we've got."

"Inside, you'll find dead Fibbers and agents. It wasn't a shootout, more like an arcade turkey shoot. One side shooting, then the other side shooting. Some of the Fibbers were bad guys, but I don't think all of them were. If any of them are still alive, patch them up and interrogate them. We need to know if anyone else was involved with Pavlovich. I don't think any of our agents had turned, but can't be positive on that either. I'll fill you in later."

"Okay. I got this. You go take care of yourself."

Drew

"That was some impressive shooting," Ollie said to Drew.

"Sorry about your friend," Drew said to Mick.

"I thought he was a friend, anyway," Mick said. "He disappointed me. Thanks for the rescue. Where did you learn to shoot like that?"

"Grandpa Ralph. He took me shooting to humor me because I told him Dad would do it if he were here. When he saw how well I could shoot already, at age eight, he thought it might be a useful skill. He said I was a natural. That's why I asked Grandpa for my own guns and shooting lessons."

"So, who were the men you brought with you?" Mick asked Ollie.

"CIA agents brought in from other areas of the country," Ollie said.

"Just as I suspected. Thank you for coming to our rescue."

"Glad we could help." Suddenly, Ollie laid his head back on the seat back, his eyes rolled up into his head, and he was out.

"We better get him to a hospital," Drew said. Mick started the truck, made a U-turn, and left quickly. He got to the emergency room parking lot and Drew helped him get Ollie inside. A nurse got a wheelchair and they lowered Ollie into it.

"What happened?" the nurse asked.

"He's a federal officer. He got shot trying to apprehend a bad guy." Drew said.

"Does he have some ID?"

"Let's take care of him, then he can show you his ID when he's able. Okay?"

"Unusual, but we'll do it that way."

"Thanks."

The nurse told Mick and Drew to wait in the waiting room and took Ollie into the back. Lynne and Raquel eventually came into the waiting room to see what was going on. They were still wearing the robes and slippers.

"You look like you just escaped from the hospital," Mick said. "We need to get you some clothes,"

"I'd like that," Raquel said. "How soon can we leave?"

"If Drew wants to wait here for the nurse to return, I can take you to my house and you can rummage through my drawers and closet."

"Let's go," Raquel said, with a nod to Lynne. Mick stood, put an arm around each of them, and led them back to the truck. Back in Green River, they found clothes that didn't look too bad on them, then showered, brushed their teeth, and refreshed their makeup before returning to the hospital.

Drew had Ollie in a wheelchair, just waiting for them to return. He had a large bandage on his left bicep and it was in a sling.

"How ya doin', old man?" Mick asked.

"Don't 'old man' me," Ollie said. "I can still beat you one-handed."

"I don't doubt it. What's next?"

"A couple of my men are here with one of the Fibbers who was still alive. They'll stay with him until the FBI arrives, then they'll take him. He swears he wasn't one of Fairchild's men and they believe him. I'll follow up with a call to the local office to ask them to investigate all of Fairchild's closest associates. I think we can call that one closed. We think we know how your parents died." He noticed Mick's look and decided to explain. "Pavlovich sold weapons in the middle east and northern Africa. We believe he paid someone to fire a missile at the plane, to take it down. We have a team trying to find out who, exactly, did it. Based on the NTSB investigation, we know where it was fired from, so we'll be focusing our investigation on that location."

"What will you find after all this time?"

"We have access to satellite images from the day it happened, so we feel sure we'll figure it out. We can't your parents back, but we can close that file, now. The life insurance company might want some money back, but you can argue that with them, since the accident was so long ago."

"It was murder, not suicide," Mick said. "They should honor the contract."

"Yes, they should."

"What about Lynne and Raquel?" Mick asked, looking Raquel in the eyes.

"What about them? Do you think they should be compensated for their pain and suffering, or something?"

"Shouldn't there be some kind of compensation for what they went through?"

"The CIA didn't cause any of this. You'll have to take that up with FBI attorneys. That's a legal issue." Ollie looked at Raquel again and she shook her head.

"I just want this whole thing to end," she said. "I don't want to drag it out for years. That's what will happen if we have to go to court."

"If the government will even let it go to court," Ollie said. "I think they would rather bury the whole thing. Maybe they'll settle, just to keep you all quiet."

"It would cost them less if they just killed us all," Mick said.

"There is that option, but let's not mention it," Ollie said with a nervous chuckle.

Ollie turned to Drew. "If I buy you a first-class ticket to fly to Virginia," Ollie said, "will you come and talk to me about a possible career move?"

"Sure," Drew said, smiling. Mick got the impression that Drew had enjoyed the action and might make a good CIA agent.

"You, too, Mick. Let me know if you're interested in working for us. Rainbow would be pleased, since some of what he told you is classified and that would keep it all in-house."

"Ms. Austin and Ms. Swensen, you've had a harrowing experience. Some of what you've seen and heard is government classified. I could swear you to secrecy, but it would be impossible for me to ensure that you don't ever say anything about this mess. I could offer you a job with the agency, but that's not my place, and I'm not sure you'd be interested anyway. Am I right?"

Both women nodded.

"Thanks, Ollie," Mick said. "Right now, I think I'm more interested in getting Raquel home, where she'll feel safer."

Drew sat up front with Ollie, while the others sat in back, Mick between Raquel and Lynne.

48

Closure

"It sounded like you knew that guy, was his name Brady?" Lynne asked Mick when they were in the truck, headed back to Provo. They had left Ollie at the hospital in Green River, in the care of his fellow agents. Now, Drew drove the truck with Lynne sitting next to him with Mick and Raquel in the back seat.

"Yeah. He was a fraternity brother in college."

"A frat brother? Why would he want to harm us?" she asked, looking past him at Raquel.

"It's a complicated story."

"Tell me."

"Are you sure you want to know?"

"I sure do. That's the most exciting and frightening thing that has ever happened to me, and that's saying something."

"Lydia didn't like or trust him from the beginning," Mick said, looking for Raquel's reaction out of the corner of his eye.

"Lydia!" Raquel said, frowning and making Mick squirm. It was probably a bad idea to bring up Lydia when he had in mind asking Raquel to marry him.

"Lynne," Mick said, taking a big breath.

"Mick!" Drew said when he realized that Mick intended to tell Lynne some of their secrets.

"I know, Drew," Mick said. "But she deserves to know the basics. I'll keep it simple."

Drew nodded once.

"Lynne and Raquel, what I'm about to tell you is government classified information. You have to promise me you'll never tell another soul. Will you agree to that?"

"Government secrets? And I can't tell anyone?" Lynne asked.

"If I can't trust you, I can't tell you. And if you break that trust, by telling anyone, we'll all go to prison."

"You're laying it on pretty thick, Mick. Really?"

"Lynne, I've never been more serious about anything."

"Oh, alright. I promise."

Mick looked at Raquel, a question in his expression.

"Me too," Raquel said. "I promise."

"Okay. Mom and Dad were CIA agents."

"Whoa, right there," Lynne said. "Are you trying to kid me?"

"Lynne, you were four when they died. What do you really know about them?"

"Okay, CIA agents," Lynne said, reluctantly.

"They were killed on the orders of a Russian arms dealer who they tried, unsuccessfully, to stop."

"You mean they actually tried to kill this guy?"

"They tried, but they failed. He must have decided to take revenge. Mom tried to defuse the situation, when the Russian came to the house just before they died. You were probably too young to remember, but Drew let him in the house, in Provo, not knowing who he was."

"He didn't have an accent," Drew said from the front seat, "so I didn't get suspicious."

"Mom got really scared and mad and asked him to leave," Mick continued.

"I vaguely remember that," Lynne said. "Why didn't they kill him then?"

"Killing him would have been murder at that point."

"I don't understand that."

"I'll explain it to you later. As the Russian was leaving the house, he told them good-bye, like he'd never see them again. I think it was his intent to kill them even then. Anyway, the Russian died recently, in Venezuela. He was a powerful and wealthy man. Even after his death, his influence caused this mess we just experienced."

"So, where does that leave us?" Lynne asked.

"Right where we are. We can't bring Mom and Dad back from the dead, so we go on with our lives. By the way, I turn twenty-five in a few weeks. Drew and I are meeting next week to discuss what to do with our inheritance."

"I want mine," Lynne said immediately.

"I know you do, and I'm inclined to convince Drew to let you have some of it now, rather than waiting another two years."

Drew nodded his head. "We'll discuss it and see what's fair. I'm still the executor of the estate, so I have the final say. So. Be nice to me."

"Thanks, Mick," she said and kissed him on the cheek. She reached over and patted Drew on the shoulder.

Mick looked at Raquel. She had a question in her expression, which he interpreted to be a plea for more information about this inheritance.

"In our parents' trust," Mick said to Raquel, "they stipulated that we couldn't get our share of the estate until we each turned twenty-five."

"I got that much," Raquel said.

"Drew received access to his share two years ago, but left it invested because he didn't need it. I'll get access to mine in a few weeks. Lynne doesn't want to wait two more years for hers."

"How much money are you talking about?"

"One third of 4.4 million dollars, or whatever it's worth now."

"Seriously?"

"Does that make you change your mind about marrying me?"

"Mick, you know I love you. I want to marry you. But I need time to process what just happened to us. The money doesn't change a thing. I wouldn't be marrying you for the money."

"How much time do you think you need?"

Raquel kissed him passionately, to let him know how she felt about him. Then she shook her head, sadly, it seemed. I don't know. Let's just wait and see.

"I'd marry you for the money," Lynne said.

"I'm sure you would, but you can't marry me," Mick said.

"Yeah. That's too bad. Can we just live together then?"

The car slowed noticeably as Drew turned his head to hear Mick's reply.

"No, Lynne. We've already had this discussion. Raquel, it's good to know that it's not my money you want. But I still want you. Marry me, please."

"Give me a little more time, Mick. I'll tell you when I'm ready."

Raquel

"Mick, you know I love you and will agree to marry you. I just need time." Raquel said. They were sitting on Raquel's living room couch, listening to music after dinner.

"Raquel," Mick said hesitantly, not sure how Raquel would react to what he needed to say. "Lydia wants to get back together. She thinks Micky and Ike need the influence of a man in their lives. I agree. I'm not sure I'm the right person to fill that bill, but the only thing stopping me is you. I want to marry you. But if you don't want to make that commitment, I may feel obligated to invite Lydia to move back here."

"Do you want to marry her?"

"I want to marry you, but I'll spend some time with her and see where it leads."

"Will you move them into your house?"

"That's one option. How do you feel about that?"

"I don't like it. It means you'll spend all your time with her and no time with me. I think I know where that will lead."

"Oh? Where is that?"

"You'll marry her, and that will close the door on 'us'. It means there will never be an 'us'."

"What choice do I have? Do you have an option to suggest?"

"Ooh . . ." she groaned. "You frustrating man. I have no good options and no suggestions for you. You'll have to make your own decisions, based on what's most important to you."

"Ooh . . . That's a copout, and you know it. This could be a mutual decision, but you're forcing me to make it alone."

"You're a big boy. You should know what you want."

"I already told you what I want. You just don't want the same thing, I guess that makes the decision for us. If you change your mind, call me, and let's hope it's not too late for 'us'."

Epilogue

"I understand why you want to talk to Drew," Rainbow said, "but why the invitation to Mick. What does he have to offer us?" They were sitting in a small conference room in headquarters, debriefing the Swensen case. Ollie was taking notes that would end up in the Top Secret case file when they were finished.

"Mick will still have to be tested and trained," Ollie said. "There's no free pass. Look at who their parents are. Odds are in their favor that they'll qualify."

"Still . . ."

"Don't worry about Mick, Rainbow. He knows too much now. We have to bring him in, to keep him quiet. It's either test him to see if he's agent material or shoot him now. Which would you prefer?"

"I see your point. Okay, bring him in and we'll test him. I guess if he fails, we can send him out with another agent, with instructions to make sure he doesn't come back."

"What about the women?"

"You mean, do we need to worry about what they know?"

"Yeah. How do we deal with them?"

"From what Drew and Mick have told me, Lynne is pretty flaky. If she revealed anything, I don't think anyone would believe her. And, if she tries to make waves, we can always discredit her, even if we have to make things up about her."

"Okay. Lies and cover-up. We can do that. But what about Ms. Austin? She would be harder to discredit."

"I have a strong feeling that she'll be out of the picture shortly," Rainbow said. "Mick is the type of person who will feel obligated to take care of his child. That means Ms. Hancock, and she doesn't know about us, so we can keep her in the dark. I give it six months before that situation resolves itself."

About the Story

This story is a work of fiction. All of the characters in the book are from the author's imagination and any resemblance to known persons is purely coincidental.

I want to thank Robert Knudsen for his comments and suggestions, also Saul Bottcher, at IndieBookLauncher.com, who designed the book cover, prepared the book for publication, and offered other professional help.

About the Author

I grew up in Salt Lake City and graduated from the University of Utah in Civil Engineering. My life revolves around my family and most of my spare time is spent with them. Together we enjoy camping, hiking, travel and get-togethers with extended family. In my quiet time, I enjoy gardening, family history, emergency preparedness, home remodeling, reading and now, writing.

I've traveled to six continents, either for pleasure or business. I survived two floods in Rio de Janeiro and a drenching rain forest in Costa Rica. I've been stung by a Ray on a California beach, I managed the construction of a graphite composite America's Cup race boat and watched it compete and win off the coast of San Diego. I managed the construction of a graphite composite prototype of the V-22 Tiltrotor aircraft. I managed the construction of five large steel wind turbines, which were installed in Washington, Wyoming and California. I managed and coached project managers in the U.S. and Canada and helped several of them earn their Project Management Professional certification. I co-authored two technical papers for the Department of Defense and spent most of my career doing technical writing of one sort or another. Other than some creative papers written in college English classes, the Gemini Gate Series was my first attempt at creative writing. This is my second.

Feel free to contact me with questions and suggestions.
Thank you.
Steven E. Wilde

Facebook: StevenEWilde_GG
StevenEWilde@gmail.com
www.stevenewilde.com